COLD

LOR...

AND

HER HERO
IN HIDING

BY
RACHEL LEE

Dear Reader,

How far would you go to keep a secret? Are some secrets better left buried, or does truth liberate, always? And at what point, exactly, does a secret between two people who care for each other start becoming a lie by omission?

These are questions my heroine, Muirinn O'Donnell, must confront when she returns to her childhood home, where the secret of her father's murder—and her grandfather's death—lies buried deep in an abandoned mine, and in the psyche of a small Alaskan coastal town.

To find the truth, she has no choice but to turn to Jett Rutledge, the man she has always loved, but couldn't have. And in unearthing the dark and terrible truths of their shared past, Muirinn and Jett must in turn reveal their own deep secrets—secrets that both bind and divide—and fight for a second chance.

But will a killer give them time?

Loreth Anne White

COLD CASE AFFAIR

BY
LORETH ANNE WHITE

First published in Great Britain 2011
Harlequin Mills & Boon Limited,
Eton House, 18-24 Paradise Road, Richmond, Surrey TW9 1SR

© Loreth Beswetherick 2009

ISBN: 978 0 263 88502 6

46-0111

Harlequin Mills & Boon policy is to use papers that are natural, renewable and recyclable products and made from wood grown in sustainable forests. The logging and manufacturing processes conform to the legal environmental regulations of the country of origin.

Printed and bound in Spain
by Litografia Rosés S.A., Barcelona

Loreth Anne White was born and raised in southern Africa, but now lives in Whistler, a ski resort in the moody British Columbian Coast Mountain range. It's a place of vast wilderness, larger-than-life characters, epic adventure, and romance—the perfect place to escape reality. It's no wonder she was inspired to abandon a sixteen-year career as a journalist to escape into a world of romantic fiction filled with dangerous men and adventurous women.

When she's not writing you will find her long-distance running, biking or skiing on the trails, and generally trying to avoid the bears—albeit not very successfully.

She calls this work, because it's when the best ideas come. For a peek into her world visit her website, www.lorethannewhite.com. She'd love to hear from you.

For Toni Anderson, who is always ready to meet me
at the water cooler on days both good and bad.
To Susan Litman, for keeping that bar raised.
And to Jennifer Jackson for believing in me.

Prologue

Seven hundred fifty feet under the Alaskan earth the air was dank, the shaft black as pitch.

Spring runoff—an icy sludge of water and mud—gushed down over him as he descended a wooden ladder slick with rot and moisture, foot by tortuous foot, into the cold womb of the earth. The small lamp on his mining cap pierced the blackness with a quavering halo of yellow, shadows lunging at him whenever he moved.

It was 3:42 a.m.

By the time he reached the 800 level, his knee was locked in pain, his fingers dead. He suffered from *white hand*—the nerves in his hands permanently damaged from the constant vibration of the heavy pneumatic jackleg drill that shuddered daily through his body as he drove blast holes into rock.

Miners got cold, they got wet and they got old as they toiled in perpetual blackness, forcing tunnels deeper and deeper into the bowels of the earth to extract ore that would be turned into bright, gleaming gold. And he was no different—his body just as battered.

Dragging his left leg now, he made his way to the scoop tram shop. He was edgy. Even at this hour, someone could be in this part of the mine. He took a tram and drove it along the tunnel to the powder magazine. Breathing hard, he worked quickly to load two bags of explosives, a couple of powder sticks, detonator caps, B-line.

By 5:02 a.m. he was tackling the knee-grinding, lung-busting seventy-story ascent to the earth's surface. He exited the shaft at the deserted Sodwana headframe, three miles away from the main gates of the Tolkin Mine, limbs shaking. Waiting for him in cold predawn shadows was a friend with a hard shot of whiskey and a ride back into town.

At 6:33 a.m., on that bleak Alaskan morning, a man-car loaded with twelve miners trundled and screeched along the black drift eight hundred feet below ground. The men—all from the small town of Safe Harbor—huddled facing each other, knees touching, clutching thermoses and lunch pails as they made their way to their workstations for the day.

The beam from the headlamp of the man sitting in front lit the rail ahead. He spun around suddenly, terror on his face as he tried to shout a warning.

But it was too late.

The blast was massive, rocking the ground above, registering on sensitive seismic monitoring equipment as far away as the university in Anchorage.

The first external agency to be notified of an unexplained explosion in the bowels of Tolkin Mine was the Safe Harbor Fire Department. Seconds later Safe Harbor Hospital was on high alert for possible mass casualties, and frantic calls were going out for all available doctors to be on standby. These calls were picked up on home scanners, the news rippling like brushfire through the small, close-knit community. Family members hysterical with worry converged on the mine site.

Adam Rutledge, head of mine rescue and the shop steward for the local miners' union, scrambled into his Draegers—mine rescue gear complete with breathing apparatus. He hurriedly contacted the members of his volunteer team.

When they reached the mine, acrid black smoke was billowing out from D-shaft and the extraction vents. At this point, no one aboveground knew what had happened eight hundred feet below. Snowflakes began to crystallize in the frigid air and a group of women shivered together against a biting wind, not knowing if their men were alive, injured or dead.

Among them was Mary O'Donnell, clutching the hand of her nine-year-old daughter, Muirinn.

Muirinn watched the rescuers tumble out of a bright yellow bus in their Draegers, led by their neighbor, Adam Rutledge—her friend Jett's father.

But a police officer flanked by burly mine security men stopped Adam and his crew at the gate. One had a gun. Angry voices carried on snatches of wind as Adam clashed with the police. A German shepherd strained against his leash, barking and baring teeth at Adam. The cop then drew his gun. Adam raised both hands, backing off. Swearing.

Muirinn grew very scared.

She knew the whole town was at war over the big mine strike, neighbors pitted against neighbors, family members against each other. That's why all the police and security men were here. Still, she didn't understand why they wouldn't let Mr. Rutledge and the mine rescue team in—her *dad* was down there.

Desperation squeezed the nine-year-old's heart.

Snow swirled thicker. Temperatures dropped.

Slowly, miners began to emerge from the earth, blackened with soot, choking from emergency stench gas released by management into the tunnels to warn them out of the mine. Muirinn and her mother stood alone as other families were reunited all around them. A few women started to sob. Their men hadn't come up yet, either.

Then Safe Harbor Police Chief Bill Moran came striding through the snow toward Muirinn and her mother, flakes settling thick on the wide brim of his hat.

When she saw the look in his eyes, Muirinn knew her daddy was never coming back.

By late afternoon, Chief Moran had examined the scene and learned of the two bags of explosives missing from the powder magazine. Positive he was now dealing with a mass homicide investigation, he'd contacted the FBI field office in Anchorage, and Tolkin Mine was locked down as they waited for the post-blast team. But the spring snowstorm had other ideas. It barreled in and powered down with a vengeance, unleashing blizzard-force winds on Safe Harbor, cutting off access to the remote Alaskan coastal community. The FBI team was unable to land in Safe Harbor for a full forty-eight hours. The television crews came shortly after, filling the few hotels and restaurants in the tiny mining town. As the story of mass murder in the North broke, it rippled across television screens south of the 49th.

Three months later, Muirinn stood beside a hospital bed, tears streaming down her face. Sheer grief had stolen her mother's life.

Muirinn was taken home to be raised by her grandfather, Gus O'Donnell, her last living relative.

Someone had planted a bomb that had killed Muirinn's father, taken her mother, and changed her life forever.

And the police never found him.

The heinous secret remained buried deep in the abandoned black tunnels of Tolkin Mine. And a mass murderer still walked among the villagers of Safe Harbor.

Chapter 1

Twenty years later

The wings banked as the pilot began a steep descent into an amphitheater of shimmering glacial peaks at the head of Safe Harbor Inlet, a small and isolated community that clung to a rugged coastline hundreds of miles west of Anchorage.

When Muirinn O'Donnell fled this place eleven years ago, those granite mountains had been a barrier to the rest of the world, a rock and ice prison she'd sought desperately to escape. Now they were simply beautiful.

Pontoons slapped water, and the tiny yellow plane squatted down into a churning white froth as the engines slowed to a growl. The pilot taxied toward a bobbing float plane dock.

She was back, the prodigal daughter returned—almost seven months' pregnant, and feeling so incredibly alone.

Muirinn clasped the tiny whalebone compass on a small chain around her neck, drawing comfort from the way it warmed against her palm. Her grandfather, Gus O'Donnell, had left her the small compass, along with everything else he owned, including the house at Mermaid's Cove and Safe Harbor Publishing, his newspaper business.

His death had come as a terrible shock.

Muirinn had been on assignment in the remote jungles of West Papua for the magazine *Wild Spaces* when Gus's body had been found down a shaft at the abandoned Tolkin Mine, a full thirteen days after he'd first been reported missing. And no one had been able to reach her until two weeks ago.

She'd missed his cremation and the memorial service, and she was having trouble wrapping her head around the circumstances of his death.

Muirinn had called the medical examiner herself. He'd told her Gus had been treated for years for a heart condition, and that he'd suffered cardiac arrest while down the mine shaft, which had apparently caused him to tumble a short way from the ladder to the ground. Muirinn could not imagine why her eccentric old grandfather would have been alone in the shaft of an abandoned mine. *Especially* if he had heart trouble.

And she was unable to accept that the dank maw of Tolkin had swallowed the life of someone else she loved.

Gus had raised her solo from the age of nine, after the death of her parents, and while Muirinn had never come home to visit him, she'd loved her grandfather beyond words.

Just the knowledge that Gus was in this world had made her feel part of something larger, a family. In losing Gus, she'd somehow lost her roots.

All she had now was this little compass to guide her.

Muirinn peered out the small window as the floatplane approached the dock, thinking that nothing had changed, yet everything had. Then suddenly she saw him.

Jett Rutledge.

The one person she'd sought to avoid for the past eleven years. The reason she'd stayed away from her hometown.

He stood at the ferry dock on the opposite side of the harbor, wearing jeans and a white T-shirt, his skin tanned summer dark, his body lean and strong. His thick blue-black hair glistened in the late-evening sun.

Muirinn's stomach turned to water.

She leaned forward, hand pressing up against the window as the plane swung around and bumped against the dock. And like a hungry voyeur she watched as the man she'd never stopped loving crouched down to talk to a boy—a boy with the same shock of blue-black hair. The same olive-toned complexion.

His son.

Muirinn's eyes brimmed with emotion.

He ruffled the child's hair, put a baseball cap on the boy's head and cocked the peak down over his eyes. Jett stood as his kid raced toward the ferry, little red backpack bobbing against his back.

The child hesitated at the base of the gangplank, drawn by some invisible tie to his father. He spun around suddenly, and even from this distance Muirinn could see the bright slash of a smile in the boy's sun-browned face as he waved fiercely to his dad one last time before boarding the boat.

At the same time a woman approached Jett, the ocean wind toying with strands of her long blond hair. Her stride was confident, happy. She placed her hand on Jett's arm, gave him a kiss, then followed the child up the passenger ramp.

That vignette—framed by the small float plane window—struck Muirinn hard.

Her eyes blurred with emotion and a lump formed in her throat. As the sound of the prop died down and the plane door was swung open, Muirinn heard the ferry horn and saw the boat pulling out into the choppy inlet.

Jett walked slowly to the edge of the dock, hands thrust deep in his jeans pockets as he watched the ferry drawing away in a steady white *V* of foam. He gave one last salute, hand held high in the air, a solitary yet powerful figure on the dock. A lighthouse, a rock to which his boy would return.

"You ready to deplane, ma'am?"

Shocked, she turned to face the pilot. He had a hand held out to her, a look of concern in his eyes. She got that a lot at this stage of her pregnancy.

"Thank you," she said, quickly donning her big, protective sunglasses as she took his hand. She stepped down onto the wooden dock, disoriented after her long series of flights from New York. Two cabs waited up on the road as the handful of passengers from Anchorage disembarked around her.

Muirinn climbed into the first taxi and gave directions to what was now her property on Mermaid's Cove, a small bay tucked into the ragged coastline a few miles north of town. But on second thought she leaned forward. "I'm sorry, but could you take the long way around town? Not along the harbor road."

Or the past the airstrip.

There was a risk of seeing Jett again if they went that way. She wasn't ready for that—even from a distance. Not now.

Not after seeing him with his son. And his wife.

Muirinn's lawyer in New York had told her that Jett Rutledge had led the search team that located Gus's body in the mine. This news had rattled her—the idea of Jett still here in Safe Harbor, still saving people when she hadn't allowed him to save her all those years ago. It was almost too painful to imagine.

Muirinn also knew from her grandfather that Jett had married in Las Vegas shortly after she'd left town eleven years ago, and that he'd had a child. The news had nearly killed her because Jett had refused to follow *her* to Los Angeles just a few months before. And when she'd learned that she was pregnant with Jett's baby, she'd been too proud—too afraid—to return home. And so she'd chosen to bear the child alone.

At nineteen, with no money and few prospects, Muirinn had ended up giving *their* baby up for adoption, a decision that still haunted her.

She'd never gotten over it.

Muirinn had also learned from Gus that Jett had joined the ranks of Alaska's bush pilots, a free-spirited breed unto themselves. And that's when she'd told her grandfather to stop.

She didn't want to hear one more word about Jett and his happy little family. It was driving her crazy with the pain of her own losses, so Muirinn had resorted to her tried-and-true coping mechanism—she just severed ties, cutting herself off from the source of her angst. And her grandfather had respected her request.

From that point on, Muirinn knew nothing more about Jett's life. She hadn't even wanted to know his wife's name. And sheer stubborn pride forbade her from ever asking about Jett again, or from coming home. Pride, and her dark secret.

All Muirinn knew for certain was that she'd lost the only man she'd ever loved through the biggest mistake of her life. One she'd never stopped regretting. Because after Jett she'd had one failed relationship after another, no man ever quite measuring up to him.

Which was why she was having a baby on her own now.

She sank back into the cab seat, wondering where Jett's son and wife were going on that ferry. It was late July. School was out. The kid might be going to a summer camp, or with his mother on a trip to Seattle. Anywhere.

It was none of her business.

Muirinn had given up any claim to Jett Rutledge a long, long time ago.

Yet a poignant sadness pressed through her, and she closed her eyes, placing her hand on her belly.

Do you still hate me so much, Jett?

What would she do if his parents still owned the neighboring property on Mermaid's Cove?

Muirinn had grown up on that cove. She and Jett had stolen their first-ever kiss down in the old boat shed, hidden from the houses by a dense grove of trees. She wondered if the shed still stood.

They'd made love for the first time in that shed, too, on a night the moon had shimmered like silver over the water. She'd just turned eighteen, and Jett twenty-one. The boat shed had become their special place, and there was a time Muirinn had thought it would all be there for her forever.

But the summer she turned nineteen, everything changed.

As the cab neared the Mermaid's Cove property, Muirinn asked the driver to drop her off at the ramshackle gate.

Bags in hand, she stood at the top of the overgrown driveway, staring down at her childhood home as the taxi pulled off in a cloud of soft glacial dust.

The scene in front of her seemed to shimmer up out of her memory to take literal shape in front of her—the garden and forest fighting for supremacy; brooding firs brushing eaves with heavy branches. Wild roses scrambled up the staircase banisters, and berry bushes bubbled up around the wooden deck that ran the length of the rustic log house.

On the deck terra-cotta pots overflowed with flowers,

herbs, vegetables; all evidence of her grandfather's green thumb. And beyond the deck, the lawn rolled down to a grove of trees, below which Mermaid's Cove shimmered.

In a few short months this would all be gone and piled high with snow. Safe Harbor was known for the heaviest accumulation among Alaskan coastal towns.

Numbly, Muirinn walked down the driveway and set her bags at the base of the deck stairs, bending to crush a few rosemary leaves between her fingers as she did.

She drank in the scent of the herbs, listening to the hum of bees, the distant chink of wind chimes, the chuckle of waves against tiny stones in the bay below. It amazed her to think that her grandfather was actually gone; evidence of his life thrummed everywhere.

She looked up at the house, and suddenly felt his presence.

I'm so sorry for not coming home while you were still here. I'm sorry for leaving you alone.

A sudden breeze rippled through the branches, brushing through her hair. Muirinn swallowed, unnerved, as she picked up her bags.

She made her way up the stairs and dug the house key out of her purse.

Pushing open the heavy oak door with its little portal of stained glass, Muirinn stepped into the house, and back into time. She heard his gruff voice almost instantly.

'Tis the sea faeries that brought you here, Muirinn. The undines. They brought you up from the bay to your mother and father, to me. To care for you for all time.

Emotion burned sharply into her eyes as her gaze scanned the living room, full of books, paintings, photos of her and her parents. For years Muirinn hadn't thought of those fantastical tales Gus had spun in her youth. She'd managed to lock those magical myths away deep in the recesses of her memory, behind logic and reason and the practicalities of work and life in a big city. But now they swept over her—there was no holding them back. This homecoming was going to be rougher than she thought.

More than anything, though, it was Gus's artwork that grabbed her by the throat.

She slumped into a chair, staring at the paintings and sketches that graced the walls. She was in almost all of them—images of a wild imp, frozen in time, in charcoal, in soft ethereal watercolor. In some, her hair flowed out in corkscrew curls as she swam in the sea with the tail of a fish. In others, Gus had taken artistic license with her features, giving her green eyes even more of a mischievous upward slant, her ears a slight point, depicting her as one of the little woodland creatures he used to tell her lived up in the hills.

Eccentric to the core, Gus O'Donnell had been just like this place. Rough, yet spiritual. Wise, yet a dreamer. A big-game hunter, fisherman, writer, poet, artist. A lover of life and lore with a white shock of hair, a great bushy beard and the keen eyes of an eagle.

And he'd raised her just as wildly, eclectically, to be free.

Not that it had boded well for her. Because Muirinn hadn't *felt* free. All she'd wanted to do was escape, discover the real world beyond her granite prison.

Sitting there in a bent-willow rocker, staring at her grandfather's things, exhaustion finally claimed Muirinn, and she fell into a deep sleep.

She woke several hours later, stiff, confused. Muirinn checked the clock—it was almost 10:00 p.m. At this latitude, at this time of year, it barely got dark at night. However, clouds had started scudding across the inlet, lowering the dusky Arctic sky with the threat of a thunderstorm. A harsh wind was already swooshing firs against the roof.

Muirinn tried to flick on a light switch before realizing that she had yet to figure out how to reconnect the solar power. She lit an oil lamp instead and climbed the staircase to her grandfather's attic office. The lawyer had said all the keys she'd need for the house, along with instructions on how to connect the power, would be in the middle drawer of her grandfather's old oak desk.

She creaked open the attic door.

Shadows sprang at her from the far corners of the room. Muirinn's pulse quickened.

Her grandfather's carved desk hulked at the back of the room in front of heavy drapes used to block out the midnight sun during the summer months. A candle that had drowned in its own wick rested on the polished desk surface, along with Gus's usual whiskey tumbler. A pang of emotion stung Muirinn's chest.

It was as if the room were still holding its breath, just waiting for Gus to walk back in. And a strong and sudden sense gripped Muirinn that her grandfather had not been ready to quit living.

She shook the surreal notion, and stepped into the room. The attic air stirred softly around her, cobwebs lifting in currents caused by her movement. Muirinn halted suddenly. She could swear she felt a presence. Someone—or something—was in here.

Again Muirinn shook the sensation.

She set the oil lamp on the desk and seated herself in her grandfather's leather chair. It groaned as she leaned forward to pull open the top drawer. But as she did, a thud sounded on the wooden floor, and something brushed against her leg. Muirinn froze.

She almost let out a sob of relief when she saw that it was only Quicksilver, her grandfather's enormous old tomcat with silver fur, gold eyes, and the scars of life etched into his grizzled face. He jumped onto the desk, a purr growling low in his throat.

"Goodness, Quick," she whispered, stroking him. "I didn't see you come in." He responded with an even louder rumble, and Muirinn smiled. Someone had clearly been feeding the old feline since Gus disappeared because Quicksilver was heavy and solid, if ancient.

The lawyer had mentioned that Gus's old tenant, Mrs. Wilkie, still did housekeeping for him. She must've been taking care of the cat, too.

As Muirinn stroked the animal, she felt the knobs in his crooked tail, broken in two places when he'd caught it in the screen door so many years ago. Again, the sense of stolen time overwhelmed her. And with it came the guilt.

Guilt at not once having come home in eleven years.

The cat stepped into the open drawer and Muirinn edged him aside to remove the bunch of keys, her hand stilling as she caught sight of a fat brown envelope. On it was scrawled the word *Tolkin* in Gus's bold hand. Muirinn removed the envelope, opened it.

Inside was a pile of old crime scene photos, most of which Muirinn recognized from a book Gus had written on the tragedy. A chill rippled over her skin.

Had Gus *still* been trying to figure out who'd planted the Tolkin bomb?

Despite the protracted FBI investigation, the mass

homicide had never been solved. Yet while the case had turned old and cold, her grandfather had remained obsessed with it, convinced that his son's killer still lived and walked among them in Safe Harbor.

Clearly, not even writing the bestseller had put his curiosity to rest, thought Muirinn.

She opened the drawer and spotted Gus's laptop tucked at the very back. Her curiosity now piqued, she decided to take the envelope and the laptop downstairs to her old bedroom and look at them in bed. Perhaps she'd learn why her grandfather had gone down into that dark shaft of the abandoned mine, alone.

Jett Rutledge reached forward and turned up the volume of his truck radio. *"I believe in miracles"* blared from the speakers as he drove, arm out the window. In spite of the dark storm rolling in, he felt happier than he had in a long time.

He'd had a hard workout, a good dinner, a few beers with his dad at the airport club, and he'd taken some time off flying. He was now going to use this period when Troy was away at summer camp to focus on his big dream project. He wanted to prepare several more proposals that would secure financing for the next phase of a fishing lodge he was building in the wilderness farther north.

He turned onto the dirt road that snaked down to Mermaid's Cove, heading for home. His parents had ceded their rolling oceanfront property to him years ago, opting to relocate closer to town themselves. His mother still worked occasionally as a nurse at Safe Harbor Hospital, and everything was generally more accessible from the new house—including his dad's physiotherapy.

Few jobs aged a man quite as fast as mining. Especially working a mine like Tolkin.

The ground at Tolkin was solid rock, which meant fewer cave-ins, fewer deaths, but it also meant the company had racked up a disproportionately large number of other injuries related to the kidney and back-jarring stress of high-impact drilling.

A miner's equipment was heavy. The men were constantly wet. Cold. The thunderous din and fumes of diesel equipment were rough on ears and respiratory tracts. And jarring along the drifts in massive trucks took its toll on bodies. So did negotiating the black ground on foot—the tunnel surfaces were invariably booby-trapped with water-filled potholes that wrenched knees, ankles and shredded tendons.

Which was what had happened to Adam Rutledge.

Jett's dad had taken his fair share of a beating, and his injuries were worsening with arthritis and age.

But he was still alive, still watching his grandson grow, and now he was helping out with communications at the airstrip, a job Jett had scored for his father. All in all, Jett couldn't ask for more.

As he neared Gus's place, he wondered what was going to happen to the old man's property now that he was gone. A thought flashed briefly through his mind that he might make an offer, join the Rutledge land with the O'Donnell acreage. But that idea led to thoughts of Muirinn O'Donnell and he instantly quashed the notion. She'd probably inherited the property. Putting in an offer would just bring him into contact with her. Jett figured he'd rather forgo the option of buying it if meant ever seeing, or talking, to her again.

His hands tensed on the wheel, anger flooding into his veins at the mere thought of Muirinn. She hadn't even shown up for Gus's funeral. That told him something.

It told him that she didn't care.

She didn't give a damn about the people she'd left behind

in this town. She'd turned her back on it all—on him—and never once looked back.

Eleven years ago, Muirinn had been doing a summer stint at her grandfather's newspaper where she'd discovered a passion for journalism. Around the same time a Hollywood production company had blown into town to do a movie on the Tolkin Mine murders, based on Gus's book. The presence of the movie crew had turned Safe Harbor upside down, and it had fired a burning coal in Muirinn's belly. She'd started going out to the set every day, reporting on the production, interviewing the actors and crew. In turn, the actor playing the part of Muirinn's father had interviewed Muirinn as the surviving O'Donnell family member. In Jett's opinion it had messed with her head, giving her a false sense of celebrity.

Then one of the crew members had suggested that Muirinn's writing was really good, saying he'd put a word in for her at his sister's Los Angeles magazine, and Muirinn had become completely obsessed by the idea.

Lured by absurd notions of fame, fortune and escape, she'd packed up her life and followed the crew to LA. Jett had literally begged her not to leave. He'd been so in love with that woman. He'd planned to marry her, never a doubt in his mind that they were meant for each other. But she'd been as stubborn as mule.

They'd argued hot and hard, and it had led to even hotter and angrier sex. Afterwards, she'd tried to convince Jett to go with her, but he couldn't. He was born to live in the wilds of Alaska. It would've killed him to move to L.A. She'd taunted him, saying that if he really loved her enough he'd do it. And Jett, feeling her slipping from his grasp, had retaliated by saying if she did leave, he'd never forgive her, never speak to her again. He'd hate her for walking out on what they had.

Clearly, she'd taken him at his word, because the next day she'd boarded that plane and he'd never heard from her again.

Muirinn had always had a way of bringing out the irrational fire in Jett, something he regretted to this day. Because even through all his anger, Jett never had managed to let Muirinn go, and it had cost him his marriage. It had cost *them*... He slammed on the brakes suddenly, on the road just past Gus's house.

A light was flickering faintly up in Gus's attic window. *Someone was inside.*

Vandals? A fire?

He put his truck into reverse, quickly backed up the road and wheeled into the rutted driveway with half a mind to alert the police before deciding it was likely just old Lydia Wilkie in there, probably using an oil lamp since the power had been disconnected after Gus's death.

Still, it was past midnight; not a time the crazy old lady would likely be up and about inside Gus's house.

He'd better check to make sure.

Muirinn's sleep was shattered by a violent clap of thunder.

She jolted upright. Then she heard it again—not thunder— a thunderous banging on the door downstairs. Quicksilver shot off the bed and bolted down the hall.

Muirinn groped in the dark to light the lamp. Holding it high, she negotiated the stairs, careful not to trip over her nightdress. She halted in the hallway, glanced at the old clock. It was past midnight. Who on earth could be beating on Gus's door at this hour?

The banging shuddered through the house again. Fear sliced into her.

She set the lamp down, reached for the bunch of keys she'd left on the hall table before going to bed. Fumbling for the right key, Muirinn headed for Gus's gun cabinet. Another wave of banging resounded through the house.

Unlocking the cabinet, Muirinn removed Gus's old shotgun. Hands shaking now, she loaded a cartridge, chambered the round and went to the door.

"Who is it?" she yelled.

Wind rattled hard at windows, swished through the conifers outside, branches clawing on the roof. Whoever was out there in the storm couldn't hear her, and the pounding began again, so hard the door shook. She sucked in a deep breath and swung the door open.

And froze.

Chapter 2

"Muirinn?"

Shock slammed into Jett's chest.

The flame in the old lantern on the hall table quivered in the wind, making shadows dance over her copper hair. But she simply stared at him, green eyes glimmering, her face ghost-white, shotgun pointed at his heart.

Jett's gaze flickered sharply at the sight of her pregnant belly under the white cotton nightdress. "What are you doing here?" His voice came out rough, raw.

Muirinn slowly lowered the 12-gauge, her left hand rising as if to reach out and touch him. Anticipation ripped through him hot and fast. But she pushed a fall of sleep-tangled curls back from her face instead, and he realized that she was shaking. "Jett?" she whispered.

He was speechless.

Nothing in this world could have prepared him for the

sheer physical jolt of seeing Muirinn O'Donnell back in Safe Harbor. Especially barefoot and *pregnant*.

The pulse at her neck was racing, making the small compass on a chain at her throat catch the light. It lured his gaze down to her breasts, which were full and rounded. Lust tore through him, his blood already pounding with adrenaline. Every molecule in his body screamed to touch her, pull her against him, hold her so damn tight, erase the lost years. But at the same time the sight of her softly rounded belly triggered something cold and brittle in him, a protective shell forming around his raw emotions.

He needed to step away, fast, before he did or said something stupid. "I didn't know you were back," he said crisply. "I saw a light up in the attic, thought it might be vandals."

She was still unable to answer, and his words hung like an inane echo in the chasm of lost years between them. Rain began to plop on the deck.

"Gus's place has been empty," he explained further, clearing his throat. "But I can see you have things under control." Jett turned to go, but he hesitated on the stairs, snared by a fierce urge to turn around, drink in the sight of her once again. "Welcome home, Muirinn," he said brusquely, then he ran lightly down the steps toward his truck, forcing himself not to look back.

"Jett—wait!"

He stilled, rain dampening his hair.

"I…I wasn't in the attic," she said.

He turned very slowly. "You weren't up there when I knocked?"

She shook her head. "I was sleeping."

"Someone was up there, Muirinn."

"It wasn't me."

He wavered, then stalked back up the stairs, flicking on the light switch as he entered the house. Nothing happened.

"I haven't figured out how to reconnect the solar power yet."

"Here, give me that," he said, taking the shotgun from her. "I'll go check things out for you, connect the power, then I'll be gone."

He snagged the lantern from the table and thudded up the wooden stairs.

Muirinn pressed her trembling hand to her stomach, trying to collect herself. Then, forcing out a huge breath, she followed him—and the light—up to the attic.

He creaked open the attic door, the movement causing a draft to rush in from the attic window behind Gus's desk. Drapes billowed out, scattering papers to the floor. Outside, the rain fell heavier, the breeze carrying the moisture in with it.

"I…I could swear that window wasn't open earlier," Muirinn said, moving quickly into the study and stooping to gather the documents scattered across the Persian rug. Her movements were awkward around her growing stomach and she could sense Jett watching her. She stilled, and her gaze slid up to meet him.

In the light of her lantern, the planes of his face were rough, utterly masculine. His mouth was shaped with a sculptor's fine precision, wide and bracketed by laugh lines that had deepened over the years. New, too, were the fine creases that fanned out from his cobalt eyes—eyes still as clear and piercing as the day she'd left town. And they bored into her now with an animal-like intensity that turned her knees to jelly.

Muirinn swallowed.

She knew he had to be thinking about her pregnancy. She also knew that he was too damn proud to ask. They were alike in so many ways.

She stood up, awkwardly clutching the papers to her belly, her cheeks flushing as something darkened in his eyes. Something that made her feel dangerously warm inside.

"It must have been how Quicksilver got in," she said quietly, trying to fill the volatile space between them. "My cat," she explained, then laughed nervously. "Gus got him for me when I turned thirteen, remember?"

"That cat can hardly be called yours, Muirinn," he said crisply. "You left him. Eleven years ago."

The implication was clear. She didn't have any rights. Not here, not anymore, not in Jett's eyes. Not even to a cat.

She moistened her lips.

Jett turned from her suddenly and crossed the room. He held the lantern up behind Gus's desk. "You didn't see this, either?"

"God, no!" Muirinn said, coming to his side and seeing shards of glass glinting on the carpet. The desk drawers had been wrenched open, too, folders lying scattered beneath the leather chair in which she'd sat only hours before. The computer tower beneath the desk was toppled onto its side, wires ripped from the back. A chill rustled through her.

"Someone was up here, Jett, while I was sleeping."

Jett yanked back the heavy drapes. "The windowpane's been shattered. Whoever came in here must have ransacked Gus's desk." He frowned, surveying the scene. "The sound of my truck must have interrupted them."

Muirinn wrapped her arms over her tummy, shivering as the rain-damp wind from the broken window whispered over her skin. "Why would someone want to go through Gus's things?"

"Hell knows," he said, studying the floorboards under the window. "But whoever did this was clearly looking for something. He might've tried to take the whole computer tower because your solar power is off, and he couldn't access the information he wanted right here."

"He?"

"There's dirt transfer on the wooden floor here, left by a boot, about a size 12. I'd say it was a guy."

Another gust of wind chased a ripple of goose bumps over her skin, tightening her nipples. Jett glanced at her breasts, then caught her eyes for a long beat. He looked away quickly, rubbing his brow as he cursed softly.

"Is it that hard, Jett?" she whispered. "Seeing me again?"

He kept his face turned away from her for a long moment.

"Yeah," he mumbled. "It is. Come—" He touched her elbow, gently ushering her out onto the landing. "We should leave the scene as is. I'll call the cops."

He pulled the attic door closed behind them, the space on the narrow landing suddenly close, the halo of lantern light too intimate. Jett had that effect on space—it shrank around him. It wasn't just his physical size; he radiated a kinetic energy that simply felt too large for contained spaces. He thrived out in the wilderness, and it was why he'd refused to follow her to Los Angeles. He'd said the city would kill his spirit, who he was.

In retrospect, Muirinn knew he was right. A crowded urban environment wouldn't accommodate a man with a latent wildness like Jett's. He was born to roam places like Alaska, the tundra, in his plane. It's why people like him came north of 60 in the first place.

Los Angeles would have been a concrete prison for him. But at the time, it had represented freedom and adventure to her—a key to a vibrant new world.

Yet, he *had* left for a while. He'd gone to Las Vegas. Where he'd gotten married. And that *really* burned.

It also made him a hypocrite.

He glanced down into her eyes, sensuality swimming into his features.

"Jett—" she said quietly.

He swallowed, tension growing thicker. "Get something warm on, Muirinn," he said abruptly. "I'm going to call this in. Then I'll connect your power and wait with you until someone from the police department arrives."

She blew out a shaky breath, nodded. "Thanks for doing this."

He held her eyes a moment longer, then jogged down the stairs without a word.

Jett stood in the brick archway, quietly watching Muirinn busying herself in Gus's rustic, open-plan kitchen. She'd pulled one of her grandfather's voluminous sweaters over her white nightgown, and she'd caught her rampant copper curls back in a barrette. He felt relieved—the other look was driving him to total distraction…or destruction. Same difference with Muirinn O'Donnell.

Damn if he hadn't gone red-hot at the sight of her on hands and knees in that cotton nightgown as she'd gathered up Gus's papers, strewn all over the attic office. There was something about her pregnant body that drove him wild. And made him incredibly sad.

Hurt.

She'd always had such power over him, yet she'd never known the extent of her control. But now, in Gus's oversized sweater, she looked small, vulnerable. Jett wasn't so sure this look was any better for his health. It aroused protective instincts in him—things he didn't want to feel for her. This was such a total shock, seeing her again, without warning. He needed to figure out what this might mean to his family. To his son.

To him.

"Hey," she said with a soft smile, as she caught him watching. His blood quickened.

He stepped into the kitchen, making sure he remained on the opposite side of the rough wood table.

She poured him tea from a stubby copper kettle, which she set back on the gas stove, still steaming. He avoided eye contact as he took a seat at the table, and accepted the mug from her.

She'd made his tea just the way he liked it, black and sweet. The fact that she even remembered cut way too close to the bone. Why *should* it matter? Truth was, it did.

Everything about Muirinn mattered.

And right now he was struggling with his emotions, trying to avoid the elephant in the room that was her pregnancy, trying to be the gentleman and not ask, yet desperate to know who the father was, where he was. Why she was here alone.

The fact that she was expecting a baby at all sliced Jett like a knife. He forced out a heavy breath of air. Civility be damned—they were beyond that. There was no way to be polite about what had transpired between them, no way to bridge the divide with small talk. So he chose a direct approach. "You never came to visit Gus," he said quietly. "You didn't even come home for the funeral. So why are you here now?"

She studied him with those shrewd cat eyes for a moment. "I came to take over Safe Harbor Publishing, Jett. Gus left me the company in his will, along with this property."

He literally felt himself blanch. "You're going to *stay?*"

Pain flickered over her features. "Maybe." She inhaled deeply, bracing her hands on the back of a chair. "The will stipulated that I could sell the business, but only after a year. That means running it myself for twelve months, or hiring someone else to do it."

"So you're here to hire someone?"

"No. I'm here to run it."

"For one year?"

"Look, Jett, I'm not going to get in your way, okay? I'm not going to cramp your style." She hesitated. "I…I saw you down at the ferry dock this morning, with your son—" She wavered again, as if not quite trusting herself to say the next words. "And your wife."

Perspiration prickled across his lip. He'd made a mistake starting this conversation now. He set the mug down, getting up in the same movement, and he stalked into the hall. "I'll just go wait outside for Officer Gage."

"Jett?" she called after him.

He halted, hand on the doorknob.

"What's his name? Your son?"

A strange emotion tore through him, raw and wild. Part of him didn't want to give the name up to her, give any part of *his* boy to her. "Troy," he said quietly, still facing the door. "Troy Rutledge."

She was dead silent for a long moment. "Troy was my father's name."

"Your father was a good man, Muirinn. I was proud to name my son after him."

"I…it just surprises me."

He turned. "Why?"

"Half the town—the union hardliners—*hated* my dad for crossing that picket line, your own father included. They called my dad a scab, called me terrible names at school, humiliated my mother in the supermarket. They hated my father enough to blow him and eleven others up with a bomb."

"It was a bad time for everyone, Muirinn." Jett paused. "But no matter what people said, you know that I always cared for your father. If Troy O'Donnell hadn't introduced me to model airplanes, to the idea of flying, I might have become a miner, not a pilot. He was the one who told me, when I was ten years old, that I could do something better with my life than go down that mine. He was a friend, Muirinn. I was twelve when he died, and I was also devastated by his murder. It ate my father up, too, regardless of what he might have said about your dad."

Emotion seeped into her eyes, making her nose pink—making her so damn beautiful. "Thank you, Jett," she whispered. "I...I needed to hear that."

"It's not for you," he said quietly. "It's for a man who knew honor, knew his home. Knew how not to deliberately hurt the people who cared for him."

She stared at him. "Do you really still hate me that much?"

Wind rattled the panes. Rain smacked at the windows. "I hate what you did, Muirinn, to the people who loved you."

He closed the heavy oak door behind him with a soft thud that seemed to resonate down through her bones.

Muirinn slumped into a chair at the kitchen table, and buried her face in her hands. If she'd known it was going to be quite so rough to see him again, she wouldn't have come. If Jett only knew what she'd gone through since she'd left Safe Harbor. He didn't have a clue just how much his ultimatum had cost her back then...how much it had cost *them*.

She should've told the lawyer to just go ahead and hire someone—anyone—to run Safe Harbor Publishing, and to put the word out that the company would be up for grabs within twelve months.

But at the same time, Muirinn felt in her heart that Gus had wanted her to come back. Why else would he have insisted she be given the small compass along with the terms of his will? She'd told Gus that she was pregnant, having a baby alone. He might have been trying to show her a way home, to remind her where her family roots lay.

Muirinn scrubbed her hands over her face quickly as she heard tires crunching up the driveway, telling herself it would be okay; she wasn't trapped here anymore. She could go back to New York anytime before the twelve months were up if things weren't working out. She could hire a publisher at any point she chose. *She* was the one in control here.

Smoothing errant tendrils of hair back from her face, Muirinn adjusted her sweater and went to meet the police.

"Could have been kids," Officer Ted Gage said as he stared at the papers scattered under the desk, thumbs hooked into his gun belt. "Incidents of vandalism often flare up during the summer holidays." His gaze tracked round the room. "Kids probably thought Gus's place was still empty."

"So you're not sending crime scene techs or anything?" Muirinn asked from the doorway.

He shrugged. "That's for the movies. We only dust for prints in major crimes. And nothing was stolen—"

"Not that I *know* of," she interrupted.

"That footprint is pretty big for a kid, Gage," said Jett. "I'd say about a size 12."

"I can point you to several kids with feet that size," he said around the gum between his teeth.

"Well, why don't you see if you can match one of them up to this print?"

"That's a lot of lab time and resources for a possible mischief or vandalism charge." He glanced sideways at Muirinn, a whisper of hostility beneath his deceptive easy-breezy style. Unease fingered into Muirinn.

"Look," he said suddenly. "I'll send someone around later. Depending on our caseload."

Muirinn was beyond exhausted now. She just wanted to go to bed. She thanked the cop, saw him out.

Jett hung back. "Would you like me to stay, Muirinn?"

She knew how difficult it must be for him to make the offer, and all she truly wanted to answer was *yes*.

"I'll be fine, thank you. Officer Gage is right, it's probably just vandalism with the place being empty and all. I can call 9-1-1 if the kids come back. Somehow I doubt that they will."

Jett didn't look so sure.

She wondered if his hesitancy was because of Officer Gage's chilly attitude toward her. Or because it seemed pretty darn clear that someone *had* been after something in her grandfather's office. For all Muirinn knew, they'd found what they'd been looking for, and had taken it. And she had no way of knowing what it was.

He reached for a pad of paper by the phone, scribbled something down, then ripped off the top sheet. "Here's my number." He looked directly into her eyes. "If you need help, Muirinn, I can be over right away. I live next door.

"Next door?"

"I've taken over my parents' house."

She felt the blood drain from her face.

His gaze skimmed over her tummy again, and she wanted to explain, to tell him that she was single; that she'd do anything for a second chance.

But he was married. He had a family.

And damn if they didn't all live right next door. Muirinn felt vaguely nauseous at the idea of facing the other woman. She told herself that she was tough, she could handle it. She'd been through enough in her life to know that.

So instead of justifying herself, she became defensive. "You're just dying to judge me, aren't you, Jett?"

"I gave up judging you a long time ago, Muirinn. What you do is none of my business."

And neither was his business hers. Yet here he stood, in her life again. And his words rang hollow.

"Look, I'm tired, Jett. I don't want to argue. I need to get some sleep."

He studied her for a long moment. "You always did get the last word in."

"No, Jett. You got the last word eleven years ago when you told me you hated me, and that I should never, ever come back."

His mouth flattened. "Muirinn—"

She swung the door open. "Go, please."

And he stepped out into the storm-whipped darkness.

She slammed the door shut behind him, flipping the lock with a sharp click. Then she slumped against the wood, allowing the hot tears to come as she listened to the tires of his truck crunching down the driveway.

Jett stood at the floor-to-ceiling windows in his living room, rain writhing over the panes as he watched the yellow glow coming from the kitchen window of Gus's house on the neighboring knoll.

He spun around, pacing the floor. What was he supposed to do?

Tell her?

After all these years?

No. He couldn't. He'd done what he had for a reason—and Gus had helped him do it.

He cursed viciously.

Seeing her pregnant now, back here in Safe Harbor…the irony just made everything more complicated.

Jett poured himself a whiskey in spite of the hour and took a long, hard swig, felt the burn in his chest. He exhaled slowly. He had no choice but to ride out this storm that was Muirinn O'Donnell. If she stayed true to form, she'd probably be gone within twelve months.

He wondered again about the father of her baby; where he was, whether they were married. There was a chance that Muirinn's husband would suddenly show up next door and join her. How in hell was he going to swallow *that*?

At least Troy was away at summer camp for a few weeks, because he was the one person who stood to lose the most in this situation. And Jett did not want his boy to get hurt.

He could not allow Muirinn to do that Troy.

There was just no way he was going to tell his son that Muirinn O'Donnell was his mother—that ten years ago she'd simply given him away in a private adoption.

He wasn't going to tell Muirinn, either, that he'd named their son after her father out of some deep need to connect his boy to his mother's side of the family.

In retrospect, Jett recognized that he'd probably been trying to tie himself back to Muirinn in some subconscious way, hoping she'd come back.

And now she *was* back.

Living right next door. Another baby on the way. Another man somewhere in her life. And before too long, she'd surely be gone again.

Right or wrong, the only way Jett could ever tell Muirinn the truth was if she somehow proved herself to him. She

needed to show that she was worthy of her own son; that
she'd stay, and not hurt Troy.

As she'd once hurt him.

Chapter 3

Muirinn awakened to a warm and sunny morning, but inside her gut a tiny icicle of unease was growing. As she poured her morning cup of decaf, she glanced at Gus's laptop and the envelope of photos that she'd put on the long dining room table.

Could that laptop and those photographs be what the burglars were searching for last night? She'd removed them from the attic and taken them down to her bedroom mere hours before the break-in. Had her grandfather really been poking into the old Tolkin mystery again? Was that why he was at the mine when he died?

Nothing made sense to her.

Muirinn blew out a heavy breath of air and looked out the window at the clear cobalt sky—blue as Jett's eyes. Her gaze shifted slowly over to his deck, jutting out over the trees next door.

An American flag snapped in the breeze, colorful against

the distant white peaks. Jett had found Gus's body—he could tell her more. But Muirinn didn't want to talk to him.

Not after last night.

She needed to stay away from him.

Her best option was to talk directly to the Safe Harbor police. She'd go to the station later today, right after she met with Rick Frankl, the editor of Safe Harbor Publishing. She'd already left a message at Rick's office for him to call her to set up an appointment. But first she wanted to look inside Gus's laptop.

Muirinn set her mug down, seated herself at Gus's rustic wood table and powered up the computer. Immediately, a message box flashed up onto the screen asking for a password.

She tried several possibilities, including O'Donnell family names, and the name of the cat.

Nothing worked.

The only way she was going to access this laptop was with the aid of a computer tech who could circumvent the password protection. She also needed a tech to help reconnect the hard drive up in the attic office. Perhaps Rick Frankl could recommend one.

Muirinn reached instead for the brown envelope and slid the black-and-white crime scene photos out. She spread them over the table. Most of the images she recognized from the book her grandfather had written years ago on the Tolkin massacre. But there were a few other images she didn't think she'd seen before. She picked one up—a shot of bootprints in shiny black mud, a ruler positioned alongside the impressions.

Muirinn flipped it over, read the notation on the back. *Missing Photo #3. Bomber tracks.*

She frowned. Quickly, she flipped over the rest of the photographs she didn't recognize, laying them all facedown on

the table. On the back of each one was a similar set of nota-
tions, all with the word *Missing* scrawled in her grandfather's
bold hand.

What did this mean?

Surely her grandfather had given up trying to actually *solve*
the Tolkin murders? Unless…she stared at the images strewn
all over the table. Unless there was *new* evidence.

No. It wasn't possible.

Was it?

She turned the images faceup again, selected a photo of a
mining headframe—a rusted A-shaped metal skeleton that
loomed over a small boarded-up shack. She flipped it over,
read the back: *Missing photo #8. Sodwana headframe.
Bomber used as entry to mine?*

She'd never heard any theory about the bomber using the
Sodwana headframe to gain access to the mine. As far as she
could recall, the old Sodwana shaft was literally miles from
the actual underground blast location near D-shaft. FBI investigators had always surmised that the bomber had been
someone working inside the mine that day, someone who'd
crossed the picket line with her father.

Muirinn realized that she didn't even know *which* shaft Gus
had been found in. Had it been Sodwana?

She shot another look at Jett's deck, inhaling deeply. He
would know…but before she could articulate another thought,
the phone rang.

Muirinn jumped at the sudden shrill noise, then, clearing
her throat, she lifted the receiver. "Hello?"

"Muirinn? This is Rick Frankl, returning your call. Welcome
to Safe Harbor—I'd love to meet with you sometime today."

Smoothing her hand over her hair, Muirinn glanced up at
the wall clock. She was nervous about meeting Rick and

taking over a small business she knew little about. "How are you fixed for time this afternoon, Rick?"

"Around noon would be perfect."

"I'll be there."

"Looking forward to it—we all are. And I can't begin to tell you how sorry we are for your loss, Muirinn. Gus was our cornerstone here. We *all* miss him."

She swallowed against the lump forming in her throat. "Thank you, Rick."

"His office is ready and waiting for you. We've left everything as it was, apart from some cleaning after the break-in—"

"Break-in?" Her hand tightened on the receiver. "When?"

"Two nights ago. Someone managed to disable the alarm system and come in via his office window."

"Was anything stolen?"

"Nothing that we can ascertain. Gus's desk drawers were ransacked and his computer was turned on, but that was it. We did file a report with the police, of course. Apparently there's not much more they can do in a case like this. The cop who responded said it was probably just vandals."

Muirinn shot another glance at the laptop, the photos spread out over the table. "Which cop?"

"Officer Ted Gage."

After finalizing the details of the meeting, Muirinn slowly replaced the handset, a coolness cloaking her skin. *Both* Gus's offices ransacked? This was more than coincidence.

And why hadn't Officer Gage mentioned this to her last night?

Muirinn quickly gathered up the photos and slid them back into the envelope. To be safe, she unlocked a drawer hidden in the side of Gus's thick, handcrafted table.

She placed both the envelope and the laptop into it, but as

she was about to shut and lock the drawer, she caught sight of a small bottle of pills in the drawer.

She picked up container and read the label. *Digoxin.*

Gus's heart medication.

Closing her fist around the bottle, holding it tight against her chest, Muirinn walked back to the window, eyes hot with emotion. Her grandfather had never mentioned his heart condition to her. But while that hurt, it wasn't surprising. Gus had routinely refused to acknowledge his encroaching age or ill health, and he used to drink all sorts of herb teas to ward off the inevitable.

Comfrey had been his favorite—knitbone tea, he'd called it. *"To knit them old bones."*

Her chest tightened at the memory of his words, and she swiped away an errant tear.

Gus had always said crying was a useless waste of time. If something worried you, you went out and fixed it. And that was exactly what she had to do now. She needed to get to the bottom of these break-ins. And she needed to know why Gus had been looking into the Tolkin Mine murders again.

Collecting herself, she locked the drawer, slipped the key and the pills into her purse, and glanced into the hall mirror. Tucking a strand of hair behind her ear, she scooped up the keys to Gus's Dodge truck.

She'd go into town, meet with Rick at the paper, and then head over to the police department.

Because now she really wanted some answers.

The truck wouldn't start.

Muirinn turned the ignition again, and it just clicked. The oil light on the dash glowed red.

Damn.

Muirinn climbed out of the cab, hoisted up her skirt and got onto hands and knees to look underneath the vehicle. Sure enough, there in the gravel was a big, dark pool of glistening liquid.

Stretching to reach under the truck, she tapped her finger lightly into the puddle so she could smell what it was.

"Muirinn!"

She jumped, banging her head on the undercarriage. Cursing, she backed out from under the vehicle and sat up, heart thumping.

"Is that *you*, Muirinn?"

She blinked up into bright sunlight at the silhouetted form of an old woman bent double, peering down at her with a bunch of purple flowers clutched in her hand.

"Mrs. Wilkie?" she said, rubbing her head. "My God, you half startled me to death!"

"Are you all right, dear? Did you hurt yourself?" she said in a warm, gravelly voice that Muirinn remembered so well from her youth.

"I'm fine." She got to her feet awkwardly, dusting her knees off. "I was just checking out the oil leak." The back of her head throbbed where she'd banged it, and her baby was kicking. Muirinn placed her hand on her belly, calming her baby and herself.

"I heard you'd come back, sprite." Mrs. Wilkie angled her head as she spoke, wrinkles fanning out from her intelligent gray eyes. Quicksilver, who'd materialized from nowhere at the sound of Mrs. Wilkie's voice, was purring and rubbing against the old lady's legs.

"I was just coming up to feed the cat, and to put some fresh flowers inside your house. I've also got some new herbs for tea. Sorry I scared you, dear."

Muirinn noted that Mrs. Wilkie's body had bowed even further to age, like a gnarled tree that had spent its life on a windswept shore. But she was still beautiful, her face tanned and creased in a way that spoke of kindness, her eyes still bright and quick. A thick gray braid hung over her shoulder, and she wore a long gypsy skirt, riotous with color. Muirinn wondered just how old the woman was now. To her mind, Mrs. Wilkie had seemed old forever, like a mythical crone.

She gave the hardy old dear a shaky smile, adrenaline still coursing through her body. "Thank you. It's good to see you, Mrs. Wilkie. I heard from the lawyer that you'd been taking excellent care of Gus, and I see you've been feeding Quicksilver, but I—"

Muirinn was about to say she no longer needed daily housekeeping services. Guilt stopped her. This woman had been here for Gus—she'd been a companion to him. Which was more than Muirinn could say for herself.

Mrs. Wilkie had lived in a small cottage down by the bay on Gus's property as long as Muirinn could remember. Even though it was now Muirinn's land, there was probably an official lease that still needed to be honored. Plus, the woman likely relied on the minimal income Gus had paid her, whatever it was.

Muirinn needed to go easy, go slow. Give things time.

"You were saying, dear?" Mrs. Wilkie was watching her intently, waiting.

"It's…nothing."

"Well, it's a terrible thing about Gus. I miss him. But it's good to see *you* back, Muirinn, and to see that you are expecting, too," Mrs. Wilkie said softly. "Are you going to have the baby here in Safe Harbor?"

Muirinn realized that she hadn't really thought that far ahead. "I… yes, I am."

"Well, if you go running into any trouble, you know where to find me. I've helped deliver my fair share of children, including my two nephews."

"I know. Thank you, Mrs. Wilkie." Muirinn was aware that Lydia Wilkie had once been a nurse who'd moved gradually into midwifery and naturopathy. She'd always had a keen interest in herbs and the natural healing practices of aboriginal peoples. When they were kids, Muirinn and Jett used to peer into her cottage window down by the water, pretending they were spying on the Good Witch because she was always boiling some herbal concoction on her blackened wood stove.

"Now, you call me Lydia," she said.

Muirinn smiled. "I can't. You've been *Mrs. Wilkie* to me forever."

Mrs. Wilkie's face crumpled into a grin. She took Muirinn's hand firmly in her gnarled one. "It's so good to have you home, sprite. Gus would be mighty pleased. Especially to have a small one around the house again."

Muirinn nodded, emotion prickling into her eyes again at the sound of her old nickname. Damn these pregnancy hormones and this trip down memory lane. "I know he would," she answered quietly.

I just wish I'd come home sooner.

Mrs. Wilkie turned, her gypsy skirt swirling around in a rainbow of color as she scuttled up the steps toward the front door. She unlocked it with her own key.

"Do you know any decent mechanics in town?" Muirinn called after her, vaguely uneasy with the idea of this woman coming and going into her house at will.

"Why, Jett next door could fix that truck for you, Muirinn. I'll just go right on inside, put these flowers down on the table and call him." She disappeared through the front door.

"Mrs. Wilkie! *Wait*—"

The old woman peeked back out the door. "What is it, love?"

"I…I'd rather call a mechanic from town."

"What nonsense. You've been away too long, sprite." She smiled. "We look after each other out here." And with that she vanished into the house.

Muirinn sank onto the bottom stair, tears threatening to overwhelm her again. She dropped her face into her hands fighting to hold it all in.

Pregnancy was making her so darn emotional about coming home.

So had seeing Jett.

Her feelings for him were still powerful—feelings for a man she could never have again.

A man she'd never stopped loving.

Jett found her sitting on stairs, crying.

His heart torqued and his throat tightened—the old Muirinn had never cried.

He shut of his ignition and got out of his truck. As he approached her, he felt his mouth go dry. She was wearing a chiffon skirt in pale spring colors. She had dirt on her smooth legs and he could see way too much of her thigh for male comfort. Her fiery hair hung wild and loose around her slender shoulders, glinting with gold strands in the sun.

"Hey," he said softly, sitting awkwardly beside her, trying to restrain himself from putting his arm around her and comforting her. "What's up?"

She sniffed, then laughed dryly as she smeared tears and dirt across her face. "God, I'm a stupid wreck. It's…it's the hormones." She nodded toward the truck. "Gus's truck didn't start. It was just a last little straw…" her voice faltered, hitched and flooded again with emotion. "I…miss him, Jett." Tears came again. *"I really miss him."*

And then he did touch her. He put his arm around her shoulders, drew her close and held her while she left her grief out. And he knew it was a mistake.

The warm curve of her breast, the firm swell of her belly against his torso, the exhilarating sensation of her thigh against his jeans…they did things to his body. Clouded his mind. With them came a raw and powerful protectiveness that surged through his chest, and Jett felt afraid—of what this could mean to all of them.

He was crossing a line. One look at her and he was falling in love all over again, when all he wanted was a reason to push her away, a reason to hate her, to despise her for what she'd done in the past.

But in this moment, the lines between past and present were blurring.

"I just wish I could have been here for Gus, then maybe… maybe this wouldn't have happened."

"What do you mean? His death?" Jett's voice came out thick.

She glanced up, luminous eyes red-rimmed from crying, and his heart squeezed all over again.

"You led the search-and-rescue team that found Gus, Jett. Tell me about it. Where exactly did you find his body?"

"Muirinn—"

"Please, Jett, everything. Step by step. I need to know."

He moistened his lips and nodded.

"When we first got the report that Gus was missing, we really had nothing to go on. Then on the thirteenth day, we got a break. A hunter called the police tip line to say he'd been on his way out into the bush almost two weeks earlier, when he'd seen Gus walking inside the perimeter fence of Tolkin Mine.

He hadn't thought anything of it until he'd returned and heard the news. We brought dogs in immediately, set them to work on the Tollkin property. They led us straight to the shaft—"

"Sodwana shaft?"

He frowned. "Yes, why?"

She hesitated. "Just wondering."

"The grate covering the man-way inside the headframe building had been pulled off. So we went down with ropes, flashlights." He paused, watching her, compassion filling his heart. "We found him down there. On the 300 level."

Muirinn's neck tensed. She swallowed. "What's on the 300 level?"

"More tunnels. Another man-way that leads further down, possibly as far as the 800 level."

"Who was the hunter who called in that tip, Jett?"

"The cops don't know. It's an anonymous tip line."

Her cheeks flushed with frustration, or maybe anger— he'd always found that so sexy, the way her complexion betrayed her emotions so easily.

"So, basically, my grandfather might've been saved if he'd just taken the trouble to tell someone where he was going that day. Why didn't he?"

"Who knows, Muirinn. You knew he was stubborn."

"But didn't you guys think it was odd that he was down there, down that shaft?"

"I had questions, sure," said Jett. "But the ME and the police went through everything. So did Dr. Callaghan. Pat had been treating Gus's heart condition for some time already. There was no evidence of foul play of any sort, if that's what you're thinking."

She bit her lip to stop it from wobbling, looked away.

"Hey—" he cupped her jaw, turned her face back to his,

and immediately regretted the impulse. "Gus was a really eccentric old guy, Muirinn, even more so these past few years. This was in keeping with his character."

Tears pooled in her eyes again, and Jett couldn't stop himself from asking. "You'd have known all this about Gus if you'd come to see him," he said quietly. "Why, Muirinn? Why didn't you ever come home to see your grandfather?"

She held his eyes, silent for several beats, something unreadable darkening her features. Then she sighed heavily. "I sent Gus plane tickets, Jett, so he could come to see me in New York."

"Yeah, he wasn't that impressed with the city. He told us about it."

Her lips flattened. "And for his birthday, I sent him a ticket to Spain. I met him in Madrid. Gus had a thing for Hemingway—he wanted to see a bullfight…" Tears spilled down her cheeks again. "Damn, I'm so sorry," she said brushing them away.

"Sorry for what? *Caring?*"

Her eyes shot up to his.

"Look, I guess I just don't understand why you didn't even come back for his memorial service, Muirinn. Or when you first heard he was missing."

"I didn't *know* he was missing!"

"*Someone* must have told you."

"I was unreachable, Jett, on assignment in the remote jungles of West Papua—"

"With no cell phone? No satellite connection, nothing?"

"Nothing." She rubbed her face. "That was the whole point of the assignment, to be inaccessible. For myself, an anthropologist and a photographer to spend some time with one of the world's last truly isolated tribes. Part of my story was to be about that sense of isolation. Our goal was to feel it."

"But you were—*are*—pregnant."

"And in good health. Women in those tribes have been bearing children in that jungle for centuries. The photographer was also a paramedic. I was not at risk."

"What if there had been an emergency?"

"That's the point, Jett. Our society can't conceive of living without phones, Internet, radios. We don't know how to cope on our own anymore. We go into a total panic at the mere *notion* of not being in contact, but it's not necessary. Besides, I grew up here, remember? My grandfather raised me to be self-sufficient."

"Stubborn is more like it," he muttered.

She glanced at him. "You disapprove of me."

Jett inhaled deeply, thinking how she'd run off pregnant with *his* baby, never allowing him to share in the joy of a pregnancy, the birth of his son.

"It's not just you that you need to think about," he said. "You have a responsibility toward a child now."

"You're still angry at me, aren't you?" she whispered.

He *wanted* to be. He needed *something* to shield himself from this woman. Anger was all he had to protect himself right now.

Jett got up suddenly, went to the truck.

"You're avoiding my question," she called after him.

"I'm doing what Mrs. Wilkie called me over to do," he said coolly, as he opened the door. "What happened when you tried to start it?"

"Nothing at all. I think it's an oil leak," Muirinn said, getting up and following him to the truck, sun burning down hot on her head as it rose higher in the clear blue sky.

He climbed into the cab. "There's a bunch of gray silt on the floor here," he said, turning the key in the ignition. It clicked but the engine didn't start. "You'll need to clean this thing out if you want your city clothes to stay all fancy," he said, shooting her a glance. "And you're going to need better sandals, too, if you actually want to get around."

"I was going into the office, to meet Rick Frankl," she replied crisply. "And then I was going to see the police chief—"

He crooked up a brow. "Chief Moran?"

"Whoever."

He turned the key again and frowned. "Oil light is on."

"Doesn't take a genius to see that."

Jett scowled, popped the hood and climbed out of the cab.

"What do you want to see Moran for? To complain about Gage?" He checked the oil as he spoke, then stripped off his shirt.

Muirinn's heart skipped a beat as her gaze tracked over his naked torso, down to the dark hair that ran in a whorl into his jeans. Heat flooded her veins and she swallowed, feeling a small bead of sweat roll down between her breasts.

His eyes darkened—he was clearly aware of the effect his naked, sun-browned abs were having on her. This made her cheeks flush red and her pulse race. "I…uh, there was another break-in, at Gus's newspaper office."

"What?"

"According to Rick, nothing was taken," she said, her voice husky. She cleared her throat. "Officer Gage responded to that incident as well. He should've said something to me, and I intend to take this up with his superior, because this can't be a coincidence. *Someone* is looking for *something* that belonged to Gus."

He was looking at her mouth. But he tore his gaze away, got down on his haunches and slid himself under the truck.

Muirinn stared at him, the way his thigh muscles flexed under the fabric of his jeans. Her mouth turned dry. This was wrong, so wrong.

"Looks like the oil sump was ruptured by something—a

sharp rock maybe," he called out from under the vehicle. "It's been leaking out for some time."

He came out from under the truck and got to his feet in a fluid, powerful movement. He reached into the cab for a rag. "A new sump, some oil and it'll be good as new," he said wiping his hands on the rag, avoiding her eyes now. He put his shirt back on, ruffled his hand through his hair and then hesitated, as if unsure, nervous.

Then he handed Muirinn her purse from inside the truck. "I'll drive you into town. I can pick up a new sump and oil while you meet with Frankl, then I'll go with you to the cops."

Anxiety licked at her. "You don't have to do this, Jett."

He moistened his lips, still avoiding her eyes. "Yeah, I do. I don't like these break-ins, either. And I don't like the way Ted Gage treated you. Besides, Chief Don Moran can be a bear at the best of times—"

"Don—is *he* chief now? As in Bill's little brother?"

"Keeping it in the family, those Morans." He smiled, but it didn't quite reach into his eyes. "Things really went to the collective Moran head when the youngest brother's wife was elected mayor. Now they think they run this town."

Jett touched her elbow gently as he led her to his truck.

"You mean Chalky Moran's wife? Who did he marry?"

He opened the passenger door for her. "Kate Lonsdale. She's been mayor for the past year now."

They drove in tense silence along the twisting dirt road that clung to the ragged shoreline, dust billowing out behind them.

Muirinn wished she could rewind the last half hour, retract Mrs. Wilkie's call to Jett. She should never have let this happen, never should have let him touch her. Because she'd seen in his eyes that, hidden behind that brittle shell, he still felt something for her. And she sure as hell felt *everything* for him.

But he was married. Out of bounds.

And Muirinn owed it to his wife, his son, to *him,* to stay away, leave the past where it belonged.

She felt him glance at her and she swallowed, cheeks flushing hot as she looked away.

And in that moment she knew it was too late. She was already in trouble.

They both were.

Chapter 4

Chief Don Moran shut his office door and motioned for Muirinn and Jett to take a seat. Through his glass walls Muirinn could see Ted Gage watching them intently from his desk across the bullpen. She could feel the other officers watching, too, and wished Moran would lower the blinds.

"What can I do for you, Ms. O'Donnell?" Moran said as he took his seat on the opposite side of his metal desk, his eyes flicking to Jett. He was clearly not surprised to see her back in town, nor was he overly thrilled about it.

Don looked unnervingly like his much older brother, William "Bill" Moran, from his father's first marriage. It was as if Don had somehow morphed into his brother with age.

While Don had been just a twenty-two-year-old rookie at the time of the Tolkin blast, Bill had been the Safe Harbor police chief. It was Bill who'd approached Muirinn's mother in the snow that day, and told her that her husband was among the dead.

Seeing Don looking so much like his brother threw Muirinn off guard. Gray images of that tragic, snowy spring morning suddenly filled her mind, and for a disconcerting moment, she was nine years old again.

She cleared her throat. "My grandfather's—*my*—house at Mermaid's Cove was broken into last night—"

"I saw the report, yes. Vandals, most likely."

She leaned forward. "I don't think so, Chief Moran. I've just learned that Gus's newspaper office was also broken into, two days ago. Nothing was taken there, either."

Moran glanced discreetly at his watch, telegraphing mild impatience. "What is it that seems to be the problem, Ms. O'Donnell?"

"I believe the break-ins have to be connected, and that someone was looking for something in Gus's papers or computer files."

His eyes turned flat, inscrutable. Silence hung for a beat. "What gives you that idea?"

Muirinn felt Jett stiffen beside her. She placed her hand on his knee to steady him—and take support from his proximity. "Pardon me, Chief, but what *wouldn't* give me that idea? Gus was—" suddenly she didn't want to mention the Tolkin file, the photographs, what Gus might have been working on. She had a bad feeling about it all, about the way the other cops were eyeing her from the bullpen.

He waited for her to continue.

"I…was just hoping that you'd have one of your men look into it."

He inhaled deeply, and stood. "We treat all our cases with due consideration, Ms. O'Donnell." His gaze lingered on Jett for a moment, his jaw tight. "And we allocate our resources accordingly. But we're extremely short-staffed, given the city budget cuts."

"Looks like you have a few men to spare at the moment." Jett interjected, nodding his head to the guys watching from the bullpen.

Moran's eye twitched slightly. "I'll see what we can do." He went to the door and swung it open, waiting for them to leave, his features expressionless.

"Thank you," Muirinn said, getting to her feet, but she hesitated in the doorway, bolstered by Jett at her side. "Chief Moran, why did it take so long to find him? I mean, my grandfather was missing for over two weeks. Didn't *anyone* see his truck parked out at the Tolkin site?"

"There was no vehicle parked out there, Ms. O'Donnell."

"What?" She shot a questioning glance at Jett. "No one told me that."

"Our assumption is that Gus hiked out to the mine."

"You're kidding. With a heart condition? That's fifteen to twenty miles out of town. In summer heat. I—"

"Ms. O'Donnell, I really am very sorry for your loss, but I can't speak to your grandfather's health condition, nor to his state of mind at the time of his disappearance. All I can tell you is that the ME determined the cause of death to be a heart attack." His voice softened slightly. "If you want to know more, why don't you go talk to Doc Callaghan? She was treating your grandfather."

"I will. I just don't understand why it took everyone so long to find him down there," she said quietly. Now that she'd actually voiced it, she was convinced that there was something seriously amiss with the circumstances surrounding her grandfather's death.

"Really, there's nothing more to it than meets the eye, Ms. O'Donnell." Moran smiled.

She met his gaze. "Yes," she said. "I'm sure it's all…co-incidence."

Jett thanked the chief for his time, then placed his hand gently on her elbow as he guided Muirinn out of the police station into the harsh sunlight. She put on her shades.

"You're shaking," he said softly.

"I—" she exhaled nervously. "I guess I am. Must be low blood sugar or something. Why didn't you tell me that Gus didn't drive out to the mine?"

"I thought you knew those details." Concern softened his blue eyes. "Have you eaten, Muirinn?"

"I…I just haven't been hungry."

"Come, we're getting some lunch into you."

"Jett, I should really just go home."

"Food first, then I'll take you home." His tone brooked no argument, and Muirinn allowed him to escort her down to a small café patio with red umbrellas near the harbor, feeling that each second longer she spent with him, the further she was headed past the point of no return.

People stared openly as they walked, and her sense of unease deepened. The rumors had no doubt rippled through town—Safe Harbor's prodigal daughter had returned. And now she was seven months' pregnant, being escorted around town by a married man.

She wondered, too, how they must judge her for missing Gus's funeral, coming after the fact to claim her inheritance.

They had no idea what remorse she was feeling at not having returned once in eleven years to see her grandfather. Even though she'd met with Gus on neutral territory over the years, she now realized that it had probably hurt Gus beyond words that she hadn't come home.

The irony wasn't lost on her.

She'd done it solely to avoid Jett, yet here he was, the man who had her back now. And she realized just how deeply she'd missed him.

And how much trouble she was getting herself into.

"Jett," she said softly as he pulled out a chair for her at a table under a red umbrella, feeling people watching. "I really don't think this is a good idea."

"Sit, Muirinn. Just eat something, and then I'll take you right home."

That was the kind of man he was. Like his father, Jett was hardwired to save, rescue. Protect. Emotion choked her inexplicably. She took a seat and a second to compose herself.

He avoided her gaze as he reached for the menu, but the small muscle at the base of his jaw pulsed. He was as conflicted as she was, and Muirinn could see it.

I'm sorry to have put you in this position. I promise to stay out of your way after today, Jett.

Jett stared blindly at the menu, unable to focus on the items. What in hell was he really looking for here, right this minute? With her?

For a brief shining nanosecond, he knew. This wasn't about trying to help her figure out what had gone down with Gus, or about helping her with the truck. *He wanted her back.*

He wanted her to prove herself to him, so he could feel safe enough to tell her about their son. So he could tell her that he wasn't married.

Mostly, he needed her to come clean about having given his baby away behind his back. He wanted to hear her say that she was sorry. He wanted to know that she'd felt remorse.

And he wanted to be sure that she was going to stay.

Only then could he tell her about Troy.

Only then could he trust himself to be near her, because his body sure as hell had different ideas from his mind.

Jett blew out a breath, and dragged his fingers through his hair. "What're you having?"

"Orange juice."

He glanced up. "You need more. You're eating for two."

"I'm not really hungry."

He flipped the menu shut, ordered a sandwich, juice and coffee. "Now tell me what's going on, Muirinn," he said as the waitress left.

"You mean with the break-ins?"

No, with you, the baby, the father, that fancy magazine job—everything.

"Yeah, with the break-ins," he said instead. "You're clearly suspicious about Gus's death, and you asked me earlier specifically if he'd been found down the Sodwana shaft. And I want to know why."

She fiddled with her napkin, her clear green eyes holding his for a moment, and a band squeezed tight across his chest. She was so strikingly gorgeous, and—though he hated to admit it—even more attractive to him now than she'd been a decade ago.

There was a new sophistication, a wisdom in her eyes, yet it was balanced by a softness that came with pregnancy, and with the pain of the loss she'd just experienced.

She'd been all wild, rough edges when she was nineteen; a flat-out challenge. He suspected that he hadn't been much different himself. Hell, they were just kids; their relationship as combative as it had been loving. It had been about the sparring, the fun. The sex.

Until it had all gone bad.

"I think Gus was investigating the old Tolkin murders—"

"Muirinn—" he interjected, leaning forward. "—Gus was *always* thinking about the Tolkin murders. That's nothing new."

"I think he might have come across some new crime scene photos, Jett." She lowered her voice, glancing at the tables around theirs. "I believe those photos and Gus's laptop could have been the target of the break-ins, because I'd removed them from his attic desk just before going to sleep that night."

Jett frowned. "What's in the laptop?"

"I don't know yet—it's password-protected. But Rick Frankl is sending a tech around later."

Unease trickled into Jett, along with worry.

Damn.

The last thing he wanted right now was to worry about Muirinn. What he wanted was space, to think. Her proximity was clouding his mind, driving his libido to distraction. He inhaled deeply. "Will you let me know what you find?"

"Sure," she said, reaching for her shades.

He placed his hand over hers, stopping her. "Muirinn? You *will* call?"

She cast her eyes down. "I don't want to have to call you, Jett," she whispered.

"Why?"

She swallowed, looked up slowly, her eyes glittering with emotion. "You're attached, Jett. You have a family. A wife."

For a very long beat he said nothing, and a heated current thrummed between them.

Don't say anything stupid here, buddy. Think of Troy.

"Where were your wife and Troy going yesterday?" she asked suddenly.

He hesitated, then lied by omission. "She was taking him

to summer camp," he said, circumnavigating the part about his divorce five years ago, knowing at the same time he'd just started digging a hole that he was going to have one hell of a time climbing out of.

"What's your wife's name, Jett?"

"Kim." At least that wasn't a lie, exactly.

Her jaw quivered and she bit her lip.

Guilt stabbed through him. He told himself he was entitled to do this, she probably had a man waiting for her somewhere, perhaps even coming to join her. And suddenly he couldn't stop himself from asking.

"What about the father of your baby, Muirinn? Where is he?"

She turned and stared out over the sea. "I'm flying solo, Jett," she said very quietly. "I'm doing this on my own."

Something hot ripped through him. "What do you mean?"

She sighed. "Things just never worked out. I...I could never seem to find the right guy."

So she'd done it again.

She'd gotten pregnant with her lover's child, and then she'd abandoned the man, not giving him a chance, *a choice,* to be a father. It instantly tempered his feelings toward her.

Jett could remember *exactly* what it had felt like. He recalled just how badly she could dig the knife into his heart, and twist.

How she might do it again—if he let her.

He cleared his throat. "And what exactly were you looking for in a guy, Muirinn?" he said coolly.

She breathed out nervously. "You, I think."

He felt the blood rush from his head.

"God," she whispered, panic flaring in her eyes. "That... that was a terrible mistake." She got up so fast she knocked her chair back onto the patio. "I…I am so sorry, Jett." She spun around, walking as fast she could.

Jett stared, glued to his seat for a nanosecond before his brain kicked back into gear. Then he leaped up, digging into his back pocket for his wallet. He dumped a wad of cash onto the table, and ran after her into the street. "Muirinn! Stop!"

She didn't look back.

Instead, she waved wildly to a passing cab.

She was in the door, and the cab was pulling off, before he reached her.

Jett watched the brake lights flare at the stop sign at the end of the block. Then the cab turned the corner and vanished.

He stood there in the street, shell-shocked.

She still loved him.

She'd never stopped.

Exhilaration mounted inside him like a wild thing, coupled tightly with fear for his child. Because she was still capable of dumping him—just as she'd obviously dumped the father of her new baby.

"If O'Donnell has accessed that laptop, it means she's seen the old man's theory," said the voice on the phone. "It's only a matter of time before she connects the rest of the dots."

"Christ, if this gets out—"

"It *can't.*"

"So what do we do now?"

Silence. Heavy, loaded silence.

"Oh, sweet Jesus, no. If something happens to Muirinn O'Donnell it's going send red flags up all over the goddamn place!"

"Then we control those flags, because—" The voice lowered. "—the alternative is far, far worse."

"What about *him?*"

"We don't know how deep he is in yet, which is why this must happen fast—understand? One step at a time."

More silence.

"Look, we can handle this—we've managed worse before, remember?" The voice went even quieter still. "Find a way. Just make sure it looks like an accident."

The phone clicked.

Chapter 5

Muirinn powered up Gus's laptap.

After fleeing Jett in the cab yesterday she'd spent the afternoon tidying her grandfather's attic office, and the evening going through the newspaper company books. Her sleep that night had been fitful, and she'd awakened late in the morning to learn from Mrs. Wilkie that Jett had quietly come around at 5:00 a.m to replace the fuel sump in the truck.

Clearly, he'd been avoiding her.

It was for the best.

Muirinn exhaled in exasperation as she pulled her hair back into a severe ponytail. She was utterly mortified by what had come out of her mouth yesterday. Even more disturbing was the spark of need she'd glimpsed in his eyes, the tenderness she'd felt in his touch.

It was all still there—their old bond, the raw, simmering attraction. She and Jett were like flame to fireworks. Always had been. There was just no way she could be in his presence, or he in hers, without things exploding.

She'd send him a thank-you note for fixing the truck, because her promise to herself—her *vow* to him—was to stay the hell out of his life until things settled down, and his wife and child returned.

She rubbed her face angrily, and clicked open the file labeled *Tolkin.*

And with slow, mounting horror, she began to read what her grandfather had written.

According to Gus, the crime scene photographs labeled *missing* in the brown envelope, had "disappeared" from the Safe Harbor Police Department's evidence room twenty years ago, during the violent snowstorm that delayed the FBI post-blast team's arrival for forty-eight hours.

Since then they'd been in the possession of retired and recently deceased SHPD officer, Ike Potter.

Over the last few years, Ike, who'd been suffering from cancer, had become a close friend of Gus's. They'd played chess regularly at the Seven Seas Club. It was during these chess games that Ike had learned the sheer extent of Gus's obsession with the Tolkin murders and his desperate need for closure, to find out who had killed his son.

This knowledge had begun to wear Ike down, and on his deathbed, Ike had told Gus that he had wanted to come clean, to make peace with the past. And he'd told Gus his story, entrusting him with several crime scene photos that had been kept in a safe deposit box up until that point.

Muirinn scrolled further.

The night of the blizzard, Ike had returned to the police station to pick up a plug-in cable for his vehicle. That was when he'd witnessed a fellow SHPD officer in the dark, with a flashlight, removing the photos from police evidence. The officer had however been interrupted by someone else coming down the hall, and he'd hurriedly trashed them with department waste that was destined for routine incineration in a few hours.

Ike had waited until the coast was clear, then he'd retrieved the photographs and hidden them himself while he tried to figure out what was going on.

The photos were of bootprints taken outside and inside the Sodwana headframe building, and of prints inside the mine allegedly made by the bomber.

Muirinn's pulse accelerated.

It was Ike's belief that the prints documented in these photos had been compromised by someone in the SHPD before the FBI team could get in, contaminating the scene and thus sabotaging the investigation.

Muirinn scrolled faster through Gus's notes, tension squeezing her chest like a vise.

But Ike had died before finishing his whole story. And for some reason, he'd never blown the whistle until speaking to Gus.

There was also no mention of *which* SHPD officer had originally taken the photos from evidence. Muirinn had no means of knowing whether he—or she—was still even a cop. Twenty years was a long time.

Blown away by what she'd just read, Muirinn sat back to catch her breath. According to Gus's notes, more than one person in Safe Harbor had covered the tracks of the man who had killed her dad, and her mom by default. Nausea—and rage—began to swirl in her stomach.

She turned back to the computer. But the notes ended, the last questions posed: *Did bomber use Sodwana shaft to access D-shaft where bomb was planted? Did accomplice stand guard at headframe?*

Accomplice?

Perspiration prickled over Muirinn's skin.

This was even worse than she'd imagined. This was a conspiracy. The burglar must have been after this information.

And there was certainly no way she could trust the cops now.

Hurriedly, Muirinn emptied the photographs onto the table, spreading them out. She separated the photos labeled *missing* from the rest, and she picked up the image of bootprints made outside the Sodwana headframe building.

Were these the prints of an accomplice?

She selected another photo—of the prints in black mud allegedly made by the bomber himself. A chill crawled over her skin as she wondered whether the man who'd made them still walked the streets of Safe Harbor.

She got up and started pacing in front of the windows, her heart beating fast. She wondered just how far someone would go to keep this old secret buried.

Could they have killed Gus for this?

Who could she turn to? Not Jett. No way. She'd made a vow—she wasn't going to mess up his family.

She clasped her hand over the little bone compass at her neck. Whatever the answers, she owed it to Gus to find them, to see through what he'd started and secure the closure he'd sought so desperately for the last twenty years.

She owed her dad.

Her mom.

And Muirinn owed it to herself to finally put the past to rest. That Tolkin blast had torn her life apart. It was part of the reason she'd come to hate Safe Harbor, and had so desperately needed to leave it. And leaving had cost her so much.

Including her first child. And Jett.

Now she had a new baby on the way, a business to run. And she had a home she could really call her own—the childhood home that her father had crossed the picket line and died to keep, the home that Gus had stepped in to save from foreclosure after her parents' deaths. This just made her more determined to stay. Muirinn truly had something to fight for now, and she was not going to let whoever had destroyed her past destroy her future, too.

She moved closer to the window, staring absently at Jett's deck in the distance as her mind raced, and she was suddenly distracted by a sharp flash of light. Then another.

Muirinn went to a corner window where Gus's powerful telescope stood atop a tripod.

She swung the massive scope over to Jett's property, bent slightly and peered through the sight, adjusting the focus.

Surprise rippled through her.

Jett.

Standing on his deck, wearing only drawstring shorts slung low and baggy on taut hips. And he was aiming binoculars at her house…directly at the window in front of which she'd just been sitting.

Had he been watching her all this time?

But now she was watching him, and he was totally unaware. "Gotcha," she whispered.

She quickly sharpened the telescope's focus.

Her grandfather's equipment was state of the art—she could make out the individual ridges of muscle on Jett's sun-bronzed torso. He looked as though he'd just stepped out of a shower, hair damp and hanging over his brow.

From the privacy of her corner window, Muirinn couldn't help but study him, panning the telescope slowly over the length of his body, going lower and lower down his abs, following the whorl of dark hair into his shorts. Heat pooled low in her abdomen and she felt her nipples tingle.

Jett suddenly angled his binoculars over to her window.

Muirinn's breathing stalled.

Jett's body stiffened as he caught her looking at him from the side window. But he didn't lower his binoculars. He stared right back at her, a slow wry smile forming on his lips.

Stepping back quickly from the lens, she dragged her hands over her hair, face flushing hot. Panic started to circle.

Muirinn quickly reached forward and dropped the blinds. As if that could wipe out what had just happened.

She paced the dining room, swearing to herself. Truly, the best thing for both of them would be for her to get out of here, to leave Safe Harbor. Soon.

But she wasn't going to do that.

Gus had wanted her to come back.

And she had too much to fight for now. Damn, she had a *right* to be here, to make a life in Safe Harbor if she so chose.

She shot another glance at Gus's laptop, thinking again about the murders.

How had she manage to end up between a rock and a hard place like this, anyway? Frustration mounted in her, and it turned gradually to anger.

Jett had a responsibility to his family, too. He had no right to spy on her like that.

Snapping the laptop shut, she glanced around. The hidden drawer under the table was still the best place to secure the computer and photographic evidence. She slid the laptop back into the secret compartment, but before she locked the drawer and pocketed the key, she removed four of the photographs labeled *missing* and slipped them into the side pocket of her cargo pants. Then she unlocked her grandfather's gun cabinet.

She was going to see that mine for herself.

She needed to stand exactly where her grandfather had stood. She wanted to match the photos to the Sodwana site, walk Gus's last steps, *feel* what he might have felt.

The mine lay farther north, and the area was isolated. Her grandfather had taught her to go prepared when going anywhere in the Alaskan bush, so Muirinn removed a .22 rifle and a box of ammunition.

Perhaps once she'd been to the mine, she'd manage to make some sense of it all.

Jett sat at his glass-topped trestle desk, the blueprints for his wilderness lodge spread out in front of him—his big dream project. But he couldn't concentrate on his future.

He hadn't been able to concentrate at all since Muirinn O'Donnell walked back into his life.

He picked up his scopes again and went back to the window, excitement trilling dangerously like a drug though his blood. He could not get her words from yesterday out of his mind. They'd lodged inside him like a big barbed hook, bleeding a trickle of hope deep into his system.

A rueful grin tugged at his lips as he saw that she'd drawn the blinds. His smile deepened—he hadn't been able to stop himself from toying with her when she'd caught him red-handed with his binoculars aimed at her house. Locking eyes with her through those scopes had been intense, sexual, even over the distance. Damn, she'd made him hard just by looking.

It had always been that way with Muirinn. She sparked the playful in him. The daring. The lust.

The goddamn pain.

Easy on the eyes, hard on the heart—that was Muirinn O'Donnell.

And now that he knew she was available, and that she still clearly wanted him, it raised the stakes.

Big time.

He swore softly.

Going near her again would be akin to touching fire. He'd get burned, and he knew it.

Even worse, Troy would get burned.

Jett put the scopes down, and returned to his desk. But he still couldn't focus on his project. And the more he sat there, the more he felt like an ass for his little episode with the binoculars.

He grabbed his shirt, yanked on his jeans and scooped up his keys.

He drove his truck over to Muirinn's house under the pretext of apologizing for scoping her out; besides, he needed to head into the village anyway, to pick up some supplies. But deep down Jett just needed to see her again. She was his addiction; always had been.

But as he pulled into her driveway, he saw that Gus's truck was gone, and Mrs. Wilkie was bustling down the front steps of the porch, bag in hand, looking flustered.

He rolled down his window, hooked his elbow out. "Lydia?" he said.

She started. "Jett! Muirinn's not here."

He frowned at the odd edginess in her tone. "Do you know where she went?"

"That's the whole thing, Jett—she went to that awful mine! I…I told her she shouldn't go alone, but you know Muirinn. She never did listen. She left in a real hurry, and she was carrying one of Gus's guns."

"*What?* Are you sure?"

"Of course I'm sure. It was a hunting rifle."

"I mean, are you sure that she went to *Tolkin?*"

"That's where she said she was going."

Jett thought about Muirinn's suspicions—the way she'd practically interrogated Chief Moran.

Had she managed to access Gus's laptop and found out more? Is that why she'd gone to the mine?

Damn—she'd said she would call him.

Angry now, and more than a little concerned, Jett suddenly slammed his truck in reverse, sped backwards down the driveway and spun out into the dirt road.

He punched down on the gas and headed north to the abandoned mine, a sense of unease digging deeper into his chest.

Chapter 6

Muirinn sped down the dirt road, fine gray alluvial silt billowing out behind Gus's truck as she made her way up through the gulley, into the valley of the Tolkin Mine.

It felt good to drive with the window down, to have the warm summer wind ripping through her long hair, the big fat truck tires under her. The wilderness of this place was whispering through her again, awakening her consciousness.

After having lived in Manhattan, traveling the world, chasing her image of freedom, Muirinn finally realized how much she'd actually sacrificed. Deep down, she knew that everything she'd ever dreamed of was right here.

But she'd needed to get beyond those granite peaks, transcend it all, see what lay beyond the horizons just to be able to return on her own terms. When she was ready.

Except she *hadn't* come back on her own terms.

She'd come on Gus's terms—the terms of his will.

Muirinn drew up at Gate 7, the main entrance to the Tolkin property, and checked the odometer—15.4 miles since leaving home. That was how far Gus would have had to have hiked with his heart condition.

Allegedly he'd done it about a month ago—in June. The weather would very likely have been warm, maybe even hot.

She didn't buy it.

That, in turn, provoked another disturbing question—had someone brought him out here? A cab, maybe? Perhaps his truck had already been malfunctioning.

But if someone *had* dropped Gus out here, why had that person failed to come forward right away when the alarm was first raised that he was missing?

And the reason she was now heading out to the mine troubled her.

Muirinn got out of the vehicle and walked slowly up to the gate. Heat pressed down on her.

A six-foot-high, rusting, chain-link fence ran the length of the property. A hardboard sign, paint peeling, clanked against a pole in the hot breeze, fading letters proclaiming the Tolkin Mine private property, warning trespassers they would be prosecuted.

The big strike had lasted over a year. Combined with the mass homicide twenty years ago, it had resulted in severe staffing and production problems for the Tolkin Mining Corporation. Development mining—the boring of new tunnels deeper into rock in order to reach fresh veins of ore—had to be scaled back, resulting in a shortage of quality ore. And new gold mines in the north had subsequently opened, producing a far greater yield. The resultant competition had killed the Safe Harbor mine, and Tolkin had finally shut its doors seven years after the bombing.

The property had sat abandoned ever since, crumbling with time and seasons.

For a moment Muirinn just stood there, snared by a surge of memories, the place coming to life with people, frantic, milling around like ants. She could hear sirens, see the acrid smoke boiling up out of D-shaft, feel the spring snow cold on her cheeks, her mother's hand icy in hers. Chief Bill Moran was walking toward them…

Clouds began to gather in the sky, suddenly darkening the ground. The air grew hotter, closer. The strange thrum of a grouse reverberated against the stillness.

Muirinn shook herself, rubbing the chill of the memory from her arms.

She glanced up at the avalanche-scarred mountains that soared up on either side of the Tolkin Valley. Their plunging chutes looked dark and ominous, although they shouldn't. They were choked with the vibrant green of deciduous summer growth that had burst from snow-scoured ground, and higher up on the peaks, avalanche lilies—a favorite food of grizzlies—had formed a verdant green carpet.

Muirinn stepped up to the gate.

The chain and lock had long ago been rusted and pried open by vandals. Unhooking what was left of the chain, Muirinn creaked open the massive gate, dragging it wide through the dirt so she could bring the truck in.

She drove through, shut the gate behind her, and traveled along the perimeter fence for about three miles until the Sodwana headframe loomed on a rise ahead, a grim, rusting, metal skeleton in the shape of an *A,* a small derelict building squatting at its base.

Just like the photo.

Muirinn stopped alongside the shed.

The windows were partially boarded up, a metal drum and old iron boxcar resting outside. Plastic flapped in the hot breeze. Her mouth felt dry.

This was a bad place, choked with the ghosts of old miners. She didn't like to think of Gus here, alone. Or down the shaft.

Muirinn retrieved the rifle from the gun box, loaded it and released the safety. She couldn't say why exactly. But she felt edgy, as if she were being watched by unseen eyes.

Wind gusted, stirring fine silt up into a soft dervish, and suddenly it was cold again, and the silt was blowing snow, and she could see Chief Bill Moran coming, looming, the grim news carried in his posture and stride… Disconcerted, Muirinn again shook away the haunting images.

This place had an eerie way of slamming present and past together, and Muirinn realized that that was exactly why Gus had come here. And why she was here now, too.

Approaching the old headframe building, the .22 clutched a little too tightly in her hand, her eyes tracked over the dry ground, trying to see where the old photos might have been taken, where some accomplice might have stood vigil on a cold morning twenty years ago as a killer trekked deep underground.

A sudden soft whoosh of breeze rustled through the alders, leaves clapping like little hands, an invisible audience watching, waiting, cheering. She glanced nervously back at the main gate. It suddenly seemed so far. Her hand touched her belly.

Maybe she shouldn't have come out here alone, but she honestly didn't know who she could turn to right now, apart from Jett. And that definitely wasn't going to happen.

Making sure her cell phone was easily accessible in her pocket, Muirinn pushed open the old door. It released an inhuman groan of protest, rusted metal grinding against the hinge.

Her heart hammered.

It was stifling inside, rank. She shivered again. Her gaze skimmed around the interior, settling on the heavy-looking grate covering the man-way as the last words in Gus's notes sifted into Muirinn's mind.

Did bomber use Sodwana shaft to access D-shaft where bomb was planted? Did accomplice stand guard at headframe?

Was that why he dragged the grate back and climbed down into that black hole?

Maybe he'd wanted to see if it was actually possible to access the bomb site underground from this shaft, and how long it might take.

No, that was pure insanity.

Her grandfather might have been eccentric, but he would never have gone down that shaft alone, not at his age, not with his heart condition. Not without telling anyone where he was going.

She propped her rifle against the wall, bent down to tug the grate off the man-way. It was heavy iron, virtually immovable. She tried to imagine Gus doing this. Sweat prickled over her body as she hefted it a few inches, then a few more, metal grating across metal until she managed to pull the grate right off. Her hands burned, smelled of rust. She'd never have gotten this off if it hadn't been removed and replaced recently.

Dank air from deep in the bowels of the earth reached up, cold, crawling right into her. Peering cautiously down into the black abyss, Muirinn was suddenly 100 percent convinced that Gus wouldn't have taken hold of the decaying old ladder rungs and climbed into that black maw alone.

But as she bent down to replace the cover, a powerful crack resounded through the quiet hills, and a slug slammed into metal just near her shoulder. A cloud of birds scattered from a clump of alders.

It took a nanosecond for Muirinn to grasp what had just happened.

Gunshot!

She crouched down, mind racing. *Must be a hunter. And I just happen to be in the line of fire,* she thought, peeking up carefully through the slatted boards just as another explosive sound boomed through the valley. A slug hammered into the opposite wall, splitting a support beam into shrapnel. A piece stabbed into her shoulder.

Muirinn gasped, clamping her hand over the wound. Blood started to well between her fingers, dribbling down her arm. The report echoed down through the valley, fading into the distant stillness.

She could hardly breathe.

That was no simple rifle. That was the distinctive explosive sound of a point three-effing-oh-three, with enough firepower to fell a moose at full charge!

Almost immediately, another shot walloped through the wall. She dived to her knees, slamming down onto her side into the dirt. Her phone clattered out of her pocket and skittered across the floor.

Grouse fluttered outside.

Someone was shooting at this shack!

She lay dead still, heart jackhammering, skin drenched with sweat. And blood.

Then came another report—this one clunking off the ironwork outside.

Her stomach started to cramp. *My baby.* Oh, Lord, she shouldn't have come here alone. Muirinn inched along the dirt on her side, reaching for her rifle. Gripping it in her hands, she wriggled over to a second window that had been boarded over. She edged up, inserted the barrel of her .22 through a large crack. She scanned the mountainside with her scopes, trying to locate the shooter.

She caught a movement in the brush, a slight glint of sunlight against metal. Someone was hiding in the bush, dressed in camo gear and hunting cap, aiming at the shed.

With shaking hands she snugged her cheek against the stock, aimed to the right of the sniper and slowly squeezed off a round.

Almost instantly the sniper returned fire, blasting the boards clear from the window. Muirinn screamed, dropping her rifle as she scrambled for cover. Shattered wood blew clear across the room, a piece glancing across her temple.

Panic and pain tore through her body.

Her weapon was no match for that kind of firepower.

Muirinn tried to crawl over to her phone. But the sniper could now see in through the window with his powerful scope, and a slug *thwoked* into the dirt just in front of her cell, shooting sand into her face.

She lurched back with a whimper, crawled into a far corner and cowered there, blood now running down her face from the wound on her temple as more slugs slammed through the shack.

The only reason she wasn't dead already was because the heavy metal boxcar outside was preventing bullets from coming through the wall. But that meant she couldn't move. She couldn't call for help.

Tears of frustration burned into her eyes. She held her stomach, feeling small cramps sparking across her abdomen.

Oh, please, I don't want to die like this. I don't want to lose my baby.

Then she heard a slug thunk into her truck outside, and the powerful odor of gas fumes reached her nostrils. Another well-aimed shot ignited the fuel with an explosive *whoosh* that filled the air with a rush. She heard the hot crackle of flames, saw black smoke rising outside the far window. Someone out there was determined to kill her.

If the shack caught fire, she'd be burned alive.

If she tried to flee, she'd be shot.

She was trapped.

Jett's truck bounced over ruts in the road as he raced north, a cone of silt roiling out behind him. His gun lay on the seat beside him. He had no idea what Muirinn was up to, but a cold instinct told him trouble awaited.

Nearing the Tolkin perimeter, he saw a plume of black smoke twisting up into the wind.

Jett slammed down on the gas and blew his truck right through the closed mine gate, smashing it back with a violent crash and scrape of metal. Spinning his tires in the fine dry dirt, he swerved and sped along the perimeter fence, aiming for the source of the smoke.

As he approached, he realized it was Gus's red truck burning.

Jett drove even faster. But suddenly a cloud of dirt spat sharply up in front of his tires. Then another. Then something thudded into the bed of his truck.

With raw, gut-slamming shock, Jett realized that someone up in the hills was shooting at *him,* trying to stop him from reaching the shed. And judging by the burning wreck of the truck and the state of the shed, Muirinn was holed up in there like prey.

Or worse.

She could already be dead.

Chapter 7

Jett skidded to a stop behind the headframe building and flung open his door, dropping down behind his vehicle as another shot slammed into the ground. Resting his rifle barrel on the bed of the truck, Jett edged up, squinting into the scope.

He saw the glint of a weapon, then a sharp movement in leaves up on the hill, as if the sniper had suddenly seen him looking and ducked.

Reining in his adrenaline, Jett forced his breath out, slow and measured, and he squeezed off a shot. The bushes on the hill rustled sharply. Then a cloud of dust boiled up into the air as the shooter fled into the mountains on an all-terrain vehicle.

Jett burst through the shed door, slamming it back off its hinge.

Muirinn scampered backwards with a whimper, blind terror in her eyes as she cowered into a tight ball in the corner. Blood and tears streaked her sheet-white face.

A terrible fear gripped Jett as he dropped to his knees, rifle to the ground as reached for her. "*Muirinn!* How badly are you hurt?"

She sagged visibly as she registered his voice. "Oh, God, Jett—"

He took her quickly into his arms, her entire body trembling like a frail aspen branch. He held her tight and she sobbed, releasing everything, giving herself fully over to him, to his care. To his embrace. And it tore into his soul. He wrapped his arms more tightly around her, a fierce, raw rage bubbling inside him.

He fought to tamp it down. Uncontrolled aggression bred rash decisions.

He needed cool.

Focus.

Jett blinked back his hot emotion and stroked her hair back from her face. "What in hell happened here?" he said, examining the cut on her temple.

She couldn't talk. Not yet. Sobs still wracked her body, choking her words.

"Shhh, it's okay," he whispered. "It's just a surface wound. But they do bleed a lot." He removed his hunting knife from the sheath on his belt and used the tip to tear back the blood-soaked sleeve from her shoulder.

"Got some wood fragments in there. I have a first aid kit in the truck, but we need to get out into the light." He helped her to her feet and led her from the shed. Coughing, eyes burning from toxic black smoke, they steered clear of Gus's smoldering vehicle.

Once they were well away from the mine property, Jett pulled over onto the side of the road and tended to Muirinn as she sat in the passenger seat, feet hanging out the door.

Putting his paramedic training to work, he cleansed the wound on her brow then applied a butterfly suture just under her hairline.

"A stitch or three and you'll be as good as new," he reassured her gently. But he had to force his voice to stay level, because inside his belly trembled with raw protective rage, and it took every ounce of control to bottle it in. He was angry with her, too, for coming out here alone.

"What happened here, Muirinn?" he asked softly as he pulled the shard from her shoulder, feeling her wince as he did. "What were you doing at the mine?" He taped the wound tightly shut, noting the ripped knees on her dust-caked pants, the deathly pallor of her complexion. His chest tightened.

"I wanted to see where Gus was found." Her voice sounded small, scared.

"I swear that idiot was trying to kill me. I thought it was over. I…I thought I was going to die, Jett. You…" her voice hitched. "You gave me—my baby—a second chance. I can't tell you how grateful I am." Tears tracked down through the dirt on her face.

He stilled his hand against her cheek.

A second chance. Was it possible for them? Could they ever try again?

He felt his body—every molecule in his system—aching to kiss her, hold her, comfort her. And Jett started to shake against his restraint, the powerful aftereffects of the massive cortisol dump to his system finally seizing control. With it his anger mushroomed.

"You shouldn't have come out here alone, Muirinn," he said brusquely.

Her mouth flattened at his admonition.

He grabbed his phone. "I'm calling the cops."

"No! Wait!" She clamped her hand on his arm, looking mortified.

"What for?"

She closed her eyes for a moment, sucking in air deeply, bolstering herself. "Gus's death wasn't an accident, Jett."

"What are you saying? Did you get into his laptop? Did you find something?"

She nodded. "Gus had new evidence on the Tolkin homicide, something that could lead to the bomber. I think he was murdered because of it, and whoever killed him might believe that *I* have seen it, and now they might be trying to silence *me*."

"Why in hell didn't you come to me with this first, Muirinn, before charging off half cocked to the mine?"

She sighed heavily, limbs still trembling, and guilt pinged through Jett. He knew why.

Muirinn was avoiding him because he hadn't been able to come clean on his divorce. She was staying away out of respect for him.

He softened his voice. "Tell me what was in those files, Muirinn."

"Ike Potter, a retired cop who worked for the SHPD at the time of the Tolkin homicide apparently gave Gus some old crime scene photographs—"

"I knew Ike. He had cancer, passed away just two months—"

"Yes," she interjected. "And just before he died, he handed Gus information from the old Tolkin investigation. Evidence that had been buried by the SHPD, never making it into the hands of the FBI team."

"*What?*"

"Hear me out." Her eyes looked glassy. She was going into

shock—pale, clammy skin, breathing too fast and light. Jett was worried about her baby.

"Muirinn, listen, we need to get you checked out. You can finishing telling me all this on the way to—"

"No! Listen to me first, Jett, please!" She grasped his hands. "You need to know this *before* we figure out who we can talk to." She swallowed hard, glancing nervously toward the mountains into which the shooter had fled. "Among the missing crime scene photos were shots of two different sets of boot prints. One set of prints was made inside and outside the Sodwana headframe on the morning of the bombing. It appears the bomber had an accomplice, Jett, someone who waited at the headframe while the bomber climbed down the shaft—"

"That shaft is *miles* away from the bomb site, Muirinn. I don't even know if the bomb site *is* accessible from Sodwana."

"I don't know, either, and maybe that's what Gus was trying to find out. But the FBI was never given those photographs, Jett. And apparently the tracks themselves were obliterated by someone on the SHPD force before the postblast team could get in. The FBI never explored that angle because there was no evidence to corroborate it."

Jett shook his head. "Muirinn, this doesn't make sense. Why would Ike have sat on this information all these years? And why suddenly hand it over to Gus?"

"Because he was dying, Jett, and he wanted to come clean. Because he was a cop, and he'd been eaten up by guilt these past twenty years. Maybe Ike sat on the evidence because he was a rookie at the time of the blast, and he was afraid of ratting out a superior officer—someone who could still be around now." She gripped his hands tighter in her urgency to get her message across.

"Gus probably felt secure in thinking that no one knew

what Ike had given him, Jett. But someone *must* have found out, someone who is still trying to keep the past buried. And will kill to do so."

Jett leaned back in shock. "So you think Gus was *murdered?*"

She hesitated, suddenly growing more pale, exhausted, drained. She glanced in the direction of the mine. "I *know* he was," she whispered. "After looking down that hole I know in my heart that my grandfather would never have gone down there on his own. Something bad happened to him."

"Muirinn," he said gently. "Your grandfather was known for his eccentricity, his obsession with Tolkin. And remember that both the ME and Gus's doctor were in agreement about the cause of his death. The police didn't voice any suspicions about foul play, either."

"The *police?* Listen to yourself, Jett! It was someone on that same police force who helped sabotage an FBI investigation into a mass murder, and who let a killer walk free. This is a conspiracy."

Jett rubbed his brow. He couldn't deny that someone had been taking serious potshots at Muirinn, and at him. And he'd seen someone in camo gear flee north into the wilderness.

The seriousness of her allegation bored more deeply into him. Along with it came an ominous chill.

Muirinn gasped suddenly, clutching at her stomach. Jett's heart lurched and he reached for her. But she shook her head, smiling wanly. "It's just kicking again," she whispered, awe filling her incredible eyes. She grasped his hand quickly. "Here, feel." She placed his palm on her belly.

Tears burned into Jett's eyes as he felt her child moving. He looked up into Muirinn's face, a sense of wonder rippling through his body. She met his gaze, and together they felt her baby move again, rolling over in her womb, and a powerful, sensual bond shuddered between them.

Jett's breathing quickened.

This was the exact privilege she'd denied him when she was pregnant with Troy. Now she was denying some other man this same sense of wonder.

Anger surged afresh through Jett, his grip on control cracking at the thought of just how close she and this little baby had come to getting killed—at the pain the father who'd sired this child would feel upon receiving news of his baby's death, regardless of whether or not he was still seeing Muirinn.

"Get in the truck," he said crisply, trying to hide his own emotions. "I'm taking you straight to Dr. Callaghan. She knows what she's doing. She's delivered tons of babies, and she's Troy's doctor."

"I'm fine, really."

"It's not you I'm worried about, Muirinn. It's your baby." Jett's words came out far harsher than he intended, but he couldn't stop himself. "You had no right going out there if you knew your life would be threatened."

He went around to the driver's side, got in, slammed the door and rammed his truck into gear. "Buckle up." He fired the ignition.

"I didn't *know* I was in danger, Jett. Not until I was shot at. I was still piecing together—"

"Oh, so you just brought that .22 with you for fun?" He hit the gas, fishtailing back onto the dirt road, taking his frustrations out on the truck. "What were you expecting—a bit of hunting along the way? I know you, Muirinn. You think you can go playing Nancy Drew without considering—"

"You know *nothing* about me, Jett!" she snapped. "You're talking about someone you last saw a decade ago."

The truth sobered him, made his eyes cool, his heart hard. His jaw tight. "You might be doing this baby gig on your own, Muirinn," he said very quietly, hands gripping the wheel tightly. "But somewhere out there is still a father who might just give a damn that his kid actually lives! You were always so damn selfish, O'Donnell."

"What is this really about, Jett?" she said quietly. "What are you really trying to say to me?"

That you gave our son away without thinking of me, and that you still haven't told me the truth.

"All you ever think about is yourself, Muirinn."

She stared at him in silence, blood beginning to trickle out from under the butterfly suture on her brow. Jett drove faster, knuckles white on the wheel.

"There is no man, Jett," she said softly.

His head swiveled. "What?"

"There is no father. I did this in a doctor's office. With sperm from a donor bank. Artificial insemination, Jett. Just me. Solo."

He stared at her in shock.

"Watch out!"

He swerved, just missing a tree on a bend, and slammed on the brakes, the vehicle sliding to a stop on the grit-covered road. He turned off the engine.

Dust settled quietly around the truck. He could hear the soft rush of wind in conifers outside, feel the cooler air against his face.

"God, I'm sorry." He dragged his hands over his hair. "I was just so worried about you, about your baby, Muirinn."

She looked out the window, avoiding his eyes.

He swore softly at his idiocy. "Why?" he said quietly. "Why'd you do it?"

"I want a child." She turned to face him, fresh tears and old mascara tracking down the dirt on her pale cheeks. Her hair was a matted mess of dried blood and silt. But she'd never looked more beautiful to him. *Or more available.*

"I want a family, Jett. I want to be a mother. What's so wrong with that? And I couldn't find the right man—a man who'd want to do this with me. So I'm doing it alone."

She really was totally free.

And she wanted all those things that he'd wanted from her all those years ago. All that wasted time suddenly yawned out in front of him. Jett didn't trust himself to speak.

Instead, he turned on the ignition.

As he drove, he tried to process everything she'd said, and a humming started in his muscles, his whole body soon vibrating like a tuning fork.

A second chance.

Was it really possible?

What would it take to get there? It would take Muirinn telling him about the boy she'd given up for adoption, that's what—that was Jett's line in the sand. He *needed* to hear this in order to find a way to tell her about Troy.

And before Jett could tell Troy that Kim was not his mom, Jett needed to be damn sure that Muirinn was committed, that she was going to stay right here in Safe Harbor, and be here for their son.

He gripped the wheel more tightly, the possibilities suddenly so frighteningly fragile inside him. But the excitement wasn't without remorse, because Muirinn could have a family eleven years ago.

With him.

Whatever move he made now, Jett told himself, his son had to come first. He owed that to his boy. Because just as easily as Muirinn had thrown it all away the first time, she had the power to do it again.

Chapter 8

Jett paced like a caged bear in Dr. Pat Callaghan's waiting room. He'd brought Muirinn straight here instead of taking her to the hospital because he trusted Pat. Her specialty was obstetrics and her office was rigged for ultrasound.

She'd also taken excellent care of Troy when Jett had first brought his tiny infant son home to Safe Harbor, feeling nervous about being a new dad at the tender age of twenty-two.

The exam room door opened suddenly, and Jett spun around.

A band clamped tightly over his chest as he saw Muirinn's wan face, the neat little plaster over the fresh stitches on her forehead, the bandage on her shoulder under her ripped shirt.

But despite her trauma, there appeared to be a subtle new determination in her stride as she exited the exam room with the doctor. Pat smiled, nodding to Jett as she picked up a clipboard and pen. "We just need to fill out some paperwork and mom and daughter are good to go."

Daughter?

Jett's heart stalled.

He could barely focus on the doctor's next words. "I had your grandfather on Digoxin, Muirinn." She filled in a form as she spoke. "It's a generic digitalis preparation."

"Could an overdose have possibly caused his cardiac arrest?"

Pat's pen stilled, and she looked up. "Well, yes. But—"

"Either way the ME would have expected to find digitalis in his system, right?"

"Yes, he would. But the ME's involvement in Gus's case was a formality, really, because the cause of death was clear, especially given Gus's preexisting condition—"

Muirinn interrupted. "Does it honestly make sense to you, Dr. Callaghan, that my grandfather hiked all the way out to Tolkin with his heart condition, and then climbed all the way down that shaft? I mean…" she hesitated. "Everyone keeps reminding me that he was eccentric. But I need to know, in your professional opinion, was my grandfather of sound mind these last couple of months?"

Dr. Callaghan placed a hand on Muirinn's arm, and smiled comfortingly. "It's always tough to lose someone, Muirinn. But I can assure you that Gus was mentally agile, if somewhat creative in thought. Plus he'd started taking daily walks on my recommendation, so he might easily have included the Tolkin property along one of his routes."

"It's fifteen miles from his house. I clocked it on the odometer."

The doctor returned to filling in her form. "That's really not far for a good hike if you take it slow, you know." She set the clipboard down. "Your grandfather had a really good life, Muirinn. He died active, busy. Not tied to a wheelchair, not in a hospital bed. Gus wouldn't have wanted it any other way."

"I know." She glanced down. "It's just that…I guess I was wondering, given the unusual circumstances."

"I don't believe the circumstances were that unusual, especially knowing your grandfather. Gus had always been obsessed with that mine, almost pathologically fixated, in my opinion. Both the ME and I were satisfied, upon examining his body, that it was the heart condition that caused his death, and resulted in a small tumble. This is not unusual in cardiac arrest."

"He was down a mine shaft."

"And according to the police, there was absolutely no sign of foul play. He'd simply been poking around there when he collapsed."

Muirinn shot Jett a glance.

The doctor smiled again, compassion fanning out in warm crinkles from her hazel eyes. "Now go and get some rest, Muirinn. Take care of that baby girl of yours."

"Thank you, doctor."

Jett swallowed against the dryness in his throat, the thought of what they could have shared eleven years ago suddenly so stark, as he led Muirinn out into the street, back to his truck.

"Did you tell the doc what happened at the mine?" he said, holding open the passenger door.

"No, I just told her I was out for a walk, and that I slipped and fell down a bank." She hesitated. "Doesn't it strike you as strange that Gus's case was basically rubber-stamped by the ME?"

"No, it doesn't." He went around, climbed in the driver's side and started the engine. "From Pat's point of view, what she said makes sense, Muirinn."

"Well, I think the ME should have done a more in-depth investigation, and done toxicology tests…something."

"Are you saying you don't trust Doc Callaghan and the ME now, either?"

She strapped herself in. "I'm just trying to figure out what in hell happened, Jett."

Jett pulled out into the small main road. "Why were you asking about Gus's medication?"

"I was wondering if he might have been poisoned. Technically, a heart attack could have been induced using Gus's own meds, in an effort to make his death seem as if it were from natural causes."

Jett focused on the road ahead thinking how absurd it seemed to be having this conversation at all. He was still trying to wrap his head around the fact that Muirinn had almost been killed, and that they couldn't go to the police with this information.

One way or another the cops *were* going to find Gus's burned-out truck at the mine, and questions were going to be asked.

This was going to come out somehow.

Bitterness leached down his throat as he thought of the historic blast, and what it had done to this town. He tried to imagine how much that bomber and his accomplice might stand to lose now, if the truth came out that they were responsible for one of the biggest mass homicides north of 60.

Who *wouldn't* kill to keep something like that quiet?

"We need to get to the bottom of this, Muirinn," he said quietly as he drove. "You need to show me those photographs, and Gus's notes."

"I don't want to involve you, Jett," she said with a heavy sigh.

"I can't let you do this on your own, Muirinn. Not now."

She sat in silence. He could sense the nervous tension rolling off her in waves.

He cursed to himself.

He didn't want this any more than she did. What he needed was some distance between Muirinn and himself, so he could try to figure some things out. Everything was moving too fast, and he was scared of what it might do to all of them.

But he was also the only one who could protect her right now.

The only emotional barrier he had left was the fact that Muirinn thought he was married. And the more he was forced into her proximity, the harder that secret was going to be to keep.

But, damn, he *needed* to keep it right now. It was the only way he'd be able to keep his hands off her.

They drove in tense silence along the twisting coast road, the late evening sun turning the ocean into beaten copper.

"Is it really a girl?" he said suddenly, thinking again that the child had no father.

Muirinn nodded as she placed her hands on her tummy. "I wanted it to be surprise, but after being in that shed, convinced I was going to die…" She inhaled shakily. "When Dr. Callaghan gave me an ultrasound just to check that everything was okay, she asked if I knew the sex, or if wanted to know. I said yes."

"You happy?"

"I am. I…I've always wanted a daughter."

"What about a son?" There was something in the tone of his voice that made Muirinn glance at him.

But Jett didn't return the look, and she couldn't read his eyes. Yet his hands had tightened on the wheel, and his neck was tense. She studied the lines of his rugged profile, his thick dark hair, his strong arms. And she loved him all over again. Age had been good to him. She wondered what might have been if she hadn't left, if they'd raised the boy she gave away for adoption. Guilt and confusion twisted inside Muirinn like a knife.

She was suddenly overwhelmed by a desperate desire to open up, spill everything about the fact she'd had a son—*their son*—that she'd given him away. But it was all too much to handle right now. A part of Muirinn even wondered if was better that Jett didn't know.

He had his own family now, and she didn't want to tamper with that.

The other part of her was afraid of how much he might truly hate her if she told him all these years later.

"Yes," she whispered, remorse thickening her voice. "I wanted a son, too."

He turned into her driveway, came to a stop and sat silent for a several beats, staring out the windshield. Then his gaze flashed to her, fierce suddenly. "Look, I can't let you stay here alone, Muirinn. Not after what happened today. You need to pack a bag and stay at my place until…until we've figured this out."

Fear, anxiety, attraction erupted in a dangerous cocktail inside Muirinn. She could *not* be forced into such close proximity to this married man, alone with him in his house, his wife away. "I…I don't think that's a good idea, Jett." Her voice caught, turning husky as his eyes bored hotly into hers, the intense stare of a hunter. Anticipation rustled through Muirinn like a wild and lethal thing.

She swallowed. "I just can't do it. I…cannot be with you, not in your house…I still have…"

"Still have what, Muirinn?" His voice was low, gravelly, his gaze drifting down to her lips.

"You know that I still have feelings for you, Jett," she whispered.

His eyes darkened, and lust etched into his face. Heat arrowed through her body, her world swirling to a narrow focus, logic fleeing.

Jett raised his hand to touch her face. He wanted her. To feel her hair, her skin, her body wrapped around his. But he couldn't go down this road again. Not yet, not before both of them had confessed the secrets between them. He exhaled slowly, lowering his hand.

Her body sagged visibly at his rejection, and her eyes glistened sharply with hurt. The pulse in her neck was racing, the emotion in her face so raw. "Muirinn, I—"

He just couldn't stop what came next. Cupping her jaw, Jett bent down, sliding his hand under her hair and he lowered his mouth to hers. His heart pounded as his lips met hers. There was no rational thought at all, as he felt her mouth open under his.

A small sound came from her throat as his tongue entered her mouth. She kissed him back, hard, desperate. And he felt the wetness of tears against his skin.

She hooked her arms around his neck, drawing him closer, her tongue tangling with his as she melted into him. Jett felt her pregnant body press against his, and something inside him cracked. His body burned as he kissed her harder, deeper. And they moved faster—urgent, hungry, angry, digging down deep for something neither of them seemed to be able to reach in the other.

Jett pulled back suddenly, rocked, breathing hard.

Muirinn stared at him in wide-eyed shock, chest rising and falling fast, cheeks flushed, panic flickering in her features.

Her hand covered her mouth, horror dawning in her eyes at the reality of what had just happened.

He didn't say a word, didn't move. *Couldn't.*

"Jett…" Tears streamed fresh down her face. She turned suddenly, flung open the door, slammed it shut, and stumbled up the stairs to her house.

Chapter 9

Muirinn's hands were shaking too hard to get the key into the lock.

Jett's truck door banged behind her. She heard his footsteps crunching on gravel, heard him coming up the stairs. She wanted to sink into the floor, be swallowed by a hole.

He stilled her hand, took the key from her and opened her front door. "I'm sorry," he said quietly, holding the door open. "It won't happen again. Please, just get your things, Muirinn," he said. "I'll wait for you downstairs."

She clenched her jaw. "I'm not coming to your house, Jett."

"Then I'll stay at your place," he said, following her into the hallway. "But it'll be easier the other way. I have my work at home."

She spun around to face him. "I never wanted to put you in this position, Jett. I didn't—*don't*—want your help." *Just as she hadn't let him help her eleven years ago when she found out she was pregnant.*

He let out a wry laugh. "You never did let anyone help you, Muirinn. You always wanted to do everything on your own. Let me help you now. For the baby's sake."

"I *can't*," she whispered.

"Look, I really am sorry about what just happened, and if I could find someone I trust to stay with you tonight, Muirinn, I would. And after tomorrow, if things still haven't been sorted out, I have a good friend who will do me that favor."

A favor.

Pain twisted.

That was the last thing on this earth she wanted from Jett. "So why don't you get him now?" she said icily.

"He's away until tomorrow."

She swallowed, humiliation filling her chest. She'd led him to this—it was as much her fault as his—and now she just wanted to be alone, in her old bedroom where she could sob her heart out. And he wasn't going to let her do that.

"Please, Jett," she said, clenching her jaw, refusing to let him see her break down further. "Please get out of my house. Now."

Frustration flashed into his cobalt eyes. "Someone just tried to kill you, Muirinn. I can't leave you here alone. As soon as possible I'll get my buddy Hamilton Brock to come stay here with you. He's an ex-Marine and does close protection work for a private company offshore. He knows what he's doing."

She turned away from him, rested her forehead against the doorjamb, shoulders slumping with fatigue. She just couldn't stay in Jett's house with his wife away. It wasn't right. It wasn't helping either of them. God, this was a mess.

"Think of your child for a change, Muirinn."

Her head whipped up. "For a *change?*"

"Yes. Someone other than yourself for a change."

"Damn you, Rutledge," she whispered, eyes blurring with tears she could no longer force back. "Will you get off your high horse! I didn't *ask* you to kiss me back there! What about *your* responsibilities—to your family, to your *son?*"

His body went rigid.

She swore softly. "The best thing I ever did was leave you and this place."

"That's in the past, this is—"

"Oh, it might be in the past, Jett, but what just happened in that truck has *everything* to do with now."

His jaw flexed angrily. He stuffed his hands into his pockets. "Muirinn, please, just get your things. Bring the photographs and laptop. We'll go through it all, and we can decide where to go from there, whether there is enough to bring in an outside agency like the FBI. You can shower and change at my place." He hesitated. "Just for tonight. At least you'll be safe."

Safe?

That's the last thing she was with Jett. Her own heart had made sure of that. *He* had made sure of that. She turned, stomped up the stairs, slamming doors behind her.

So she was angry with him. Well, he was angry with himself. Jett slammed his fist against the wall.

A door banged upstairs.

He dragged both hands over his hair and cursed. *Idiot!* He should never should never have touched her. But it had just happened.

He swore again.

What else was he supposed to do now? They couldn't go to the cops. And he didn't know who else to trust, apart from Brock, who'd arrived in town only seven years ago and had no connections whatsoever to the Tolkin blast.

All Jett had to do was keep his hands off her for maybe forty-eight hours, max, until he could reach Brock. But the more he was with Muirinn, the more he wanted her. And the longer he tried brush the fact that he was divorced under the carpet, the more onerous the deception became, and the worse it was going to be to tell the truth.

Not to mention the truth about Troy.

Her words sifted into his mind: *"I wanted a son, too."*

Well, she could have damn well had one if she hadn't given him up for adoption, right? He stalked across the living room, furious with himself and his own out-of-control libido.

Gus's silver tomcat watched Jett as he paced, its tail flicking like an irritating metronome. He scowled at the creature, then strode into the kitchen, looking at Gus's things, anything to distract himself while he waited.

He picked up a small tin of herb tea, prepared by Mrs. Wilkie, no doubt. The label said *comfrey*. He opened the tin, shook the thin furry dried leaves, put it back, then picked up another tin. Chamomile. He set it back, stared at the foxglove bells in a copper vase on the long wooden table, the basket of vegetables in the kitchen. Mrs. Wilkie was still doing her thing, as if Gus were still here, as if nothing had changed.

But so much had changed—the echoes from a murderous blast two decades ago still rippling into the future.

Jett felt bad for the old woman. Gus had always been good to her, and he knew Lydia Wilkie was deeply fond of him.

If Muirinn was correct—if Gus *had* been murdered—Jett was going to make damn sure the bastard paid, and that an end was finally put to this case. He stalked back through the living room.

There were photos and paintings of Muirinn everywhere.

Claustrophobia reared up and came down on him with sharp teeth bared. He swung around, feeling short of breath.

And there she was.

Standing in the brick archway with her bag in hand, her ripped pants still caked with silt from the mine, her hair still matted. Gone was the feisty redhead. She looked more like a forlorn orphan.

"I need to leave a note for Mrs. Wilkie to feed the cat," she said stiffly.

"Fine."

She got a notepad from the hall table, her movements tense, mouth tight. She'd been crying again. God, he felt bad, putting her through the ringer after all she'd gone through today. He had no right to kiss her, and here he was telling her that she needed to think of something other than herself, while he'd acted like a selfish ass. What must she think of him?

"Muirinn... I... "

She looked up.

I'm not married. And I still love you.

He clamped his mouth shut.

She returned her attention to scribbling a note for Mrs. Wilkie, purple petals falling onto the back of her pale hand as she inserted the corner of the paper under the big copper vase on the table. She removed a key from her pocket and unlocked a drawer hidden into the side of the table. And gasped, hand flying to her mouth.

"Muirinn, what is it?"

Her eyes flared to his, panic on her face.

"It's gone! The laptop—it's *missing!*" She rummaged frantically. "The envelope with the photos—that's gone, too!"

She yanked the drawer out further.

"Maybe you put the laptop somewhere else?"

"No, Jett! It was *here*. All the evidence is *gone*..." Her eyes flickered as she remembered something. "Except for these—" She fumbled to unbutton the side pocket of her cargo pants.

With a shaking hand she held out a set of crumpled black-and-whites. "I took these four photos with me to the mine so I could compare them with the area around the Sodwana shaft."

He placed his hand over hers, stopping the shaking. "Come," he said firmly. "I'm taking you home. We can think about this later."

Jett handed Muirinn her bag as they entered the hallway of his house. "I'll set up the spare room for you," he said. "Bathroom's that way."

She walked slowly into the living room, bag in hand. Pale evening sunlight slatted through skylights in a high, vaulted ceiling, and windows overlooking the sea yawned up from natural wood floors—Jett's love affair with the sky evident in the renovations he had made to his parents' old home.

"Are you absolutely sure you didn't put that laptop somewhere else?" he asked as he walked into his kitchen.

"Of course I'm sure." She took in the décor as she spoke. Mounted photographs graced his living room walls—aerial shots of caribou racing across a frozen tundra below the wingtip of a plane, black-and-white images of antique airplanes, family pictures. Muirinn stalled suddenly in front of a photo of Jett and his son, Troy in the cockpit of a small plane.

Her throat closed in on itself.

Troy looked so much like his father; smoky dark lashes, ink-black hair, bright white teeth in a broad smile. But his eyes were green, and he had a slight smattering of freckles across his sun-browned cheeks.

He was around the same age her son would be now—
their son.

The thought stung.

Slowly, she turned her attention to another photo, this one
of Jett, Kim and Troy on Jett's boat. Kim was beautiful—
blond with pale blue eyes. Jett had his arms around both his
wife and child. The family vignette made Muirinn flinch.

She could feel Jett watching her from the kitchen
entrance, silent.

Tearing her attention away from the photos, Muirinn
made her way to the bathroom, forcing herself not to look
back at him.

While Muirinn was bathing, Jett warmed soup he'd made
with vegetables from his garden and caribou he'd shot last
August. He struggled to concentrate on the task at hand,
and not think of Muirinn naked and pregnant in his bathtub,
in his home.

Back in his life after all these years.

He heard her come out of the bathroom and head into the
spare room. He buttered some toast and dished the soup into
bowls, the sensation of her mouth, her taste, her kiss curling
back into his mind as he watched the steam.

He carried the plates out and put them on the low coffee table
in front of the sofa, then went to his drafting table and quickly
began rolling up his blueprints. He didn't want her to see them,
didn't want her asking about his life, his future. His big dream.

He needed to stay focused on just getting her through
whatever in hell was going on—and keeping himself from
getting too close.

"What are those?" she said appearing in the doorway.

He tensed. "Just some plans for a wilderness lodge I'm
building farther up north."

"Where up north?" She came closer, toweling her hair, wearing soft sweats, her scent clean, soapy.

He didn't answer the question. "Soup's on the table."

Muirinn padded softly into the living room and sat on the sofa, tucking her feet under her.

She ate while Jett studied the four crumpled photos she'd given him.

"Good soup," she said.

He glanced up. Color was returning to her cheeks. Relief washed softly through him. "Tell me again what Gus wrote in his laptop about these," he said, positioning the photos next to each other on the coffee table.

"Those four images were among the photos allegedly removed from police evidence before the arrival of the FBI postblast team. That one—" she pointed with her spoon, "—shows bootprints outside the Sodwana headframe building. Apparently, those were left by the bomber's accomplice."

He looked up, catching her eyes, and the memory of their kiss shimmered between them. Her cheeks flushed and she cleared her throat, returning her attention to the photos. "And those two sets of tracks in the dark mud were apparently left by the bomber himself."

Jett tapped a photo with his finger. "The ruler next to the prints outside the Sodwana shaft indicates that the accomplice wore a size 12 boot. I figure the print up in Gus's attic was also a size 12."

Muirinn set her bowl down and rubbed her arms, as if she were cold suddenly. "You think it was actually the *same* guy who broke into my house?"

"Hell knows. The ruler next to these other prints in the darker mud shows that the bomber wore a size 10 boot." He frowned slowly as he studied the photo more closely.

"They're odd tracks," he said, a whisper of unspecified foreboding rustling down his spine. "It looks like the guy was dragging one foot, or something."

She nodded, watching him intently.

"What else did Gus say about these prints, Muirinn?"

"That's all. His notes just ended in midstream."

"Did he have a theory about *who* might have left these tracks?"

"No."

"So Gus figured—with Ike Potter's help—that an accomplice stood guard while the bomber went down to the 800 level, then walked about three miles underground to D-shaft where he planted the bomb?"

"It appears that way."

"And you think Gus went out to the mine to check out this theory?

"Except I don't believe Gus actually intended to go underground," said Muirinn. "He just wouldn't have done that."

Jett sat back. "That's one helluva trek underground."

"Which means the bomber must have been in good physical shape, right?" she said, pushing a strand of damp hair back from the bandage on her forehead.

Jett caught the scent of her shampoo.

"Or very determined." He got up suddenly, walked to the windows. He stood with his back to her, hands thrust deep in his pockets as he stared out over the ocean.

"That part of Tolkin had also been shut down due to low yield at least four years prior to the blast," he said quietly, trying to imagine the scenario. "Only a guy who'd worked that part of the mine before it was shut would even begin to know where to go in those abandoned tunnels, alone."

"So you think the bomber was likely a veteran miner?"

He nodded, pursing his lips. "Plus, he was an explosives expert. At least that's what the FBI thought." Jett rubbed his brow, that unspecified sense of foreboding gnawing deeper into him.

Muirinn sighed heavily. "I wish we could find someone we can trust who knows more about tracking, Jett."

"What use would a tracking expert be? The boots that made those prints would've been thrown out years ago."

"Yes, but maybe an expert could tell us something more about the *men* who made those prints. You said yourself the tracks in the black mud looked odd, like the bomber was dragging his leg or something."

Nausea swirled in his stomach.

The thought that several people in this town were protecting a mass murderer galled him. "Whoever that bomber was—" he said quietly, watching the water "—he sure as hell trusted his accomplice."

"What veteran miners might have that kind of a bond, Jett?"

He could feel her watching him intensely. He was nervous about turning around, meeting her eyes again.

"Those kinds of bonds do develop in life-and-death professions, like mining." Jett said softly. "Think about it, Muirinn. Each day those men enter a cage that is dropped miles down straight into the earth. There's no day down there, no night. Just total darkness. And there's this awareness of the tons and tons of rock and gravity pressing down over your head, held back only by manmade tunnels." He exhaled, thinking of his dad, and what Adam Rutledge had been forced to endure each day of his working life—a life that had made him a cripple.

He turned slowly to face her. "Those men are faced daily with inevitable accidents, death."

She cast her eyes down, and Jett knew she was thinking of her own father.

"Some of them deal with this threat by becoming fatal-ists—they just put their life in God's hands each day and go down into that mine."

"Is that what your father did?"

"No." He shook his head. "My dad didn't believe in fate. He was what they call a perfectionist. He used to say Tolkin killed only foolish miners. He said it was smarts, not God, that would keep him alive. He learned to know that rock like he knew the backs of his own hands, Muirinn. He'd study it carefully, figure how to slant drill holes at just the precise angle, put in just the right amount of explosive—enough to shatter it apart without disturbing the drifts where men worked, or endangering lives."

"So Adam was an explosives expert. Plus, he'd have known that closed-off part of the mine?"

"What are you saying?"

"Nothing. I was just wondering how many explosives experts worked Tolkin at the time of the blast."

"A lot," he said crisply. "Look, I don't like your insinua-tion here. My father—"

"I'm not saying Adam had anything to do with murders, Jett!" she interjected. "I'm just saying that your father would know those veteran explosives experts, and I was thinking that maybe he could *help* us."

Jett's chest tightened, his thoughts turning grudgingly to the odd bootprints in the black mud. "If my dad knew anything, Muirinn, anything at all, he would've told the cops a long time ago."

"And they could have buried it, just like they buried those crime scene photos that Ike gave to Gus and erased the prints."

He held her gaze, his body growing cold.

"You were explaining about the bonds that develop between miners, Jett," she urged softly.

He didn't like where she was going with this. He didn't like anything about this line of questioning. "The perfectionists were also the best producers," he said coolly. "Which meant they earned the largest bonuses, sometimes even coming out financially ahead of the mine managers. As a result—and because they knew how to stay alive—that young and ambitious miners often tried to latch onto a perfectionist—to work under him, to learn the craft. Those bonds are legendary in the industry."

"Who latched onto your dad, Jett?"

Silence hung between them for several beats. "Where are you going with this, Muirinn?"

"Nowhere. I'm just interested."

He studied her a long while. "Chalky Moran."

Her eyes widened. "A *Moran?*"

He gathered up their empty soup bowls and carried them to the kitchen.

Muirinn came up behind him, not daring to get too close. "Chalky is the younger brother of the police chief, Don, right? The one you said is married to the mayor?"

"Yeah." He rinsed the bowls, not looking at her.

"What is Chalky Moran doing now?"

He snorted, gave a wry smile as he stacked the bowls in the drying rack. "Chalky went into real estate when he left the mine. The Lonsdale family owns a good percentage of the buildings in town."

She hesitated. "Is he still tight with your dad?"

He slapped the dish cloth down abruptly. "Yeah. They still go fishing and hunting together." His eyes crackled with tension.

"Jett—" She almost reached out to touch him. But he visibly flinched and stepped past her, making for his booze cabinet. He poured himself a whiskey, then held up the bottle to her. "I take it you're not drinking at the moment?"

She shook her head.

"Can I get you anything else?"

"No, thank you."

He stalked out onto the deck, clearly needing space.

Muirinn felt guilty for being here at all. She sank wearily back onto the sofa, and closed her eyes.

She'd angered Jett by talking about Adam. She hadn't meant to. Muirinn was merely curious as to what kind of bond might motivate someone to keep the heinous secret of mass murder, and perhaps even kill for it twenty years later.

The image of Adam Rutledge hobbling out of that yellow bus in his Draegers sifted up from Muirinn's subconscious, and her thoughts turned again to the odd prints in the black mud...

No, it wasn't possible.

Besides, someone with Adam's disability was not likely to be able to negotiate a seventy-story climb both ways, plus hike a total of six miles underground. She'd seen herself just how crippled Adam had been on the day of the blast—it was burned indelibly into her memory.

Adam was a rescuer, not a killer.

Jett came inside to refill his glass.

Muirinn was nestled into the sofa cushions sound asleep, breaths coming soft and light, her eyelids fluttering with some private dream. Her hand rested on her rounded tummy.

He set his glass down, fetched a soft blanket and draped it carefully over her, tucking the corners in.

Then he sat and watched her sleep as the hours ticked by. The sky turned indigo, then deep purple as the midnight sun hovered just below the horizon.

Her hair had dried into soft springy ringlets, the auburn color rich against her pale skin. Her lips were parted slightly as she breathed. Unabashedly, Jett allowed his gaze to trace the curve of her breasts, her swollen belly. Lust grew hot inside him, hardening his groin with a sweet aching need.

He lurched to his feet suddenly, tension torquing too tight for comfort. He poured another shot of scotch, went back outside.

It was almost midnight now.

An eerie green summer aurora borealis pulsed across the sky, and the scent off the ocean was fresh. He leaned against the railing, watching a ghostly cruise ship move silently over the water. He sipped his whiskey.

Warmth spread through his chest, the taste of peat smoke, silky, smooth. Gus had bought him the bottle to celebrate Troy's tenth birthday. Jett missed the old man. He owed him.

Without his help, Jett would have lost his son.

Gus had never spoken to Jett about Troy's start in life, not after that initial phone call when he'd alerted Jett to the fact that Muirinn was giving their baby up for adoption.

During that call, Gus had told Jett that no matter what Jett chose to do about his son, Gus was never going to talk to Muirinn about it or interfere in any way. That was between Jett and her, but Gus had wanted him to know that Muirinn was giving away his child.

Jett suspected that Gus had been hoping he'd contact Muirinn, and that they'd work out their issues and become a family.

Instead, he'd gone to Vegas, secured custody behind Muirinn's back, and then married Kim. For reasons that had seemed so right at the time.

Jett started suddenly as he sensed Muirinn coming up behind him. She leaned against the railing beside him, careful not to get too close.

He ached to reach out, touch her.

"It's so beautiful," she whispered, staring at the silent, billowing curtains of northern lights, a reverence in her voice. "I didn't realize how much I missed this view."

Jett closed his eyes for a moment, her scent, the sound of her voice, tumbling his mind into a confusion between then and now. He slanted his gaze to her.

Her red hair was a wild mass of curls, her skin like porcelain in this haunting light. Again past shimmered between present, and she looked all of nineteen again. And he felt all of twenty-two. And just as desperate for her. For all the wrong reasons.

He took a deep slug of his whiskey. "Maybe you should consider leaving Safe Harbor for a while, Muirinn. Until this is sorted out."

She stiffened. "Why?"

"Because then you'll be safe. Your daughter will be safe." He slugged the rest of the whiskey back hard, relishing the burn.

And so will I.

She gripped the balustrade with both hands, staring out over the ocean, features tight. "I hear what you're saying, Jett," she said crisply. "And I did think about that. But I refuse to allow someone who murdered my father, and my mother by default, to kill my grandfather and to now scare me and my daughter out of our own home."

He tensed.

"You're really going to stay in Safe Harbor? Long term?"

"Damn right I'm going to stay."

His pulse quickened.

He had to tell her. He couldn't keep this secret any longer.

But by the same token, she hadn't told him yet that she'd borne his son. She was keeping her own secrets. She might never tell him. What would that mean for them, if she couldn't be honest?

Jett could not go forward without complete honesty and openness. Not this time.

"I owe it to Gus, Jett, to finish what he started, to find the answers. How *could* I leave now?"

"Just as easily as you did the first time."

Her mouth opened. She stared at him in shock.

He clenched his jaw, said nothing. Alcohol, adrenaline, lust, the memory of her kiss—all of it simmered in his blood. He needed barriers. Truth.

Pebbles clattered softly down at the shore with the incoming tide, and he felt her glaring at him.

"Look, I'm sorry," he said. "I just think it might be best if you left town for a while."

"For your sake, Jett? Or for mine?"

"For all our sakes," he said crisply. "I don't think it's a good idea for you to be here."

"Believe me," she whispered almost inaudibly. "I don't want to be here in your house right now, either. This was your idea, not mine. And tomorrow morning I'm going home. I'm going to do this on my own."

"And what are you going to do at home, alone? Sit there with a loaded shotgun in case your attacker comes back?"

"It's better than sitting here." She spun around, stalked toward the open sliding doors. "Or you can get that friend of yours to watch over me!" she called over her shoulder.

"Gus should have gone to the feds with this right away— you know that!" he yelled after her. "He should've handed that evidence over the minute Ike Potter gave it to him! Before someone could steal it. I have no idea why he didn't."

She turned inside the doorway. "Maybe, Jett, he had his reasons. Personal ones."

"So personal he ended up dead?"

"Maybe he wanted to be sure of something before he went around accusing people and screwing up lives."

Jett laughed harshly. "Yeah, wouldn't want to screw up any more lives now, would we, Muirinn?"

She turned her back on him and went inside, slamming the door behind her.

Chapter 10

Muirinn awakened at the sound of a sharp rap and the bedroom door opening. She blinked, momentarily disoriented before realizing that she was in Jett's house, that it was Saturday morning. Shafts of gold sunlight angled through the blinds, and Jett stood in the doorway, hand on the doorknob, a fresh white T-shirt molded to his torso.

His jeans were faded, seductively low slung, his hair damp from a shower. Those cobalt eyes lasered into her, and the set of his jaw was defensive.

He wasn't handsome, thought Muirinn as she sat up, reflexively bunching the sheet up over her chest. To her mind, handsome meant pretty, and this man did not qualify. There was nothing gentle about his physique at all. Jett looked rough, rugged—like the wilderness he'd grown up in, the place that defined him. The place he loved.

Something stirred in Muirinn's heart, an insistent voice that told her she needed to follow through on her threat last night and get the hell out of this man's hair, pronto, before they both got hurt again.

"Breakfast's almost ready." His gaze tracked over her as he spoke, and she saw his fist tighten on the door handle, cording muscles along his arm.

"Good morning to you, too," Muirinn said, reaching for her robe. His eyes followed her hand, a dark lust shifting into his features. Muirinn sensed his anger, too, rolling off him in quiet waves. After eleven years of silence, she'd invaded his space, his house.

His marriage.

And she felt awful. But the hot, sexual, intensity in his eyes invaded her body and, in spite of herself, warmth surged through her belly.

He grunted, closing the door softly.

Muirinn blew out a breath of air, tossed back the covers and pulled on her robe. Cinching the belt around her nonexistent waist, her attention was drawn to a framed photo of Troy on the dresser. She picked up the frame and, in privacy, carefully studied Jett's son. Pain twisted deeper, uncorking memories of giving birth to a baby boy, of how it had torn her apart to hand him over—feelings she'd managed to lock down in a part of her mind.

Feelings now being stirred back to life by Jett.

She wondered where their child was now, who he'd become. A wave of anguish and fresh guilt crashed through her, stealing her breath.

Muirinn set the photo down, inhaling shakily. Would their son perhaps try to find his real mother and father someday? Would he hate her for having abandoned him?

Would he ever understand?

Would Jett? If she told him?

Perhaps there truly were some secrets better left buried.

Or did that just lead to more tangled webs, more ruined lives, as Jett had so brutally reminded her last night.

Muirinn found Jett frying eggs and bacon in the kitchen, and the scent made her realize that she was starving.

He glanced up, and her heart squeezed again at the sight of him.

"Can you grab some napkins?" he said, jerking his chin toward a cupboard near the bookshelf. "They're in that drawer through there."

Muirinn moved into the open-plan living room, and reached for the drawer, but stilled as the cover of a familiar magazine spine on the bookshelf caught her eye. A copy of *Wild Spaces,* the high-end travel magazine for which she wrote. Her pulse quickened.

She glanced toward the kitchen, but Jett had his back turned, busy at the stove.

Muirinn quickly pulled the magazine off the shelf, flipping it open to where the corner of a page had been folded over. Shock rippled through her as she registered that Jett had bookmarked a feature *she* had written.

Again, she shot a glance toward the kitchen. Jett had disappeared around the corner.

Muirinn quickly replaced the magazine, knocking a book over as she did. And stacked behind that book she found every issue of *Wild Spaces* from the past year, along with a DVD of a television show that had filmed Muirinn on assignment in the Sahara, where she'd been working on a story about the Dogon tribe in the Homburi Mountains near Timbuktu.

Muirinn's heart began to race—he'd kept in touch by following her career. While he'd told her that he never wanted to see or hear from her again, he'd been reading her stories, watching her on TV.

She hurriedly flipped open the cover of another magazine. This one had a corner turned down marking the page that contained her own bio; *Muirinn O'Donnell grew up in a remote coastal town in the Alaskan wilderness....*

Her vision blurred.

He still cared. Always had. But while he'd been keeping tabs on her life, she'd been doing everything to isolate herself from his.

"Want coffee with—" He froze, plates in his hand, as he saw what she was looking at.

Silence thrummed between them.

He turned abruptly, set the plates on the dining table with a clunk, stalked back into the kitchen and returned with the coffeepot.

He set it down heavily, motioned for her to take a seat, taking one himself. The look on his face was thunderous, his body tense, a dark and powerful undertow humming through him.

"You *subscribed* to them?"

"Sit, Muirinn," he replied coolly. "Your breakfast's getting cold."

She came right up to him, standing above him, the magazine in her hand. "Why, Jett?" she whispered. "Why have you got my magazines?"

The muscle at the base of his jaw began to pulse, a small vein swelling on his temple. "Muirinn—"

She wagged the magazine at him. "How'd you know I wrote for them?"

He said nothing. The wind outside soughed through the pines. His chest rose and fell heavily, his fist tightening around his fork. He was bottled rocket fuel, ready to blow. And she wanted him to blow.

"Talk to me, Jett!"

He dumped his fork onto the table, anger smoking into his eyes, his glare so direct and intense her cheeks flushed hot.

He lurched to his feet. "Get dressed when you're done eating," he said crisply, gathering up his plate, still full of food. "I need to do some work on one of my boats."

"Now?"

"Yeah, now."

She grabbed his wrist. "Don't—" she said, glowering at him. "Do not walk away from this."

He stilled, vibrating under her touch, his features like cold granite. He was so close she could smell soap, the warmth of his skin, the fresh scent of laundry.

"So it's okay for *you* to walk?" he said darkly. "To just up and leave Safe Harbor, to never look back? But not for me?"

"How did you know where I worked, Jett?" she said quietly, still gripping his wrist.

"Gus told me."

Anxiety edged into her. She glanced at the photo of Kim and Troy, thinking of her own baby. "He told you what?"

Jett held her eyes for a long, loaded beat. "Muirinn—"

"Tell me!" Her voice went higher and she hated it. "How did you know where I was?"

Did Gus tell you about my baby?

He glanced down at her hand gripping his wrist. Embarrassed, she let him go. He stepped back from her, and sighed heavily as he raked his hand through his hair. "Gus said that after California you went to Nevada."

Nerves tightened, memories of giving birth, the adoption in Vegas. Her eyes began to burn, her pulse to race, the tension of not telling him squeezing her chest, wanting to burst out. Fear stopping her from allowing it to.

"Did he say anything else? About Nevada?"

He held her eyes for a long, loaded beat, and she felt as if he knew something. "Should he have, Muirinn?" he asked very quietly.

She swallowed, her hand going automatically to her tummy. His eyes followed the movement to her belly. "He said that after Nevada you went to London for two years, and then to New York, where you got the job with *Wild Spaces*. I subscribed to the magazine."

"Why, Jett?"

"Because I was interested!" he snapped. "Wouldn't you be? Oh, wait. Why would *you* be interested—you who didn't bother to come home once in eleven years to visit your own grandfather. Or me."

Her cheeks flushed hotter. "Why in hell would I visit *you*, Jett? You went and got married! You who wouldn't deign to come with *me* to California. But you went off and got married in Las Vegas!" In spite of her best efforts, tears pricked hot into her eyes. "And then I *couldn't* come home, could I? Because you couldn't be there for me anymore."

He went stone still.

"That's the reason?" he said, very quietly.

"The only reason."

He paled. The muscle at his jaw pulsed and his eyes sparked. It made them fierce blue.

"What did you think, Jett?" she said, emotion balling painfully in her throat. "That I could come home to watch you with a new wife, and a new… " her voice hitched on the thought. "A new baby when, when I had just…"

Given ours away.

But the words wouldn't come.

She just couldn't tell him about his son—not right now, maybe not ever. She cast her eyes down. "The news of your marriage nearly killed me, Jett," she whispered hoarsely. "It's the reason I never came home, and it's the reason I need to get out of your house now, because…"

"Muirinn—"

She looked up slowly, swallowed at the rawness she saw in his eyes.

"I'm not married, Muirinn."

Speechless, she stared.

"What…what do you mean?"

"Kim and I separated six years ago," he said quietly. "We've been officially divorced for five."

Her skin felt hot, then ice-cold as the sea breeze wafted through the open window, blowing strands of hair across her face. The stitches Dr. Callaghan gave her yesterday began to throb on her temple. "But I saw you," she whispered. "With Kim down at the dock."

He cleared his throat, a range of emotions twisting his features. "Kim and I have an amicable relationship, Muirinn. She's great with Troy. She offered to take him to camp." He tilted his head slightly toward his drafting table. "I'm working on a large project, and I was going to use the time while Troy was away to finish it, draw up proposals for more funding."

Muirinn drew in a shuddering breath, and reached for the back of the chair, her mouth dry.

Her entire world had just been turned on its head and was spinning wildly. Suddenly, everything seemed possible, wide open, no bearings. "So…you and Kim share custody?"

Something flickered through his eyes. "No," he said softly. "I have custody of Troy. It's complicated."

She couldn't speak.

She just stood there staring at him, reality fading into the sound of wind in the pines, the crunch of waves down in the bay.

How many times had she looked into those cobalt eyes, heard those same sounds when they were in the shed by the water? They seemed to be melting past into present, the lost years crumbling to dust at her feet, and Muirinn was suddenly disoriented.

He took a step closer to her. Gently, he removed the magazine clutched in her hand, and set it on the table.

Muirinn's heart began to race.

He reached up, touched the side of her neck, his palm warm against her cheek. She shivered.

"I used to watch that video, Muirinn," he whispered roughly. "I'd look at your face, your smile for the camera…" His fingers closed around the back of her neck. "No matter what I said all those years ago, I couldn't *stop* caring about you."

He slid his warm hand slowly down her neck, and along her shoulder, slipping it under her robe, exploring the curve of her shoulder, the feel of her skin. He lowered his head, breathing her scent in deeply on a shuddering breath, his mouth so close to hers.

Heat arrowed to her belly, and her world spun, everything whirling into a wild blur around her and Jett, as if they stood at the heavy and silent eye of a kaleidoscopic storm.

"And I never stopped wanting you back," he whispered, blue eyes devouring her, his body trembling with hunger.

"It was impossible to go down to the ocean, to see that shed on Gus's beach and not remember that last night."

The night we made our son.

She swallowed.

The night we fought so bitterly and parted with such stubborn anger in our hearts.

Her eyelids fluttered as he slid his palm down the length of her arm, causing her robe to fall back off her shoulder. She was vaguely conscious of the wind increasing outside, the faint tinkling of chimes down at the boat shed.

"That night…you told me you hated me, Jett." Muirinn's voice came out thick. "You were so angry—you said you'd never speak to me again if I left."

"Would you have come back if I hadn't said those things?"

"Yes," she whispered, tears forming in her eyes, rolling down her cheeks. "God, yes. I would have come back, I would have come home to you."

His mouth twisted as he fought to control something inside himself.

"I've made mistakes, Jett," she said quietly. "Terrible mistakes. And I wanted to come back. I wanted to call you, to talk to you, to tell you that… "

That I was pregnant with our child.

He waited, willing her to finish, his eyes lancing hers, his entire body vibrating at some dangerous, elemental level.

But her voice cracked. "…then I heard you'd married and it was too late."

He closed his eyes for a moment, tempering the raw volcanic power of his own emotion. He moved his hand lower down her arm, encircling her wrist like a large cuff. "Did you love me?" he whispered roughly.

"Always." The word came out on a breath, soft. Urgent.

He drew her closer, so close her swollen belly pushed hard up against his pelvis. Her vision blurred as she felt his arousal.

She reached for his hand, placed it on her abdomen. He splayed his fingers, exploring the rounded shape of her tummy, and the shudder of a sigh escaped his chest. Closing his eyes, he slowly moved his hand to her waist, then up to her breast.

Muirinn's breathing became shallow as he rubbed his thumb over her nipple. His lips opened slightly, lust swilling black into his eyes as he felt her nipple harden under his finger.

And Muirinn couldn't focus on anything other than the pure sensation of his touch. To finally feel his hands on her body—to feel him wanting her, to know he always had—went beyond words, beyond her wildest dreams. Beyond all logical thought.

Shaking against his control, Jett drew her even closer, and Muirinn slid her hand up the back of his neck and guided his mouth down to hers. A groan escaped Jett as his lips met hers.

And something inside him snapped. He yanked her tight against him, thrusting his fingers up into the thick hair at the nape of her neck, as he crushed his mouth down hard onto hers.

Hunger blinded Muirinn as she felt him forcing her lips open, his tongue tangling, warm, salty with hers. He slid his hand up her thigh, under her robe, cupping her buttocks under her nightgown as he pulled her even tighter against his hard, hot body. Against the length of his erection.

An exhilarating wild heat coursed through Muirinn as this man who'd fought so hard to control his feelings for her finally lost it in her arms, moving faster. She hooked her leg around him, as he cupped her buttocks, lifting her up into himself as he kissed her deeper. Muirinn placed her hand between his thighs, relishing the rigidity of his erection under the rough denim of his jeans, oblivious to anything but the desperate, sweet, aching urge to have him inside her, all of him, as close to him as she could possibly get. She began to fumble urgently with his zipper.

He pulled back suddenly, eyelids heavy. "Muirinn—" his voice was hoarse, intense. "Are you sure?"

"Yes," she whispered. "I've never been more sure of anything."

Chapter 11

Jett eased Muirinn back onto the mattress of his double bed. She was naked, hair spreading out in a fiery halo of curls over his pillows.

Soft summer sun filtered through the floor-to-ceiling windows in his bedroom, warming his bare skin as he stood over her, staring down at her with tenderness and wonderment in his heart. He couldn't believe that she was actually here, in his bed, *all his,* beautiful in the glow of her pregnancy. And the lost years between them seemed to melt into a liquid sensation that knew no time.

Jett needed to take her hard, hot, fast—he needed to possess her—but he was afraid. He didn't want to hurt her.

And he wanted this to last.

She smiled up at him, lowering her lids as she studied his naked body unabashedly, drinking in every inch of him. His arousal grew hotter, heavier between his thighs as her scrutiny lingered there.

Lust shifted her features, glazing her eyes. She sat up, reaching out for his hands, the movement parting her legs, deepening her cleavage. Jett's mouth went bone dry as she took his hands, drew him closer.

She rolled a condom onto him, her movements smooth, tortuous, teasing, along the length of his erection. Jett's eyes rolled back and his vision swam with swirls of scarlet and black as she coaxed him with rhythmic strokes. He wasn't going to be able to make this last.

Quickly, he got to his knees, and gently placing a hand on each knee, he parted her thighs.

Muirinn felt his tongue, lips, and a silent cry swelled in her chest. Pregnancy had changed things in her. Everything felt fuller, more swollen, nerve endings heightened to excruciating sensitivity. She began to shake almost instantly as his tongue entered her, pressure, blood, building low inside her.

And she shattered, gasping between breaths and rolling contractions.

His control snapped. He flipped her quickly onto her side and, spooning his body against her back, he entered her from behind. The penetration in this position was shallow, but still she gasped as her body accommodated his size.

He moved, slowly at first, then faster, harder, hotter.

Muirinn clamped her hands down on the mattress, nails digging deep into the sheets as she came again, exquisite rolling waves of contractions seizing hold of her body. But she wanted more, the orgasms just seeming to increase her need, not satisfying something deeper. Because even in his hunger, Jett was being careful, not going deep enough.

Breathless, her skin now slick with perspiration, she swung

around, and pushed him onto his back. Holding his wrists above his head, she straddled him, and eased slowly down onto him, controlling the depth of penetration herself.

Muirinn threw her head back, and closed her eyes, savoring the sensation of Jett inside her.

She began to rock her pelvis against his, feeling the swell of her tummy rub against the rough hair low on his abdomen. He clamped his hands suddenly on her hips, guiding her. Faster, urgent.

Bracing her hands on his shoulders, hair tumbling forward over her face, he rocked her faster, harder. She grew breathless, dizzy.

The wind outside increased, branches tapping on the windows.

His fingers suddenly dug hard into her hips, and he stilled. She looked down into his eyes, and he bucked up in one hard thrust, releasing. And she came again, this time powerful, blinding.

She sank down onto him in a pile of loose, jellylike limbs. And she saw that he had tears in his eyes.

Muirinn gently kissed away a salty drop as it tried to escape down a tanned crease at the corner of one eye. He smiled at her—so open, so warm, as if all barriers between them had crumbled.

But they hadn't.

Because the pressure to tell him about the baby she'd given away had just mounted intensely inside her, but the prospect of his reaction was now even more daunting.

This thing between them was so precious, so gossamer fragile, she was absolutely terrified to shatter it right now.

And that fear of losing it all again made her feel especially vulnerable.

But he wrapped himself protectively around her, nose

nuzzling into her hair, breathing in her scent, and they lay like that, listening to the branches tick on against the window. "Sounds like another storm coming," he murmured against her neck.

"Doesn't matter," she said softly. "I feel safe here."

Jett grinned, but inside he felt suddenly edgy.

Never had he been so fulfilled by the act of sex, but neither had he been left so empty, needing so much more. Because he wanted it all now.

He wanted Muirinn to stay with him and Troy, for them to finally be the family they were always supposed to be. But he had to do this right. He had to find a way to carefully broach the subject of Troy, and the thought daunted him.

The last thing he wanted was a major confrontation with Muirinn. The last time they'd fought it had cost them both. Dearly.

Because he could see now just how much she'd suffered, too.

But the longer he hid the truth from Muirinn, the worse it was going to be.

He closed his eyes, thinking, imagining how it could all still go so wrong.

The wind was picking up outside, beginning to buffet the branches of a pine against the deck railing. Jett got up, wrapping a towel around his waist. He stood at the windows.

Whitecaps were flecking the inlet, and he wondered if he should bring his boat on shore. He reached for the binoculars he kept on the dresser, and scanned the water and mountains in the distance. It looked like bad weather ahead, judging by a dense band of cloud beyond the peaks.

"What are you doing?" Muirinn said from the bed, her voice husky, warm.

"Just looking."

"For bad guys?"

He laughed, his chest expanding with affection, warmth. He glanced back at her.

Muirinn's fire-gold hair tumbled in a mass of tangled curls over creamy white shoulders and breasts, and her cheeks were flushed, eyes glowing. He couldn't let her go again. Not ever.

He turned back to the window, tension whispering inside him, a movement from Gus's house next door suddenly catching his eye. Jett panned his scopes over to the property next door. "Lydia Wilkie's on your deck again," he said, adjusting the focus.

Muirinn sighed. "She's *always* in that house." She got out of bed, wrapping the sheet around herself, and came to stand by his side. "I guess my grandfather liked the company."

"Does she bother you?"

"Maybe. No. I don't know." Muirinn hesitated. "I was going to tell her that I didn't want her housekeeping services. Then again, once the baby comes…" her voice trailed off.

Jett's hands tightened around the scopes. "Are you really going to stay?" He made sure there was no emotion, no inflection in the question.

She bumped him playfully. "How could I not, after that."

He grinned. "I'm serious."

Her smile sobered. "My roots are here, Jett. I don't have any family left, but this is where I feel a sense of belonging than anywhere else. I had to leave to learn this, and I want my daughter to feel that same sense of identity."

He inhaled deeply, a fragile hope flaring like a burning coal inside him. So much could still go haywire. They needed time. They needed less pressure. But this case, Gus's files, Tolkin, their own secrets—it was all putting the delicate beginnings of this new relationship into a pressure cooker, with a timer set to blow.

He thought again about the prints in the dark mud, and it hit him suddenly. "You know, I have an idea. Do you remember Trapper Joe?"

She frowned, pulling the sheet higher over her breasts. "You mean that old hermit who used to live way out in the bush?"

"That's the one. He still lives in the bush, and if *anyone* can tell us anything at all about those prints, it's Trapper Joe."

"He's a nut job, Jett."

"Yes, but his tracking ability is also borderline psychic, Muirinn. Last year he helped our SAR crew track down a missing twelve-year-old boy who got separated from his family on a hunting trip. For three weeks we found no sign of him at all. Everyone had given up. Even the family. And then one night old Trapper Joe shows up like a shadow out of the forest, and he just walks into the woods, and starts tracking. He found that kid in two days. Alive."

"Maybe Joe had something to do with the kid going missing in the first place. I wouldn't put anything past him. He always reminded me of an old stray wolf preying around the outskirts of town, looking to steal anything anyone left out."

Jett shook his head. "I've seen what he can do, Muirinn. Sometimes he comes into town, goes to the outfitters store on Main Street. He doesn't talk to anyone, but he watches them. He studies the way people move, the way they dress, what shoes they wear. I'd swear he can identify the prints of just about everyone in Safe Harbor."

"Okay, so he found a kid, and you're sold, but—"

"He was also at Gus's funeral, Muirinn. I think helping us will mean something to him."

She went dead still, color leaching from her face. "Why didn't you tell me he was at the service?" she whispered.

"You didn't ask. I saw Joe at the back of the church

during the ceremony. When I looked again, he was gone, like a ghost."

"Why?" she asked softly. "Why do you think Trapper Joe came to the funeral?"

"Because Gus was one of the few villagers Joe actually did communicate with. I saw him at Gus's house a couple of times over the years. I figured they were friends, in some weird way. Well, as much as Joe could be a friend to anyone."

"Where's Joe now?"

"He runs a trapline up north, has a camp out there."

"Maybe we should go see him, Jett. Even if Joe can't tell us anything about those prints, I'd like to know why he really came to the funeral. Maybe Gus spoke to him about his suspicions."

Jett nodded. "I'll fly us in, as soon as you're dressed." He tilted his head toward the window. "We should go before that weather behind the peaks rolls in. It'll also give us an opportunity to check out those ATV tracks from the air. Besides—" Jett wavered suddenly, then smiled. "There's something else I want to show you."

"What?" Eyes so clear and green and open looked into his. "You'll see."

A smile ghosted her lips. "A secret?"

"No," he said quietly. "I'm tired of secrets, Muirinn."

She swallowed, forcing a smile that never quite reached into her eyes, nodded and left the room.

And Jett's whispering unease intensified.

Perspiration beaded the woman's lip. She swiped it away angrily with the base of her thumb. "What part about making it look like an accident did you not understand?"

"It was supposed to seem like a *hunting accident*—"

"Shooting up an entire shed, blowing up a truck?" She swore at him.

He jabbed his finger at her. "Do not swear at me. I am not a goddamn *murderer.* The woman is pregnant. Besides, we've got the laptop and photographs—"

"She's seen them!"

"So? She won't be able to prove a damn thing without them."

"But she can *talk.* And the fact that she hasn't reported the theft of the laptop, *or* the shootout at the mine, tells me she doesn't trust the cops. And that in turn tells me she's read the old man's files."

Panic shot across the man's features. "Do you think she's told Rutledge?"

"Of course she has." She inhaled shakily, pressing her hand against her sternum. "We've *got* to do something. This can't get out. We cannot be exposed."

"What do you propose we do, then?"

Her eyes darted, bright, manic. "The only thing we *can* do. We nip this in the bud. Now. We take them *both* out of the picture."

The man shook his head. "For God's sake, no. I can't do this. I am not a killer."

"Oh yes you are," she said. "Twelve men died in that mine because of *you*—"

"But I didn't—"

She held up her hand. "It doesn't matter. If this gets out, you *will* spend the rest of your life in prison."

She gripped his shoulders with both hands, perspiration shining on her forehead. "Think ahead. Think clearly. Think of the future." She paused, her mind racing. "It'll be easier to go after her alone, first. We find a way to abduct her, quietly. We take her out to the cabin, alive. And we use her to lure

Rutledge out into the bush. Then we make them both vanish."
She clicked her fingers near his ear. "Into the wild, a trip into
the bush gone wrong. It happens often enough."

Nausea roiled in his stomach.

He couldn't look at her, be with her. He went to the
bathroom instead, and threw up.

Leaning on the basin, he stared into the mirror, no longer
recognizing the man who stared back at him. He swore,
swiped his hand hard across the back of his mouth.

Twenty years had passed. And it still wasn't over.

Chapter 12

As they drove to the airstrip, Muirinn asked suddenly, "How come you were the one to get custody of Troy, Jett?"

His heart skipped a beat, but he kept his eyes focused on the road ahead. "Kim was okay with it."

Muirinn waited, but he volunteered nothing more. She turned in the car seat, back to him, staring out the window, and he sensed the shift in her mood. They'd just shared a deeply personal experience, and here he was holding back. Again. His hands tensed on the wheel.

As they neared the turnoff she spoke again, not looking at him. "What actually happened between you and Kim? Why didn't things work out?"

"You happened."

She shot him a glance. "I don't understand."

He heaved out a sigh. "Kim knew that I'd never gotten over you, Muirinn. She knew she'd always walk in your shadow, and she just got so darn tired of trying to *be* you, to take your place in my heart."

And she knows you'll always be my son's mother. Your eyes look back at her every time she looks into Troy's.

"Separating was for the best."

Silence filled the cab of the truck.

"Did she love you, Jett?"

Guilt gnawed at him. He'd tried so hard to trick himself into forgetting about Muirinn, to love Kim fully. He moistened his lips, nodded. "Yes, very much. She's a good person, Muirinn. A good...mother. And I loved her back, in my way. But Kim's happier now. She has a new man. It was the right thing to let her go."

"What does she do?"

"Nurse."

"Like your mom?"

He nodded. "Yeah. She gets on real well with my mom, and my dad, too."

Her hands fidgeted in her lap, restless. He neared the gates to the airstrip.

"Do you ever think that some secrets really are better left buried?" she asked softly as they drove through the gates.

That subtle sense of foreboding rippled through him again. "Why?" He pulled up alongside one of the hangars, where his plane was parked.

"Because maybe the truth is worse."

"What makes you say that?" He removed his shotgun and ammunition from the gun box, then opened the passenger door, holding his hand out to her.

She didn't take it right away. Instead, she looked directly up into his eyes. "What if we know the killer, Jett?"

He studied her for a moment, conscious of the growing

sound of a single-engine prop coming in for a landing. The airstrip wind sock was stiff, pollen blowing on dry, warm wind.

"I'm sure we will know him, Muirinn," he said, frowning. "It's a small town, and someone's been living here among us, keeping this old secret for a long time."

She clasped his hand, and he helped her out. She stilled in his arms for a moment, and Jett's chest ached. Damn, he loved her. Even more, if that was possible. Yet, oddly, he could feel her slipping from his grasp even as he held on. "Muirinn, what's worrying you?"

She inhaled deeply, a strange emotion crossing her features. She pulled away and rubbed her face, suddenly angry, conflicted by something. "It's nothing. I'm fine."

That icicle of unease that had crystallized inside him earlier burrowed a little deeper. He handed her the shotgun. "That's my plane over there," he nodded toward a stubby de Havilland Beaver parked in the hangar. "I'll be right back—just going to check in with the guys, tell them where we're headed."

She took the gun from him, unable to meet his gaze. Jett was really worried now. She was hiding something from him, and it was eating at her. Anxiety snaked through him. If she suddenly confessed to him that she'd given up his son for adoption, he was going to have to explain what he'd done— how he'd gone after Troy behind her back, how he'd raised her boy without ever telling her.

It wasn't going to be pretty. She was going to be hurt, furious. She might never forgive him.

He stalked over to the Safe Harbor Air offices, a sense of things closing in and pressing down on him with the low pressure cell and changing weather.

Muirinn slowly turned around inside the hangar, taking it all in.

A dusty tarp covered something large in the far corner.

She walked over to it, her eyes adjusting to the light. Propping the shotgun against the wall, she lifted up a corner of the tarpaulin. Underneath was the fuselage of a small plane, partially built, without wings. Curious, she peeled the cover back some more. Dust motes floated up into the dim shafts of light.

She recognized the shape of the fuselage from the little models her father used to have hanging from the ceiling of his old workshop—the planes he used to dream of flying up in the sky as he went down into the earth each day to toil in the blackness of the mine. A lump formed in her throat at the irony, and Jett's words filtered into her mind.

"If Troy hadn't introduced me to model airplanes, to the idea of flying, I might have become a miner, not a pilot. He was the one who told me, when I was ten years old, that I could do something better with my life than go down that mine."

At least her dad had passed on his love of planes to Jett and, in doing so, something of him still lived on. But whoever had been building this plane seemed have stopped some time ago. The fuselage was thick with dust. Muirinn yanked the tarp back fully, coughing as she did. She froze as saw the name that had been tentatively stenciled on the side.

Muirinn of the Wind.

Her heart caught in her throat. With trembling fingers, she reached up, smoothed off the thick layer of dust.

As she did, a shadow behind her blocked the light.

She swung around, heart thumping. She'd clean forgotten the gun, everything.

Jett stood silhouetted in the entrance, posture rigid. "What are you doing?"

He came up to her, reached for the tarp and jerked it back across the fuselage, covering the name, as if to hide a corpse, something offensive that shouldn't be exposed to the light of day, to human eyes.

"It's a Tiger Moth, isn't it?" she said softly. "Like the models my dad had, like the ones in Gus's photos from the war." A sudden rush of memories squeezed to her chest as she spoke.

Muirinn could almost smell her mother's baking again, hear the sound of teaspoons chinking against china, the patter of rain against the window. She could see Jett—her young neighbor on whom she had the biggest crush—building model airplanes with her dad as her mom served tea and cookies.

"De Havilland Tiger Moth, a replica," he said, watching her eyes. "I was building it when you left. It was going to be a surprise."

"You never finished her. Why?"

His eyes darkened. "Because you left."

She swallowed hard.

"We should go, Muirinn. This weather will bring rain by tomorrow, if not sooner."

"You named her for me," she whispered. *"Muirinn of the Wind."*

He said nothing.

She reached up, touched his face, her heart aching. "I love you, Jett," she whispered. "God, I love you."

He took her in his arms suddenly—hard, fierce—and he kissed her mouth. She melted into him, kissing him back, her world swirling away in a blur of time.

Someone coughed loudly. "Hey, you two lovebirds!"

Jett stiffened, and shock rippled through Muirinn. She pulled back. Adam Rutledge stood at the entrance to the hangar, hands stuffed into pockets of his coveralls as he grinned broadly.

"Adam!"

"Dad?" Jett said. "I didn't know you'd be here today."

Adam came forward, his smile broadening in his tanned, lined face as he held his hands out to Muirinn. "I heard you were back. Welcome home, Muirinn!" He clasped her shoulders firmly. "You're looking fine, girl. Wow, all these years. It's real good to see you." He shot his son a quick glance, not managing to hide a flicker of concern.

Jett scowled subtly, warning his dad to shut up, not to mention the kiss. Or the pregnancy.

He didn't. Instead, Adam stepped back, slapped his son affectionately on his shoulder. "The guys in the office told me you were here. I came to see where you were headed."

"I'm taking Muirinn up for a spin before that weather over the ridge rolls in."

He nodded, eyes thoughtful as Jett declined to elaborate. Adam stuffed his hands back into his coverall pockets, turned to Muirinn and smiled warmly. "Well, I hope Jett's going to bring you around for Sunday lunch tomorrow, Muirinn. The missus likes to cook up something special for the weekends." He cast another quick look at his son. "Too bad Troy won't be here."

Jett smiled, but the light didn't quite reach his eyes. "Yes."

"So, you coming tomorrow?"

"Wouldn't want to miss Mom's cooking."

"See you both Sunday, then." Adam hesitated, something unreadable creeping into his eyes, a worry, perhaps, that his son was going to get hurt again by this woman. "Fly safe," was all he said.

Jett nodded.

Muirinn watched as Adam hobbled toward the hangar entrance. His injuries and arthritis had worsened over the years, and he was dragging his left leg with each awkward swing of his gait. While still strong and solid, mining had clearly taken its toll on Adam Rutledge's body, thought Muirinn. She wondered if he was in constant pain. Jett followed her eyes, a frown crossing his features. "Come," he took her elbow, turning her away from watching his dad. "Time to fly. You got those photos with you?"

She nodded, looking back over her shoulder, eyes still trained on Adam as he crossed the grass outside the hangar.

"Muirinn?"

She shook herself. "Sorry," she said softly. "I just can't help wondering what it might be like to have my parents around, too." Her eyes were soft. Sad.

"Hey," he tilted her chin up. "We're going to do right by your parents, Muirinn. We're going to get to the bottom of this, and we're going to find justice. Someone will pay."

She bit her lip and nodded.

Before flying out to Trapper Joe's, Jett flew northeast of town, guiding his barrel-chested plane between the avalanche-scoured peaks that surged up either side of the Tolkin Valley. The plane's characteristic growling made headsets necessary to talk without yelling.

Through the blur of the spinning prop, Muirinn recognized the old headframes of Tolkin Mine coming into view ahead. She shuddered involuntarily at the memory of being under fire in that dank shed.

Jett dropped altitude, banking his craft tightly along the flank of the mountain, then suddenly he pointed. "Down there!" The mouthpiece gave his voice a tinny quality. "See them? ATV tracks, along that dry portion of narrow mountain trail." He dipped his wings sharply, and followed the tracks, the de Havilland's belly almost skimming the tips of the trees.

The trail below them crossed a dry creek bed, then disappeared into forest. Lifting the nose sharply into the blue sky, he banked and flew low over the tracks again.

"Are you sure those are the sniper's tracks?"

"I saw dust kick up when the shooter fled. The only thing you can drive up those trails is either a four-wheeler or a dirt bike. And look, the tire marks lead straight from his hide above the Tolkin Mine site to the trail there."

Anxiety unfurled inside Muirinn. "And where does the trail itself lead?"

"Up through the saddle in the mountains over there—" he pointed. "And then back down into the drainage on the other side of this ridge. You can go all the way along that eastern river drainage back to Safe Harbor, approaching the town from the other side."

"So the shooter could have come from town?"

"Or from one of a handful of remote hunting or logging camps up the next valley."

Jett pointed the nose of his craft northward and, as the foothills faded behind them, the horizon grew flat and endless. Below them a herd of caribou fanned out in a thunderous race across the plain, spooked by the buzz from his prop.

"Down there," Jett said suddenly as he buzzed low over the forest again, just skimming the treetops.

Below them, miles of aquamarine lake shimmered between white shores and dense forest. He pointed to a small log cabin in a clearing cut along the north end of the lake. "That's what I've been working on. A high-end, rustic fishing lodge that will attract clients from places like New York and Texas. There's also a big market for this kind of thing in Germany and the Scandinavian countries."

He dipped his wing sharply left, swooping over the

clearing. "The main lodge will go over there." He pointed. "With satellite cabins along the shore there." He pulled up the nose of the Beaver and flew west, the rugged craft rattling and growling. "You can see how that tributary from the Tuklit River feeds in at the head of the lake over there. Perfect for salmon fishing."

Muirinn peered down through the side window as Jett banked the plane for her. A massive grizzly appeared, lumbering along the shallows of a pebbled spit.

He grinned as he caught sight of it. "Brown bear, wolves, caribou, moose—it's God's country, Muirinn."

She turned to look at him. "Those blueprints in your house—they were for this place?"

He grinned again, a wicked slash of white against tanned skin, his mirrored glasses glinting under his helmet. She'd never seen him like this, in his plane, in his element. Pure, happy, all-male.

And Muirinn realized with a start that they had always, at the core, been exactly the same.

While she'd seen those granite peaks as a rock prison, so had he. Only he'd been able to escape, up here, with wings. And because of it, he'd found freedom. To leave and return whenever he wanted, on his own terms.

While she'd left and hurt the people she'd loved the most.

Jett tilted the de Havilland's nose upwards, and they climbed again before leveling out over a wide valley of muskeg. A male moose with full set of antlers jerked his head up at the sound of the plane, and took flight through tussock as they buzzed over him.

Muirinn felt her heart soar as the vista took hold of her soul. Almost subconsciously, she placed her hand on Jett's thigh. "This is gorgeous," she whispered.

"I wish I could have brought you up eleven years ago, Muirinn."

She glanced at him, unable to read his eyes behind the mirrored shades, but she knew what he was saying. Maybe if she'd found this freedom with him, instead of looking for it away from him, they'd still be together.

A family.

Because if she'd stayed, she'd have kept their son.

Muirinn's mood shifted as her thoughts turned to the adoption. *How would you feel about me if I told you about our baby?*

He shot her a concerned glance. "What's up?

"Nothing." She forced a smile. "I was just thinking how good it is to see you happy, Jett."

And how I'd hate to do anything to destroy that.

They flew farther north in silence, the vast beauty brooking no conversation. Or perhaps it was a looming sense of foreboding as the sky grew darker, more oppressive.

Jett took the plane down alongside a sullen river. He landed on a gravel bar, wheels bumping wildly over the spit next to the wide and silent body of water. His prop slowed as they came to a halt near a crude wooden rack hung with strips of drying salmon flesh.

A deathly silence seemed to descend over the plane, broken only by the pop of hot engine metal, and the sharp *krak* of a raven perched high on a dead snag.

A cloud of midges hovered over discarded salmon guts at the water's edge. Two scarred dogs were eating the scraps. They growled, heads low, then scuttled into the brush as Jett climbed down from the pilot's seat.

The air felt sticky, close.

He helped Muirinn down from the plane, suddenly keenly

aware of his hunting knife at his hip. And as they crunched over a small stone beach, Trapper Joe appeared, his grizzled form silently separating from the dense shadows of the trees, shotgun in his hand. He watched them approach, lowering his weapon only when he recognized Jett. He pushed his cap back on his head, nodded his greeting.

A silent man.

A secretive man.

A man like so many before him who had fled north, escaping something—perhaps the law, or a dark secret— hoping to hide from the past in this vast and isolated wilderness, under the cover of the long, dark winters. It was out here that men like Joe hoped to start another life. But invariably that didn't happen. Because the problems came with them. And Trapper Joe's problems, his secrets from south of the 49th parallel, were hidden behind bloodshot eyes, too much whiskey, sun-baked and wind-worn skin. And silence.

He was a man of indeterminate age who lived completely off grid. A survivalist, with only his dogs for company.

No one knew his story, where exactly he came from. Local lore pinned him as an escaped con from Down South. The kids Muirinn grew up with used to say he had murdered a man. Adults, however, pegged him for an ex-cop. One who'd gotten on the wrong side of his badge. They cited Trapper Joe's almost paranoid avoidance of local law enforcement as proof.

But regardless of Trapper Joe's secret, those who knew of his ability to track found his art almost mystical.

"Joe—" Jett nodded, showing the old trapper the bottle of whiskey he'd brought with him, not wasting words on a man who didn't like to use them. "We were hoping to show you something, ask your opinion."

Joe narrowed his eyes onto Muirinn.

"This is Muirinn O'Donnell, Gus O'Donnell's grand-daughter."

Trapper Joe said nothing, just turned and led Muirinn and Jett through the trees to the clearing where his camp had been set up.

Mosquitoes buzzed in a small cloud. Two Husky-Malamute crosses got up, growled. Joe waved them away, and they retreated a few feet to lie silently, watching, like barely tamed wolves. Again, Jett reminded himself that his knife was handy. Joe ducked under a tarpaulin that served as a deck cover and led them into the log cabin, motioning to a camp chair and sawed-off log for seats. Jett placed the bottle of whiskey on the Formica table.

The interior smelled of wood smoke and the cloying scent of wet dog fur. Strung along one wall were an assortment of animal traps and a pair of old gut snowshoes. Joe went to his woodstove, poured coffee, black. "Got no cream," he said, plunking the chipped mugs onto the table.

He sloshed a dollop of whiskey into his own, offered the bottle to Jett and Muirinn. Both declined with a shake of the head.

Joe took a seat, his eyes still fixated on Muirinn. It made her feel uncomfortable. Jett tried to break the ice. "You haven't seen Muirinn for a long time, huh?"

"Gus said you were a looker. He was right."

Muirinn flushed. "Thank you."

"You weren't at his funeral." Joe's voice was creaky, as if from disuse, but it didn't disguise the accusation in his words.

Guilt washed through her. "I was stuck out in a jungle, in Irian Jaya, the Indonesian half of New Guinea." She found herself trying to justify her absence again. "It's one of the last places on earth where there are still tribes that have had no contact with the rest of the world, and no one could get news to me," she said, *needing* Joe to understand. "It was part of the project, to feel as cut off from communication as the locals of the area."

He sipped his coffee, eyes unwavering. "Even though you was pregnant?"

Muirinn felt her cheeks warm again. "I was entering my sixth month. My doctor said everything was good. Plus, our photographer was a qualified paramedic." Muirinn cleared her throat, feeling small, judged. "Gus must have really meant something to you, Joe, for you to have trekked all the way into town for the service," she said.

He studied her in silence. "What do you want me to look at?"

"These." She slid the four photos onto the table.

He pursed his lips, gray whiskers standing out. He tapped his dirty fingers on two photos. "These two were taken down inside the Tolkin Mine."

Muirinn glanced at Jett, heart pattering. They'd been hoping to avoid too many specifics. But she couldn't lie now—not if she wanted his trust. "Yes. How do you know?"

Joe picked up one photo, his thatch brows lowering as he examined it more closely. Then his eyes shifted up slowly, warily, and met hers. "What you want to know?"

"Is there anything at all that you can tell us about who might have made those prints?"

"Why?" he said quietly.

Muirinn exhaled cautiously. She'd hoped it would be easier. But Joe had read enough already to make Muirinn believe that if she were less than honest, he'd clam up. She needed his trust. "Gus was trying to solve a mystery."

"The bombing."

She nodded.

Jett leaned forward. "Joe, the reason we came out here to see you was—"

"Was because you don't want anyone in town to see these," he cut in, shaking his head. "Gus spent years trying to solve this thing."

"Did he ever discuss it with you?"

The trapper didn't respond. He just stared at the photos.

"Joe," Muirinn said, leaning forward, "my grandfather believed that the bomber had an accomplice, and that means there are at least two people who might still be out there trying cover up the murder twenty years later." Muirinn paused. "These photos recently came into Gus's possession, and those prints could belong to the men responsible for killing my father. And, yes, right now it's best that no one knows that Gus had these. It could be…dangerous."

"You think it was what got Gus killed?"

"What makes you think he was killed?" Jett asked, very quietly.

"No way Gus went all the way down that shaft alone. No truck. Nothing. It didn't smell right to me." Joe wavered, as if weighing the potential blowback for what he was about to reveal next. He cleared his throat. "Two people were at the mine with Gus the day he died."

Muirinn's pulse quickened. Jett placed his hand on hers, warning her to go slow with Joe.

She swallowed. "What makes you say that?" she said, voice cracking.

"Prints. I saw them at the scene. Left by a man and a woman." A nerve began to twitch under his eye. "They were with Gus. And they killed him."

Chapter 13

Muirinn's heart thudded. But suspicion unfurled slowly through her. "How do you know this, Joe?" she asked very quietly. "Were you there?"

He moistened his lips, lifted his cap and scratched his head. "I went to look after I heard they'd brought up his body. That's when I saw the tracks. They told me Gus was not alone when he died."

"But how could you tell?" Muirinn asked. "There must have been police and rescue personnel tracks all over the place—"

"My own prints included," interjected Jett.

His gaze shifted to Jett. "The SAR people's boots have individual identifying marks in the heel lugs, right?"

"That's right," said Jett. "It was something we started after that kid and his family went missing in the bush. We did it so that trackers like yourself wouldn't confuse our prints with the prints of the missing."

"So that trace from you and your team could be excluded right off. Cops issue boots, too. I know who wears what shoes. You get a good mantracker, he can tell a whole story—like finding a fossil. You can build the whole damn dinosaur. You can see who came first, who walked on top afterwards, what the weather was like."

Again, Muirinn was reminded of the old rumor that Joe was ex–law enforcement, or ex-military. It fit. It was why Jett had thought Joe might actually be able to help them.

But what he was saying raised more questions.

"Why did you go to the mine after they'd brought my grandfather up, Joe? Was it because you didn't buy what the police were saying about his accident?"

He shrugged, avoiding eye contact suddenly. "I liked Gus," he said, as if that explained it all. The fact was Joe found very few reasons to like any humans at all. If he was admitting a fondness for her grandfather, it probably meant a hell of a lot.

"And you didn't think to mention this discovery of yours to the Safe Harbor police?" Jett said.

He cast a withering look at Jett. "I mind my own business. They can mind theirs."

"Tell me about the prints, Joe. What led you to believe my grandfather was murdered?" Muirinn swallowed the sharp lump swelling in her throat as she spoke. Jett reached out, covered her hands, and she realized they were clenched tightly in her lap.

Joe drained his coffee, swiped the back of his hand hard across his mouth and splashed a few fingers of straight whiskey into his mug. "This is how I read it. Gus was on the Tolkin property, and he was looking for something. He had a flashlight with him—"

Muirinn threw Jett a questioning look.

Jett nodded. "He did. A flashlight was found with his body."

"So that tells me Gus went there to poke around somewhere dark, maybe look down a shaft. His prints were going back and forth between the Sodwana headframe and D-shaft."

"Like he might be timing how long it would take between the two points underground?" Muirinn offered.

Joe nodded. "Yep. Like that. But he's not feeling well, okay, or maybe he's tired, or he's thinking and pondering, or confused, because he shuffles some, sits down a couple of times."

"As if he might have been short of breath, or his heart was giving him trouble?"

"Yep. That would do it. Then tracks from two people intersect with his, and they stop and talk to him. You can see this from the prints."

Joe's whiskey-coffee breath was strong, and Muirinn felt slightly queasy. She glanced out the door, suddenly craving clean air. Suddenly afraid of what Joe was going to say.

"You okay, Muirinn?" Jett said softly, hand on her shoulder.

She nodded, mouth dry.

"What can you tell us about those two sets of prints that intersected with Gus's tracks?" Jett said, taking over for her.

"One set was made by a man, hiking boots, size 12. Other set was probably from a woman. 'Bout a size 6."

"A woman? You're sure?" said Jett.

"Well, could be a young male, but the prints looked like a woman's running shoes to me, and the gait was more like a female. So my take is that this couple comes up to Gus, they stand and they talk. Then they start walking with Gus back to Sodwana. Then they stop and there's a tussle. And from that point on, the prints change. Woman is walking on one side, man on the other. Gus in the middle. Tight formation. The couple's gait is sort of angled in toward Gus, like they was pushing him, escorting him. And then Gus's stride, the depth of depression changes, like he is reluctant, leaning back, maybe collapsing, dragging his feet a bit."

Muirinn swallowed, nausea deepening.

"By this time, they're getting close to the headframe building, and their trace gets all messed up with all the other prints that came later. Police-dog prints all over them, too."

Silence.

Heat intensified in the cabin as the sun baked down outside.

A mosquito whined near Muirinn's head, and one of the huskies whimpered softly, paws twitching in his dream as he slept near the door.

Jett broke the gravitas.

"Why does that scenario say murder to you, Joe?"

"Because it tells me Gus was forced to the headframe building, and then I figure he was forced down into the shaft by those two people, because, like I say, Gus wouldn't have gone down there alone." He shrugged again. "Maybe once down there on the 300 level, in the dark and heat, the stress of it all gave him the heart attack. Thing is—those two people never told anyone he was down there. That's murder in my book."

Muirinn tensed, perspiration prickling over her lip. "What else could you tell, Joe?"

"The prints went back to D-shaft, just the two sets, no Gus this time. And they went to where two vehicles were parked behind the main D-Shaft buildings. The woman got into one vehicle, and the man into the other. Both vehicles had standard truck tires, one with winter tread and a real heavy oil leak. Left a black puddle."

Muirinn chilled. An oil leak. Winter tires.

Gus's vehicle?

Maybe he *had* driven out to the mine, and one of those

people had driven his truck back to his house to hide the fact that Gus was ever at the mine.

She glanced at Jett. He hadn't touched his coffee. Neither had she.

A soft wind began to swoosh through the stunted conifers outside, a pine cone clunking onto the metal roof.

Jett cleared his throat. "Joe, Gus's housekeeper said he was gone three days before he was actually reported missing. Then it took another thirteen days before we found his body down the shaft. And you're saying you could read all this information from prints that were made on the day of his death? Because those prints would have been over two weeks old."

Joe's eyes narrowed. "The time lapse is what helps tell me the story. Who was there first, who came after. There was rain the night before Gus went out to Tolkin. His prints, and the prints from the man and woman, were made in wet mine silt. Then they baked solid under hot sun for the next couple of weeks. That gray glacier silt bakes good as damn clay. Easy to see what prints were made atop of those."

Muirinn thought of the fine gray silt Jett had pointed out when he'd come around to fix Gus's truck. It could have come from the shoes of one of the two people who'd forced Gus down the mine shaft, after they'd driven Gus's truck back to his home to cover their tracks. "How come the police or SAR didn't look for any of this?" Muirinn snapped suddenly.

"It wasn't being treated as a crime scene, Muirinn," Jett said quietly. "To be honest, we were all just looking for an old and eccentric man who'd wandered off."

Muirinn's mood darkened. "And how do you know those two photos were taken down inside Tolkin Mine?" She pointed angrily to the crime scene shots Joe said were taken underground.

"Mud down there is very black, especially at the deeper levels. Anyone can see this was shot in a tunnel."

"And what can you tell us about those underground prints?" Muirinn's voice came out thick.

Trapper Joe studied them for a long moment. He got up, opened a drawer and retrieved a big old-fashioned magnifying glass. He pored over one of the photos in silence. Muirinn swatted at a small cloud of bugs, the smells in the cabin growing more cloying as the sun rose and the heat baked down.

"See there—" Joe pointed with a blackened fingernail. "And there—the smoothness in the lugs of the sole on the one side? This man favors his right leg. His left is injured, and from this wear on the sole, it's a permanent disability."

An unspecified chill stole into Jett, despite the heat in the cabin.

Joe held their eyes for a moment, running his tongue over his teeth, waiting. But neither Muirinn nor Jett offered him more information.

He grunted, turning his attention to the next photo. "From the ruler alongside this underground print, *these* tracks were made by a size 10 winter work boot, Vibram sole, standard mining issue. You can still buy these from Big Bear, the Safe Harbor outfitter on Main. This trace was made by a well-built man, solid, judging by the depths of the boot depressions, maybe 'bout five-eleven if we're looking at an average ratio between foot length to height. His limp is pretty bad—it would be real obvious to anyone watching him walk." Joe creaked his chair back, got up and began to imitate the limp, conjuring up the man's movement from the prints. One long stride, a swing of the left hip, then a short stride accompanied with a drag of the leg. "And he was getting tired. Like this." Joe dragged his left leg more.

The chill deepened in Jett as he watched Joe, an image of another man filling his mind, a man who made the exact same movements Trapper Joe was making.

A man both he and Muirinn had just watched hobbling out of the airport hangar.

He felt Muirinn glance at him, but Jett did not meet her eyes. He stared instead at the table, telling himself it was nonsense—lots of men working Tolkin had these kinds of injuries, not just his father. It was an occupational hazard.

And five-eleven was a pretty damn average height.

Joe piled the photos neatly, and pushed them abruptly back toward Muirinn. "If I was a betting man," he said looking at Jett very intensely, then Muirinn, booze and the scent of stale sweat wafting across the table as he moved, "I'd say the owner of those boots worked the mine. 'Cause—" he watched Jett again "—if this man went down to the 800 level at Sodwana and hiked all the way underground to the blast site, he'd have to know where he was going. He'd have worked that section before it was shut down, known those tunnels and rock like the backs of his own hands. And he'd have to know his explosives." He rubbed his stubbled jaw. "You ask me, you're looking for an experienced miner who was blasting rock in that old section before it closed. To be that experienced, I reckon he wouldn't have been younger than thirty at the time of the blast. Add four years from when the Sodwana section was closed, then another twenty years since the blast—your bomber is older than fifty-four. Could even be in his sixties now."

Jett felt the blood drain from his face, but he said nothing. Again, he told himself that tons of miners could fit that profile.

What if we know the killer, Jett? Maybe some secrets really are better left buried.

He felt sick.

Joe was watching him oddly. Heat and claustrophobia closed in on him. He needed to get out of this place.

Jett lurched to his feet and stomped out of the cabin.

Muirinn and Joe followed him. "Jett?" Muirinn said, placing her hand on his arm, but he shrugged her off and kept walking. "That storm is going to be coming in soon. We need to leave."

The wind blew hotter and harder, a soft rushing sound beginning in the tops of the conifers as they walked in awkward, ominous silence back to the plane, Joe following behind, shotgun in hand.

As they took off, Joe stood watching them from the beach below, until he was just a tiny speck alongside the wide brown river in a vast and lonely wilderness.

Muirinn sat quietly, watching Jett. His hands were tense on the controls, a muscle at his jaw pulsing. She knew he had to be thinking of his father—how could he *not* be?

Because she sure was.

The image of Adam Rutledge hobbling out of the hangar was burned fresh into her brain, and Joe had mimicked Adam's movements so exactly it was almost as though he'd morphed into Adam himself for a ghostly split second.

"Do you trust him?" Muirinn said as the plane reached elevation and leveled out.

"Joe?" Jett exhaled heavily, features grim. "I trust him not to go to the cops, if that's what you mean."

"I mean, can you trust that he knows what he's talking about? About those prints, that man and woman. The two vehicles." She hesitated. "The limp."

"Joe might be short on words, but not brain cells. He's sharp. I told you what he did with that kid."

Muirinn peered down at the ground below as they flew.

"That could have been Gus's Dodge leaking oil at the mine, Jett," she said softly. "And there was gray silt in his cab. If those two people were walking in wet silt at the time, it would have caked to their boots, and it would explain how so much got into the bottom of Gus's truck."

He shot a sharp glance at her. "So you figure Gus drove his own truck to the mine, and either that man or woman drove it back?"

She closed her eyes, resting her hand on her tummy, tired suddenly. "I don't know what to think," she whispered.

Silence hung for several beats, broken only by the whine and rumble of the engine.

"I guess I'm scared of the truth, Jett, of what we might find," she said softly. "If it's all connected—the Morans, the police—the truth could blow this town and families apart again, just as if we'd planted a bomb in Safe Harbor ourselves."

Jett said nothing, eyes focused dead ahead as he flew.

And Muirinn's mouth turned dry.

It wasn't just the town that would blow apart. If they found out that Adam did have something to do with the death of her father, the truth could shatter for good the fragile beginnings of their relationship.

Muirinn sneaked another look at Jett's rugged profile. She understood something crucial now—the lies that could bind, and divide. Because as much as she wanted justice for her father, for Gus, for her mother, she sure as hell didn't want to blow Jett's life out of the water, or her chances of a future with him.

Muirinn sat back in the seat, a sense of looming, unavoidable disaster ahead as they came in to land at the Safe Harbor airstrip.

"I'm going to fly you out," Jett said suddenly as the plane taxied to a stop on the grass.

"What?"

He helped her down from the plane. "I want you to pack your bags, and then I'm going to fly you to Anchorage, see if we can get you on standby to New York."

"*Why?*"

He led her back to his truck. "Because this is more serious than I thought, Muirinn. And it would be safer for you and your baby to go home until this is settled."

He yanked open the cab door, waited for her to get in. But she just stood and stared at him, dumbfounded. "Jett," she said, "I told you, I'm not going back to New York. I'm staying in Safe Harbor for good. This is my *home*."

Jett swallowed, tension beginning to roll off him in hot dark waves. "Please, get in."

She climbed into his truck, her mind racing, and he slammed the passenger door closed.

He started the engine and drove her back to Mermaid's Cove in unnatural silence, his features gray. "Please, *talk* to me, Jett," she demanded. "What the hell is going on with you?"

"Nothing. I just want you and the baby to be safe."

Urgency bit into Muirinn as he ushered her into his house. And she couldn't take it anymore. She swung around to face him as they entered his house. "Jett—"

He waited, laser eyes burning into her.

"You don't want me in New York because it's safe," she said, feeling as if she were going to the gallows with her next words. "You want me way out of the way while you deal with this, because you think your *father* might be involved."

"Look, Muirinn, if you're thinking my dad had anything to do with that bombing just because he has a limp, you're way off base!" He tossed his flight jacket onto the sofa and thumped his shotgun onto the table. He was nervous. Edgy. He aimed his index finger at her, eyes glinting cold. "My father tried to *save* your dad, but the security and the cops wouldn't let him and his mine rescue crew in."

"Why wouldn't they let Adam in?" she urged softly.

He glared at her.

"Because he was a union stalwart, okay? I didn't understand that when I was twelve, but I learned later it was because Adam Rutledge was a shop steward, and he was vehemently anti–scab labor. That made him an enemy of Troy O'Donnell, and an enemy of all those other men who crossed the picket line daily to earn a dollar to support their families, and to stop the banks from foreclosing on their mortgages."

He vibrated with anger, eyes darkening at her accusations.

"There was a court injunction against Adam and the union executives, prohibiting them from being on Tolkin property, Jett. Remember that? And *that* is why they wouldn't let him in to allegedly save my father."

Jett lowered his voice dangerously. "That doesn't make him a *murderer,* Muirinn."

"So what size boots *does* he wear, Jett?"

Silence.

"How tall is he?"

Pulsing, darker silence.

"Jett, it does fit. Your father was an explosives expert. He worked that section of the mine before it was closed. And Chalky Moran had latched onto him—Adam was Chalky's mentor, you said so yourself. Chalky could have been the accomplice, Jett. You also said Moran blood runs thick in this town. Think about it—why would Ike Potter, a rookie cop at the time, sit on those photos? Because it must have been a Moran who took them. And a Moran was also police chief at the time. Bill Moran could have destroyed Ike's career. And after Ike had left it so long, he must have gotten scared, because he'd have been implicated in a conspiracy to cover up mass murder if he'd come forward at a later stage."

Jett paled, his skin tightening over his bones, his eyes growing dark and hollow. The clock in the kitchen ticked loudly, and Jett felt sick. All that old crap resurfacing from that dank hole in the earth.

Too many goddamn secrets.

Why had she come back anyway—just to dredge up all this old stuff again?

"Jett—" she reached to touch his arm, but he drew back sharply and shook his head. "Do not touch me, Muirinn."

Hurt arrowed through her eyes. "I'm sorry, Jett," she said softly. "I was just connecting the dots. The limp, the left leg injured—"

"No! No freaking way, Muirinn."

"There's one way to find out, Jett. You could at least speak to him."

He swore again. Muirinn was forcing his mind to go where it didn't want to go, where he *couldn't* allow it to go. So he fought back instead, lashing out at her because he needed to strike out at the very idea itself.

"My father wouldn't do it. He's just not a murderer."

"And what makes you so damn sure? Just how far might *you* go to protect *him?* As far as…" she paled suddenly as the implication hit her. She instinctively placed her hand over her belly. Jett's expression tightened.

"What were you going to say, Muirinn?"

She shook her head, looking ill.

"You were going to say as far as trying to kill Gus? To shoot at *you?*"

Her mouth opened in protest.

But he raised his hand. "Don't even *think* it, Muirinn. My dad is a savior, a *rescuer*—"

"Maybe your father is the reason Gus did not go straight to the FBI with Ike's photos, Jett. Have you considered that? Maybe he wanted to be sure. Maybe Gus didn't want to hurt you or your family. And his hesitation got him killed."

Jett watched her hand on her belly, tore his eyes away and fixed them on her face instead. "My father," he said very quietly, "could not have blown up the men he used to sit elbow to elbow with in the Miners Tavern—"

"He didn't drink with those men during the strike, did he? When things started to get bad, when the town was divided, I'll bet Adam started drinking down at the union hall, along with the other stalwarts."

"Dammit! He did not try to cover this up! It's inconceivable. My father would never, ever hurt Gus. Or you." He stalked to the window, paced, dragging his hands over his hair. "For God's sake, Muirinn, there is just no way in hell my dad would try to murder his own grandson's mother!" He stalled as he realized what had just come out of his mouth.

He swung around, staring at her.

Her mouth opened slowly, and her face went ghostly white.

Time stretched, her eyes growing into huge dark-green pools of shock, horror.

"What did you say?" Her words came out hoarse.

He inhaled deeply, then released a heavy shuddering breath. "I said, my father would not harm his own grandson's mother." He paused. "The mother of my son."

Chapter 14

Muirinn felt the blood rush from her head.

"I...I don't understand."

Desperation twisted into Jett's face, and Muirinn's gaze slid slowly over to the photo on the wall. She stared numbly at the image of a smiling Troy sitting on Jett's lap in the cockpit of his de Havilland Beaver.

"Troy?" It was a rough sound that came from low in her throat. A sound she didn't recognize as her own.

Jett said nothing, grief, angst, agony wrenching his powerful features. And Muirinn knew.

"How?" It was all that would come out.

"You gave him away."

"How did you *know?*" she whispered hoarsely.

"After you told Gus that you were having a baby and had agreed to a private adoption, he called and told me. He gave me the name of the lawyer the adoptive couple was using."

She swayed, catching the back of the sofa for balance, unable to speak, face muscles in a vise.

"I sold everything I could, Muirinn—my bike, my fishing gear, my boat—and I flew down to Nevada, and I fought for my son. I wasn't going to see my boy, my own flesh and blood go to another family—"

"But *how* did you do it? How did you get him?" The words were barely a whisper.

He inhaled deeply. "I told the lawyer that I was the real father, that my child was being given away without my consent, and that I would fight for my rights every goddamn step of the way. The lawyer informed the adoptive couple, and they decided not to contest me. They didn't want a child on those terms, Muirinn. And they released the baby into my care."

Her stomach turned to water.

"And Kim?"

"I'd met her just after you left town—she'd come up here for a nursing job. We started dating, and she offered to fly with me to Nevada to get my son. I was grateful for her help, Muirinn. I was a twenty-two-year old guy who knew zip about infants. But Kim did."

Emptiness, exclusion clawed at Muirinn's insides. She'd been so terribly desperate, so alone and hollow after giving up her child. Missing her baby so terribly much. Meanwhile, Jett and some young nurse had him, warm in their arms. Without her knowledge. Tears swam into her eyes, blinding her, and they rolled down her face. She didn't care.

Their son. Troy. Living here with his real dad in Safe Harbor all these years, right next door to her grandfather. The lost years, the lost potential, the sense of betrayal—it was too vast, too painful to comprehend.

"So my grandfather *knew* that Troy was my son, and living

here?" She couldn't quite grasp that Gus had not once, not ever, told her any of this.

"Yeah, Muirinn, he knew. Gus told me you were having our baby because he didn't want his grandchild being raised by some other family. He wanted to give me the tools to make my own choices, because he felt it was my right as a father. I think, Muirinn, that Gus truly believed I would contact you, talk some sense into you, bring you home and make things right. But I married Kim instead, while we were in Vegas. And when Gus found out, he let things be. He was just happy to be able to watch his grandson growing up next door, anonymously."

The sheer scope of the deception—of Gus's deception—was suddenly suffocating, drowning her.

"Why…why didn't Gus tell *me* you had our son?"

"Maybe he would have if you'd ever bothered to come back to Safe Harbor to visit." The bitterness in Jett's voice sliced into Muirinn like a knife. "Or maybe he didn't tell you because I ended up marrying Kim, and Gus didn't want to mess with my marriage for Troy's sake. Kim was a good mother, Muirinn. Maybe Gus didn't want to force you to return out of some misguided sense of obligation and break up our family. Hell knows. Gus was different. He did his best. He wanted the best for you, too. He knew how desperate you were to escape this place, to 'grow,' he called it. He just wanted you to be free."

"Why *did* you marry Kim?" she whispered, feeling utterly defeated. "So soon."

"She loved me. I loved her back in my own way. I never thought I'd ever love anyone again the way I loved you, Muirinn. And I really needed her help with Troy. It was her idea to get married in Vegas, to return to Safe Harbor as a family, and it seemed right at the time."

"And your parents?"

"They know. I told my mom and dad. How else was I going to explain the sudden appearance of a tiny baby in my life?"

Muirinn's grip on the back of the sofa tightened as she felt her legs beginning to buckle.

"What about everyone else in town?"

Jett's eyes pierced hers. "Safe Harbor has clearly been pretty damn good at keeping secrets and minding its own business. I personally never said anything to anyone, and no one ever asked anything about the baby, even if they did have their suspicions. Dr. Callaghan knew Troy wasn't Kim's child. But everyone treated her as his rightful mother."

"Oh, God." Muirinn moved around the sofa, and slumped weakly down onto it. She looked up through her tears. "What about Troy, what does *he* know?"

"He thinks Kim is his mother."

"You lied to me," she whispered, then lurched back to her feet. "You bloody hypocrite. *That's* why you have custody of him, and Kim doesn't! She isn't his *mother.*"

"Don't—" He pointed his index finger at her. "Do not go calling *me* a hypocrite. *You* hid Troy from me. You gave him away to strangers. You have no right to call *me* a liar."

"How could you not tell me, even after we made love!"

"I needed to be sure."

"Of what?"

"He's ten years old, Muirinn. If I tell him that Kim is not his mother, everything he has thought to be true in his life will have be reevaluated. I'm not ready to turn his entire world upside down only to have you walk out on us again."

"I told you I was going to stay!"

"Muirinn," he said quietly, his hands trembling. "I still don't know for sure that you mean it. God knows you felt nothing leaving before."

She stared at him. "What do you want from me, Jett? What more can I do to make you trust me?"

He came up to her, took her hands in his. "I wanted time, Muirinn. Time to be sure that I wasn't making a mistake in opening that door to talk to you about Troy." His eyes bored hotly into hers. "And maybe part of me deep down felt that you needed to come clean first, and tell me what was my *right* to know—that you'd borne my child and given him up for adoption."

"And *my* right?"

"What right? You chose to leave. You *chose* to give him away. You never tried to find him again."

"I wasn't allowed to! It was part of the adoption arrangement. What was I supposed to do, Jett, when I found out that our last night together made me pregnant? I had no choice. I was alone. I had nothing. You told me you hated my guts, and never wanted to see me again."

"I said those things out of blind fury because you were abandoning everything we had, Muirinn!"

Her mouth tightened, and with the sense of betrayal surged anger. "All these years I could have watched him grow," she said quietly, bitterly. "Stolen away because no one told me."

"You didn't come home. You never once looked back—"

"That doesn't mean I didn't regret having done what I did! Giving my baby away was the worst mistake of my life, and I have never stopped regretting it. If…" her voice hitched. "If I'd only known there was a way back, a way to set things right…"

His eyes glistened, emotion ripping at him, daring him to crumble and break.

She swore softly. "So it's okay for you to have secrets, but not me?"

"I didn't want to hurt Tr—"

"Do you *honestly* think I'd hurt Troy?" she snapped. "Do

you think I wouldn't move heaven and earth trying to do the right thing by my son? Do you think I purposefully set out to hurt you, or *anyone* else? If that's the case, then to hell with you, Jett. Because I never stopped loving you." Tears streamed fresh down her face as she pushed past him, stalked to the spare room, grabbed her bag and started shoving her things into it.

"What do you think you're doing?" he said from the doorway.

"Getting out of your hair. Once and for all."

He grabbed her arm as she marched past him. "Muirinn, wait. We need to talk about this—" but she shook him off with force. "Get your hands off me!"

He let her go, undeniable rawness shimmering in his eyes. Yet under all the pain, she could still see his love. And that made it hurt all the more. She felt like crawling into the abyss that had yawned open at her feet, and just curling up and dying.

She stormed into the living room and grabbed a shotgun and a box of shells from his gun rack.

"Muirinn—"

She slung her bag over her shoulder, flung open his front door and stormed out in the purple northern night.

"Muirinn, dammit, don't be so stubborn. Get back in here!"

She halted in the driveway, turning around. *"Stubborn?"* She raised her hand palm up, warning him not to move one step in her direction. "If you come after me, Jett, I *will* shoot you."

"It's not safe out there."

"And I'm safer with *you?* You've hidden my son from me for ten years, Jett." Her voice shook. "What else are you hiding? The fact that your father killed my family?"

"My father is not involved, Muirinn."

"Oh? Then you shouldn't have any trouble asking him about it. Or are you going to just ignore it, sweep that under the carpet, too?"

"You're doing it again, Muirinn! You're running away instead of facing things—facing me—working this out with me!"

"Oh, be a man, Jett, and face your own damn father before you can talk about facing me!"

She stomped off down the path and disappeared into the grove of woods between their properties.

Panic seared through Jett, followed by a crushing wave of sheer desperation. He knew Muirinn's temper—she *would* pull the trigger if he went after her now.

And he was worried about her baby, the stress he'd inadvertently put her under. Guilt beat at him. He still had to keep her safe, and he couldn't call the cops. This thing had spiraled way out of control, and he had no idea who might be involved.

So he called one man he did trust—his friend, Hamilton Brock, an ex-Marine who'd served in two Gulf wars. More than anything, Jett trusted Brock with his life. Brock also volunteered for Safe Harbor Search and Rescue and he'd put his life on the line for the team more than once.

As always, Brock was game to help Jett out, and said he'd be right over. Jett thanked him and hung up the phone, thinking about how his father had also regularly put his life on the line for men trapped in the mine.

Then you shouldn't have any trouble asking him about it. Or are you going to just ignore it, and sweep that under the carpet, too?

Muirinn was right. He had to talk to his father. Now. No matter what he discovered, he had to face this.

Jett waited in his truck at the top of Muirinn's driveway for Brock to arrive. He wound down his window and stuck out his elbow as he saw Brock's SUV approach.

"I left a message on her voice mail to say I was sending someone around. She didn't pick up, but I'm pretty sure she heard it. She should be expecting you."

Brock gave his twisted grin. "No problem." He hesitated. "You okay, bud?"

"Yeah. You just keep an eye on her, okay? I'll explain later."

Brock reached out his window, smacked his palm on the hood of Jett's truck. "No worries. She'll be waiting for you, safe and sound when you get back."

Jett drove to his parents' house. The northern night was dusky, but not dark. There was no moon, and an eerie stillness.

He slammed on the brakes suddenly as a coyote darted out from a bush and froze in his headlights.

Heart hammering, Jett waited for the animal to gather its wits and trot into the trees before putting the truck in gear.

But the incident had rattled him further.

What else are you hiding, Jett? The fact your father killed my family…you going to sweep that under the carpet, too?

The deep gut-honest truth was that Jett *had* thought briefly of his father when Muirinn first showed him Ike's photos, when she'd mentioned his dad's kinship with Chalky Moran. And Jett *had* brushed those thoughts right under his mental carpet. He didn't want to think it remotely possible that his dad might be the bomber, even though all the signs had been staring him in the face.

Could he have seen it years ago?

Had he subconsciously avoided facing the truth?

And how much better would that make him than the rest of the people who'd tried to bury the evidence—like Ike Potter or the cop who'd removed the photos?

Jett pulled his truck into his parents' driveway and sat for a moment, fighting his worst fears.

He *had* to ask his father outright. No matter what the consequences. Because he'd said it himself to Muirinn, the time for secrets was over.

Jett banged on the door.

His mother opened it, belting her robe around her waist.

"Jett? What is it? Goodness, you look awful. Come on in."

"I need to speak to Dad."

Worry flared in her eyes. "What's going on?"

Jett stepped past his mother and into the mudroom. He lifted up one of his father's work boots just as his dad came through the living room.

"Jett?"

He didn't reply. He turned the boot over, read the size on the Vibram sole. Size 10. His chest tightened.

He looked at his father.

Adam Rutledge stared at the boot in Jett's hands, then lifted his eyes slowly and met Jett's gaze. He said nothing, but Jett's heart sank at the expression on his father's face.

He put the boot down, marched into the living room, straight for the booze cabinet. "Want a drink, Dad? Because I sure as hell need one." He poured two fingers of scotch and downed the shot. Eyes burning, he poured another.

Jett's father limped into the room, cobalt eyes intent on his son. Jett watched his father's distinctive hobble. It was just as Trapper Joe had demonstrated—the perfectionist, an explosives expert, a veteran miner who bore the battle scars of Tolkin in his body.

And what scars did he bear deep in his soul? What secrets were buried there? What guilt?

"Where did you go in the plane today, son?" Adam said, jaw tight. "Who did you go see?"

"Trapper Joe. Gus had some crime scene photos of the bomber's prints down in the mine. Did you know that?"

His father swallowed. "No," he said quietly.

"We took those photos to Joe to see what he could tell us about the man who made them."

"Then you came here, to look at my boots?"

"Because the prints were made by a veteran miner with size 10 feet and a lame left leg—an explosives expert who had an accomplice waiting up at the Sodwana headframe while the bomb was planted."

Jett paused, giving his father a chance to offer some explanation. Some denial. But his father remained silent, neck muscles bunching, the fingers of his right hand twitching at his side.

"Did you do it dad? Did you 'fix' the strike by planting that bomb, killing twelve men?"

"Jett!" His mother admonished from the doorway.

"Stay out of this, Mom," he said coolly, eyes focused solely on his father, *willing* him to deny it, to offer some explanation, anything.

Instead, Adam Rutledge's face turned ash-white.

Nausea gushed up into Jett's throat, mixing with the acrid heat of whiskey. But he had to see this all the way through. He had to pick a side, and that side had to be justice. It was the *only* recourse, the only way to end the secrets, heal the rifts in this town.

It was also the only way to make things right with Muirinn.

He slugged back the last of the whiskey, slapped the glass down.

"Did you kill Gus O'Donnell, too?"

His father tensed visibly, saying nothing. Jett's mother started sobbing uncontrollably.

He turned to his mother. "Did *you* know that Dad rigged

that blast, Mom?" His voice remained ice cool. "Did you suspect what he'd done? Or did you just turn a blind eye that help bury it like the rest of this godforsaken town?"

Her sob turned into a wail, and Jett's heart plummeted even further.

He stared at his parents, eyes burning. "You're not going to deny *any* of this?" he said, unbelieving.

His mother just cried softly. His father glared, his body humming with tension.

Shaking with anger, Jett stormed out of the house, his entire world shattered.

The screen door slapped dully closed behind him, the sound echoing into the pale, moonless night.

Waves of violent anger, pain, regret all churned through him as he marched toward his truck.

The screen door suddenly swung open behind him, and Jett tensed, hearing his father hobbling out over the gravel.

"Jett!"

He couldn't face him.

Jett climbed into his truck, started the ignition and slammed the gearshift into reverse. He wanted to get the hell away from here. But he couldn't—he just could not hit that accelerator. His father had admitted nothing yet, and Jett still wanted desperately to believe that his dad was coming over to tell him it wasn't true, that there was some rational explanation for it all.

Staring dead ahead, fists tight on the wheel, he listened as his father's footfalls crunched over the gravel, coming nearer.

He turned slowly to look at him—the face he knew so well and had loved so deeply all his life. The face of a man he'd respected, the man who'd taught him so much.

His father clamped his hands down over the open window. "It was a mistake, son," he whispered hoarsely. "A *mistake*."

Jett felt sick.

He shut his eyes tight, gripping the wheel, his ears ringing as he fought the urge to punch down on the gas, flee from things he didn't want to hear.

His father's arthritic hands gripped the door tighter, gnarled knuckles white. "The blast wasn't supposed to kill those men, Jett," he whispered urgently. "They were not supposed to *die!*"

Chapter 15

The knowledge that his father was a murderer swilled dangerously inside Jett. "So you did do it," he whispered. "You're the killer."

"The blast was just going to be a warning, Jett, to spook management and scabs. We'd been without work for almost a year, and union funds were depleted. There was no more strike pay coming, and the longer those scabs kept working, the longer management could handle the strike, and the longer half the men in this town stayed unemployed. People were losing homes, they were being forced to leave town. The strike was killing this place—that mine was the only goddamn gig in town!"

"So you tried to fix it all with a *bomb?*"

"A warning! There were not supposed to be casualties, son." Adam's eyes glittered feverishly in the glow of the northern night. "The man-car carrying those men was not supposed to trigger the trip wire. The ore car—which is wider and has a third wheel that sticks out—that was supposed to trigger the explosion. But I was cold, wet. It was a long climb, a long hike underground, my fingers were numb from white hand. I... I must have gotten the trip line too close to the track. God knows, Jett, I have not lived a day without regretting what happened."

Jett couldn't even look at his father. "You killed Troy O'Donnell," he whispered. "You tore Muirinn's life apart."

"It wasn't supposed to happen, you've *got* to believe that!" Anguish torqued through his father's voice. He gripped the door tighter. "I did it for you, son. For your mother. We were desperate. If the mine stayed operational with scabs, it meant that men like me—the veteran miners who built this place— would go bankrupt. And if we couldn't buy stuff in the stores, the shops were going to go under, the support industries were going to go under, the whole damn town was going to go under. We would have lost our house, *everything.*"

"You murdered people to keep the house I now live in," Jett said quietly. "I used to admire you, Dad." He shook his head. "I used to be so damn proud of you."

"I did it so we *could* remain proud. So I could care for all of you."

The irony hit Jett hard—the things people did for love, the secrets they hid, the lies that bound them, the ripple effect down through the generations. The lingering poison.

He thought of what he'd done to Muirinn, and she to him—for love.

"The deaths were a mistake." Adam whispered again. "But I never did *anything* to hurt Gus. Nor would I ever try to harm Muirinn. I am not a murderer, son."

Jett turned slowly to stare at his father. Tears glistened on the man's rugged cheeks. A man Jett had always looked up to. Admired. Now he could barely even look at him.

"Who was your accomplice? Chalky Moran?"

His father's mouth shut in a grim line. Silence hung for several beats. A coyote yipped somewhere on the outskirts of town, hunting neighborhood cats.

"It's in the past, Jett." Adam said almost inaudibly. "It's over. Can't we just leave it in the past?"

"It's *not* over." Jett ground the words out through clenched teeth. "Gus O'Donnell *died* because of those photos Ike Potter gave him. And Muirinn and her baby almost died, too, because someone out there is *still* prepared to kill to keep this secret."

"I swear on your mother's life that I had *nothing* to do with that," Adam said hoarsely.

"Then who did?"

"I don't know anything about that."

"Start with your accomplice. Was it Chalky?"

Silence.

So the identity of his accomplice was a secret his father still wanted to keep. A sick coldness slicked down inside Jett's belly. "Step back from the truck," he ordered quietly.

"What are you going to do?"

Jett didn't know what he was going to do with this mind-blowing news—that his father was the mass murderer who'd evaded an FBI manhunt.

He needed to think, process. Someplace where he could find distance, objectivity.

"What would *you* do, Dad?"

Silence.

"Step back from the truck," Jett repeated through clenched teeth.

And he drove off, leaving his father standing in a settling cloud of dust, his eyes burning with tears—the tears of betrayal.

Jett did not drive home. He headed instead for the unprotected cliffs to the west of Safe Harbor. It was a place that drew him in both good times and bad.

Easing his truck onto the grassy verge, he cut the engine. The night was clear, dusky, the sun not far below the horizon. But the peaks themselves were hidden by a dark band of storm clouds—the pending front was beginning to move in. He called Brock. "Everything okay there?"

"All quiet," Brock said. "Nothing going on apart from the old tenant awake, light on in her cottage down at the bay. Otherwise, nothing but raccoons."

Jett killed the call.

He stared out over the ocean, watching the timeless heave and pull of the dark water, listening to the soft crunch of waves at the base of the cliffs. And he tried to process the knowledge that his own father was responsible for a mass murder, a case that had been mothballed, never solved, the truth buried by people in this town that he'd loved so deeply.

A pod of killer whales, sleek as mercury, ribboned through the swells below, hunting seals as the midnight sun began to rise again over the distant peaks.

The world in beauty and death.

Beginnings and endings.

It was time for justice to be done, for the past to be put to rest. For new beginnings.

But to do that Jett would have to take his own father down. He rubbed his brow.

All he had to do was pick up the phone and call the FBI, tell them that his dad was a killer.

It wasn't as easy as one might think.

As the day brightened, Jett drove to the airstrip, picking up a bagel and coffee on the way. He wanted to get his plane into the air, get above it all during those rare dawn hours when the world was still pure. When he came back down to earth, he'd face his duty. He'd call the feds.

He parked his truck and headed on foot out onto the airfield, coffee in hand. Dew glistened on the grass, and on the wings of his plane as they caught the first warm rays of the sun.

After one more phone call to Brock, who said all was still calm at Mermaid's Cove, Jett swung himself up into his cockpit.

Muirinn watched dawn breaking over the sea, the loaded shotgun resting in her lap. All night she'd sat, absently rocking in her grandfather's bent-willow rocker, thinking about Troy.

Her son.

Another tremor of emotion ran through her body, and she placed her hand over her stomach.

Two children.

A son and a daughter.

Again her eyes filled with moisture. But with it came the anger, the profound sense of betrayal. And so it had been all night, waves of intoxicating exultation washing through her, alternating with shafts of bone-deep sadness at the sense of time lost with her son, exhausting her.

One thing Muirinn knew for sure was that as much as she might spark and simmer and clash with Jett, he was—and always would be—the father of her son. And she was not going to leave Safe Harbor.

She was going to give birth to her daughter here, raise her baby girl in this town, and watch her son grow into a man—from a distance if necessary.

She'd run the paper. Be a mother. Grow vegetables in the garden and show her daughter how to collect clams, just as Gus had shown her.

And God help anyone who tried to take that away from her now.

Because no matter how hurt Muirinn might be, Jett had done an incredibly bold thing going after his child, alone. It was the kind of move that defined him. He had a rock-solid core of values he was not prepared to compromise. And he valued family.

Then she thought of Adam Rutledge, and cold anxiety surged fresh through her. He was family, too. But she had to believe that Jett would do the right thing, and see justice done.

She had to believe in *him*.

Even if the rift between father and son meant she and Jett could never be together.

Finally, she slipped off, eyes closing as sleep claimed her.

Sun was hot on Muirinn's face when a noise in the hallway startled her awake.

Someone was inside the house.

She raised the shotgun, heart in her throat. "Who's there!"

"It's just me, Muirinn. Oh goodness, child, put that gun down. What on earth is going on?"

"Mrs. Wilkie?" Muirinn swallowed, disoriented. "I…it's nothing. I was having—" she laughed, embarrassed. "Just a bad dream."

The old woman frowned and tutted. "It's the baby. The hormones can do it to you. I've never had children myself," she said, setting her basket down on the kitchen counter. "But when my sister, Margaret, was pregnant with my godchild, she had vivid nightmares all the time. Chamomile tea really helped." She tapped her basket, smiling warmly. "I brought you some scones for breakfast, baked in my wood oven. And strawberries, fresh from Gus's garden."

She removed a cluster of smiling daisies from the basket, and busied herself emptying the older foxglove blooms from the copper vase and rearranging the daisies in their place.

Mrs. Wilkie had left the front door wide open to the bright morning, and a soft warmth drifted inside on the sea breeze. Muirinn glanced nervously at the door. She knew there was a bodyguard outside, yet she was suddenly filled with an unspecified sense of trepidation.

"I'll make you some chamomile tea, dear. It'll be good for those nerves, and for the baby." Mrs. Wilkie shuffled into the kitchen and took down one of the tea tins Gus kept on the shelf. "With a few sprigs of mint. You used to like that mix as a child, remember? I used to make it chilled for you in the summer."

Muirinn felt surreal, as if she couldn't believe the past events had actually happened, that she'd slept in a rocking chair with a shotgun. That this woman had just walked into her home with a basket of flowers and breakfast. Maybe she was just confused by the heat of the sun that had been on her face while she slept. Still, it seemed strange that Mrs. Wilkie hadn't really asked about the gun. Or mentioned the bodyguard outside.

"I…I'd love some tea. Thank you." Muirinn clicked the safety on her weapon, got to her feet, set the gun against the wall and stretched her back. Not only was she thirsty, she was starving.

Chimes tinkled in the breeze, and Muirinn glanced at the open door again. "Did you see anyone outside, Mrs. Wilkie?"

Mrs. Wilkie glanced up. "No, why?"

Muirinn frowned, wondering what had happened to the bodyguard Jett had sent over. Perhaps he was laying low, or maybe he'd left when the sun came up. Which was odd.

"Is everything all right, Muirinn, love?" Mrs. Wilkie asked, concern creasing her brow.

"I'm fine. Will you stay and join me for breakfast? I wouldn't mind the company."

"Of course I will, dear." Mrs. Wilkie reached for another china cup. "But no chamomile for me—" she grinned. "I need caffeine in my tea." She spooned a different herb mix into another small teapot, poured in boiling water and set both pots on the table with a little mat.

The tea was good, different from the way Muirinn remembered, but that might be because her mouth was so dry and fuzzy from adrenaline the night before. She sipped from her cup as she watched Mrs. Wilkie buttering scones, her bright gypsy skirt swirling around her ankles as she moved, her long gray hair caught back in a colorful scarf. It was comforting to watch her. Equally comforting was the soft, warm sensation that was beginning to flow outward through her chest, her body. With mild surprise, Muirinn realized that this tea was working fast—too fast. A faint dawning of fear whispered in her brain, but she couldn't quite harness the thought. Her mind was growing foggy. Then she heard voices outside the door—a man and woman.

She glanced at Mrs. Wilkie, her vision suddenly blurry.

Mrs. Wilkie was watching her intently, smile gone.

"Did…did you hear…that…" *Oh God, she couldn't talk, her tongue was thick and slow in her mouth.* Muirinn tried to lift her arm. It was heavy, as if she were trying to move through syrup.

Panic struck her heart, but she couldn't seem to react to it, to think straight.

"Mrs….Wilkie…"

The woman said nothing.

Muirinn's brain swirled as she squinted at Mrs. Wilkie, the colors of her gypsy skirt morphing into a chromatic blur. The purple foxgloves lay on the counter behind her. So pretty. Pretty…as poison. It struck Muirinn suddenly—foxglove contained digitalis. The same medicine Gus had been taking.

Years ago Gus had told Muirinn that dried foxglove leaves could easily be confused with comfrey. He'd liked to drink comfrey for his health. But foxglove would stop your heart, he'd said.

Muirinn tried to look up into Mrs. Wilkie's eyes, to read what was going on. But her vision was too hazy, a halo seeming to shimmer around the woman's body. Mrs. Wilkie knew about herbs. She'd made Gus's tea blends.

She could have given him foxglove.

Mrs. Wilkie had also just mentioned her sister Margaret's pregnancy. Margaret was married to Old Man Henry Moran. And Margaret's child—Mrs. Wilkie's godchild—was Chalky Moran.

Jett's voice rumbled into Muirinn's fading consciousness. *Moran blood runs thick in this town…*

Mrs. Wilkie was protecting her godchild, her flesh and blood—and she'd put something into Muirinn's tea!

My baby… Muirin had get out of here, get help.

She tried to stand, bracing her weight on the table. But she slid slowly down to the floor as her legs buckled out from under her.

Mrs. Wilkie moved forward quickly.

Muirinn reached out her hand, trying to mouth the word *help.* But nothing came out.

Lydia Wilkie crouched down, stroking Muirinn's long, soft, red hair. "Sleep, child," she whispered softly. "You'll be with Gus soon. This town needs peace now. The past must sleep." Wilkie's eyes closed, tears spilling down her cheeks.

"Go in peace, my child," she whispered as Muirinn's world faded to black.

Chapter 16

Adam Rutledge had long dreaded the day his son might discover the truth about the Tolkin massacre.

But after twenty long, tortuous years of guilt and nightmares, Adam had dared hope that Jett might just be spared knowing what his father had done. But it wasn't to be. His nightmare had come true.

Not only that, but from what Jett had just told him, the toxic secrets from the mine were oozing up to rip lives apart all over again, and Adam could not—would not—let that happen.

He wheeled his Jeep into Chalky Moran and Kate Lonsdale's driveway, slamming on the brakes. Hobbling quickly up to the door, he banged loudly with the base of his fist.

No answer.

Adam went around back and saw that Chalky's big white van was gone. Peering in through the windows, he could see their gun cabinet hanging open. This felt wrong—way wrong.

As far as Adam knew, the only other people who knew what had really gone down on that cold spring morning twenty years ago were the Moran brothers, and now maybe Chalky's wife, Kate Lonsdale.

When the bomb had ended up killing those men, Chalky had turned in desperation to his brothers, and Don and Bill Moran had instantly rallied around their own, closing ranks to protect Chalky. Because of that, Adam had been spared, too.

Adam knew just how deep Moran blood ran, and just how much they all stood to lose if this got out, especially now that Kate was mayor. But just *how* far would they go to keep the old secret buried?

Could they have killed Gus?

He shuffled painfully back to his Jeep, the arthritis in his hip and knees acting up the more he moved. He called Jett on his cell phone, but the call went straight to voice mail.

Adam cursed. His son had disowned him, cut him off. He couldn't blame him, but he really needed to talk to him now.

Adam started his ignition and raced over to Mermaid's Cove. But Jett's driveway was empty, his truck gone.

Tension squeezing across his chest, Adam rushed over to the O'Donnell house, thinking maybe he'd find Jett there. But his son's vehicle was not in the O'Donnell driveway. Neither was Gus's red Dodge. The front door of the house, however, hung wide open.

Adam dragged his disabled leg up the stairs, pain worsening, making him break out in a sweat. He raised his fist to rap on the open door. But as he did, he caught sight of Lydia Wilkie hurriedly clearing dishes off the table. She glanced up, and at the sight of him in the doorway, a look of sheer horror—then panic—crossed her lined features. Her eyes were puffy, as if she'd been crying.

"Lydia?" he said, stepping into the hallway. "Is everything all right? Where's Muirinn?"

She seemed unable to speak for a moment, rooted to the spot, looking as though she'd flee if Adam weren't blocking her exit.

A chill trickled down Adam's spine.

His gaze tracked the room quickly. He saw two teacups and a half-finished breakfast on the table. An overturned chair lay across the room. A shotgun rested near a bent-willow rocking chair facing the window, and a woman's sneaker lay upturned in an odd position near the door.

The chill deepened.

"Where is she, Lydia?"

She swallowed, eyes flicking round the room. "I...don't know. She had a fight with Jett, just packed up all her bags and left in the truck," Lydia said quietly. "I came in to clean up."

She was lying. He could see it in her eyes.

Raw fear raked down Adam's throat as the horror of what might be happening dawned on him. He bent down and picked up the shoe. "Is this Muirinn's?"

"It must have fallen out of her bags. She left in a real hurry."

Adam limped over to the rocking chair, picked up the shotgun and checked it. It was loaded, a round chambered. He glanced at Lydia who remained frozen in place. "Did Chalky come get her?"

She said nothing.

"*Where*, Lydia! Where did they take her?"

"I don't know what you're talking about."

Adam cursed, gesturing at her with the gun. "If she dies, Lydia, *you* go down for murder!"

"And if you go after Chalky, we *all* go down. I know what happened in the mine, Adam," she said hoarsely. "You're in the same boat if this gets out."

"No," he said coldly. "I am not in the same boat. Because the difference, Lydia, is that *I* don't care if I go down now. I never intended to kill anyone twenty years ago, and I sure as hell have no intention of letting anyone else die now. This has to stop, even if it means turning myself in to the FBI."

He stormed out of the house, taking the gun with him. He tried again to call Jett from his Jeep. No answer. Lydia came rushing out the door after him, but Adam slammed the gearshift into reverse, hit the gas and shot like a wild man down the driveway, spinning backwards onto the dirt road in a spray of dirt and stones.

He raced for the airstrip.

If Jett was unaware of what had just happened to Muirinn, and he was not at home, there was one place he would be. His plane.

Sweat soaked his shirt as Adam drove faster, pain burning into his knees and hip. He hit Redial, steering with one hand, willing his son to pick up. Because there was no one else he could call. If Chalky had taken Muirinn, the Morans would be circling the wagons again.

That meant the police were the enemy.

The mayor was the enemy.

And there was no time to get FBI or state troopers in. He wasn't even sure there was still time to save Muirinn's life.

But he sure as hell was going to try.

Preparing for takeoff, Jett caught sight of his father, a pitiful figure hobbling fast over the tarmac, waving his hand high in the air. Jett started the engine, the prop of his Beaver turning over a few times then whizzing to a choppy blur. He opened the throttle and began to taxi out onto the runway.

But his father angled sharply across the field ahead, trying to cut him off. And as he neared, Jett saw the determination and grit on his father's face. And he a chill touched the base of his spine as he realized that Adam was carrying a shotgun.

He braked the plane and pushed back the sliding window.

"Muirinn's gone, Jett!" Adam yelled as he approached the plane. *"They took her!"*

He removed his earphones, hoping to God he'd heard wrong. "Where is Hamilton Brock? He was supposed to be guarding the house!"

Puzzled, his dad looked up. "No one else was there, except Lydia Wilkie. There were signs of a struggle inside the house, Jett. I think Chalky took her in his van—it wasn't at his house. If we can get up in the air fast, we might still see it."

Jett's stomach flipped over in dread. He quickly leaned over the passenger seat to swing open the door. "Get in!"

His father struggled to climb up, and Jett grasped his hand and helped haul Adam up. Their eyes locked for a second, tension simmering between them.

"Put the headset on," Jett snapped, as he turned to rev the de Havilland's engines. They took off into a brisk early morning headwind, and Jett noted that the distant bank of clouds to the west was closing in as he listened to his father relate how he'd rushed over to Chalky and Kate's place, found the van missing, saw the gun cabinet open and then raced to Mermaid's Cove.

"Lydia might even have given Muirinn some sedative or something because there were cups on the table, and she was trying to put everything away in a real hurry."

An image sifted suddenly into his mind—purple foxglove petals falling onto the back of Muirinn's hand as she left a note for Lydia Wilkie under the vase.

Gus could have been poisoned, Jett, a heart attack induced.

Had Lydia helped them with Gus, too?

Had she given Gus something—like digitalis tea made from foxglove—that had stopped his already damaged heart?

Jett's stomach lurched at the thought.

Could it have been Chalky who shot at Muirinn that day at the mine?

Jett recalled the ATV tracks that had headed up the mountain toward the eastern drainage. "Kate Lonsdale's family has always had land up north, up the eastern valley," Jett said coolly. "There's an old cabin on the property. They could be taking her there."

Reaching elevation, Jett dipped the de Havilland's wings sharply to the right, taking his craft out of the headwind and circling back. The dark bank of clouds to the west loomed closer, stray drops of rain beginning to fleck the windshield. The storm was moving in faster than had been forecast.

Jett flew up over the ridge and dropped low into the adjacent eastern valley, flying in a northerly direction as his father scanned the dirt road below with binoculars for signs of a vehicle.

Suddenly, through the trees, Adam caught the dust plumes of two vehicles racing north along the twisting track. He tapped Jett's arm and pointed.

Jett buzzed lower over the trees.

"Chalky's van!" his father said, scopes fixed on the column below. "And Gus's truck in front."

Panic whipped over Jett's chest and his hand tightened on the controls. He told himself he couldn't afford to panic. He *had* to stay focused if he was going to get Muirinn and her baby out of this alive.

He inhaled slowly, forcing his breath out in a slow, controlled fashion as his mind raced. The police were out of the question. He couldn't even call for SAR help—many of the SAR volunteers were tight with the Safe Harbor cops, and any radio chatter could be picked up. Jett didn't know who he could trust. He wasn't even sure now if he should have trusted Brock.

They had no choice—he and his father had to handle this on their own. And they had to be damn creative about it.

He shot his dad a glance. Adam's eyes met his, and a current of understanding passed between them. "We'll get her, son. I swear, we *will* get her." And Jett knew from the look in his dad's eyes, that despite everything in their past, they remained united on this one thing.

Jett nodded, and his father quickly went back to tracking the vehicles.

The dirt road below began to climb along the edge of a talus-filled canyon, and the trees thinned. Jett swooped down lower behind the vehicles, wings almost brushing the tips of the conifers.

But as he did, dust suddenly boiled out from behind the vehicles as the drivers sped up, realizing that they were being pursued by air. The van at the rear, without four-wheel drive, began to sway wildly on the steep dirt road, veering closer and closer to the cliff edge.

Jett's heart leapt to his throat.

Then the back doors of the van were flung open, and a body came tumbling out the back. It bounded hard on the dirt, all arms and legs as it rolled over the edge of the cliff and plunged down into the ravine, bouncing over rocks as it plummeted all the way down into the narrow crevice hundreds of feet below, until it disappeared into choking brush.

Jett's stomach lurched. "It's Brock," he whispered, praying that Muirinn was still alive inside the van.

Tilting the nose of his Beaver, he suddenly veered sharply up and over the next mountain.

"What are you doing?"

"They're going to have an accident and hurt Muirinn if we stay on them like that." Jett's face felt tight. "We have to assume that they're heading for the Lonsdale cabin. We can get there ahead of them."

"What if they second-guess us and turn back?"

Jett reached forward, switching radio channels. "There's only one road that leads north up the eastern drainage area, which means there is only one way out," he told his father. "We'll block the exit."

"How?"

"Like this." Jett radioed into the SAR dispatch. He said nothing about Muirinn or the Morans, only that he was in the air and had witnessed a man go down the mountainside. "He's hurt pretty bad, if he's even alive."

Grimly, he relayed the GPS coordinates indicating where Brock had fallen into the canyon. "You'll need to set the chopper down on the road. It's the only place to land," he said. "Get some guys to climb down, you'll find where he broke through brush and rolled over the edge. You're going to need ropes carabineers—full gear. I'll try to get out there as soon as I can get my bird landed," he lied.

By the time he signed off, the emergency chopper's rotors were spinning back at the helipad. The helo would be airborne and squatting smack in the middle of that exit road within minutes, followed hot quickly by ground ambulance and EMT personnel.

"If the Morans turn back now," he told his dad, "The road will be blocked." *With people who can help Muirinn.*

He flew low, following the course of the slow, meandering river in the eastern drainage, until his father pointed.

"There! That's the cabin. Down there in that grove of alders."

Jett began scanning farther along the river for a place to set his craft down.

Crouching in the dense alder and willow brush that surrounded the log cabin, Jett and his father waited for the vehicles to arrive. Between them they had a rifle, shotgun, two hunting knives, a can of bear spray, and several bear bangers—explosive cartridges that screwed onto pencil flares.

The minutes ticked by slowly. Rain began to come down heavily, and the sky grew dark and low with thunderclouds. The air felt hot, electric, in spite of the wind that rustled the tops of the conifers in the surrounding forest.

Suddenly, a plume of dust rose above the bush in the distance, and Gus's truck appeared. It pulled up in front the cabin and Kate Lonsdale jumped out. Face flushed, she rushed to the cabin door, hurriedly fumbling with keys to open it. She had a rifle slung over her shoulder.

Jett's pulse quickened. He placed his hand on his dad's arm, cautioning him to hold their position until the van arrived. "Wait until the driver gets out," Jett whispered. "Or we might risk them bolting. We'll never make it back to the plane in time, and we could lose her." His dad nodded, eyes fixed on Mayor Lonsdale opening the door.

Jett scanned the layout of the clearing, unsure of his plan. He wanted to get Muirinn away from them before they could get her inside the cabin, where they would be able to hole up with weapons.

A second plume of dust rose above the bush, blowing like spindrift in the increasing wind as the van approached.

Treetops were now beginning to sway with a soft hiss and

warm rain made his shirt cling to his body. Jett could sense the air pressure changing, too, a feeling of electricity in the air. They needed to hurry, or they might not be able to get the plane out again if the storm brought lightning.

He made a sign with his hand to show his father that he was going to sneak around to the far side of the cabin, where he could use the cover of vegetation to get closer to the door. There he might be able to head them off as they tried to carry Muirinn in.

He was just settling into his new hideaway when the van pulled up.

Jett's heart began to drum loudly in his ears, but ice-cool anger held him tight, fiercely focused.

Trees swayed violently. Heavy wind rushed through the trees now, cones and branches crashing down into the underbrush. Thunder rumbled in the distance. Not a good time to be in dry forest. Most fires out in the wild were sparked by lightning, and the effect could be devastating.

Chalky emerged from the driver's side of the van. Hurrying around to the back, he swung open the doors. Out jumped Bill Moran himself, still a strong hunter and outdoorsman in his early sixties. Bitterness leached into Jett's mouth at the sight of the old police chief.

It would've been Bill who'd thrown Brock out of the van.

Jett inched closer, peering through the leaves, wondering what his dad was thinking on the other side of the clearing. Adam Rutledge had as much—and more—to lose as the Morans did.

Could Jett trust him to pull through?

He *had* to.

Jett had to believe that the man he'd loved and respected and looked up to all these years was still inside that crippled body somewhere, and that he'd do the right thing when it came down to it.

The roar of the wind grew louder, and the sky darker. Lightning glimmered in purple clouds in the distance, followed by a rumble of thunder in the peaks. The rain came down in a sudden heavy sheet, releasing the musky scent of soil that had been dry for too long.

Chalky and Bill began to ease Muirinn out of the van, holding her up by the arms.

She's alive.

Jett's heart caught in his throat, and rage swelled in him.

She was gagged, bound, covered in dirt, her legs buckling out from under her as they tried to get her to stand.

Every molecule in his body screamed to blast out of the bush shooting wildly, but he forced himself to stay put. One wrong move could get them all killed.

Kate came back out the door, yanking a hood over her head as she ducked through the rain and ran toward the men, rifle in her hand.

Chalky moved away from Bill and Muirinn to shut the van doors, and Jett raised his weapon, sighting carefully down the barrel, Chalky in his crosshairs. He hooked his finger through the trigger guard, slowly put pressure on the trigger—then hesitated.

He'd never shot a man, and something deep in him resisted now.

It was wrong, in spite of what Chalky had done. This was not the way to end the secrets and lies and deaths of the past twenty years—it would be playing into the same game. Jett just couldn't do it. He would not allow Troy to one day look at him the way he'd been forced to look at his own father.

Instead, he slowly reached for the bear banger in the side pocket of his pants.

But before he could release the small trigger that would shoot the explosive cartridge out from the end of the pencil flare like a rocket, his father startled him by standing up suddenly and crashing out of the brush.

Everyone froze.

Kate was the first to react. She swung her rifle into position at her shoulder, aimed at Adam and pulled the trigger without a breath of hesitation. Almost simultaneously, Jett fired the banger.

It hissed from the flare, exploding like a grenade in a flash of light and sound behind Kate's head, sending her shot wild.

Kate dropped into a crouch, arms protecting her head as her rifle clattered to her feet.

Chalky ran toward his wife, thinking she'd been hit. He dropped to her side as Bill released Muirinn to lunge for his weapon in the back of the van. Muirinn crumpled to the dirt on all fours, and immediately started crawling for cover behind the van, drenched in rain and mud.

Bill swung his weapon into position and aimed at Adam. He pulled the trigger just as Adam blasted a slug from his shotgun.

Kate shrieked as a gaping hole tore through Bill Moran's chest and he was thrown backward against the white van. Chalky swung round, jaw slack, raw horror tearing across his face. *"Adam?"* he said in shock, still unaware that Jett was in the brush behind them. *"What in hell are you doing?"*

"It's over, Chalky," Adam's voice was thin, barely discernable over the beating rain as he raised his shotgun again. Wobbling slightly on his feet, he took aim at Chalky, who was still hunkered down, his arm around Kate. "The past ends right here. Drop your weapon."

Chalky slowly set his rifle on the ground at his side, his ghostly-blond hair slicking against his face with rain. "Adam, if *we* go down, you go down ten times worse," he said, desperation snaking through his voice. "*You* planted that bomb. *You* killed those men."

"And I will pay for it. We *all* will."

Jett reached for another banger, his body hot, humming with tension. Rain dripped into his eyes as he hurriedly screwed the cartridge onto the pencil flare, then fired.

The blast exploded right near Chalky and Kate's heads and they were momentarily stunned.

Jett used the instant to lunge forward, releasing a jet of bear spray on the pair huddled on the ground, incapacitating them further.

He coughed himself, eyes burning, rain drenching him, as he took their weapons and ran to the van. He grabbed a coil of wire from the back of the van. "Get Muirinn," he yelled to his father as he rushed back to Chalky and Kate. He bound them tightly, back to back, his mind racing.

Thunder clapped above them and rain drummed down even harder. Over the trees in deep purple clouds, white streak lightning stabbed down to earth with a violent crack. They had to get out, now, before one of those bolts started a wildfire. Even in heavy rain, flames could grow and roar like the wind.

Rushing around to the side of the van, Jett dropped to his knees, reaching for Muirinn who was huddled ghost-white on the ground behind the wheels of the van.

Where was his father?

"Jett!" she whispered, as she clutched him. "Thank God you came!"

He gathered her up, quickly checking her out. Her pupils

were dilated. And her pulse was thready. "Are you hurt anywhere?"

"No, just…drugged."

"What did they give you?"

"I don't know, but it seems to be wearing off."

"The baby?"

"She's still moving, I felt her kick." Muirinn glanced over his shoulder. "Jett, I'm okay. Your father—go to him!"

He whipped his head around. With shock he saw his dad splayed motionless, facedown on the ground, blood seeping out of a dark stain under him.

"He was hit, Jett. Bill got off a shot before he went down."

Jett scrambled over to his dad and rolled him over. Adam's head flopped back.

Lightning streaked from the sky again, cracking into trees a few yards away. Thunder boomed right over their heads. The wind roared, flinging debris at them from the trees.

Jett hunkered over his dad, protecting his face from flying twigs and cones, and his father's eyes flickered open. He was alive, breathing, but his dad had been shot in the gut, and the bleeding was bad. It was beginning to come out his mouth.

Muirinn shook Jett's shoulder. "Fire!" she said in an urgent whisper at his ear. "I can smell smoke."

Jett glanced back toward where the lightning had struck. Under the noise of the wind, he could hear the ominous crackle of flame taking hold in tinder-dry brush. He had to get Muirinn back to the plane, had to try to take off in this storm. Or they would die, consumed by fire in this desolate place.

He turned back to his dad. Adam's face was a cold, gray color that Jett knew well. Adam coughed up blood. "Go, son," he croaked. "Take her. Go. Start again."

"I can carry you, Dad—"

He shook his head slowly. "Go, please. I won't make it."

Jett hesitated. In the corner of his eye, he saw Chalky and Kate desperately pulling against their bonds, rain puddling around them.

Adam reached up suddenly, clutching at Jett's shirt. "It's better this way," he whispered. "I'd die in prison. And your mother would die just knowing I was in there. She didn't know about the bomb, Jett. This is right, the way it must be. Be…good to your mother. This…is…" His father went suddenly still, his hand flopping back down to the dirt as life left him.

Jett's eyes burned. Tears ran with the rain down his face. He felt Muirinn at his side again. He glanced up at her, anguish ripping through his chest. Her hair was plastered with rain to deathly pale cheeks, her eyes dark hollows.

His duty was with her now, with the baby.

His father had died to save the mother of his child—the daughter of the man he'd killed two decades ago.

But what about Chalky and Kate? He couldn't just leave them bound and incapacitated in the face of a fire. That was akin to murder.

Jett took note of the wind direction. If it held course, the fire would move to the east—it might even sweep past.

He cupped Muirinn's face in his hands. "The de Havilland is about a mile upstream. We can go along the bank. Do you think you can make it?"

She looked into his eyes. "We *have* to make it, Jett."

His father was right—the past had been put to rest, and he had to move forward, protect his woman, build a future. And if they made it out alive, he'd do anything, *everything,* to make sure they were together—her, him, Troy, the new baby girl. And his heart swelled with fierce energy.

"Start going to the river, Muirinn. Head upstream to the plane. Wait for me there."

"What about you!"

"Go! Now! I'm going to see if there's a radio in the cabin."

He hesitated for a split second, making sure Muirinn was moving toward the river, then he rushed into the Lonsdale cabin. He found the radio, set it to the right channel, and placed an emergency call to Search and Rescue, saying only that two people were injured at the Lonsdale cabin, and a fire was closing in. He had to yell as the storm played havoc with reception. "They'll be on the east side of Wolverine River! Downstream of the cabin!"

Thunder crashed again. A branch smashed down onto the roof. Jett signed off.

He'd call the FBI in Anchorage as soon as he got the plane down. If the SAR team didn't find them, an FBI manhunt would. There was nowhere for them to go, but into the wild.

Dashing out into the rain, he used his knife to cut Kate and Chalky loose, still dazed and disoriented. Holding a gun to their heads he said, *"Run!"*

They stared at him blankly, shivering, drenched. "Now! Or I'll shoot." He jerked the barrel of his rifle toward the trees. "Go that way, head for the river, downstream, cross it. I told the SAR guys you'd be there on the other side. Do it and you might escape the fire."

They took off, scrambling and stumbling into the bush as he fired into the dirt behind them for good measure.

Hands shaking as the aftereffects of the adrenaline dump took hold of his body, Jett raced after Muirinn.

They reached the plane, and Jett managed to take off into the sharp, gusty crosswinds. They flew into the deluge, water writing in pearly strings across the windscreen as they peered through the spinning prop blades.

Jett felt Muirinn's hand on his knee, and his eyes darted briefly to hers. And in that instant he knew that if he could bring her safely through this storm they would be able to finally bury the past, and find a way to a future. Together.

And nothing in this world would ever be able to tear them apart again.

Chapter 17

The past was finally being laid to rest—on all levels.

SAR crews had airlifted Kate Lonsdale and her husband, Chalky Moran, to safety, and they were now being held by the FBI for questioning in Anchorage, the town reeling from the news that their mayor and police department were implicated in the murders—from twenty years ago and today. Media crews had descended on Safe Harbor en masse, and towns-folk were finding solace in finally seeing their story told, the old wounds cleansed—and healed—for good.

The FBI had also taken Lydia Wilkie into custody. In an effort to lessen the charges against her, she had confessed her role in the case.

She'd told FBI investigators that just over a month ago she'd gone up to clean Gus's office while he'd stepped outside to smoke his pipe. Lydia had seen the "missing" crime scene photos of the Tolkin bombing on his desk, and she'd been unable to stop herself from reading what was on the screen of his laptop. That's when she knew that Chalky, her nephew and godson, was in serious trouble, along with his brothers. Lydia knew what had happened in the mine twenty years ago, and she was aware that it had been Don, then a rookie officer, who'd removed the crime scene photographs at his brother Bill's request. It was Bill and Don who'd then returned to the mine during the storm, and destroyed the tracks.

Lydia had gone straight to talk to her sister, Margaret, Chalky's mother. And the Morans had quietly closed ranks, asking Lydia to help them kill Gus.

Lydia said she was devastated by what she had to do, but she'd done it to save her family. She already knew what medication Gus was taking, and the small amount of dried foxglove leaves added to his comfrey tea, in combination with his medication, should have killed him, making it look like a natural progression of his illness.

However, Gus had been impatient to get to the mine that morning and had barely touched his tea. The toxin had thus not worked right away, and Gus had driven out to the mine.

In desperation, she had phoned Chalky, and in a panic, Chalky and Kate had headed out to the mine where—just as Trapper Joe had indicated—Gus was feeling ill, and succumbing to digitalis poisoning. They made him climb down the shaft, where his heart had finally stopped.

They'd then driven his truck home.

However, when news of Gus's absence finally hit the papers, someone passing by on a hunting trip remembered having seen Gus at the mine. And that's when the search dogs were brought in. But upon locating the body, Don was able to persuade the ME and Dr. Callaghan that there was nothing suspect about how they'd found Gus.

Lydia had also been the one who'd removed the laptop from the table drawer, and she'd administered a sedative in Muirinn's tea, but not enough to kill her—the Morans had wanted her alive so that they could use her to lure Jett.

Hamilton Brock had not been so fortunate. He'd been shot and killed with a police-issue handgun.

Jett would never forgive himself for leading Brock into mortal danger. His buddy had no idea what he'd been dealing with. Even he hadn't grasped the sheer gravity of the situation at the time. But the main thing was that he'd flown through that storm, and he'd landed Muirinn and her baby safely.

Go, son. Take her. Go. Start again.

His father was right. Adam had given his life to atone for the sins of the past, and it was now time to move forward—in Adam's memory. In Troy O'Donnell's memory. In honor of all those who'd died and suffered because of the tragedy.

Jett entered the hospital room just as Dr. Callaghan was completing Muirinn's ultrasound.

He'd had Troy fetched home, and the boy was sitting in the waiting area. Jett had spoken to his son, telling him everything.

Muirinn smiled as Jett neared her bed. "Dr. Callaghan says everything looks good."

The doctor looked up as she covered Muirinn's tummy with the sheet. "Everything seems okay, Jett. There's no evidence of anything at all in Muirinn's bloodstream. Whatever Lydia Wilkie administered worked through her system very quickly. The baby would have felt similar woozy effects, but the good news is that we're into the third trimester, everything is fully formed and her vital signs are all good." She smiled warmly, hazel eyes twinkling. "Mother and daughter are going to be just fine."

Jett stole a glance at the image still up on the ultrasound monitor, and his heart contracted so tightly at the sight of the blurred human form that he felt tears burn. He reached for Muirinn's hand, looked into her amazing green eyes, into the lost years. And he didn't need to say the words—they were finally sharing what they'd missed the first time around.

A pregnancy.

He smiled, throat thick with emotion. "I have someone I want you to meet."

Her face changed, anxiety creeping into her green eyes. "He's *here?*"

Jett nodded. "I had him flown back. We need to be together now." He paused. "I've told him, Muirinn. I've told him that you're his mother."

Muirinn's heart began to patter, nerves dampening her palms. She moved up into a sitting position, her entire being focused on that doorway.

Troy appeared—the dark-haired boy she'd seen on the dock. In the photos. Jett's son.

Her son.

He hesitated in the doorway, glancing up at his father. Jett nodded encouragement, and Troy stepped into the room. His hair was the exact same inky-black as Jett's, his skin tanned. Big green eyes fixed on her—the same unusual moss-green as her own eyes.

"Troy," she said, her voice coming out soft and strange to her own ears. She felt so afraid. So fragile…so worried she'd scare him away.

Silently, he walked up to her bedside, his gaze riveted on her, his little mind processing so much.

He was clearly not a shy child—his walk showed a young confidence, a latent curiosity. And Muirinn loved Jett even more for being a good father, a father who could foster and nurture this sort of character in his son. It was the kind of confidence that would serve him well in life. Yet apprehension showed in his eyes, in the way he fisted his hands at his sides.

Muirinn ached to hold him, squeeze him so tight, grab back all the childhood that had been lost to her.

"I've heard so much about you, Troy."

Troy nodded, silent.

"Jett told me you're named after my father."

"He died before I was born." His voice brought tears into her eyes. Her son. A second chance…it was overwhelming. The tears spilled over and ran down her cheeks. She laughed nervously, reaching for a tissue to wipe them away.

"My dad said Troy O'Donnell taught him about planes, and that's why my dad is a pilot."

Muirinn tried to swallow around the incredible emotion balling painfully in her throat. She nodded. "He…he was your grandfather."

Troy nodded all too sagely for his years. Warming easily to the conversation in between glances at his dad for reassurance. "I know. My dad told me. And that makes Gus my great-grandfather."

"What did your dad tell you about me?"

Troy shot another glance at his father. But Jett stood quietly to the side, letting his son direct things where he needed them to go. Troy turned back to Muirinn.

"He said he always loved you, and that you are my mom. But that you couldn't be here right away. That you needed time."

Muirinn was unable to talk. She looked at Jett, his gaze held hers.

Then little Troy's mouth flattened, and he drew a breath in

deep, as if he were mustering courage. He glanced at Muirinn's tummy, then down at his shoes, then up again. "Can I touch it?"

"The baby?"

He nodded fiercely.

"Yes," whispered Muirinn, taking his hand, her heart breaking at the sensation of it in her own. She placed the little palm on her belly, on top of the covers. "If you wait you might feel her move."

He narrowed his eyes, focusing intently, a boy raised here, in wild country, open about life and death. The way she liked it. The way Muirinn wanted it to be.

"There," she whispered. "Did you feel that?"

His green eyes flared, and his mouth dropped open. "Was that the *baby?*"

"Yes." She smiled. "That was your sister."

"Cool!" He grinned, a bright white slash of teeth against his tanned skin. All kid again. The kid she'd glimpsed at the dock, the child she'd envied Jett for having with all her being. The child she had not known was hers.

Jett stepped up, placing his hand on his son's shoulder. "The nurse outside has ice cream for you, Troy. I need a word with Muirinn, and then she needs some rest."

Troy grinned at her, bounded out.

Muirinn didn't trust herself to speak for several long minutes. "Thank you, Jett, thank you so much. He...he's..." Tears streamed again, and she couldn't talk at all. Jett took her into his arms. "It'll take a while," she said between sniffles into his shoulder. "I'm just so happy to be able to watch him grow."

"You really are going to stay?"

She'd told him over and over again, but Jett was almost afraid to believe it, to accept that, this time, it really might happen.

"I wouldn't leave for the world, Jett. Everything that is precious to me is right here in Safe Harbor."

He stood silent, energy raging like wildfire through him. Why in hell was he so scared?

Because he really didn't want to screw up this second chance.

Then he came right out and said it—not the way he'd planned, but because he was terrified he'd miss the opportunity. "Marry me, Muirinn. I don't want secrets, I don't want boundaries." He hesitated, suddenly panicking that she'd say no. "I just want you. I always have."

She stared at him in silence, and Jett felt perspiration prickle over him. "We can finally be a family, Muirinn," he said, voice rough with emotion. "The way it should have been."

She inhaled deeply. "I've wanted nothing more, Jett," she whispered.

"Is that a yes?"

She nodded, tears flowing down her cheeks. "All these years…" she swallowed, wiping her eyes. "I…I never dreamed I could have a second chance."

And he gathered her into his arms, and kissed her. Never again would he let her go. This time she was here to stay.

December.

Muirinn stepped up and placed a twelfth long-stemmed white rose alongside the eleven others on the small cairn of mining rocks. On top of the cairn rested a miner's hat with a headlamp.

She lowered her head and said a silent prayer for her father, for her mother, for the families of all the men who had lost their lives that tragic day. And she prayed for Adam Rutledge, and for Hamilton Brock.

For the future.

For the sins of all fathers to be forgiven.

Then, solemnly, she returned to her pew in the tiny church where her family stood.

Jett slipped her hand into his. He was holding Arielle, her two-month-old daughter, bundled up warm in his arms.

He and Troy had helped name her—after a mermaid. From Mermaid's Cove. In honor of Gus, who had once made Muirinn believe that she, too, had been brought up from the sea.

Muirinn closed her eyes as voices rose in hymn, and she said a special prayer for her grandfather. But she didn't need to. Because she felt him here, watching over them, just as she felt the tiny bone compass warming against her chest. Gus had shown her a way home.

He'd shown her true north.

It was snowing softly when they left the church, having finally laid the miners' memories to rest. The town could now move forward, and the future had started with winter snows blowing in over the sea.

Jett put his arm around Muirinn, drawing her close. Arielle was tucked in under his jacket, warm as a bun, and Troy ran ahead, jumping into new snowdrifts, Christmas lights twinkling in the town.

Jett's chest swelled with fierce devotion, happiness, and he leaned down and kissed his bride-to-be.

She smiled up at him, snowflakes like white confetti dusting her red curls.

It was these simple pleasures, thought Jett, that made it all worthwhile, and the fresh snow was redolent with promise of a long winter. A time of rebirth.

Because in the spring, they would marry, and it would all be new again.

And he couldn't be more happy. He had his family at last.

"I'm going to finish her," he said suddenly, as they walked trough the drifts, arm in arm.

"Finish what?" her voice was dreamy, soft.

"*Muirinn of the Wind.* I'll do it over the winter, give her wings. She'll be ready to fly by summer."

Muirinn looked up into her man's deep-cobalt eyes. "I love you, Jett. I always have."

"I know," he whispered.

She laughed, and he kissed her softly on the mouth, thinking of the tune that had been playing on his truck radio when he'd driven past Gus's house and first glimpsed that light up in the attic.

I believe in miracles.

And today, he did.

* * * * *

HER HERO
IN HIDING

BY
RACHEL LEE

All the characters in this book have no existence outside the imagination of the author, and have no relation whatsoever to anyone bearing the same name or names. They are not even distantly inspired by any individual known or unknown to the author, and all the incidents are pure invention.

First published in Great Britain 2011
Harlequin Mills & Boon Limited,
Eton House, 18-24 Paradise Road, Richmond, Surrey TW9 1SR

© Susan Civil Brown 2010

ISBN: 978 0 263 88502 6

46-0111

Harlequin Mills & Boon policy is to use papers that are natural, renewable and recyclable products and made from wood grown in sustainable forests. The logging and manufacturing processes conform to the legal environmental regulations of the country of origin.

Printed and bound in Spain
by Litografía Rosés S.A., Barcelona

Dear Reader,

It is so sad to me that a subject I first picked up in *Lost Warriors* years ago is once again relevant, and probably more so than ever. The struggles our soldiers face when they return home are enormous. Some may never be able to find peace. And, of course, domestic abuse continues as a plague.

I write to tell a good story, not to preach. Part of that storytelling for me must involve the exploration of the human heart. It is how we find each other, thus finding shelter amid life's storms, that endlessly fascinates me. How do two people cross a long, uncertain bridge to the point of trust where love can blossom? Each of us finds his or her own way to that place and the paths are varied. The journey to the oasis we call love is endlessly fascinating, endlessly touching.

Most of us have sorrow or pain in our past. Finding comfort and love is probably one of the most important journeys we take. For only a heart filled with love has love to give. I hope you enjoy this tale of two devastatingly wounded hearts as they strive for peace and happiness.

Hugs,

Rachel

To all the heroes in hiding from pasts they struggle
to make peace with.

Rachel Lee was hooked on writing by the age of twelve, and practiced her craft as she moved from place to place all over the United States. This *New York Times* bestselling author now resides in Florida and has the joy of writing full time.

Her bestselling CONARD COUNTY mini-series (see www.conardcounty.com) has won the hearts of readers worldwide and it's no wonder, given her own approach to life and love. As she says, "Life is the biggest romantic adventure of all—and if you're open and aware, the most marvelous things are just waiting to be discovered."

Chapter 1

Snow flurries began to blow before Clint Ardmore left Conard City with his truckload of supplies. By the time he reached the county road leading to his ranch, it became apparent that winter was arriving. Big flakes whipped about in the wind, threatening a whiteout later when the temperatures dropped enough to make the snow nearly as fine as sand. As it was, the flakes reflected his low beams sufficiently to make the already dark afternoon seem darker.

Winter pleased him. He liked the cold, the snow, the isolation it brought to his ranch. Not even the most determined salesman or missionary would try to make it up the road to his house, and the neighbors to whom he leased his land for their own stock were undoubtedly pulling the last of them in. Soon his ranch would become exactly what he wanted it to be—a hermitage he left only out of necessity.

At least that was his cheerful expectation until he caught sight of a gray figure staggering alongside the road.

Hell, no one ought to be out here on foot. Cussing under his breath, he jammed on his brakes and pulled over. The snow was only just beginning to stick, so he didn't skid. Some drunk, no doubt, lost in the middle of nowhere. But whatever this person was doing out here, there was no way he could be left to wander alone in this weather. From here to the nearest ranch—his—it was another ten miles.

Clint climbed out and slammed the truck door. The wind had taken on a nasty bite, presaging a deadly night for unprotected humans.

Still cussing—he possessed quite an amazing vocabulary of cuss words in several languages—he stomped back toward the staggering figure in gray. The snow continued to swirl, thick enough to be almost fog-like. He really needed this, he thought. Now he would have to drive back to town in this damn storm to make sure this idiot didn't freeze to death out here.

It wasn't until he was only a few steps away that he realized the idiot was a woman and, worse, a woman dressed only in a gray sweatshirt and pants. And when she lifted her head at his approach, he saw a shiner that would have looked appropriate on a boxer, not on a tiny woman with straggly blond hair and blue eyes the size of saucers.

At least they became saucer-size when they saw him.

Well, he could kind of understand that. He was a large man, well over six feet, and years in Special Ops had given him a need to stay in shape that wouldn't quit even though he'd left the military well behind him. Then there was his face. The faces on Mt. Rushmore looked less stony.

Too bad.

"Hey, lady!" he called. "You're going to freeze!"

She staggered another step, then turned and started to run. Only she couldn't quite run, because her feet didn't seem to be cooperating, and moments later she tumbled facedown on the shoulder.

At once he raced to her side and squatted. "Lady..."

"Go away!" she cried. "Get away from me!"

"I won't hurt you," he said, making his voice as gentle as when he talked to his horses. Not exactly second nature, but he knew how.

"No! No! Get away from me."

Another time, another place, he might have been happy to oblige. But not out here. Not even on a sunny day. Not when she had a black eye like that, which might mean a bad concussion.

"Easy," he said quietly. "Easy. I won't hurt you, I swear. But you'll freeze out here."

Then he reached out to help her up and realized he might as well have tried to lift an angry mountain lion. She started fighting the instant she felt his hands, kicking and swinging and trying to scratch him.

Experience came to his aid. Keeping his hold as gentle as he could, keeping her back to his chest to minimize the damage to himself, he lifted her. "Shh," he said soothingly near her ear. "Shh. I'm just going to take you to a doctor."

"No! No!" She wriggled wildly. "He'll find me! He'll find me!" There was no mistaking the terror and desperation in her voice.

"All right, then," he agreed gently, all the while wondering why he was making such an insane promise. "All right. But how about you come home with me and get warm? You'll freeze out here."

"I don't care! He'll find me!"

"Nobody's going to find you at my place, I swear. I promise you'll be safe…."

He kept murmuring soothingly, taking care to keep his grip without hurting her. She fought a little longer, but she didn't have a whole lot of strength left, and soon enough she began to sag.

He shifted her a bit, so his hold was more comfortable, then swung her up and began carrying her toward his truck. A car drove by, slowing down, but he barely glanced at it before it sped up. He didn't recognize it, so it didn't belong to the only other rancher on this road before it dead-ended. He felt a fleeting suspicion, but dismissed it. If someone were following her in a car, he would certainly have caught her long since. Probably someone visiting. Not that he cared.

"No doctor," she said again, but her blue eyes had begun to look hazy.

"No doctor," he agreed. "Just a warm fire and some food."

Then she said something that tore at his heart. Her huge blue eyes focused on his face, and she said, "You're not him."

Then she passed out.

Kay Young returned to woozy consciousness to find she was lying on a soft sofa beneath a heap of quilts near a cheerfully burning fire. Dimly she realized it felt odd to be warm, because she had been cold for so long, so very long. But she no longer felt frozen to the bone.

When she tried to move, however, everything hurt, from her head to her feet, and she groaned. The pounding in her head alone nauseated her, and the world around her spun.

At once she heard a sound; then a stranger with a hard, harsh face was squatting beside her. "Shh," he said softly. "You're safe here. I promise. Shh. You might have a concussion."

"I have to go," she said weakly, struggling against pain, a swimming world and the quilts. "He'll find me. I can't let him find me." *Run!* The word shrieked in her brain, burned into every cell. *Escape! Flee!*

"Easy, lady," he said quietly. "Easy. You're hurt. No one's going to find you here. No one."

"He will," she said desperately, terror clutching at her insides with bony, knifing fingers. "He always finds me."

"Easy," he said again. "There's a blizzard outside. No one's getting here tonight, not even the doctor. I know because I tried."

"Doctor? I don't need a doctor! I've got to get away."

"There's nowhere to go tonight," he said levelly. "Nowhere. And if I thought you could stand, I'd take you to a window and show you."

But even as she tried once more to push away the quilts, she remembered something else—this man had been gentle when he'd found her beside the road, even when she had kicked and clawed. He hadn't hurt her. Not like her ex-boyfriend.

Terror receded just a bit. She looked at him, *really* looked at him, and though his face might have been granite, she detected signs of true concern there. True kindness.

The terror eased another notch, and she let her head sag on the pillow. "He always finds me," she whispered.

"Not here. Not tonight. That much I can guarantee."

And she believed him. Oh, God, she believed him. "Thank you," she murmured finally.

"I heated up some broth. Let's see if you can hold a little bit of it down. Do you feel sick to your stomach?"

"Yes."

"Maybe a couple of crackers first, then. After that we can try broth. I'll be right back."

She watched him straighten, amazed at his sheer size. Everything about him looked as if it might have been carved out of the nearby mountains. As he walked away from her, other things began to penetrate. She was in a warm room, a cozy room, with walls that looked like a log cabin. The furnishings were sparse but colorful, and they looked comfortable. The fire blazed merrily in a stone fireplace.

Nothing, absolutely *nothing,* about this place seemed in any way related to her tormentor or her experience since…since when? She didn't even know how long she had been in hell, how long ago she had begun to fear men. All men. Everything in her head was a jumble.

Oh God. She allowed her eyes to close, let her aching body relax at last. Oh God. Maybe she had truly escaped.

Maybe.

"Crackers?"

Her savior had returned with a small plate holding a dozen soda crackers. Only then did she realize, nauseated or not, that she was famished. Moving gingerly, she pushed herself up against the arm of the couch. He didn't try to touch her, not even to help. That seemed like a good sign.

She held the plate on her lap and nibbled at a cracker.

"I'm Clint Ardmore," he said.

"Kay Young," she answered, surprised at how weak she sounded. "May I have some water?"

"I can't believe I forgot that." He hopped up immediately from the roughly hewn coffee table on which he'd been sitting. "Would you prefer something carbonated? Maybe ginger ale or club soda?"

"Ginger ale, please."

He vanished once again, returning a minute later with a tall glass of soda. "I didn't put ice in it," he said. "I figured you need to warm up, and this is already chilled from the fridge."

"That's great. Thanks." She sipped it with relief, feeling it wet her mouth and burn a little. Her stomach liked it, and soon she was eating another cracker.

"Is it settling?"

"Very well." More ginger ale, another cracker. Somehow he no longer seemed frightening. But how could she be frightened of a man who was practically hovering in concern, a man who had given her his name without asking hers?

"You have one hell of a shiner," he said.

She looked at him. Again that granite face reflected genuine concern.

"He hit me," she said simply. Hard. Multiple times. But she didn't add all that.

"I could have guessed that," he said. "I should call the sheriff."

"No!" Panic erupted again, and he grabbed the soda from her hand right before she spilled it. "No! He'll kill me if he finds me!"

"Easy. Easy. Okay. No sheriff for now. Nothing tonight. Nobody can move in this storm anyway. You just rest. We can talk about everything tomorrow."

Tomorrow. For the first time in what felt like an eternity, she dared to believe there would be one. "I'm sorry," she said finally, staring at the crackers that still rested in her lap.

"No need. I can tell you've been through hell. Just take it easy. You're safe now."

And she believed him. For now, anyway. She looked at him gratefully as her panic subsided, then resumed eating.

"I'm still dizzy," she remarked. "On and off."

"That sounds like a concussion. You might be dizzy for a while."

It was then she noticed that her sweatshirt had turned dark green. Another shiver of panic. "What happened to my clothes?" Her gaze darted to his face, and for a moment the world turned into a carousel before settling again.

He frowned. "You don't remember?"

"Remember what?"

"Your clothes were wet from the snow. I helped you change into one of my sweat suits. You said it was okay."

Something far from pleasant started dancing along nerves that were already on the edge of shrieking from pain and terror. "I don't remember."

He swore. "Well, that settles it. You're seeing a doctor tomorrow. If you won't go to him, I'll get him to come to you. This sounds like a really bad concussion."

"He might find me," she said again, plunging back into the nightmare. "He said he was going to kill me!"

"No one will find you. I'll figure out something."

"Oh God, oh God…" And then she started to cry.

A fine freaking kettle of fish, Clint thought as he banged around in his kitchen, slamming pots a little harder than necessary as he tried to decide what the *hell* he was going to cook for himself, because he hadn't eaten all day. A terrified, injured woman in his living room, crying her eyes out, looking for all the world as if she'd been beaten and maybe tortured, who couldn't even remember letting him help her into dry clothes, who wouldn't let him take her to a doctor, not that he could anyway in the midst of this blizzard….

And all he wanted was his peace and solitude. He had a book to write, a deadline to meet, and he'd had enough of the real world to last him a lifetime. Enough so that it had stuck firmly in his craw and simply wouldn't be dislodged. And now the real world had landed on his doorstep, invaded his solitude and brought all its problems with it.

But what the hell was he supposed to do? A day, he promised himself. Two at most. He would convince her to talk to the sheriff, to see the doctor, and he would send her safely on her way to wherever she was from, where she would have family and friends and others who were far better suited to helping her through this than a crusty hermit like himself.

Finally he gave up all thought of creating some culinary masterpiece, his one indulgence, and settled instead on cocoa and some cinnamon rolls he'd bought earlier. He made enough for two in case she thought she could eat.

What kind of man would treat a woman that way and leave her so terrified? But he knew. He really didn't need to ask the question, because he'd known men like that. One of the things that lodged in his craw. He'd worked with them. They would get all messed up on the job, then take it home with them and treat their wives and girlfriends, and sometimes even their kids, like enemy combatants. He knew them too well. And he wished he didn't. So what if they were a minority?

At least *he* had the sense to realize that his training and experience had made him unfit for society. But God almighty, now he had that waif in the next room depending on him, and all that stuff about honor and duty and protecting the defenseless was rising up like the opening curtain on another nightmare.

Another cuss word escaped him under his breath. He stacked everything on a tray and carried it into the other room.

Kay was lying on the couch, her eyes closed, so still she might have been dead. His heart nearly stopped. He knew the dangers of concussion all too well.

"Kay?"

He set the tray on the coffee table and felt concern clamp his chest in a vise. "Kay?" he repeated.

No answer. Did he dare touch her? If she was unconscious, she would never know, but if she woke with a stranger touching her, he might set off her panic again.

"Kay!" Loudly. A command.

Then, to his infinite relief, her eyes fluttered open. "Kay," he repeated, more quietly.

Slowly, very slowly, her gaze tracked to his face. "Mmm?" she asked drowsily.

"I brought cinnamon buns and cocoa. Do you want to eat something more?"

"I...yes." She tried to push herself up a little more, then squeezed her eyes shut. "The world keeps moving."

"It'll stop. Just wait a few seconds before you open your eyes again."

She followed his suggestion, and when she looked at him again, her gaze remained steady.

"Cocoa?" he asked. "Or a bun? Or should I get the chicken broth?"

She hesitated, then said, "Cocoa sounds better."

Pushing the tray to one side, he sat on the low table and faced her, passing her a mug. She cradled it in both hands, though he couldn't tell whether she was seeking the warmth or worried it might spin away. Then she sipped, and her expression told him it was okay. He didn't need to run for a bucket. The cocoa would stay down.

Relieved, he reached for his own mug. "So what happened?" he asked finally.

"My...boyfriend."

His ire rose. "Your *boyfriend* did this to you?"

"My ex. Yes." She sighed and closed her eyes a moment. Her hands trembled, and he almost reached to take the mug from her.

"I can't remember much," she offered hesitantly. "It's all mixed up."

"That's okay." He tried to sound reassuring. "Concussions do that." And trauma, but he didn't add that. What was the point? Words wouldn't change her situation.

"Thank you," she said finally.

"For what? I haven't done much."

The corners of her mouth quivered, a sight that distressed him. Crying women were not his forte.

"For saving me," she said simply. "Thank you for saving me."

That was when he knew his troubles were just beginning.

Chapter 2

Wrapped around the mug of cocoa, Kay's fingers began to warm. At first they burned and tingled painfully, but then they began to feel normal again. She sipped the hot cocoa gratefully and glanced at the man who had retreated to the easy chair on the other side of the coffee table. Somehow that retreat made him seem even safer.

"Where am I?" she asked finally.

"On my ranch," he replied. "About twenty-five miles outside of Conard City, Wyoming."

"Wyoming?" The thought shocked her. How had she come to be so far from home? Had she really been trapped for that long? "I live in Texas!"

His face seemed to stiffen a bit, but she wasn't a hundred percent sure. Reading him was like reading runes—apparently you had to know the language. "That's a long way," he said finally. "You want to tell me what happened?"

"I can't...right now." Her mind recoiled from the memories, unwilling to remember the nightmare. "I can't," she said again, her heart accelerating.

"That's okay," he said soothingly. "I don't need to know. It can wait."

That was a pretty generous statement coming from a man who had picked her up off the roadside and welcomed her into his home. She felt she had to offer him something. "I ran," she said finally. "We were at a rest stop and he thought I was unconscious, and when he went inside, I ran. I ran..." Her voice trailed off, and she closed her eyes.

"You ran a helluva distance," he said. "The nearest rest stop I can think of is about nine miles from where I found you."

"I run marathons," she said simply.

A soft oath escaped him. She looked at him then, and there was no mistaking the anger on his face. She wanted to shrink and hide, but there was no place to go, not now.

But moments later his face settled back into impassivity. Of course, he wasn't mad at *her,* she thought. Not like *him.* This was a different man, one who was trying to help her. He had been nothing but kind.

"So you're from Texas," he said presently. "I spent some time there, years ago, mostly in Killeen."

She started. "Really? That's where I'm from."

"Small world sometimes."

"Or very big." Her words seemed to hang on the air. She wasn't quite sure what she'd meant, except that maybe now the world seemed more threatening than it had before Kevin. Into her small world, evil had come, a kind of evil she had once thought would never intersect with her life.

"Yeah," he said presently, "it can be."

As if he understood. Perhaps he did.

"I…tried to get away from him," she offered. God, it was so hard to speak of it. "He kept following. I moved three times, and he found me every time, and now…" Her voice broke. She couldn't continue.

"You're away from him now."

"Yes. Now." She squeezed her eyes shut. "But for how long?"

For a long time there was no sound but the crackling fire and keening wind. Then he asked, "You moved three times? Different towns?"

"Different states."

He swore. She jerked her head back, feeling the inescapable stab of fear, then relaxed when he didn't move a muscle.

"That's bad," he said quietly.

"You can't hide anymore," she said. "Not anymore. Not with the Internet."

"So it seems. And restraining orders might as well be written on toilet paper."

"You can't get one when you move to a new state. The judge asks where your proof is that he'll follow you. So the last time I didn't even try."

He shook his head. "By the time the restraining order is broken, you're already in too much trouble for it to do you much good."

"Yeah. I've learned that the hard way." She bit her lip, still clinging to the cocoa mug as if it were a lifeline. "That's why I don't want to let anyone know where I am. He'll find me. He always does."

He nodded but didn't say anything. She watched his stony face, trying to read something there, but couldn't. He was a man, and she ought to be frightened because Kevin had indelibly taught her that no matter how nice a guy might seem at first, he could turn into a monster.

But Clint Ardmore didn't know her yet. She was new to him, so regardless of what kind of man he might be, it was still too early to have to fear him. And she would be gone before it reached that point.

At least that was what she needed to believe.

"Okay," he said at last. "I won't even call the sheriff. At least not tonight. We can talk more about it when you're feeling a bit better."

She hated that he sounded grudging, but there was no way she could ignore his concession, even if he didn't want to make it. "Thank you."

"As to this concussion…I'm no doctor, but there's one thing I know for sure. I can't let you sleep too long or too deeply tonight, so you'd better make up your mind that I'm going to be waking you often. And if that means shaking you, I *will* shake you."

She didn't want to be touched. Not by anyone. Fear clogged her throat, even though she understood the sense of what he was saying. "I…only if you have to."

"Only if I can't wake you by banging a pot next to your ear." Then he surprised her by lifting one corner of his mouth in an almost-smile. "Can you live with that?"

"I think so."

"Don't worry about attacking me," he added, the smile deepening enough to seem almost real. "You already tried that and didn't even put a scratch on me. So if you wake up frightened and strike out, it's okay."

That was meant to calm her? Yet in some odd way it did. "I don't remember attacking you."

"Most likely not. You were pretty out of it, between the concussion and hypothermia. But yeah, you tried to defend yourself even when you were weaker than a newborn kitten."

He seemed to like that she'd defended herself, although she couldn't imagine why. It *did,* however, make her feel better about herself. Even totally out of it, she'd put up a fight.

"Anyway," he went on, "the blizzard alone should be enough protection for tonight. But I'll make sure everything's locked up tight. Don't usually have to bother, but…" He left the thought unfinished and shrugged.

"Thank you." It *would* make her feel safer. "And thank you for your hospitality."

Now *he* looked distinctly uncomfortable. "I wouldn't have left a stray cat out there tonight. Would have been inhuman."

Now how did he mean that? She wished she could peer behind the emotionless facade of his face and get an inkling of how this man thought.

No, maybe not. Maybe she didn't really want to know what went on inside him. Tomorrow she would be gone, as soon as the blizzard let up enough and…

"Oh my God!" The words escaped her before she could stop them.

"What?"

"I just realized. How am I going to get out of here?"

"I'll take you to a bus or something when the roads clear."

"No, you don't understand! He took my purse. I don't have any ID, no credit card, no money! Oh, God, I'm trapped!"

Just as she started to spiral into fresh panic, he stopped her with one word of command.

"No."

She gaped at him. "What?"

"I said no. Don't do it. Don't wind yourself up. I can help you out with all of that. Trust me, you'll be on your way again as soon as possible."

From something in the way he said it, she believed him. He didn't want her here any more than she wanted to be here.

It was a weird kind of hope, but it was a hope she had to cling to.

Besides, she reminded herself, she'd always found a way to run before. Always. She just needed to wait to gather her strength and lose the mental fog that seemed to be slowing her brain.

She finally ate one of the rolls he offered, and even downed another cup of cocoa. The heat from the fire began to penetrate enough that she threw back the quilt and lay there in the oversized green sweats he had put her into. "My toes are burning."

He looked at her feet. "I'm not surprised. They were getting close to frostbite. But they look a healthy pink now."

She hadn't even considered all the horrible dangers when she had taken her chance to flee the car wearing nothing but her grey sweats and running shoes into a cold Wyoming afternoon. With absolutely no thought of what she should do or where she should turn, she had fled. She hadn't even risked trying to hide at the rest stop in the hopes that someone else would drive in and she could seek help.

"I guess running like that wasn't my smartest move."

"I don't know, but from what little you've told me, it may have been your *only* move."

"It seemed like it." Then she stole another glance at him. "I couldn't have made it much farther, could I?"

"I don't know. Willpower can sometimes accomplish near miracles. I'm glad we'll never have to find out, though."

At least not this time, she thought miserably. Kevin had grown bigger than life in her mind, more like a nightmare monster than a mere man. "You know what I can't understand?"

"What's that?"

"Why he keeps coming after me. Why can't he just let me go? I go as far away as I can get, and he still comes looking. I just don't get it!"

He shook his head. "I'm no psychologist. I don't get why he abused you in the first place."

"I can understand that better than him tracking me like this. I mean, he has a temper. He blows up. At first I was even able to forgive him. But..." She shook her head. "I don't get it."

He suddenly leaned forward, almost like a striking snake, and she shrank back instinctively.

"Don't ever," he said, "*ever,* forgive someone who hits you. *Ever.*"

She blinked, wondering what the hell was behind that, but then he leaned back and reached for his own mug as if he hadn't just vented that moment of passion. "Creeps like him," Clint said quietly, "once they cross that line, they just keep on crossing it like it was never there."

That much made sense. She nodded. "I guess you're right."

"I know I'm right." His gray eyes seemed to burn. "You can't erase the lines and then draw them again. The lines get blurred, and it almost never works. Especially if they get a taste for power or inflicting fear."

She felt her mouth sag open a little and quickly closed it. They were definitely having a discussion about something that reached far beyond Kevin, but she couldn't imagine what it was.

He rose quickly, mug in hand. "Want more?"

"I'm fine, thanks."

He headed swiftly for the kitchen, as if he wanted to get away from the whole conversation.

Not that she could blame him. She didn't exactly like it herself.

She lay there, mug in her hands, staring into the dancing fire, wondering more about her rescuer than she should. He seemed like a troubled man, and that made her uneasy.

But, she reminded herself again, she would be out of here as soon as she could manage after the storm passed.

In a day or so she would never have to see Clint Ardmore again. There was absolutely no point in trying to figure him out, not when she was going to shake him off her heels like the dust along the road of what was evidently going to become a permanent flight.

God. She wanted to weep, but the tears wouldn't come. Just as well. She didn't want to annoy her rescuer. But how the dickens was she ever going to get out of this mess? The one and only time she'd managed to get Kevin charged and thrown into jail, he'd gotten out in less than two years.

Apparently it was a far worse crime to kick your dog than beat your girlfriend. And it was a lot harder to prove domestic abuse, too. The second time she'd gone to the cops, Kevin had denied he was even in town. Since he lived four states away and hadn't done anything stupid, like buy gas with a credit card or rent a hotel room, the prosecutor had shrugged and dismissed the charge for lack of proof that tied Kevin to the assault. There were so many more important cases to pursue, after all.

The wind hammered the windows, making them rattle behind the curtains, and she looked around uneasily. Kevin had to know she had taken off running. He might have wondered if she had been picked up along the road, maybe by a long-distance trucker, but he probably wouldn't have wondered for long. The roads had been deserted, maybe because of the approaching storm, and the stop had been a brief one, brief enough that she had heard him shouting her name in the distance as she hid in a thicket of trees before dashing off again.

No, he wouldn't know which way she'd gone, but he'd probably figured out pretty quickly that she wasn't running along the highway. That would have been the first thing he checked.

So he might stay in the area, looking for her.

Regardless, she couldn't afford to have her name turn up in a police blotter or anywhere else he could find it by means of the Internet.

So what now?

The question loomed darkly, without answers. Finally she pushed it away, promising herself she would think about it in the morning, after the throbbing in her head eased and her thoughts cleared.

Because right now even *she* could tell she was far from being at her best.

A male voice called her name sharply, and she started. "What?"

She looked around and saw Clint sitting on the coffee table again. The mug was no longer in her hands.

"You've been sleeping about half an hour," he said.

"I didn't even realize I'd dozed off."

He nodded. "You're exhausted. But we still have to watch out for that concussion. Sorry, but I'm going to make this a long night for you."

"I understand." She did. Moving carefully, she tried to sit up, but the room tilted and spun so much that she had to close her eyes.

"Do you need something?"

"The bathroom. But I'm dizzy."

"Let me help you. Keep your eyes closed."

She expected him to take her arm, help her to her feet and guide her. But instead he lifted her from the couch like a doll and carried her. She definitely did *not* like that. She hated being reminded that he was so much stronger than she was. It was all she could do not to fight him as fear grabbed her anew.

But then he let her feet slide to the floor and steadied her with an arm around her waist.

"Wait a minute," he said, "then open your eyes."

She did as he suggested, and when she opened her eyes the room appeared stable. It was a small bathroom, just the essentials, with little extra room.

"This is the most dangerous room in the house," he reminded her. "Don't move quickly, don't turn or tip your head, and hang on to something every time you move. If you get dizzy, just holler. I'll be right outside the door."

"Thanks."

With care and extreme caution, she managed to take care of her needs, but when it came time to walk to the door, she felt unsteady enough to call out.

"Clint?"

He entered swiftly, offering immediate support. "Let me carry you," he said this time. "The sweatpants could trip you."

So it hadn't just been an exercise of male dominance when he had lifted her before. Relieved, she didn't argue, and this time she felt no fear when he picked her up. He laid her back on the sofa as if she were fragile enough to shatter.

"How's your head?"

"Still aching," she admitted.

"I'm sorry I can't give you aspirin. But with a concussion, that could be dangerous. And I don't have anything else."

"That's all right. It's reminding me I'm still alive."

Something flickered across his face, so quickly that she couldn't quite read it. She suspected that stoniness would make him a difficult man to deal with. At least with Kevin she had always known just what kind of trouble was on the horizon, even if she couldn't stop it or escape it.

"Can I get you anything?" he asked. "Food? Soup? A drink?"

"I'm really thirsty," she admitted. "Would you mind? Ginger ale?"

"Not a problem."

She let her head rest against the pillow, listening to the hammering storm outside. The thick log walls protected them from most of it, but through the closed windows she could hear the keening of the wind, and sometimes the glass rattled before the strength of it. Not even Kevin, she assured herself, could be out looking for her in this. Thank God.

But what was she going to do when it passed? With no identification or money, or even her debit card, how could she start running again? Fear and grief grabbed her in as tight a grip as the throbbing headache, and for a few seconds she couldn't even draw a breath. Never before had he trapped her quite this effectively. Always before she'd been able to gather enough resources to run again.

Well, she would find a way, she promised herself. She always had before.

"You're going to be all right."

She moved her eyes slowly until she could see Clint standing beside her, holding out a tall glass of ginger ale. For a moment he seemed to swim, then the world stabilized again. "Thanks." She reached out and took the glass, and only then realized that she needed to sit up straighter to drink.

Clint apparently saw the problem at the same instant she realized it. He took the glass back and bent to help her sit up against the pillow. "I guess I must be tired," he said. "Missing the obvious."

"Do you never miss the obvious?"

"I miss very little." An edge in his tone warned her away, though from what she didn't know. Silently, she accepted the glass back.

He rounded the coffee table and sat in the easy chair on the other side. A book lay open on the end table, and he picked it up to start reading again. Apparently he didn't feel like conversing.

Which ordinarily would have been fine, but Kay discovered her own thoughts scared her. She didn't want to be alone inside her own head. But how could you converse with a man who was doing a passable imitation of a brick wall?

A native caution when dealing with men kept her silent. She didn't want to irritate this man. From his size and strength, he could present an even bigger threat than Kevin, even though he hadn't done a thing to indicate he might be that kind of person.

She sipped her ginger ale, and a sigh escaped her. At once he spoke.

"Are you all right?"

"Just unhappy with my thoughts."

"I can understand."

Maybe he could. She dared to look at him again and found he had set the book aside.

"I guess I should apologize," he said finally, his tone level, his face unchanging. "I've been a hermit for a while. By choice. I seem to have lost the social graces."

"I'm not asking for social graces," she said truthfully. "You've been very kind to a stranger. I don't want to intrude more than necessary. It's just that my thoughts keep running in circles. Unhappy circles."

"You've certainly got enough to be unhappy about."

It might have been a question, a suggestion or an end to the subject. From what she had seen of him so far, she guessed it was probably a signal to end the discussion. So she took another sip of ginger ale and focused her attention on the fire. She could take a hint. In fact, she was probably hyper-alert to hints, thanks to Kevin.

But Clint surprised her by not returning to his book. "I suggest you plan to stay here for a couple of days." The invitation sounded grudging, and she looked askance at him.

"Why? You said you're a hermit by choice."

"Maybe so, but it seems to me you need some time, some *safe* time, to make plans and figure out your next move. You can't just run out of here the instant the storm ends. And I can provide the safety you need."

He said the last with such calm confidence that she wondered who the hell he was. Or what he had been before becoming a hermit. Not even the most sympathetic cop had ever promised her that much. No, they had been full of warnings and advice, most of which included getting as far away as possible as fast as possible.

"Kevin," she said finally, "is like a bomb. There's no telling when he'll go off, and anyone in the vicinity is probably at risk."

"I've dealt with bombs, and I've dealt with worse than Kevin." A frown dragged at the corners of his mouth but didn't quite form. "Trust me, I can keep you safe."

"The *cops* couldn't keep me safe."

"They couldn't be there round the clock," he said flatly. "And cops don't have my training."

She hesitated, then just blurted it out. "Who are you? *What* are you?"

His gaze grew distant, as if he could see through the walls and well past the blizzard beyond. A shiver ran through her. "I was special ops for nearly twenty years. And I was good at it. *Very* good."

She didn't know how to respond to that. Should she congratulate him? Admire him? But no. Something in that rigid face told a very different story. "I don't want you to have to go back to that. To relive it."

At that the facade cracked, and he looked startled. Then the stone returned. "Sometimes," he said after a moment, "you don't have a choice."

Chapter 3

The night passed without further conversation. Either weariness or the concussion, or a combination of both, kept causing her to nod off. Every half hour or so, he woke her, then let her fall back to sleep.

Then, finally, she knew it had to be morning because she awoke to the smell of frying bacon. The aroma made her mouth water, and she realized she was ravenous. When she pushed herself cautiously upright, she was delighted to realize the room no longer spun. The crazy carousel was gone.

Her head still ached, but not as badly, and most of the pain she felt now was in her cheek and around her black eye. There were aches and pains from running in the cold, from the other blows Kevin had heaped on her, but nothing she couldn't ignore.

Moving carefully, pulling the legs of the sweatpants up as she walked, she made her way to the bathroom and freshened up a bit. Then, upon returning to the living room, she pulled one of the heavy curtains back and looked out on the still-raging blizzard.

It was early yet, still dark outside, but even so, she could tell visibility probably didn't extend much past the porch railing she could barely see, buried as it was in snowy drifts and further concealed by wildly blowing snow. Even after the storm passed, just getting out the front door would probably prove to be a challenge.

"Good morning."

Startled, she almost jumped but managed to remember her unsteadiness in time. Gripping the window frame, she turned to see Clint standing in the doorway of his kitchen. "Good morning."

He gave a half-smile. "Glad to see you can get around. Are you hungry?"

"That bacon smells wonderful."

"I thought it might. Do you want eggs and toast with it?"

"Please. Eggs any way you like."

"Can do."

He turned and vanished back into the kitchen. "Coffee?" she heard him call.

"Please. Black."

Apparently she wasn't quite back up to snuff. Realizing she had begun to feel shaky, she made her way back to the sofa and sat. At least now she could sit upright. Last night's ginger ale still sat on the coffee table. It had gone flat, but that didn't keep her from drinking it down in one long draft. Heavens, she was thirsty.

Clint returned just long enough to set a mug of steaming coffee in front of her, then vanished back into the kitchen. He'd added a couple of logs to the fire, and the flames leapt high again, making the room toasty. The fire also cast enough light that she didn't feel any desire to turn on one of the lamps.

It was like being in a warm, cozy cave, she thought. Surrounded by thick walls, safe from predators. But as she'd learned all too painfully, safety was an illusion, one that, in her life, rarely lasted for long.

There was a wooden table with three chairs in one corner of the room, and it was there Clint served their breakfast. He waited for her to get there on her own, watching her as if measuring her steadiness, but not intervening. She didn't want to admit, even to herself, how ready she was to sag into the chair by the time she got there. It wasn't that far, but never before in her life had she felt so weak.

Of course, she hadn't eaten much for days.

Clint apparently believed breakfast should be the day's biggest meal. She found herself looking at platters heaped high with toast, bacon and scrambled eggs.

"That's enough for an army," she remarked in surprise.

"I think you're hungrier than you realize," he responded.

"I think I'm going to prove you right." She was famished, in fact. Except for the cocoa and soda last night, and the crackers and little bit of cinnamon roll, she hadn't eaten in days. Whatever Kevin had intended to do with her, feeding her hadn't been part of it. Three days, she figured. Three days since he'd kidnapped her from Killeen. But that was just a guess, since she'd been stuck in his trunk a lot of the time.

"Want to tell me what happened?" Clint asked.

"Not really." But she knew she would tell him anyway. If the thoughts wouldn't stop running around in her head, where could the harm be in speaking them out loud?

"Eat first," he suggested. "That's the most important thing."

It was. With a shaking hand, she helped herself to healthy portions of eggs, toast and bacon. Hungry though she was, it still seemed difficult to focus on chewing and swallowing. The better she felt, the more the urge to flee grew in her. She had learned that when she held still, danger would find her.

And she could no longer believe it wouldn't find her, regardless of what this man promised.

"So what do you do?" he asked. "For a living."

"Whatever I can. Usually that's waiting tables. It's one of the easiest jobs to get when you're new in a place."

"Do you enjoy it?"

"Mostly. The money is good enough if you work in the right restaurant."

"Do you have any savings?"

"Probably not anymore." Her mood sank again, and she poked at the food on her plate with her fork.

"You know, you should call your bank and tell them your credit card or whatever was stolen on the day you were kidnapped."

"No!" Panic gripped her heart in an icy fist. "Don't you understand? He always finds me somehow. If I poke my head up, they'll want to know where I am. They'll want to know where to send another card. They'll want me to sign things. Once that happens, he'll find me."

He sighed. "You're right, I guess. Sorry, I'm still kind of an electronic Luddite. I keep forgetting that somehow everything is available if you just know how to look for it."

"It seems like it. Almost twenty years ago, the post office stopped giving out forwarding addresses so stalkers couldn't follow people who moved. Maybe that helped back then, but today you can get the address of anyone in the country for a few dollars. And if you have more than a few dollars, apparently you can find out a whole lot more. I'm not sure exactly how he does it, but once I've been in a place for a while, Kevin finds me. Three times now. How the hell do you hide?"

"Actually," he said slowly, "you *can* hide. But it'll involve a lot of changes. We can talk about it later."

She offered to help with the dishes, but he declined, telling her it was better for her to rest. Twenty minutes later, he rejoined her in the living room.

"Do you need to shower?" he asked before he sat. "I can get you some more sweats."

"Maybe later on the shower." She needed one, but she wasn't confident enough of her stability yet, and she sure didn't want to have to ask this stranger for help with *that*.

"Sure. More coffee?"

He freshened her mug and got one of his own before settling into his easy chair. The storm outside kept right on ripping around them. He tilted his head to one side. "This isn't going to blow over soon."

"That's okay," she said. It gave her a few additional hours of safety before she would have to figure out how to move on again.

"I suppose it is."

No, she realized, it *wasn't*. Not for him. He was a self-confessed hermit, and now he was stuck with an invader until such time as he could reasonably boot her out the door.

"I'm sorry," she said.

"For what?"

"Imposing on you like this."

"Oh, for the love of Pete!"

She shrank back against the pillows. He was an unknown, and she hadn't meant to anger him. He could do almost anything to her.

But he remained firmly planted in the chair, though he looked disgusted, a change from his usually unrevealing attitude. "Look," he said, "I know neither of us likes this situation. I prefer my solitude, and you'd sure as hell prefer not to have a lunatic ex-boyfriend trying to kill you, chasing you everywhere you go. But you know what? Sometimes we don't have a choice. We just have to do what needs doing. And right now what needs doing is giving you the safety and space in which to recover. So what if it disturbs my sacred solitude?"

"I'm still sorry," she said, weakly, not sure whether she was sorry for angering him or for the whole damn mess.

"Quit apologizing. You don't have a thing to apologize for. I know I'm not exactly a warm, fuzzy kind of host, but if you think I resent the fact that you need help and I'm here to provide it, you're wrong."

"Okay." She wanted to get away from this topic as quickly as possible.

But even though he could have dropped it there, he didn't. Evidently he had plenty of thoughts on this subject.

"You have rights, and I have responsibilities," he said flatly.

Now, that really did confuse her. "What rights?"

"You," he said, "have a right to exist without terror. You have a right to expect the rest of us to step up and get you away from this guy, since he seems hell-bent on following you wherever you go. You have a right to expect help, and apparently you haven't been getting it."

"But you have rights, too."

"Hell, yeah, but I can protect my own."

"And you don't have a responsibility to me."

"Oh, yeah, I do."

She tried to shake her head, but as soon as she did, she remembered her concussion as pain stabbed her head. "I'm nobody. You don't owe me a thing."

"You're not nobody. You're a human being, and that gives you certain rights in my book. And I'm a human being, and that's enough to make me responsible to do what I can for you."

Her mouth opened a little as she stared at him. She couldn't remember anyone ever putting it like that before.

He leaned forward, putting his mug on the coffee table, then resting his elbows on his knees. "You want to know one of the reasons why I prefer my own company?"

She wasn't sure she did, but he didn't wait for her answer.

"Because too many people have forgotten their responsibilities. Too many people look the other way, or take the easy path. Anything but put themselves out for someone who needs help."

"Not everyone is like that."

"Of course not. But too many are, and I'm sick of them, frankly. All this talk of personal responsibility that people toss around overlooks a very important fact."

"Which is?"

"That your personal responsibility doesn't end at the tip of your own nose. Or at your own front door."

She bit her lip, then ventured, "You've thought a lot about this."

"I spend a lot of time thinking about responsibility. My own. Accepting it. Then deciding what it should have been all along."

She longed to ask him what had put him on such a personal private quest, but didn't dare. There was a darkness in this man that she could feel all the way across the room. It lurked in his gray eyes like a ghost. Maybe it was best not to know.

He picked up his mug again and sat back, sipping slowly while minutes ticked by.

"Any family?" he asked abruptly.

"Me?"

"You."

"No. I oh, do you want to hear the whole story? It sounds like a cliché."

"A lot of life is made up of clichés. Tell me whatever you don't mind sharing."

She looked down and realized her hands were twisting together. She forced herself to separate them and lay them flat. Then she shrugged a shoulder, ignoring the ache. Apparently Kevin had hit her there, too. Not that she remembered, there had been so many blows.

"My mother died of an overdose when I was four. Nobody knew who my dad was. So my grandmother took care of me until she died of a heart attack when I was thirteen. After that it was foster homes. Six of them. I don't think I was easy to deal with. And there's nobody else."

"You made it through high school, though?"

"Yeah. Yeah, I did. I always wanted to go to college, but I had to take care of myself and kept putting it off and then…well, Kevin…" She bit her lip again, unable to meet his gaze.

"Tell me about Kevin. About the beginning."

She hesitated, unable to imagine why he wanted all this information, but reluctant to tell him it was none of his business. He'd rescued her in the middle of a blizzard where she probably would have died except for him. That gave him a right to know, she supposed. Especially since he was still helping her.

"Kevin was okay at first. Really nice. It was a long time before I realized that I was tiptoeing around all the time because of his temper. It took me even longer to realize he couldn't hold a job for more than a month or two, and finally I gave up even trying to tell him to look for work. So I did something stupid."

"And that was?"

She drew a long breath. "I started skimming my paycheck."

"You what?" He sounded utterly disbelieving. "How can you skim your own paycheck?"

"I got a raise and didn't tell him. I'd go to the bank and split the deposit, put the extra money into a savings account. I meant to save for school."

"And you didn't tell him."

"No."

He sighed. "That's a warning sign in huge red letters. But I suppose he had you so intimidated by that point that you didn't even recognize it."

"Not really. I just did it. I didn't exactly think about all the reasons I felt the need to. When I look back, I feel stupid."

"No, don't. You have no idea how many people, doing the best they can in whatever situation they're in, look back later and think they were stupid. It's never stupid. It's the best you can do at the time."

"Thanks. I still feel stupid."

"So let me guess. He found out about the savings account."

She nodded. "That was the first time he beat me."

"And then he was oh so apologetic, swore he'd never do it again and took the money."

"Yeah. Like I said, stupid."

"Stop saying that. It's amazing how manipulative these bastards can be. It's like they're born knowing how to get what they want. So okay, that was the first time the line got crossed. And it got worse, right?"

"Yeah. With time. Until finally he broke my arm and left my face such a mess I couldn't go to work, and my boss actually came to the house. He took one look at me and dragged me to the hospital, then called the cops."

"Ah, a responsible person arrives on the scene. Amazing."

In spite of herself, she felt the unbruised side of her face lift in a slight smile. "My boss was a good man."

"I agree. So Kevin went to jail?"

"That time."

"But he got out."

"Of course. Less than two years later."

"I think I can pretty much write the rest of the story." He sipped his coffee and closed his eyes for a moment. When they opened, they held an ice that should have frightened her, but somehow it didn't. Maybe she was too tired, too battered. Maybe she just couldn't rustle up any more terror.

"Take my word for it, Kay Young, as long as you are in this house, that man will not lay a finger on you."

Deep inside she shivered, because she believed him, because she feared the kind of protection he was capable of providing. Special Ops? Yeah, he could protect her.

"I don't want you to get into any trouble on my account," she blurted.

He smiled, but not pleasantly.

"I won't," he said. "Trust me, I won't."

She dozed off again, and when she woke, she felt disoriented. Not because she didn't recognize the cabin or the fireplace, or Clint sitting across the way in his chair reading. No, it was something even more basic than that.

Almost before she opened her eyes, she asked, "What time is it? What day is it?"

He looked up from his book. "It's Friday, December twelfth and it's just after one in the afternoon."

"Five days!"

"Since he took you?"

"Yes." She looked around, trying to center herself somehow. "What state did you say this was?"

"Wyoming. Conard County, Wyoming, to be more precise."

She squeezed her eyes shut. "Sorry. It's like things are jumbled."

"That's normal enough, I suppose. How's your head feel?"

"The headache is almost gone."

"Good. That's probably why you're trying to sort things out."

"I didn't know he had me so long."

"No?"

"No. He kept me in the trunk a lot. He didn't feed me. He hardly gave me any water."

"He would be wise not to come near you while I'm around."

She looked at him, amazed by the calm way he spoke, as if such threats were commonplace in his world. Not a ripple of emotion showed on his face. Oddly, while his obvious self-control was horrifying in a way, it also reassured her far more than a display of anger would have. Far more.

Outside, judging from the sound of the wind, the storm still raged. Hard to believe it had gone on so long. Hard to accept that she was trapped in more ways than one.

"I've got to figure out what to do."

"Relax," he said. "I'm already figuring it out."

"Why should *you* do that?"

He shrugged. "Why not?"

"Because it's *my* problem?"

"It's mine now, too."

She realized he meant it. That was no token statement. "I can figure it out."

"You've been figuring it out for a few years now. Let somebody else help you for a change." He closed his book and placed it on the coffee table. "I'm not trying to take over, it's not my place. You can make all the decisions yourself. But I have a few suggestions."

"Like what?"

"For starters, we call the sheriff."

"No! Then I'll be in the blotter. I'll be in the newspaper, like last time I made a complaint. I don't want him to know I'm still in the area!"

He waited a moment before speaking. When he did, his voice was so calm it seemed at odds with the situation. "Are you planning to run forever?"

She bit her lip so hard it hurt. "No," she said finally, feeling her eyes sting. "No."

"Then we need to deal with the problem. The sheriff here is a man I'd trust with my life, and I don't say that about many people. If I tell him what's going on, he'll guard your secret with his life. Your name won't be in any blotter or any report."

"You're sure?"

"Like I said, I'd trust him with my life. In fact, there are a few people hereabouts I can say that about. So trust me on this one."

"And if I do?"

"Then we're going to ask the sheriff to find Kevin. Find him and nail him good. It's not just beating you up anymore, Kay. It's kidnapping. Across state lines. That's a federal crime, and that son of a bitch is going away for life."

A spark of hope ignited in her, but then flickered out. "He has to be caught first."

"Trust me, we'll get him. One way or another."

"But it's just my word against his." That hadn't been enough before.

"Well, I think some photos of your face will make a point. And the other injuries he gave you."

She touched her cheek lightly with her fingertips. "I must look awful."

"You look like someone who was hit in the side of the head with something heavy. Like a tire iron."

She almost gasped. "How did you know?"

"Did you look in the mirror when you went to the bathroom?"

"No." No, she had avoided that like the plague. It was bad enough to endure the pain, but she'd been afraid to look for fear he'd ruined her face for good. How could she work as a waitress with a messed-up face?

"If we can't get the sheriff out here soon, I'm going to ask you to let me take some pictures myself."

"Why do we have to wait for the sheriff?"

"I think it's more evidentiary if he does it. Well, actually, he'll probably ask one of his female deputies to do it. From what I saw when I helped you change into those clothes yesterday, you were beaten all over."

She covered her face with her hands, pierced by a shame she couldn't explain. Why should she feel shame? But she did, and it was deep and burning. She felt hot tears begin to run, but no sobs accompanied them. She'd learned, a long time ago, to cry silently.

At least her stranger-savior didn't evince any annoyance. He just let her cry. Later, when the tears dried and she dabbed at her face with the sleeves of the green sweatshirt, he rose, returning a minute later with a box of tissues and a fresh cup of coffee.

She took the tissues gratefully, dabbing her face, blowing her nose. "Sorry," she said.

"No need."

The coffee tasted as if it had been freshly brewed, and she sipped it with pleasure. She hadn't really tasted anything before, had just been going through the motions, but now, for the first time in days, she discovered she could savor something simple. Something good. "You like it strong. So do I." She gave him a smile with the half of her face that still felt mobile.

He acknowledged her words with a small nod. Evidently he didn't run to social pleasantries.

"When are you going to call the sheriff?"

"As soon as you're ready to give me identifying information."

"What kind of information?"

"The car he was driving, what he looks like, his full name, where he kidnapped you from."

"Okay." She drew a deep breath. He was right; she couldn't keep running. And this was as good a place as any to make her stand, if only because she seemed to have an ally.

An odd ally, one who apparently had chosen to stand beside her on principle and nothing else. But maybe that was the best kind of ally—one who expected nothing from her but merely felt her situation deserved his help.

Yes, that was best, she decided. That way there was no chance of the kind of messiness she'd run into with Kevin.

"I'll give you whatever information you want."

He nodded again and rose. "Just let me get a pad and pen."

She waited, holding her mug in both hands, afraid to nurture even a spark of hope. For all she knew, she was about to sign her own death warrant.

But even death seemed preferable to living like this any longer.

Chapter 4

Clint got his cordless phone and returned to his easy
chair, putting the pad on his lap. Kay had answered his
questions, and he'd scribbled down the answers. It was
time to call the sheriff, Gage Dalton, even though the
roads for miles around were impassible.

He didn't need the sheriff to protect Kay here at
his house. He needed the sheriff to keep eyes out for
Kevin.

He scanned the pad to refresh his memory of what
she had told him before he dialed. His notes were even
more abbreviated than his speech, but he had a good
memory.

A memory that was suddenly jogged as he scanned
the description of the car.

God! Reaching back to the moments when he had
been carrying Kay to his truck, he remembered a car
passing them and slowing down. He couldn't be sure it

exactly matched her description, because by then they'd been approaching whiteout conditions, but it came close enough to give him a minor adrenaline jolt.

If that had been Kevin, then there was now a chance he had a pretty good idea where Kay was. Because the road dead-ended, he would have had to backtrack, and he would have at least an idea that Clint had taken her to his ranch. And worse, if he'd scanned the license tag, it would be easy enough to find out exactly where Clint lived. So if Kevin checked around and found that Kay hadn't gone to the police or into the hospital, he would be virtually certain that she was still with Clint.

In this storm he would be as immobilized as everyone else, but after the roads were cleared...

A thrum of anger started beating in time with his heart. He didn't say anything to Kay, though. She was already skittish enough. So skittish he wanted her to hear every word he spoke to the sheriff so she would know he hadn't betrayed her in any way.

But even as he punched in the non-emergency number, his mind was beginning to turn over plans for making his cabin safer.

"Conard County Sheriff's Office," said the froggy voice of the dispatcher. Rain or shine, blizzard or forest fire, Velma was always at the other end of the line.

"Hi, Velma, this is Clint Ardmore. I need to talk to Gage."

"Well, honey, I'll see what I can do, but as you can imagine, we're trying to help folks who got themselves into a passel of trouble by not staying home in this crud."

"Sounds to me like you didn't stay home, either."

Velma laughed, a sound similar to a braying donkey. "Honey, I only have to *walk* a couple of blocks. Gage is out somewhere with a crew, trying to pull a family out of a ditch. Say… Micah's not too far from you. Want me to have him drop by?"

Micah Parish was another of the handful of local people that Clint would have trusted with his life. But he looked over at Kay and wondered if she would be able to take it. She was twisting her hands again, and biting her lip, looking ready to jump out of her skin.

On the other hand, now that he'd recalled that car, he couldn't forget it.

"How," he asked Velma, "can Micah get here?"

"He's plowing his way in. You're on the route." All the deputies had plows on the fronts of their official vehicles exactly for times like this.

"Give me a sec, Velma."

"Sure."

He put his hand over the mouthpiece. "Kay? One of those guys I'd trust my life to?"

"Yes?"

"He's going to be driving past here. Talking to him would be better than waiting for the sheriff. Apparently he's pretty tied up with people who have storm trouble."

Her hands tightened around each other until her knuckles turned white. "You're sure?" she finally asked hesitantly.

"Well, if he comes here, you can make sure he doesn't write anything down. Maybe that would make you feel better. And I can't think of a better person to have my back."

Finally she nodded. "Okay. Okay." But she didn't sound happy.

He took his hand from the mouthpiece. "Velma? Yeah, that would be great if Micah would stop by. I really need to talk to him."

"Consider it done. I'll call him now."

"Thanks."

When he disconnected, Clint put the handset on the table beside him. "It'll be okay," he said, feeling once again as if he was trying to calm a frightened horse. He'd calmed frightened men in battle, but this was a whole different thing, calling for a different kind of patience, a kind he wasn't sure he had enough of.

He ran through an assortment of cuss words in his head, because he was sure if he said any of them aloud she would shrink away again, and as much as he had tried to harden himself over the years, seeing a woman shrink from him brought back enough memories to fill a dump truck and make him feel like an utter bastard.

The phone rang. It was Velma. "Micah is plowing his way up your road right now. He said to thank you for those reflector posts you put up last year."

Clint gave a rare chuckle. He'd lined his driveway with the things after a blizzard almost as bad as this one, because his drive was long enough, and winding enough, to be impossible to find under heavy snow, and even more impossible to clear. "Tell him thanks for clearing the road for me."

"You'll just have to clear it again later," Velma advised him. "The snow is going to stop soon, but the wind will keep up until tomorrow. Like holding a flood back with a broom." On that positive note, she disconnected.

Clint looked at Kay again. She appeared to have sunk into unhappy recollection. "Micah will be here soon. He's plowing his way to the door."

He watched her eyes widen and fill with fear, and then gave her points for quickly getting a grip on her emotions. "Okay," she said on a tight breath.

Nothing he could tell her would reassure her. She was running on an awful lot of trust right now, and as someone who'd learned to trust very few, he could understand that.

Micah arrived fifteen minutes later. They could hear the engine strain as he approached, pushing heavy snow out of the way. Then he left the vehicle idling. They heard the stomp of boots on the porch as he shook the snow off, and at the sound, Kay shrank visibly.

Clint stifled a sigh and went to get the door, letting Micah in with a cold blast of air and swirling snow. Micah was every bit as big as Clint, broad and well-muscled, but far more exotic looking thanks to his Cherokee heritage.

Clint had to force the door closed against the wind, then latched it firmly.

"Damn," Micah said. "Somebody moved Antarctica up here."

"It's bad," Clint agreed as they shook hands. "Coffee?"

"Hot and black."

But something else had to come first. "Come meet my guest."

Micah's black-as-night eyes slipped past him and found Kay, who sat up and was looking at him with evident terror.

"Well, hell," Micah said. "Who the devil beat her up?"

* * *

Kay sat on the very edge of the couch, poised to run even though there was nowhere she could flee. Another man, another dangerous man, this one older but every bit as huge as Clint. She felt like a mouse facing two lions.

"Kay," Clint said, "this is Deputy Micah Parish. Micah, Kay Young."

"Howdy," Micah said. Then he pulled off his jacket, revealing a tan deputy's uniform and badge. He hung the coat on the peg by the door. "First the coffee. Then the talk. I've been on the road for three hours now, and the heater in the damn truck is barely working. Too much wind, I think. Engine's not getting very warm."

"Take a seat. I'll be right back. Kay, you want more coffee?"

She managed a slight negative shake of her head as she tried to cope with the fact that after running from a man for three years, she was now dependent on two of them, both of them looking as if they could do a lot more damage with their bare hands than Kevin could do with a tire iron.

Micah stepped farther into the room and settled on the one remaining chair. He seemed to know that the easy chair was Clint's preferred perch. He held his hands out to the fire for a minute, then turned toward her slowly. She shrank back.

"Easy, girl," he said quietly. "Nobody here is gonna hurt you."

She didn't exactly have any choice now except to believe him. Cold comfort.

Clint returned with two mugs and passed one to Micah.

"Thanks," Micah said, as Clint settled into his chair. "So is this what it looks like?"

"Maybe. But maybe worse."

Micah sipped his hot coffee, then returned his dark gaze to Kay.

What were they talking about? Her? She wished she could hide behind the sofa pillows. And yet she sensed no threat in those exotic eyes.

"My wife," Micah said.

She managed a slight nod.

"My wife was on the run from an abusive ex-husband when I found her. There was a storm, not as bad as this, but still a storm. She was driving too fast, so I pulled her over to warn her to slow down. I got to know her terror pretty quick."

Something inside Kay seemed to pop. Maybe the bubble of fear and apprehension. She relaxed a bit. "Did he follow her?"

"Yeah, he did."

"Where is he now?"

"Well, he tried to kill her. So I had to kill him."

She sagged then, as the last of the tension seeped out of her. She looked at Clint and realized he was prepared to do the same if necessary. Oh, Lord, she didn't want anybody to die, but she was beginning to think there was no other way out.

Clint spoke. "He kidnapped Kay from Texas and got her this far before she managed to escape."

"Kidnapping is good," Micah remarked. "Especially across state lines."

"It is?" Kay could scarcely believe she had heard right, and fear began to trickle along her spine.

"It's very good," Micah said. "The Feds can usually get a maximum sentence on a case like that."

"I'd like that," Kay admitted, trying to relax again. "I'm so tired of running." Her chest tightened, and she had to fight back tears. Tired. Yes she was tired. Tired to the very bone. At last she felt secure enough to settle back more comfortably on the sofa.

Micah nodded and then turned back to Clint. "So tell me what you have."

"First, Kay doesn't want her name on any records. Not until you catch the guy."

"I can do that."

Kay released another relieved sigh and let her eyes close for a minute. Thank God. She listened as Clint related the information she'd given him, Kevin's name, age, even his social security number, and the description of the car. And then the description of her abduction and mistreatment. Brief though the account was, she found it painful to listen to. And even though she had been the victim, she could hardly believe it. It sounded so different coming out of Clint's mouth.

Micah took the pad from Clint and turned to a fresh sheet. "Some of this can go in the record. I'll need it to put out a BOLO." But even as he started to write, he paused and looked at Kay. "Not your name. We don't need *your* name now, okay? Nor do I need to tell anyone where you are. But he already knows you escaped in these parts so that won't tell him anything he doesn't know."

"Thank you."

Micah finished writing down the information, then ripped the sheet off the pad. "I can get this out right away. I'm going out to the car to get my camera, so I can take some pictures of you. You probably won't want me to see everything, but the fresher the photos are, the better, and my camera is time and date stamped. It's evidence, all right?"

She nodded, compressing her lips. "Okay." This was going to be so humiliating. Somehow, displaying her wounds seemed like an admission of her own failures.

Micah's face gentled. "If I could get a female deputy out here, I would. Maybe after the wind dies down. But right now it's just me, and we don't need lawyers arguing about whether those bruises were too old to have occurred during the kidnapping."

She hadn't thought about that, but she could see his point. From somewhere she found a bit of resolve. "Okay," she said again. If she had to face Kevin down in a courtroom again, she didn't want to be accused of lying, like last time. Or, if she *was* accused of it, she wanted proof that she wasn't.

She put her hand to her head as Micah rose and went to get his camera.

"Headache?" Clint asked immediately.

"No. I don't know. I just can't seem to get my footing. It's like things are changing so fast."

"When we've been through a really bad time, it's harder to adjust to changes for a while."

"Maybe." But it was even harder to let go of her fear. "I don't really know how to relax anymore," she blurted with sudden realization.

"I know that feeling all too well. It takes time, a lot of time, to realize you can climb down from the ceiling safely."

She supposed he would know. But then Micah came back in with the camera, and she faced more humiliation. However, he didn't ask for much. He squatted right in front of her.

"I'm going to take pictures of your face," he said gently. "Just your face. If it's hard to move, say so, and I'll do all the moving."

"I think I can do it."

He started snapping. The flash was on, of course, which made her keep blinking, but since this wasn't a fashion shoot, she didn't think it mattered. He must have taken a dozen photos of her face from different angles before he said, "Anything else you feel comfortable showing me?"

"Her back," Clint said.

She started to protest, but he spoke first. "Kay, we can get your back without offending your modesty. I'll help."

So she stood up, away from the furniture, and let Clint pull up the back of the sweatshirt until her entire back and shoulders were revealed while she clutched the front securely to her breasts.

"Well, hell," Micah said again, and the flashes started. "Any more like that?"

"All over her," Clint said. "But I think you've got the worst ones." He let the sweatshirt fall back into place.

"Make a note of the others," Micah suggested. "I'll get Sara out here tomorrow, assuming we've finished rescuing fools."

Kay made her way back to the couch and sat, resting her face in her hands again, at least as much as she could without making it hurt worse. Not that she didn't hurt all over, but the wound to her face seemed to dominate her awareness much more than her back or the rest of her.

Micah stayed only a few more minutes, then remarked that he had to get on to other things. Kay noticed that Clint followed him out onto the porch, brutal as the weather was, and the two men stood talking for a couple of minutes.

But she was past caring what they might be discussing. Fatigue was washing over her in waves again, and she didn't have the energy to fight it. She reached for the quilt, moving gingerly, and pulled it up over herself as she tried to burrow into the couch as if it were a private cave.

Enough, she thought. Enough.

Silent tears spilled down her face, but she hardly noticed them as she hid from the world and quickly slipped into sleep. Sleep, it seemed, was her last refuge.

Outside, Clint had more important matters on his mind. "I think this Kevin guy may have seen me pick her up along the road. A car came by as I was carrying her to my truck, and it slowed down. I thought at the time it was someone heading up to the Rivers place, but when she gave me the description of the car, I started to wonder. I didn't take all that good a look. We were getting into whiteout conditions."

Micah rocked a bit on his heels. Snow whirled like tiny tornadoes just beyond the porch, and some of it blew into their faces, stinging. "Not good. You want someone out here?"

"You can't spare anybody right now. Besides, I can keep her safe in the house."

"Yeah." Micah rubbed his chin. "That sumbitch probably won't be trying to get around in this weather anyway. All right, I'll get everyone on alert. If we're lucky, he's stuck in a snowbank somewhere."

"We can hope." But Clint wasn't the hopeful type. He'd had too much experience with Murphy's law. He always prepared for the worst.

"Do you have everything you need? Food? Fuel?"

"Do you need to ask?"

Micah chuckled. "No, I guess not. We come from the same school." He started to step off the porch, then looked back. "You know, I could take her to my place."

Clint knew exactly what he meant. Micah understood his need for solitude, at one time had even shared it.

"No," he said. "No. I took this one on, and I'm not pushing it off on anybody else. Besides, it could put your family at risk, and you can't be there round the clock."

Micah gave a nod of acknowledgment, then waded through the snow to his truck. With a wave, he headed out.

Clint stood outside in the biting wind and snow awhile longer, listening to the fading sound of the deputy's engine. The wind was fast filling in the gap left by the plow.

The world could be such a sorry place. Enough to make a man feel ashamed of being human. But not always. He might find his comfort in the basic innocence of nature. What could be purer than a world covered in fresh snow? But even as he looked out into the wrath of nature, he knew life-and-death struggles were going on all around him. The difference was most of those struggles weren't about power, just survival.

So what did that leave a man? Atonement. Basic atonement.

And a small part of his atonement was waiting right inside his living room.

Chapter 5

Kay awoke from a miserable sleep in which both the pains in her body and nightmares had disturbed her. As her eyes opened, she was surprised to see a propane lantern on the coffee table, providing the only light in the room except for the fireplace.

Away from the light, in the darker corners, the firelight made shadows dance and flicker. She turned her head and saw Clint in his easy chair, a shadowed figure himself.

"The power went out," he said when he saw her wake.

Since she could still hear the wind keening like a banshee, she had a pretty good idea why. "Oh." She struggled with the quilt she had managed to tangle all around herself until she could sit up a little higher.

"Need anything?" he asked. "We're pretty much okay, except we won't have running water until the power comes back on. I've got enough stashed for drinking and cooking, but I can't offer that shower right now."

"That's okay." What else could she say? It was only now, anyway, as her injuries began to mend, that she noticed how grimy she felt. Still, she could stand another few hours.

"I was thinking, though, that if we don't get power back soon, I can heat up some water and make you a bath. A small bath, but I can do it."

"That's kind of you, but maybe we better save the water." She was touched by his caring.

"Well, I don't imagine you got the chance to clean up during your abduction and I know how important that can be psychologically."

She tried to smile, but mostly she was surprised by how much he seemed to understand. Understanding had been lacking in a lot of her life. For the first time since he had found her, she felt a flicker of real warmth toward him.

He stood. "Do you need something to drink?"

"I'm fine right now."

"Okay. I'm going to go out and walk around a bit, make sure the wind isn't doing any damage. Shouldn't take me long."

She nodded, but her instant response wasn't exactly positive. Logically it made sense that he would want to look for wind damage, but emotionally she felt terrified that he might really be looking for something—some*one*—else.

Stop it, she told herself. There was no reason on earth to think that Kevin could possibly know she was here, or that Clint would be worried about it.

But long conditioning refused to let her relax. Fear seemed to have engraved itself on her very being.

She listened as he pulled on his outerwear to go out and face the furious elements. Then the door slammed and she was alone, and for the first time in a very long time, being alone didn't feel safe.

God, she was a mess. And getting messier by the moment, it seemed. After living in survival mode, always looking over her shoulder, it seemed that even the hint of safety had shattered her coping mechanisms.

She couldn't help it. She sat up completely, putting her feet on the floor, then waited tensely. Kevin had stripped her of her last sense of security, even self-deluded security.

She tried to think about Clint instead. An enigma, she decided, with a pockmarked soul. Good at heart, but damaged. Badly damaged. Like her. God knew what wounds *he* carried, and he didn't seem likely to tell her.

But even in the midst of her own selfish fear, she could feel a twinge of genuine sympathy for him. Just from occasional things he'd said, she suspected that he'd put himself in his hermitage less from general disgust with people than from disgust from himself.

But maybe she was reading too much into things. Maybe he'd meant exactly what he'd said about being fed up with selfish people. Even if that were true, she didn't believe that was the sum of it. The man had a side he kept showing in spite of himself, a generous side enhanced by a strong sense of duty.

And he was protective. Imagine him understanding her unwillingness to expose her wounds to Micah. Almost as if he understood that they were more than just external bruises but a mark of her shame. And then his thoughtfulness in the way he had helped preserve her modesty while revealing her back and shoulders to the camera.

No, he might be trying to turn into stone. He might think he'd looked into the face of Medusa and was now just rock. But that wasn't true. Not at all. No one with a heart of stone would have cared for her the way he had.

She almost gasped when he came back in. Instinct made her turn sharply toward the door, to be sure it was him, and she almost groaned as she rediscovered all her bruises. "Oh God," she whispered as the wave of agony passed through her.

He never paused to drop his jacket or kick off his boots. He came shooting over to her like a bullet and squatted in front of her. "What's wrong?"

She had to struggle to get her breath back. Each time she inhaled, it hurt again. "I just moved wrong," she gasped finally. "I think my ribs may be bruised."

"I wouldn't be surprised. How bad does it hurt?"

"It's going away."

"You're really going to have to consider seeing a doctor as soon as we can get out of here."

"I'll be *fine*." She sounded angry, but she was actually terrified by the thought. If she saw a doctor, another person would know she was here. And how the hell would she pay for it, anyway?

He remained squatting in front of her as snow began to melt off his jacket and boots. "Okay," he said finally.

"Okay?"

He gave her a crooked smile. "There's no point in having this fight right now, when all I could do is get us stuck in the snow."

"Oh." In spite of herself, one corner of her mouth lifted. "Yeah, it would be stupid to argue now."

"We'll revisit this in the morning." He rose and went to remove his outerwear by the door. Then he fetched a ragged towel and mopped the small puddles he'd left on the floor.

"How is it out there?" she asked, desperate for the distraction. Breathing was getting easier, and slowly she sank back against the pillows.

"Frankly? Awful. It may have stopped snowing, but you couldn't prove it by me. The wind is a killer. It's a good day for staying in your lair and sitting by the fire."

"Sounds like it." And but for him, she would be lying under a snow blanket, probably until spring, when someone found her and named her Jane Doe. She squeezed her eyes closed for a minute, seeking some kind of balance internally. No point in thinking like that. It hadn't happened. Instead, she was warm and safe.

For now.

"Pain?" he asked.

She opened her eyes and found him in his chair again. "No, not really. Just wrestling with demons."

"Sometimes it helps to call a time-out."

"I'm still trying to find a way to do that."

"It can take a while." He drummed his fingers briefly on the arm of his chair. "I'm not much of a distraction," he finally said. "I don't talk much. Hell, I even quit playing poker, not that it's much fun with only two players."

"Trust me, I'm not complaining. You've done more for me than most people ever have."

He shook his head. "I've done very little. Don't build me up into something I'm not."

Surprise washed away her other thoughts. Could he really feel that way? Even cops who were supposed to protect her had done less than this man, especially when measured against his obvious preference for solitude. "I think you underrate yourself."

"No, I've just taken a good hard look at myself."

"But…" She stopped. Arguing about the kind of man he was wouldn't help anything at all. It might even anger him. And he certainly wouldn't listen to her, because she didn't really know him. "I'm grateful to you. Very grateful."

"Probably," he acknowledged. "And probably more than I deserve. Are you getting hungry?"

She recognized the quick change in subject as a warning and let it lie. He didn't think he deserved her gratitude. God, talk about a pair of wounded souls!

"I run by my internal clock these days," he went on, "and I could use a sandwich. Tuna sound good?"

"It sounds great."

He was up and out of that chair as if he'd just been released from Old Sparky.

She watched his back as he walked toward the kitchen and felt a quiver of interest in him as a man, the first sexual impulse she'd felt since Kevin had beaten her the first time.

No, she warned herself. Don't let that happen. No men. Ever again. And certainly not one who preferred living alone. That was borrowing trouble, and she already had enough of that on her tail.

But apparently there was a part of her that hadn't died in the assaults of the last three years, a part that still wanted to believe in happily-ever-after and a man who could make her feel good things again.

Stupid. All a bunch of myths, as well she ought to know. In the end, she could rely on no one but herself for her happiness and safety.

But sometimes logic was a cold companion, and the heart refused to be silenced. Her dreams might lie shattered around her, but they still had some life.

The question, really, was whether it was worth trying to put them back together again.

No, she decided. It would be too dangerous. Far too dangerous to ever risk herself again.

Clint returned with a couple of plates and napkins. He placed one plate on the coffee table in front of her, the other beside his chair. He disappeared for a minute into the kitchen again and returned with two glasses of ginger ale.

"Thank you," Kay said.

"Eat up, and if you want more, there's plenty."

Tuna on rye. A lot of tuna. She doubted she would be able to eat all of one sandwich, let alone another. "Oh, this is good," she said after she had savored a bite.

He gave her his almost-smile. "I eat a lot of tuna. If I didn't make it well, I would be an unhappy, hungry man."

A little laugh escaped her, a small one in deference to her bruised ribs. "What's that about necessity?"

"The mother of all invention."

"Yeah."

His smile deepened a shade. "You're going to be all right, you know."

She paused, a mix of feelings flooding her. "How can you know that?"

"Because you've got spunk."

That warmed her. She wasn't sure he was right, but the compliment warmed her anyway. What had she done, after all, except what she'd *had* to do? She sipped her ginger ale and took another bite of her sandwich.

"So what do you do?" she asked him.

"I'm a writer."

"What kind?"

He shrugged. "I do some action-adventure novels, mostly for fun. It's a way to pay bills. Then I write other stuff."

"What kind of stuff?"

He hesitated. "I write a lot about ethics."

"Really?" That piqued her attention. "Do you mean papers or articles or what?"

"I've written a number of journal articles, and one book on what they call 'Just War Theory.' Basically, discussing what situations can justify fighting a war."

She forgot her sandwich and looked at him with amazement. "I thought only professors did that kind of stuff."

"Well, a few of us out here don't teach, we just think too much."

It sounded almost like he was joking, but she couldn't be sure. "I wasn't putting you down, I'm just kind of amazed."

"Yeah, me and Thoreau. Backwoods philosophers."

"But you must need a lot of education to get to the point where you can write journal articles the way you do."

"Over the years, when I was in the military, I took a lot of classes. Somehow they eventually added up to a PhD."

"Oh, wow." She stared at him, impressed.

He waved a dismissive hand. "No biggie. The military pushes education. They make it easy to take classes."

"But you went all the way."

He shook his head. "It was an escape."

She longed to ask how that could be. "Maybe I'll get to college eventually."

He nodded. "I believe you will."

She wished she could be as certain.

"Any idea what you'd like to study?"

She shook her head. "Not yet. I've thought about things like being a nurse, but I don't know if I could pass all the classes."

"Well, college is great, especially the first couple of years. They give you an opportunity to try on all kinds of things for size. You'll find what you like."

"I hope so. I don't mind waiting tables at all, but I have so many questions about things. And as time passes, I seem to get more curious."

"Curiosity is good."

"So this book you wrote—*Just War Theory*? What is that?"

"It's a lot of philosophical thinking about what can morally justify war. People have been asking and trying to answer that question for a long time. People with consciences, anyway."

"And your book?"

"Well, I did the usual overview, then put my own spin on some of it."

She sensed she wouldn't be able to understand if she pressed him any further. "I hope someday I'll know enough so I can read it."

"It's dry, unless that's your thing."

"Was it successful?"

"That depends on what you mean by success. It didn't make me rich. But it's being used in a number of colleges and universities."

"That's success."

"Getting read is success."

She smiled and reached for her sandwich again. "I guess so. Being ignored would be awful."

"In this business, it would be a death knell. Much better to annoy people."

"Really? Why?"

"Because it stimulates discussion. Nothing makes me happier than when my e-mail box gets full because a new semester has begun and a bunch of people want to argue with me."

"I honestly can't imagine that. I think it would intimidate me."

"It makes me rub my hands with glee."

She laughed, then winced. "I don't think that's me."

"Maybe not. We're all different."

And he was definitely a puzzle. A hermit who liked to argue with people. By e-mail. So he hadn't totally cut himself off, he'd just set up barriers. High ones, evidently, ones that guarded him from everything except intellectual interaction.

She could understand that. It would be nice if her world would resolve into that kind of neatness.

But not *exactly* that kind of neatness. She didn't think she was built to live alone and intellectualize things.

Before Kevin, she'd always had a large circle of friends she liked spending time with. After Kevin, that first time, when she had thought she was safe again, she'd rebuilt her circle.

Then she had learned to avoid connections, because every time Kevin found her again, she had to give them up. It was painful to have to run again, but even more so if she had to leave behind people she cared about.

She invested nothing of herself in life anymore, nothing beyond trying to get by. So how was she different from Clint?

She lost her taste for the sandwich and slipped the plate back onto the table, wincing as she did so.

"Full?" he asked.

"Full enough." Full enough of *everything,* including her own misery.

"You know," he said slowly, "I can heat up that water and you could soak a bit. It might help with the aches and pains."

"But I don't want to waste your water. We don't know how long this might go on."

He shrugged. "If worse comes to worse, I can melt plenty of snow in front of the fire. It's not like we're in the middle of the desert."

She had to smile at that. "I guess not."

"So let me make you a bath. You need to soak out some of the soreness."

She had to admit that sounded good. "If you wouldn't mind?"

"Lady, I'd rather be busy any day than staring at the walls. I can't even work right now with the power out."

"Then I'd love a bath."

"Consider it done as soon as I'm through eating."

"Thank you."

He was as good as his word. Astonishment took her when she saw the number of huge pots he had. "Do you cook for an army or something?"

"You can never have too many pots for an emergency. I wouldn't cook in these, they're too thin, but they're great for boiling water."

Which he managed to do in surprisingly short order by using both the propane stove and the fireplace. When he at last called her to the bathroom, steam was rising from the tub. A couple of candles burned on the rim, safely out of the way, shedding extra light to compensate for the thin gray daylight that came through the single window.

"It's too hot, obviously, but I'm going to add cold water now. You tell me when the temperature's right."

So she sat on the toilet beside the tub while he added cold water, then stuck her finger in to test. Finally she said, "It's probably just about right now."

"Okay. I'll leave it there, then. I'll keep another pot on the stove in case you want a reheat." He paused. "By the way, if you want more hot water, don't be too modest to ask. I can walk in here backward."

He also brought her a fresh set of sweats, blue this time, and a couple of clean towels. Then he set a bottle on the edge of the tub. "Shampoo, if you want it. I don't have any of those fancy bath salts, though. Sorry."

She was touched that he would even think of such a thing. "I don't use them anyway."

"If you need anything at all, just call me."

Her first thought as he closed the door behind him was that she hoped she didn't have to call him for anything. Then she remembered that he had redressed her after finding her. It wasn't like she had anything he hadn't already seen, even if she didn't remember the moment.

Moving gingerly, she shed the sweats she wore, steadied herself with a hand on the side of the tub and eased into the water. It was actually a bit too hot, but she didn't care. She would get used to it quickly enough, and the hope of easing some of her aches overrode everything else, even the desire to be clean again.

She didn't even try to move once she had settled into the water. It rose to her neck if she sank just a little, and she laid her head back against a towel, closed her eyes and let the heat do its work. God, it was heaven.

When was the last time she'd felt safe enough to indulge in such a luxury? She couldn't remember. For a long time now she'd taken showers, hurrying through them. Five minutes max, because she couldn't forget how vulnerable she was when bathing. That was another legacy of Kevin. When you never knew when you were going to need to run, you didn't let yourself get into a situation where you couldn't get away quickly.

Her eyes flew open as ice rattled against the frosted glass window over the tub. Nothing out there. Nothing. She was safe, she reminded herself. Clint was just outside that door, near enough to hear a single cry. Nasty as Kevin could be, she doubted he could stand up for long to Clint. Nor could he get her very far in this storm.

No, she was safe. She willed her body to recognize that and relax again. It would have been so nice to nod off right now, but an acute awareness of her nakedness, and thus her vulnerability, wouldn't allow her.

She wondered if she would ever get past this constant insecurity and fear. Maybe, if Kevin went to prison for twenty years, then after a few years she could relax again.

But that kind of security was something she could only dream of now; it was nothing she could really believe in. Not yet.

There was a knock on the door, and she started, realizing the bath had begun to go cold. She must have nodded off right in the middle of thinking about her own fear.

"Kay? Are you all right?"

"I guess I fell asleep."

"That's good. Need more hot water?"

She considered it. "No, thanks. I'm just going to wash fast and get out of here." Because the fears that lurked in the corners of her mind were trying to bite again, insisting that she remember she was *never* safe. Not even now.

"Okay. Holler if you need help."

The heat had done its job, though, and she found it easy enough to wash herself with a bar of soap and a washcloth. Then she submerged her head to wet her hair and stifled groans as she shampooed. She was feeling better, yes, but not perfect.

Finally she submerged her head one more time and ran her fingers through her hair, working the shampoo out.

No, not perfect, but much better. With a toe, she pulled the plug and let the water start to drain.

She was feeling a whole lot better by the time she reached for the side of the tub and realized she couldn't get out.

Getting in had been a lot easier than trying to lever herself up. Dammit! Her arms and sides screamed at the effort of trying to lift herself. Now what?

She tried again, but the pain only got worse. And now she was shaking and getting cold. Oh, this wasn't fair!

But what the hell was fair in life? Not a damn thing.

She gave it one more try, and a cry escaped her as her muscles and ribs rebelled.

"Kay? *Kay?*"

She pressed her forehead to the edge of the tub, mad at her own helplessness, embarrassed beyond belief, ashamed by her weakness and hating this situation. Hot tears stung her eyes.

"Kay?"

The door opened, and she knew what he saw. A black-and-blue woman, naked, clinging to the side of a tub she couldn't even climb out of. Why couldn't she have just died out there in the snow? Then it would have been all over. No more pain, no more shame, no more embarrassment...

"Ah, lady," he breathed, and she realized with horror that his mouth was right beside her ear. "Hold on," he murmured. "I'll get you out of there."

To her infinite relief, she felt towels settle over her body, felt him tuck them around her from her shoulders to her knees.

"It's okay," he said. "Hold on just another second."

Her heavy wet hair was lifted from her shoulders, and she felt him wrap another towel around her head.

"Now," he said gently, "I'm going to lift you as carefully as I can. I can't guarantee we won't lose a towel, but I'll try. Okay?"

"Okay," she said, hating herself, fighting down those awful, hot, helpless tears. "I'm sorry."

"Don't be sorry. No need. Every single person on this earth needs help sometimes."

She kept her eyes tightly closed as his arms worked their way gently around her. As she had feared, the towels slipped a bit and his callused hand met the smooth skin of her hip. He stopped at once and struggled to pull the towel back over her.

"Don't worry about it," she whispered finally. "Nothing you haven't seen anyway." And maybe humiliation would kill her right now.

"Nicer than most I've seen by far."

She realized he was trying to joke, probably to make her more comfortable. She bit her lip as he began to lift her. Inevitably his arms and hands found some of her bruises, and she caught her breath more than once.

But by and large the towels stayed in place, even if his skin did keep brushing hers. At least he was wearing long sleeves.

She expected him to set her on her feet, at which point her stupid modesty would fall with the towels to the floor, but he surprised her. Moving carefully, he carried her back into the living room and laid her on the couch. An instant later, the quilt settled over her.

"I'll get the sweats," he said. "Then I'll leave you to dress."

"Thank you." Finally she opened her eyes and watched as he went back to the bathroom. He returned quickly with the clothing and placed it on the coffee table. When she dared to glance at his face, her heart sank.

The stone facade had returned, as impenetrable as when she had first seen him. Worse, he wouldn't even look at her. She must repulse him. Damn, that hurt as much as anything.

She didn't know what kind of approval she was seeking from this man, but it sure didn't help to feel that she was just an ugly burden he wanted to be rid of.

But was that fair? He'd been so kind. She couldn't blame him if he found all her bruises repugnant, and found her repellant for not having been able to stand up to Kevin. Not when she felt that way herself.

"Let me know when you're done." And then he disappeared into the back of the cabin.

Stifling further groans for fear he would come riding to her rescue again, she managed to sit up and work the towels over the parts of her that were still wet. Like a brand, the remembered warmth of his hand seemed to remain on her hip. The touch, she realized with a kind of wonder, hadn't repulsed her, or made her want to flee.

That alone marked a major change in her course. Since Kevin, she had hated to be touched in any way. *Any* way. Thoughtfully, she put her hand over the spot and pressed. That accidental touch had actually felt *good*.

Which left her with something to think about as she worked her way into the sweat suit and tried to roll up the legs so she wouldn't trip on them.

"Clint? I'm decent."

He returned at once to gather up the towels, except for the one wrapped haphazardly around her head. He paused, looking at her, and seemed almost hesitant.

"Do you," he finally asked, "need help with your hair?"

She wanted to tell him no, to just let it be, because that would have been her instinctive response before. But something had changed. Something had shifted, and she couldn't even tell what had happened.

"Would you mind?" she asked just as hesitantly.

"No." Short and brief. "Hold on a second."

He took the other towels away, and then a couple of seconds later he returned with a fresh towel and a comb.

"Sorry I don't have a brush," he said, indicating his short hair with a gesture. "I'll be careful."

He walked behind the sofa and spread the dry towel over her shoulders. Only then did he remove the damp one from her hair. She felt the heavy weight fall to her shoulders.

"Now lean back until you're comfortable."

She followed directions, feeling almost as if she was split in two, the old Kay watching in amazement as the new Kay let a man comb her hair.

He was almost unbelievably gentle. When he found a knot, he worked it carefully, never yanking.

"Where'd you learn to comb hair?" she asked finally.

"Horses," he said, with something like a short laugh. "Manes tangle. Your hair's a lot finer, though."

"It tangles really badly."

"Not that badly." He kept working, taking his time, taking it easy with her. She actually enjoyed his attention and could scarcely believe it.

"So," she asked after a few more minutes, "do you have horses?"

"I own a couple, but I have a friend take them over the winter. I like to ride a lot, but not in the winter, so he sees to it they get plenty of exercise."

"Sounds like a good friend."

"He is. It's also his business, so I don't have to feel bad about stabling them with him. He's really good with them. They come back every spring fat and happy and a pleasure to ride. I don't have his touch, so every summer I manage to work some kinks into them, and every winter he irons them out."

She laughed a little. "What kind of kinks?"

"Oh, they get a little stubborn. A bit fussy. Gideon's tried to figure out what I do wrong, but so far he just fixes things and can't tell me where I mess up."

"So he knows what to do right but can't tell you how to do it right, too? That's weird."

His hands stopped combing, just briefly, then resumed their work. "Well, actually, he does tell me something."

"What's that?"

"He keeps saying, 'Clint, you just gotta open your heart to those mares.' Damned if I know what he means."

Oh, Kay thought with a pang, that made *so* much sense. And it was a pity he didn't understand. Or maybe he didn't want to understand. She could sure grasp not wanting to give heart-space to someone or something.

"There you go," he said. "I have a rubber band if you want it off your shoulders until it dries."

"Thanks, it's fine. The fire should dry it fast." And she was so sorry he was done combing. The attention had touched her in ways little had in a long time.

"Feel better?" he asked.

"Tons. It's so nice to be clean again."

"Yup, that helps a lot."

No doubt he spoke from experience, especially since he sounded so certain, but she didn't feel she could ask.

After he'd cleaned up the mess from her bath, he brought her another mug of coffee. "Still no power," he remarked. "I'd lay odds at this point it'll be out all night."

"Well, I certainly feel cozy enough."

He gave her that half-smile again, the one that didn't quite crack the stone. He'd pulled back again from the place they'd nearly reached before her bath. She relaxed a little more, glad that the barriers were back in place. She didn't want the intimacy they'd shared because of her bath and hair any more than he did.

Or so she told herself. But she wasn't quite believing it anymore.

And that scared her as much as the lurking threat of Kevin.

Chapter 6

As soon as he could think of a good excuse and didn't think it was too soon, Clint announced he was going back out to check for wind damage.

Stepping out into the icy blow both shocked him and relieved him after the heat in the cabin. And not just the heat from the fire.

Crap. It was the mildest cuss word in his vocabulary, but he settled for it largely because he was making a strenuous effort to avoid using language that might singe Kay's ears. For a woman who'd been through all that she had, there seemed to be an innocence at her core. Maybe a kind of naiveté. Although he had to admit his own blighted soul hardly provided a good measuring stick by which to gauge anyone else.

The blowing snow that stung his skin, along with the wind that could suck the life out of him in a matter of minutes if he shucked his jacket, at least brought some balance back.

He was a monster. He was the bad guy. He was Kay's worst nightmare, even if he was pretending to be her savior. What Kevin had done to her was nothing compared to the things he himself was capable of. Things he'd done. Things he'd had to do.

Although *had* was a word choice he still wasn't comfortable with. Yeah, he'd done what was necessary to follow his orders and complete his missions. At the time, that had seemed to be enough. It was only later, during the dark night of the soul, that an honest man had to ask himself why he'd allowed himself to be twisted to such ends.

Why the hell he hadn't just drawn a line in the sand and said "No." Because at some point, you had to take responsibility for your actions.

Yeah, as he'd said to her, everyone did the best they could at the time, but that rang hollow in some deep interior place. For him, at any rate, which was why his book on Just War Theory set off so many negative reactions. Because he didn't just write about the responsibility of nations, he wrote about the responsibility of *individuals*. Like himself.

He cussed again, letting out a stream of colorful words in several languages, and kicked at the snow as if he could release some of his spleen on nature.

Okay, so he'd had to help the woman. No escaping that. But *desire* her? God almighty, she was wounded, damaged, frightened—and justifiably so. What the hell was wrong with him, that he could find her so attractive? And he didn't want to blame it on being alone too long, didn't want to blame normal male urges, none of that stuff, because in the end, *he* was responsible for everything he felt and said.

That was why he had a brain. To turn away from temptations that might condemn him to an even deeper circle of hell.

He bent and scooped up snow in both bare hands, squeezing it so hard some of it melted and water ran between his fingers. He held it until his hands turned numb, then dropped it.

Control. That was all it took, and he'd been working on his self-control for a long time. It ought to be strong enough to deal with this distraction.

Ought to be.

"Hah," he said, the word snatched away by the angry wind. Sharing his cabin with that woman was proving to be a circle of hell all its own, because the beast in him was waking, the beast with the primal urges.

Turning suddenly, he stalked around the cabin, making one last check, then re-entered. Kay sat up quickly, then relaxed when she saw him.

"Don't relax," he said shortly. Her eyes widened. Good.

He kicked off his boots and dumped his jacket. Then he went to sit in his chair, facing her tensely across the coffee table.

"What's wrong?" she asked.

"Me."

"Are you sick?"

"Sicker than you know." He closed his eyes, then decided to go ahead and do it, just do it. He needed her to look at him with the fear he deserved. It would help keep him in line.

"I'm going to tell you something," he said finally.

"I'm listening."

"You should be very afraid of me." He heard her gasp.

Then, her voice, hesitant, "Why?"

He opened his eyes, sure the bottomless abyss of his soul must show there. He sure hoped it did. "Because I'm a monster.

"What do you mean?"

"You have no idea what I'm capable of. I make Kevin look like a tyro. I'm a trained killing machine. I've maimed, I've terrorized and I've killed. The fact that it was my job is no excuse. I *know* what I'm capable of, and Kevin doesn't even begin to approach my capacity for evil."

Her blue eyes had grown huge, but he was annoyed to see that she didn't shrink back.

He leaned forward. "Do you think," he asked in a low voice, "that we get to check our consciences at the door and never accept responsibility for the things we do under color of war?"

"I...never thought about it."

"Most people don't. Why should they? They never have to walk into hell. But those of us who have...we're never the same again. That's why so many vets have all kinds of psychological problems, you know. Because society breaks the contract."

"What contract?"

"The one that says 'We sent you. Do this in our name, and we waive all the usual moral rules for you.' Which implies a responsibility shared among all of society, don't you think?"

She nodded, still wide-eyed.

"They promise us an absolution they can't give. Whether they give us parades or put flashy bumper stickers on their cars, tie yellow ribbons on things or call us heroes, they *cannot* give us absolution because it's not theirs to give." He ran his fingers impatiently through his short hair.

"So they say, 'Go do this in our names, and we'll call you heroes.' But what they really mean is, 'Go out and fight for us, do horrible things in our name, drop your civilized veneer and then come home and act like it never happened. Act like *we* aren't responsible for what we asked you to do. And sure as hell don't ever tell us about it.'"

"Oh, Clint…"

He brushed aside the soft sounds of sympathy. "But there's another part, too. Those of us who do the dirty work not only have to live with it, but we have to accept the responsibility for having done it. We don't get to squeeze out of it. We see it every time we close our eyes. And we have to ask ourselves why we just didn't say no."

"How could you have said no? I mean…you don't know what it's going to be like until it's too late."

"Well, that's the trick, you see. They found out during the Second World War that men are actually opposed to killing each other. Only one in four soldiers in battle actually fired their guns."

"Wow."

"Exactly. So they developed a gaming system. Haven't heard about that, have you? They train you on lifelike video games before you ever hit the field. You wouldn't believe how many soldiers I've heard say, 'It was just like a video game. Until afterward.' Afterward, when they start picking up the pieces of bodies. But by that time, you're in a kill-or-be-killed situation, which is all the push you need to cross the line. And then the next line. And the next. And then those lines will never exist again."

"No?"

"No. Because afterward you get pissed. And scared. And a whole bunch of other things that push you past the boundaries of basic morality. Your buddies are dead or maimed. You're being attacked. And you stop thinking, because you can't afford to think. Not until much later."

At least this time she didn't try to say anything.

"And some of us lucky ones get extra training, extra brainwashing, and get sent into situations where we do things the movies try to clean up and make look heroic. But believe me, there's no heroism in it. You get there one step at a time, and once you're in it, there's no way out. So you just do it. Mostly because if you don't, your buddies could pay for it. No soldier ever fought for a flag, or for mom and apple pie. No, we fight for the guy beside us."

She closed her eyes for a moment, then opened them. She ought to be avoiding his gaze, but she wasn't. Was she crazy?

"I'm so sorry," she whispered. "So, so sorry."

A kind of frustration filled him. "Don't you get it, Kay? I'm telling you I'm a monster."

"I don't think a monster would be telling me all this with such obvious self-loathing."

He swore, and this time he didn't spare her ears. Worse, she didn't even flinch.

No, instead she showed a spark of the fire that had been missing since he found her, a fire he'd been sure must have been there all along, because she had *survived*.

"You need to stop doing this to yourself," she said hotly. "The world is full of people who've been pushed into the same situation. That doesn't make any of you monsters."

"No? Then what the hell does it make us?"

"People," she said flatly. "Ordinary people. People shaped by extraordinary circumstances. Do you think I've never thought of slipping a knife between Kevin's ribs? Do you think I've never fantasized about killing him? Oh, I've planned it a dozen ways. What does that make *me?* Another monster?"

"*You* didn't do it."

"Mostly from lack of opportunity." She looked down and picked at a bit of fuzz on the sweatshirt she wore. "I plan to do it if he comes after me again. I want to get a gun."

Something inside him cracked a bit, a painful crack. "Don't do that," he said hoarsely.

"Why not? I can't keep living like this."

"You won't want to live with yourself afterward. Trust me on that. You will *hate* yourself. Let someone else take care of it."

"Who else? No one else has taken care of it except that time he went to jail, and then he just came back."

"I'll do it then, dammit!"

"No!" She almost screamed the word at him. "No. You have enough to deal with. Do you think I want Kevin on your conscience, too?"

That crack inside him became wider, deeper, and so painful he could have ripped the cabin apart with his bare hands. "Don't trust me," he said again, his chest so tight he could barely squeeze the words out. "Don't ever, ever trust me."

"I already trust you."

"Don't. You don't begin to understand the rage I live with. I've seen some of my buddies, some of the best people in the world, take it out on their wives and kids. *I am not to be trusted.* Under any circumstances. This demon inside me could burst out at any moment."

She bit her lower lip and looked down, pulling another bit of lint free, then looked up and met his eyes again. "I'll take my chances."

He swore and jumped up from his chair, unable to hold still another minute. He paced the room like a panther on the prowl. He hoped she could see the building danger in him, hoped that she would just shut up and let him walk it off.

Damn, he wanted to pound his fist into a wall, but he wasn't idiot enough to break his own hand just to break the cycle of his thoughts. Finally he came to a halt as far as he could get from her without leaving the room, faced the wall and pressed his forehead to the rough wood. He breathed deeply, leashing the monster again. Because he had to. Because he needed to. Because every time he leashed the damn thing, it got a tiny bit easier.

He hoped letting it out had scared her good. For her own protection. But now he had to put the monster back in its cage.

Then, freezing him in place, he felt a touch on his forearm.

"Clint," she said softly. "Clint…"

It was too late. Turning, he wrapped her in his arms and pulled her tightly to him, crushing her mouth beneath his.

Because, heaven help him, he needed the human touch. The human warmth. The feeling that he was still, somewhere deep inside, good enough for someone.

She astonished him. After her first gasp and a helpless groan that barely penetrated his awareness—that almost, but not quite, reminded him that she hurt all over—she raised her arms and wrapped them tightly around his neck.

As if she never wanted to let go.

Oh, God, the crack grew even wider, the pain flooding him, and in an instant he became helpless before the need, the anguish, the hunger.

That helplessness shocked him back to his senses. He couldn't afford to lose control. Never again.

Struggling against needs that bound him more tightly than even her arms, he tore his mouth from hers, then forced her arms from around his neck. He pulled back, just a few inches, but enough for salvation.

Her eyes opened slowly, sleepily. Her mouth looked bruised now, too, and he hated himself.

"Clint…"

"I need to cool down. I'm going outside."

Something sad flickered across her face, but she nodded. He made himself wait just long enough to be sure she was able to get back to the couch.

Then he strode out into the storm he never should have come in from to begin with.

Idiot!

* * *

Kay didn't know what to do. She'd thought she had lost the ability to feel pain for anyone else. She'd thought she had put her softer emotions in as tightly locked a vault as possible, leaving her to live on a steady diet of fear and caution.

But now she discovered that she was still capable of feeling as much pain for another person as for herself. Maybe even more.

And the person she felt it for was out there in the storm, probably trying to put his demon back in its cage.

She had her own demon, but suddenly she felt it was nowhere near as bad as what Clint was dealing with. The amount of self-hatred he'd shown her had been frightening. For all she beat herself up about what she had done or hadn't done with Kevin, how she had failed herself and shamed herself by not being stronger, nothing she had been through could possibly compare with what Clint was going through right this very minute.

And she didn't know what she could do to help. That pained her, too. Here he was, taking care of her, promising her protection, and she couldn't do a thing for him. If anything, she seemed to be awakening the very things he was trying to put to sleep.

At that moment, if there hadn't been a storm outside, she would have fled just to spare him. Except that would spare him nothing, nothing at all. He would hate himself if she ran, hate himself even more if she got lost—or, worse, *caught*—out there.

God, the helplessness Kevin had made her feel didn't even come close to this.

Finally she couldn't stand sitting there thinking any longer. Biting her lip against the aches and pains, she stood and went into the kitchen. Maybe she could cook something for dinner. Something to show her appreciation for the way he'd taken care of her.

Just one little thing to tell him that he mattered, too.

"What are you doing?"

His voice startled her, and she turned as quickly as she could. She hadn't heard him come in, but now he stood in the kitchen doorway, filling it, and from what she could see by the dimming light of the propane lantern she'd carried in here with her, he didn't look exactly happy.

"Cooking," she said, hoping she sounded steadier than she suddenly felt.

"You shouldn't be doing this. You're still a mess. You could get hurt."

"I'm fine. It's not that strenuous. I found a can of clams, so I'm just making chowder."

He stepped in closer. "Smells good." He sounded grudging.

"It'll smell even better in a couple of hours." She reached for the cutting board to dump the last of the diced potatoes into the pot, but he snatched it before she could lift it and scraped the potatoes in for her.

"Don't forget your ribs."

"Thanks." She wanted to ask if he was feeling any better but decided that would be foolhardy. He was so close now that she could have reached out to touch him—*would* have done so, if it were up to her, because she yearned to re-establish the link they had been building, however warily. But that was all shattered now, she supposed. And there was no telling, given what had happened earlier, how he would react to her touch. "I prefer," she started, then had to clear her throat. "I prefer to make it with half and half, but milk will do. I'll just add a bit of butter for richness."

"I'm sure it'll be wonderful."

She tried a smile and was relieved when there seemed to be a slight softening in his face. Maybe he'd walked off some of his mood, although it wouldn't help except to postpone things. But sometimes, as she had learned, even a break would do.

"What can I do to help?" he asked.

"Find me a pot lid. I couldn't look in the lower cabinets, I'm afraid. And this needs to simmer for a while."

"You'll need to step back a bit."

She did, and he bent to pull a lid out of the cabinet beside the stove. He put it on the pot. "Anything else?"

"That's it for now."

He turned the lantern, which sat on a small island, and pumped it so that it burned brightly again. Then he looked at her. "You need to get back to the sofa, Kay. You're looking pale."

"How can you even tell in this light?" she asked a bit querulously, but her body was telling her the same thing. How long would it take to get her strength back? she wondered. She definitely felt shaky and suspected rubbery knees awaited right around the corner.

Without a word, he took her elbow gently and guided her back to the couch. So where had the monster gone?

Had he buried it temporarily in the snow outside? Probably. She was good at burying things sometimes, too.

After he saw her settled, he disappeared into the kitchen, only to return about ten minutes later with fresh coffee for both of them.

"Thanks." She accepted hers with pleasure. She'd thought about making a pot, but in a strange kitchen, feeling as she did right now, she'd opted to stick with something for dinner. Finding the coffee and then wondering how he preferred to make it had seemed like one task too many.

"The chowder will need to be stirred from time to time," she told him. "Just letting you know, in case I fall asleep again."

"I can do that."

She had not the least doubt that this man could do just about anything he put his mind to. That alone was intimidating. He was obviously extremely smart, and experienced in so many things. What did she have to say for herself? Very little. She could wait tables, she could run, she could even cook decently. Beyond that, she had no accomplishments to show for twenty-six years on this planet.

A sigh escaped her.

"Is something wrong?" he asked at once.

Some monster, she thought. His concern for her was overwhelming, and certainly more than she had known since her grandmother died. She decided to be blunt. "I was just thinking about how little I've accomplished with my life."

"That probably depends on how you're measuring it."

A little laugh escaped her, and her ribs twinged. "*Now* you sound like a professor. Or maybe a shrink."

"Shrinks are good. Some of them, anyway. They don't let us make excuses, they just tell us that we aren't doing as badly as we think, and while we're at it, maybe we need to change some things."

"You've been to one?"

"Extensively."

"Doesn't seem like he helped you much."

"I'm still here."

She almost winced at that, because of what it said about the parts of hell he'd visited in order to reach this point in his life. Suicide? It had crossed her mind a couple of times. She suspected it had crossed his even more.

"Well, what would a shrink tell me, then?" she challenged him.

"I don't know you well enough to even guess. But I'm fairly certain she would tell you to stop beating yourself up over the things Kevin did."

"And if I managed that?"

"That it's time to look for new ways of dealing with this problem."

"What ways?" The words burst out of her. "Don't you think I've tried?"

"I'm sure you have."

"Then what?"

He raised his hand, absently covering his lower face as he thought. "Shall I tell you what I can offer?"

"Sure." She doubted it was much, short of killing Kevin, and she'd been serious when she'd said she didn't want him to be responsible for that.

He dropped his hand. "If we don't put that sucker away for life, then I know some people who can get you a new identity. Everything, top to bottom. Impenetrable. That jerk would never find you again."

She felt her jaw drop a little. "Really? That's possible?"

"It's more than possible. People do it all the time. But the folks I know are experts who can do it all legally, and so well your new persona would be seamless."

For some reason she found that amazing. Yes, she knew about fake identity cards. In fact, as a waitress, she'd learned to look out for them. She knew some people changed their identities to escape a crime, but they often got caught anyway. And she didn't believe a thing she saw in the movies about how to hide under an alias. "How is that possible?"

"You need to know the right people in the right places. And I'm not talking about the underworld here."

"Fantastic," she whispered. "But how could I pay for it? It must be expensive."

"It would be free. A favor. But first, let's see if we really need to go that far. If we can get Kevin into a six-by-eight cell for life, none of that will be necessary."

"Maybe not." She sighed again, turning the possibilities around in her mind. "I could really be someone else?"

"If that's what you need. So let's say you could be someone else, Kay. What would you do with a truly fresh start?"

It still boggled her mind. "I...I don't know. I never thought about it."

"Well, think about it now. Because one way or another, before you leave this house, you're going to have a new life."

She almost shivered when she saw the determination in his eyes. This man was capable of things she could barely imagine, and she believed all the way to her bones that he accomplished *any* task he set for himself.

"I'd save up money and go to college," she said.

"I'd fix it so you could get financial aid. Scholarships and loans. No reason to wait. You'd have to work while you're in school, like most students, but you wouldn't have to save up first."

"That would be amazing."

"So what would you do with that gift? It's not one many of us get."

"I know that. I'd want…I'd want to help people somehow."

One corner of his mouth lifted. "There's a beautiful soul locked up inside all that fear."

"I don't know about that. It's just that…" She hesitated. "The places I've been, I'd want to make it easier for other people who are there, too. Kids in foster care. Battered women. I know what desperation is like."

He nodded. "Life hasn't crippled you yet."

That comment interested her. She turned it around, thinking about it, and finally said, "Maybe not."

"Definitely not," he said firmly. "You've been hobbled, but not crippled. Once we take care of that bastard, the sky's the limit for you."

Did he really mean that? How could he? As he said, he didn't know her very well. But still, she liked what he seemed to see in her, something beyond a terrified woman forever on the run. Not just a rabbit in perpetual flight from a fox. She smiled a little, liking the way that made her feel. Almost like an infusion of emotional strength. "Thank you."

"Just calling it the way I see it."

Moving with care, she pulled her legs up beneath her and sat cross-legged. Once she achieved the position, it felt good, moving stress points around and giving a break to some of the more painful spots.

But the best thing of all was that for the first time in a long time, she actually felt the stirrings of hope.

And all because of the stone-faced, self-confessed "monster" who sat across from her. Maybe *he* wasn't as crippled as he thought, either.

Chapter 7

The storm wound down overnight, bringing a morning that sparkled with brilliant sunlight. The power still hadn't come back on, though, although it hadn't been terribly missed. They'd managed just fine without it. The fire had kept the living room warm, and the propane stove in the kitchen made it possible to cook and make hot beverages. What more did you need? Kay wondered.

She had pulled back the curtains to look out, noting that the wind had buried the driveway again, the one that deputy Micah had plowed out only yesterday. She wondered if Clint had some kind of plow, too. She couldn't imagine trying to clear all of that by hand.

"Get away from the window."

Kay jumped and turned swiftly, dropping the curtain. Clint had just returned from the back of the house, where he'd evidently gone to change into a fresh flannel shirt and jeans.

"What? Why?"

"Just stay away from it."

"What aren't you telling me? Has something happened?"

"Phones aren't working."

Even she could tell that was misdirection. "Clint? Don't lie to me. For God's sake, don't lie. Do I have a reason to be afraid of being seen?"

He hesitated long enough to give her an answer.

"Oh God," she said shakily. Feeling suddenly weak, she tried to stagger to the couch. He crossed the room in a flash to steady her. When she was sitting, he squatted in front of her.

"What do you know?" she asked on the merest breath. "What didn't you tell me? Clint, I *have* to know."

After a moment, he nodded. "When you gave me the description of Kevin's car yesterday, I thought I might have seen it."

"When? Where?"

"Right after I found you. I was carrying you to my truck. Now, before you panic, let me tell you I'm not *sure* it was him. I wasn't paying that close attention, because I was more concerned with you. Plus, the snow had started to blow pretty badly, so I didn't have a clear view. But a car *like* his passed us and slowed. At the time I thought it was someone going up the road to my neighbor's place."

"Oh God." Her stomach sank like a stone. Had Kevin really come that close to tracking her down? Had she been saved only by a matter of minutes and this man? "Oh God."

"Kay, I can't be sure it was him. Neither can you."

"But you're worried enough that you don't want me by the window."

"That's just common sense. In case. We don't know that he knows where you are."

"But he *could* know I'm here."

His reluctance was obvious when he nodded. "Don't worry, lady. I won't let him get to you."

"How are you going to prevent that?"

His faced hardened again. "I have ways."

She closed her eyes, feeling the panicked wings of terror beating throughout her body. Not Kevin. Not again. Not as she'd just begun to hope.

"Kay." Clint touched her arm. She opened her eyes reluctantly. "I told Micah about it. They'll be watching like hawks, too. But I'm going to take some more precautions."

"What kind?"

"I'm going to make sure he can't get into the house without waking the dead."

Still shaken, she watched as he kept his word. Below each window, he placed hazards that would trip anyone who tried to climb in. On the rear and side doors, she watched him set up what he called "trip wires." If anyone opened them from the outside, a noisy shower of objects would fall.

He gave the front windows, the ones where she would be most exposed, extra treatment; he nailed them shut. With each blow of the hammer, she winced, realizing that safety had been an illusion, that once again she was in a prison of terror.

"Why didn't you tell me?" she asked. "Why?"

"Because you weren't in danger of any kind during the storm. You needed to rest."

"I needed a lie?"

"It wasn't a lie. I can't be sure it was him. Nor can you. I'm just taking precautions."

"I want a gun."

"I keep them locked up. For good reason. And I don't need one to take care of this guy."

"But what if *I* do?"

He shook his head. "Too dangerous."

"Dammit, Clint!"

He just shook his head again. Then he squatted in front of her and took her shoulders. "Listen to me. Guns are dangerous. What happens if you get scared in the dark and think I'm him?"

"I'd never mistake you for him."

"When you're scared, everything looks like a threat. Do you have any training?"

"No."

"Can you be absolutely sure you'd shoot? Because if you don't, and he gets close enough, then you've armed *him*. Trust me on this one, Kate, if he's fool enough to try to get in here, he'll have his hands fuller than he can possibly imagine, and I don't need a gun to make him regret it."

"Maybe *you* don't."

"Okay, you want a weapon? How about a fireplace poker? Or a tire iron? You can hide it right here beside you, and if he ever gets that close, you can do enough damage with one blow to put him down until I can take him out."

She finally accepted his reasoning, though it didn't make her happy. "Something he can't pull out of my hand. He's strong."

"I'll figure it out."

"But he could still hit me first."

He shook his head, his gray eyes never wavering from hers. "Kay, I'd have to be dead to let him get that close."

God, what a thought. What an image he painted of himself. She couldn't help it. Terror was driving her, and he was the only anchor she had. She leaned forward and wrapped her arms around him, clinging.

At first he froze, as if he'd become the stone he pretended to be. Then, almost cautiously, he slipped his arms around her, gently, oh so gently, and just let her cling.

"I'll protect you," he whispered. "I swear it."

But at what cost? It was a question she didn't dare ask.

By midmorning it was easy to see that Clint had become restless. She wished she could feel that much energy, but evidently her body still demanded rest. Finally he went to one of the windows and looked out.

"I need to plow the drive."

"Do you need to go somewhere?"

"If it becomes necessary, yes." He turned from the window and looked at her. "You'll be safe," he said. "Nobody can approach this house right now because of the snow. Somehow I think it would take more guts than Kevin has to hike his way in here."

"Really?"

"A man who beats up on women is a coward."

"Or crazy," she said quietly.

"Do you think he's that crazy?"

"I don't know."

"Then ride in the truck with me. It won't take long. Just let me get the thing started so the cab is warm for you."

"Thank you." She let a sigh of relief escape her. Yes, it might be beyond Kevin to hike his way through all this snow, but a few years ago she would have thought it beyond him to pursue her across the country, too. Not only had he done that three times now, but he'd actually abducted her. Crazy? Yeah, he was crazy.

He went outside and started the truck. She could hear it roar a bit at first, then listened as it came around to the front of the house. The vehicle sounded none-too-happy about the volume of snow it had to push.

Then Clint stomped back in, shaking snow off his boots. "Let me find you something to put on your feet. And I have an extra jacket, though it'll probably swallow you whole."

"That'll just make it warm," she said with a smile. For some reason she felt like smiling. Maybe because he cared enough about her feelings not to leave her alone. Maybe because she was actually going to get out into the sun and fresh air for a little while.

He brought her several pairs of thick socks and knelt to pull them on her. "My feet are way too big," he said. "If I gave you a pair of my boots, you'd trip for sure. So I'll carry you to the truck, okay?"

She didn't mind the idea at all, oddly enough. She looked at the top of his dark head as he worked the socks onto her and felt a swelling appreciation for him. He could be incredibly kind and thoughtful, and he cared for her as if she were as precious as Limoges china, and as delicate. Nobody, absolutely *nobody,* had ever done that for her. Not even her earliest memories of her mother included this kind of care.

After the socks came a gray nylon parka. He zipped it up, even though it bagged on her and fell almost to her knees. Then he rolled up the sleeves, no easy task, but at least her hands were free.

Next he offered her big, thick blue mittens. She managed those by herself and then giggled at the way they flopped loosely at the ends of her fingers.

Even Clint smiled. "I'm sure you must be in there somewhere."

"That's the story, anyway."

At that, a chuckle escaped him. Then, without further ado, he swept her up, one arm beneath her knees, the other around her shoulders. It never ceased to amaze her that he was so strong. And where that had once frightened her, now it made her feel safe.

Probably a dangerous way to feel, she thought. She couldn't trust *herself* right now, couldn't trust her own feelings, and he clearly wanted no part of human entanglements. The only thing this man could offer her was more pain, just a different kind of pain.

He carried her out to the truck and deposited her in the already-warming cab. He went back to lock the front door, then climbed in beside her.

His vehicle was an older Suburban, heavy and powerful, but it still resisted a bit when it bit into the deep, heavy snow. He kept it in low gear and managed the manual transmission like a pro as he steadily moved forward and back, clearing away the snow with the plow blade attached to the front.

"She gets cranky about this," he remarked. "But then, she's not a snow plow."

"How long is your drive?"

"About eight-tenths of a mile. You'll know when we get to the end because there'll be a wall left by the plow that went through during the night."

"The plow already came?" Her heart lurched a bit as she realized the roads were now open. Kevin, if he knew where she was, could come at any time.

"I heard it about four this morning. It'll probably be back later, too, and I'll have to bust out again."

"Do you have to do this often?"

"Depends. We've been getting more snow than usual the last couple of years. There've been winters, though, when I haven't had to do this but two or three times."

It took nearly a half hour, but they finally cleared the right side of the driveway and reached the wall he'd promised. Clint put the car in Park and muttered.

"What's wrong?" she asked.

"I just need to loosen that mess a bit. Stay put."

So she waited while he climbed out, opened the back of the truck and pulled out a heavy-duty shovel. She hated sitting there, doing nothing as he started chopping at the huge snowbank the plow had pushed across the end of his driveway. It looked hard. It was nearly as high as he was tall, and she could only imagine the effort he was expending trying to loosen it.

But finally he seemed satisfied the truck could do the job. When he climbed back into the cab with her, he was sweating from the heavy labor.

"Here we go," he said. He backed up about twenty feet, then floored the accelerator. "Hang on."

She braced in time. The Suburban hit the wall of snow hard, jerking her a bit against her seat belt, but she managed to stifle a cry as her bruises shrieked. A moment later they burst through, and he pushed the snow all the way to the far side of the road, slamming it into the snowbank over there.

He looked at her as he backed up again into his own driveway. "Once more," he said. "Can you handle it?"

She nodded, this time bracing even harder. "This could be fun, under other circumstances."

A laugh escaped him. "Yeah, if you weren't already so sore."

Once again he broke through what was left of the snow pile and drove the snow across the road. Then he performed a three-point turn and headed back up the driveway, this time clearing the other side.

"Are you okay?" he asked, when they finally pulled up in front of the house.

"Yeah. I'm fine." Except that tensing again and again had once again made her aware of every bruised muscle in her body. The pain would pass, though, and she didn't want to tell him.

But Clint was a perceptive man. Little escaped him. When he came around to lift her out and take her inside, he scanned her face. "What hurts?"

"Just some of the bruises."

"Not your ribs?"

"I can't even feel those anymore."

A little smile danced in his eyes. "Next time stay in the house."

"I don't think so."

The smile in his eyes reached his mouth. "Up to you." Then he scooped her up and carried her back inside. "I'll help you get unwrapped as soon as I stow the truck."

As soon as he closed the door behind him, she let a groan escape. Damn! She hadn't realized just how much of her hurt. Now all her muscles were shrieking again.

Biting her lip, she pulled the mittens off. Hot. She was getting hot in front of the fire. At least she could manage the jacket.

But it was so big that the task proved difficult. The zipper kept wanting to stick, because she couldn't grab the material to straighten it out. Finally she sagged backward and told herself to just wait.

But God, she was sick of being helpless. Helpless with Kevin, and now helpless in her own battered body. Every time she started to get a handle on her life again, Kevin appeared to blow it all up once again. And this time…this time he'd left her truly helpless. Unable to run, unable to even get out of a damn jacket.

Her anger was coming back, she realized. Replacing fear as her primary motivator, it began to seethe hotly inside her. Good. When she was angry, she took care of things. All kinds of things. Anger more than fear had enabled her to uproot herself again and again. Anger kept her going when fear would have frozen her.

Furious, she grabbed at the zipper again, and this time it slid downward more than half way. Now if she could just pull her arms out of these sleeves, she could get the damn thing off.

"Let me help you."

She hadn't heard Clint come back in and gasped at the unexpected sound of his voice. Then she said, "I want to do it."

"I can see that. And I don't blame you. But let's just do it the easy way this time."

Before she could protest, he pulled the stupid jacket right over her head.

"There. It's gone."

Relief and annoyance warred inside her. "Thanks. But I want to do things myself."

"I get it," he said. "Believe me, I get it. But when help is handy, what's the point of making yourself even sorer?"

Logic.

She didn't want logic right now. "Do you have any idea what this feels like?" she demanded. "I can't even get out of the tub on my own. Or pull off a stupid jacket."

"I know exactly what it feels like."

She paused in the middle of her angry tirade and looked at him. Something in his face made her heart sink. "How do you know?" she asked quietly.

He looked away, shrugging. "I've been wounded, too."

Oh God! She suddenly felt so small. Of course. Why hadn't she guessed that? Because she was so self-absorbed she couldn't feel a thing for anyone else?

"Do you want those extra socks off?" he asked after an uncomfortable moment.

"Please."

And this time she didn't object to his help or insist that she could do it herself. It seemed like a small bit of autonomy to give up for a man who had already done so much for her. A man who clearly needed to feel useful just as she did. A man whose reasons were much the same as hers, even if probably far worse in degree.

"Thank you," she said when he'd removed all but one pair of socks.

"No problem. Maybe we'll get the power back soon."

A safe subject. "I'm not really missing it," she offered. "You have a cozy place here."

"I like it." He rose, socks in hand, and started to walk away. Then he looked back. "Take it easy on yourself, Kay."

"You're one to talk."

"Obviously." One side of his mouth lifted a bit. "Always easier to talk than do."

"Isn't that the truth." But she tried to smile back at him.

For a few seconds he didn't move. It almost seemed as if they were locked in each other's gazes, as if some quiet kind of understanding passed between them. Then he looked away as if he didn't want the connection to continue. "Oh, before I forget..."

He walked over to the door where he'd dumped his own outerwear. He bent to pick up something, and as he returned, she saw it was a large tire iron.

"I promised you a weapon. Hold it by the bent end so you can get a good grip."

She took it from him cautiously. With that simple gesture, he'd brought the nightmare back into the room. Slowly she looked up at him. "I need this to end."

He nodded. "I understand *that,* too."

She had absolutely no doubt that he did.

Clint couldn't settle, and he knew exactly why. Senses and instincts honed by so many years in dangerous situations wouldn't allow him to sit back and relax. Was it likely Kevin would try to come up to the house by way of the drive? Absolutely not. He had to know he would have no chance if he announced his arrival.

So that left hiking through the snow. It would be nice to think he wouldn't attempt it, but despite what he had said to Kay, Clint was convinced that Kevin was insane enough to try just that.

Why? Because to Clint, Kevin read like a man who had tired of the chase. Maybe it had excited him for a while to know he could find Kay when he wanted and show up to terrify the hell out of her. But he had moved well past that when he'd abducted her, had moved into a crazy place that said he was through with the chase and wanted to finish it for good, regardless of the consequences to himself.

Clint had studied abnormal psychology in some depth because it fascinated him. And he knew about obsessions, including sick obsessions.

The obsession dictated the actions, Clint thought. And Kevin's obsession could only be ended in one way.

What was more, once the obsession reached full blossom, as it apparently had with Kevin's abduction of Kay, then it goaded, pressed and drove, demanding resolution, and the faster the better. It could not be repressed for long.

Kevin would most likely come by night, under cover of darkness. In the wee hours, when he would assume everyone in the house was asleep. Well, Clint didn't plan to sleep. With that snow out there, Kevin's approach should be clear enough, unless he camouflaged himself. Which was always a possibility. Crazy did *not* equate to stupid. In fact, it was often the contrary, especially if crazy included an element of paranoia.

Even if Kevin hadn't grown paranoid as a result of being sent to prison, he was probably paranoid by now. With good reason, since he had to be aware that it was possible his victim had told the police she had been abducted, and that there might be dozens of people looking for him right now.

A sane man would disappear, but Kevin wasn't sane. Oh, he might be sane enough by legal standards, but he wasn't sane by any other standard. He was probably hiding somewhere, fighting his compulsion to end this, waiting just long enough to convince himself that people would believe he'd moved on.

But Clint wasn't going to fall for that one. So how long would the guy judge that he needed? Impossible to know for sure. Maybe a few more days. At most. Because his obsession would goad him past patience, too. He would want this over and done with.

And of course he would have no idea what a formidable opponent he would be facing once he entered the house.

Clint performed a mental checklist. The guy would wait, hoping the heat would lessen. Then he would want to observe the house for a while to figure out how many people were inside. He could do that while he waited, now that the storm was over.

But there was another wrinkle, too. Assuming that *had* been Kevin who'd driven by them on the road, how could Kevin be sure Kay was still in the house? Clearly, merely by turning around a few miles up the road and backtracking he would have figured out that Clint had taken her there to start with.

But how could he be sure she hadn't been taken elsewhere since then?

For one thing, it would be easy for *anyone* to find out if she was in the hospital. Equally obvious was the likelihood that Clint hadn't taken her anywhere else because of the storm. In fact, it was unlikely that Kevin, even if he'd been nearby, would have seen Micah come to the house, given the state of the roads.

So that left what? The fact that Clint had brought Kay to his place and still had her. The fact that the guy couldn't be sure the cops hadn't been advised of Kay's abduction and his own description. In fact, it was likely they had been. But the truth was, all of Kay's attempts to keep her presence secret had probably been wasted from the moment Kevin saw Clint rescuing her.

Clint almost swore, then remembered Kay was nearby. He didn't want to worry her, much less unleash a stream of questions he couldn't adequately answer.

So okay, another few days maybe, enough for Kevin to feel things had calmed down and plan a stealthy approach to the house. But that would be the max, because Kevin's internal demons would be driving him.

A couple of days.

Not very long.

Chapter 8

The phone rang in the early afternoon, announcing that at least part of the world had started to return to normal. Clint answered it and found Deputy Sarah Ironheart on the other end.

"Hey, Clint," she said cheerfully. Her husband, Gideon, kept Clint's horses for the winter, and despite himself, he'd become a part of the Ironheart family.

"Hi, Sarah."

"Micah said I needed to come by and take some photos of your guest."

Clint froze. His mind spun through a series of possibilities very fast. Then, "Sarah, I think it would be a very good idea right now if we didn't advertise that the law knows Kay is here."

She fell silent for a few seconds. "You think he's watching?"

"I think he'd be a fool not to be. And I want him to think the heat's off."

"Are you sure about that?"

"I promised her we'd end this. If you don't run across him on the roads, then the end is going to happen here. And frankly, the sooner the better. This guy strikes me as a mental case. He's not going to wait long."

Sarah didn't hesitate. "I could come in civvies and take her out of there."

"And what if he sees?"

"Good point. Okay. I'll talk to Micah and Gage, and see if we can't set up some loose surveillance. Or at least keep some cars near your place."

"My bet is that he won't come by road. And I don't want him scared off, because he'll just come after her another time."

"You believe that?"

"Absolutely. This guy is obsessed, and there's only one way to end it. And I honestly don't think at this stage in his obsession that he's willing to wait for her to move on again. Or even wait very long to come after her here. What if she disappears for real? I don't think he's willing to risk that."

"All right, then. We'll see what we can do to help without being seen. But don't be surprised if you get a call from Gage. He won't be happy."

"Gage has done enough undercover work in his life. He'll get it."

When he hung up, he found a very pale Kay watching him.

"I'm sorry I'm causing you so much trouble."

What had brought that on? He ran his conversation with Sarah back in his mind and remembered the phrase, *Frankly, the sooner the better.* He could well imagine how she'd taken that.

Ordinarily he would have let it pass without explanation. He cared very little about what most people thought of him, but somehow he already cared what Kay thought. Part of him reared up to object, but it didn't stand a chance, not against that look on her face. Especially when abuse had made her so vulnerable and left her feeling like something to be kicked to the curb.

"I just want you out of danger as soon as possible. That's not the same as wanting to get rid of you as soon as possible."

She nodded, but her expression didn't change. He guessed she didn't believe him. And then she asked, "So we're bait in a trap?"

"Maybe."

"There's no maybe about it. It's the best way to get at him."

Then she closed her eyes, as if that admission had taken the last of her strength, and all the vivacity that had begun to return to her seemed to drain away.

Hell. He didn't want to be responsible for this. He didn't want to make her feel bad, but he wanted even less than that for her to care enough that he *could* make her feel bad. There was no future in it for either of them. Best if she just perceived him as a weapon to use to get free of Kevin.

But the truth was, she was too nice to look at other people that way—even him. He'd seen it already, in her concern that *he* not wind up with Kevin on his conscience. As if his conscience would note the weight added to the tonnage it already carried.

He swore under his breath. The cracks inside were getting wider, and dammit, he wasn't sure he wanted to fill them up with cement again. He should have turned and walked out of the room. Immediately.

Instead, looking at her wan, sad face, something else took over, something visceral, and he walked toward her, not away from her. He'd never felt like this before about anything that didn't involve life and death, but somehow that woman's hurt seemed every bit as important to him as his own survival.

He sat on the couch beside her, then gathered her onto his lap as carefully as he could manage when every cell in his body wanted to play the caveman.

Her eyes flew open, and her lips parted in astonishment.

Quit now, he told himself. Stop!

But he couldn't. He simply couldn't. This woman made him helpless in ways he hated, in ways he couldn't fight. In ways that knocked his barriers flat.

He lowered his head, needing to kiss her. Needing to let her know that at least one person in this world didn't think of her as trash to be kicked and then kicked aside.

And this time he needed something far gentler than the earlier crushing kiss he'd given her. He needed to feel like he wasn't a monster.

As his mouth settled over hers, he felt her gasp, taking breath from him, saw her eyes widen, then flutter closed. She accepted his kiss as if she'd been waiting for it forever.

Ah, God, he thought as a new pain washed over him—a longing for an ordinary life, one that hadn't been blighted by his own failures. One that hadn't proved he was a monster at heart.

The yearning was so intense he couldn't break its grip. Just a few moments, he promised himself. Just this little bit and no more.

His lips moved gently on hers, asking, not demanding, a desperate question asked with utmost care, more care than he'd felt in a long time.

She answered tentatively at first, then as if she felt a hunger of her own. And she probably did. She must be as desperate as he was to know she wasn't just human garbage.

But it wasn't long before that caring yielded to something more basic. He didn't know who did it first, but their tongues met, engaging in an ancient dance. And with that shift, the hunger in him changed, too. His loins throbbed with long-denied needs, and the warning voice in his head yelled at him to stop.

But he couldn't stop. He needed this. He needed *her,* because somehow, in some way, she offered an absolution he couldn't find elsewhere.

She tore her mouth away, gasping for breath, but offered not a bit of resistance when he swooped in again for another kiss. He felt her melt against him, and almost before he knew what he was doing, his hand found her breast. Oh, man, she felt perfect against his palm, and he wanted to rip away the fabric that prevented him from feeling her skin. He found the strength, from somewhere, to keep his touch gentle when everything inside him screamed for him to just mount her now, to bury himself in the beauty and forgetfulness her body offered.

A small moan escaped her, and he felt her arch up against his hand, seeking more. Even through the thick fabric of the sweatshirt he could feel her nipple harden, just as he was hardening, and a flash of pure triumph ripped through him.

She wanted him, too. Every bit as much.

And all rational thought was fast flying out of his head, leaving him a prisoner of need.

His hand slipped up under the shirt, pushing it out of the way. More. He needed more, and he needed it *now*.

But just as he tore his mouth from hers and moved to take her exposed nipple into his mouth, she gasped and cried out.

Reality came back in one crashing instant. What the hell was he doing?

He lifted his head and looked into her frightened face. "Kay?" He struggled to regain his footing. "Did I hurt you."

"I'm sorry," she said, and huge tears began to fall. "I want…oh, God, I'm sorry." She struggled to pull the shirt down.

He helped, and when she wiggled as if to escape, he quickly helped her by shifting her to the far end of the couch. "Kay?"

"I'm sorry," she said, her voice breaking. "I'm sorry!" Then she turned her face against the back of the couch, and wracking sobs shook her.

What had he done? He didn't know. But the only thing he could think of to do for her now was to move away, to go sit in his own chair and give her space.

She cried for a while, and he just sat helplessly watching, figuring that even a hug might be taken amiss right now. He couldn't offer any solace at all, and that made him crazy.

"I'm sorry," he said, when her sobs began to ease. "I'm always doing that."

"Doing what?" she asked brokenly, her voice muffled against the back of the couch.

"Hurting you. I always hurt people." And he was damned if he knew how to fix it when he did.

"It wasn't you."

"What?" He was sure he'd misunderstood her.

She turned then, groaning a bit as she twisted until she faced him. "It wasn't you," she said in a tear-thickened voice. "Clint, don't blame yourself. It was me. *Me!*"

"You? You didn't do anything. *I* did."

"No, you don't get it. I wanted you to kiss me. But I can't. I *can't.*"

He was beginning to get it, and blackness seeped into the edges of his mind. "Why?"

"Because…" She gasped, almost a sob, and closed her eyes. "He raped me."

That did it. Clint rose, shoved his feet into his boots and then stepped outside into the bitter cold without even a jacket. He needed that cold, because right now his hands itched, absolutely *itched*, to wrap themselves around Kevin's throat. Or smash something. As if they had a mind of their own.

He couldn't let Kay see this. He couldn't risk expressing his rage to her. He didn't want to see her shrink from him again. He didn't think he could bear it.

But the urge to kill had never been stronger, and he had to walk it off. Rage clouded the mind, deadened the senses, and he couldn't afford that for Kay's sake, if nothing else.

He walked all the way around the cabin four or five times, not counting, fighting down the man he no longer wanted to be. The man he might have to become again to save Kay.

He looked up at the heavens, sending a blast of rage upward. What had that chaplain said to him? Oh, yeah, God has broad shoulders, and a curse can be a prayer, too. Yeah. Sure.

Except a lot of the time he didn't think God was listening. Nor should he, when you came right down to it. No reason to listen to Clint Ardmore, human monster. Probably already damned for eternity.

But what about Kay? he asked silently. What about Kay? She didn't deserve this.

A gust of wind blew snow into his face. No answer at all. But it reminded him that he was getting perilously close to hypothermia, and nice as it might be to just lie down in the snow and kiss off all the pain, he couldn't do that.

Not now. That woman inside was depending on him.

He took a couple of deep breaths, realizing that the rage was subsiding. He forced himself to let go of the last of his tension, as well.

Certain now of his self-control, he headed back inside. He kicked off his boots, his eyes seeking Kay. She was sitting stiffly on the couch and didn't even look around.

Oh, this was not good.

"Kay?"

"What?"

"Are you okay?"

"Whatever would make you think that?" she asked, her voice brittle.

Ah, hell. "What did I do now?"

"How could you have done anything? You were outside."

He wasn't buying it. In stocking feet he padded over and sat on the coffee table facing her. Some instinct told him that he needed to be close to her right now.

"Talk," he said.

"What's there to talk about?"

"Look, I'd tell you I'm sorry I kissed you, but I'd be lying. What I'm sorry about is what happened to you. And I feel so damn helpless. I can't fix it, Kay."

"Why would you think I expect you to fix anything?"

She wasn't looking at him, and little flags were beginning to pop up in his head. He knew a lot of psychology, and he began to suspect something.

"Do you think," he said slowly, "that I walked out of here because I was disgusted with you?"

"Of course you did! Don't bother trying to lie to me. I know what I am. Damaged goods. I can't even…I can't even…" Her voice broke, and she looked away. "I am so disgusting."

"Disgusting? That's the last thing you are. Do you want to know why I walked out of here? The real reason?"

She darted a look at him, then averted her gaze again.

"The real reason I walked out of here was that the monster inside me was getting loose. I wanted to kill someone. I wanted to kill Kevin. I did not, absolutely *did not,* walk out because I was disgusted with you. There is not one disgusting thing about you."

"Yes, there is," she said, her voice small.

"Why? Because you were raped? Like that was a choice you made? That dirt is all on Kevin, not on you. Even if life had forced you to stand on a street corner and turn twenty-dollar tricks, you wouldn't be disgusting. And there's most definitely *not* anything disgusting about you because you were raped."

She was silent so long that he began to fear he'd hurt her again. But then, still in a small voice, she said, "I think I'm worth more than twenty."

He almost chuckled in his relief, but caught himself, knowing it could well be exactly the wrong response. "More like a grand, maybe."

She looked at him from the corner of her eye. "There was a time I would have priced myself considerably higher."

"Well, I would, too, but I figured you'd think I was exaggerating."

Slowly she turned her head to look at him. A slight smile flitted over her mouth, but then the haunted expression returned. "I'm not worth anything right now."

"Why in the world would you think that?" But he suspected.

"Because I...can't. I wanted you to kiss me, and then I froze. I panicked. I'm...broken."

He sought words carefully. "Life breaks us all in one way or another. But if we try, we can put the pieces back together. It takes time. And we won't be exactly the same person we used to be. But we *are* whole again."

"Is that what you've done? Put yourself back together?"

"In my own rather crude way, yes. Still not done with the reconstruction, but working on it."

"With plenty of defensive walls."

He nodded, admitting it.

"I don't seem to be able to build those very well."

"I don't advise it, actually. Right now it doesn't seem to be working too well for me."

"What do you mean?"

But that was one question he wasn't prepared to answer, either to her or to himself. Because he didn't know what to make of all the fault lines that had begun cracking open inside him since this woman had come into his life. He didn't know if they would remain, or what his interior landscape might look like once the earthquake was over. Best to just remain silent.

She waited, then let it go. Unlike a lot of women he'd known, she didn't seem to feel a need to peck him open like a juicy seed until she knew every little nook and cranny inside him. He appreciated that, especially since he had some ugly nooks.

"I'm sorry," she said after a while. "I've barged into your hermitage, busted your solitude and created one emotional upheaval after another."

"Call it fresh air."

Her eyes widened. "What do you mean?"

He gave her a wry, pained smile. "Sometimes even hermits need to deal with something besides the cobwebs inside their own heads."

"Oh."

He could see that turning around in her head; then a cute, almost impish, smile appeared. "So I'm a feather duster?"

"Big-time, lady," he said. And finally he let a laugh emerge. "One really big feather duster."

He had to give it to her, she bounced back fast. He could see her muscles uncoiling, even as life began to return to her face.

That didn't mean the problems were over. By no means. Snakes had a way of going into hiding, then popping up again at unexpected moments. But Kay apparently had a resilient nature, and he liked that.

There might be some lessons there for him to learn, too.

Because, he finally admitted to himself, he was getting just a bit weary of nursing his own psyche.

The day remained sunny, the wind steadily growing calmer. Perfect conditions for Kevin, Clint thought as he walked from window to window. As the sun heated the snow on the roof, a few icicles began to grow around the eaves. Good. The more of them the better. If they grew big enough, they would become deadly. Handy weapons, and a bar to invasion.

He heard a clatter from the kitchen, and went there to find Kay struggling to pull out pots.

"Let me help with that," he said instantly. "What do you want to do?"

"Cook. I'm going to go crazy sitting on that couch worrying and thinking. I need to be busy, and you said you liked my chowder."

He should have thought of that. "The chowder was great."

"I think I saw a chicken in your refrigerator."

"Yeah, sometimes I actually cook myself."

She gave him a small smile. "Do you mind if I do?"

"Not a bit. I'll help, if you want." He pulled the chicken out and put it on a plate on the counter. "Kinda hard to wash it, though," he remarked. "No power, no running water, remember?"

"Oh, I forgot about that." She stared at the chicken, frowning faintly.

"Well, if we don't get power back soon, it'll spoil. I don't know how well the stuff in the fridge is keeping cool. So let's risk it. We just need to rinse it as best we can and then make sure it's fully cooked." He paused. "In fact, I probably ought to take what I can and put it in a snow bank to preserve it."

She touched the chicken. "It still feels pretty cold."

"But sooner or later, opening the fridge is going to warm it up too much." He sighed. "For a self-sufficient type, I'm standing here wondering why I never bought that generator I've been looking at for the last two years."

"We all have questions like that to ask ourselves."

"I suppose." He helped her wash the chicken by pouring water over it from the huge pot of water that still sat on the stove.

"Any lemons?" she asked him.

"As a matter of fact…" He opened his pantry, asking, "How many?"

"At least two."

She thanked him as she accepted them and placed them on the counter. "Pepper?"

He opened another cupboard and handed her the peppermill. "Salt?"

She nodded and took that, too. "Roasting pan?"

He dug that out of the back of another cupboard.

She regarded him. "Do you put *everything* away?"

"Why?" The question surprised him.

"Because I usually leave salt and pepper on my counter in easy reach."

"Oh." He shrugged. "Training. Stow everything."

"Navy?"

"Marines."

"Ah."

"But if you want, I can start leaving things out."

She gave him a humorous little smile. "And drive yourself crazy? I don't think so. I'll adapt." Her smile faded, and she bit her lip. "I guess I won't be here that long, anyway."

He didn't know how to answer that. If he agreed, she might think he was in a hurry to get rid of her again. And even if part of him thought that would be best for both of them, he didn't want to make her feel that way. If he disagreed, he might make her think she would never be able to get on with her own life. Lose-lose, he thought.

She turned back to the chicken, rubbing it with olive oil she'd found herself, sprinkling it inside with salt and pepper, then squeezing the lemons over the skin. To his surprise, she shoved the two halved and squeezed lemons into the cavity instead of tossing them.

"What's this?" he asked. "I've never seen anyone do that before."

"Lemon chicken," she offered. "I hope you like it."

"Sounds good." He didn't mind acting as if he were inexperienced in the kitchen if it made her feel good about what she was doing.

A sprinkle of salt on the outside of the chicken and then she placed it in the roasting pan. "All ready," she announced. "Thirty minutes at four-twenty-five, then fifty-five minutes at three-seventy-five."

He turned on the oven for her, letting it preheat. "Anything else?"

"Depends on what you want with it. I usually make this with yellow rice."

"Hey, I have that." He went back to the pantry and brought out a bag. "Too bad we can't use my rice cooker."

"You have a rice cooker?"

"I eat a lot of rice. Leftover habit from my time abroad."

She looked at him again, her eyes full of questions. He gave her credit for not asking them. "It'll cook well enough on the stove top," she said finally. "I don't have a rice cooker at…my place."

He noted she resisted the easy and obvious choice of the word *home*. That opened one of the cracks a little wider. This woman, he thought, didn't really have a home. Probably hadn't felt she had one for years. Maybe for a brief time with Kevin she had thought she was making one, but along with all the other things he'd done to her, the bastard had probably succeeded in making *home* a dirty word.

He stopped himself cold. He couldn't afford these thoughts. He sought his way back to safer ground. "I couldn't exist without one. It lets me make perfect rice without paying attention, and I tend to get distracted when I'm working."

She nodded but didn't say anything. Well, what was there to say?

"Anything else you need?"

"Not just yet. Vegetables later, if you have any."

"I've got a load of them in the freezer out in the garage. Probably most anything you could want."

"Then when it's time, we'll decide." Then she asked, "Am I keeping you from working?"

The answer was simple, though far from complete. "No power, no computer. So I get a holiday." But he also knew he couldn't keep on standing here and talking to her. Talking was dangerous. It created bonds. It might even reveal too many things he didn't want to reveal. But she'd expressed boredom, and he felt obligated to keep her occupied in some way. Occupied enough that she wouldn't notice his prowling as the evening grew closer.

"Listen," he said, "you like to read, right?"

"I love it."

"Then I've got something to show you."

Violating all his personal rules of privacy, he led her down the hallway and opened the door to his office. Ceiling-to-floor bookcases lined the walls, like battlements around his desk and computer. "If you see something you want and can't reach it, call me. I'll get it down for you."

"Thank you!" She looked genuinely pleased and excited. "I love books. I always wished I could have a library."

"Well, it's not exactly that big." But still way more than she could have when she was always being forced to move. He waved to the left. "Fiction on that side, nonfiction on the other. Most of it's in alphabetical order by author name, if you want to look for something in particular. Otherwise, happy browsing."

He left her then, needing to escape. Needing to get away from whatever it was in this woman that kept calling to him. Needing to get away from watching her explore the inner sanctum where he had never allowed anyone before.

Some might think that odd, but he knew better. Looking at a man's library was like looking into his soul. If she realized that, she could learn a lot about him from browsing those shelves.

And he couldn't imagine why in the hell he'd given her the opportunity.

She heard Clint go into the kitchen and slip the chicken into the oven. Since he had a windup timer on his counter, she assumed he set that, too. Browsing the books totally absorbed her. She found it difficult to imagine actually being able to own so many books. Even if she could have afforded to buy so many to begin with, she would have had to leave them behind every time she had to run. And that would have hurt.

She finally found a well-thumbed sci-fi novel, *A Canticle for Leibowitz.* Clearly Clint had read it a good many times, and for some reason the post-apocalyptic setting appealed to her. Distraction, maybe leading to some interesting thinking, especially since Clint seemed to have read it so often.

She returned to the living room to find him absorbed once again in his own book. There was an easy, non-threatening companionship in being able to sit across from him and read. She needed the break.

Most especially she needed the break from her own thoughts. She couldn't bear to remember how much she had wanted to be held by Clint, as if his desire could wash away the stains she felt all over her soul. Stains that had prevented her from taking what he offered. She couldn't bear to think about how broken she was.

But she also couldn't bear to think about the fact that Clint seemed convinced that Kevin would try to get at her here. If Kevin had an ounce of sense, he would have fled far and fast, awaiting some later opportunity to get at her. Keeping her forever living on the edge of fear and always looking over her shoulder.

But Clint didn't seem to think Kevin was going to do that. And Clint knew a lot more about these things, and he had enough confidence in his knowledge to seem certain. In this, she was inclined to trust Clint more than herself. After all, with all Kevin had put her through, she had never, ever thought he would kidnap her.

What was more, when she thought about it, at long last she admitted Kevin might be insane, clinically insane, not just garden-variety crazy. After all, a sane man, someone with even a partial hold on reality, would have left her alone after that prison stint, wouldn't he?

And while it terrified her to think Kevin might come after her again in the next few days, it terrified her less than spending a week here, then moving on to a new place only to discover he'd found her again.

Because despite what Clint said about getting her a new identity, she couldn't believe Kevin wouldn't find her no matter what.

Staring blindly at the page in front of her, she realized that she'd endowed Kevin with both omniscience and omnipotence. Logically, that was ridiculous, but experience insisted otherwise. No matter how carefully she tried to cover her tracks, sooner or later he showed up again. Like some kind of inhuman demon who could track her by scent or something.

Was *she* losing her grip on reality? Did she really think Kevin was something more than just another ordinary, albeit mean, human being?

Horrifyingly enough, that seemed to be exactly the place she'd reached. And logic was a poor answer to experience.

She didn't realize she'd made a sound until Clint spoke. "Something wrong?" he asked.

She hesitated. How much did she want to reveal to this man, who was still basically a stranger she was trusting only because she had to? On the other hand, running around in the circle of her own thoughts wasn't getting her anywhere.

"I just realized that I'm thinking of Kevin as something more than human."

He tilted his head a little. "How so?"

"I've begun to think of him as omniscient. As in, I'll never escape him for long, even with a new identity."

He nodded slowly. "I can understand that."

"No, it's crazy."

He put his book aside. "It's *not* crazy, Kay. Do you know the best way to learn something?"

"How?"

"Through experience. And the more emotionally charged the experience is, the better and more indelibly we learn it." He gave her a smile that was almost bitter. "You're talking to the expert in learning lessons that way."

She bit her lip, fighting back an inexplicable need to soothe him somehow. She knew she wasn't capable of that, but she wished she could anyway.

"So he's followed you from town to town, what? Three times now?"

She nodded.

"I'd begin to wonder if I had a demon on my tail, too."

A relieved sigh escaped her. "That's how it feels."

"Of course that's how it feels. How could it not?"

She couldn't answer, just looked at him, waiting, hoping that somewhere in his educated mind and broadly experienced life he might find an answer for her.

But he surprised her by taking another tack. "I know Kevin," he said.

She gasped and started to curl inward as terror began to wash over her. No, he couldn't! Was this a trap?

"Wait," he said harshly. "I don't mean I know him personally. I mean, I know his type."

She closed her eyes and fought to get her breath back, to still her madly beating heart.

"I'm sorry," Clint said. "Poor choice of words."

"It's okay," she managed. Finally she could breathe again, and her heart rate settled to something approximating normal.

"I'm too used to being alone," he muttered. "I don't put a guard on my thoughts, and now they're spilling out my mouth without due consideration."

"It's okay," she said again. "Damn, Clint, you beat yourself up more than I do."

One corner of his mouth lifted. "Maybe."

She released another long breath, stabilizing emotionally. "You were saying?"

"That I know his type. He's obsessed. That's all it is. He's obsessed enough with you that he wants to control you completely. You got away once when he went to jail. But he found you, only then you got away again. And again."

She nodded. Her eyes felt hot, though she wasn't sure why. God, she was a mess.

"Anyway, he discovered that he enjoyed chasing you. There was fun in finding you after you thought you were safe and then tearing your safety away from you. What he was teaching you was that he *did* control you. No matter how far you ran, or how often."

She gave a jerky nod.

"But this abduction is a new thing, Kay. It means the obsession is changing."

Her heart stopped, then resumed a more rapid beat. "What do you mean?"

"He's tiring of the chase. He's getting bored with the way it was. So this time he took you with him, intending to teach you that he was not only in control of your life, but also your death. He's at a point where he wants to trade you for a new obsession. He's tired of his sport."

"God." She barely breathed the word.

"But he can't get rid of the obsession until he proves his ultimate control and gets rid of you."

"I knew he was going to kill me!" The words burst from her.

"That would be my guess," Clint agreed.

The expression on his face would have terrified her if she hadn't realized by now that it wasn't meant for her. "So he'll come?"

"He'll come. His sickness will drive him to it. He's not going to let you escape. Unfortunately for him, I have other plans."

Chapter 9

The power came back on while they were eating dinner. Kay looked up as she heard the refrigerator compressor kick on.

"Well, that's a good sign," Clint said. But he made no move to turn on the lights, just left the candles they had been using burning.

"Yes," she said. He was probably eager to get back to work. Eager to return to his escape from the world. She couldn't blame him, even though the thought that he might spend hours locked away at his computer while she sat alone in the living room made her feel depressed. Surely she couldn't have become emotionally dependent on him so quickly?

But maybe she had. Once it was clear Kevin would never stop hunting her down, she'd stopped making even loose connections with other people, because she knew that would only add to the pain when she had to run again.

This man had taken her in and offered her safety. Moreover, in more ways than one, he was promising long-term safety. Of course she had started to make a place for him in her heart.

And that was foolish, because she would have to move on again. Even if Clint did manage things so that Kevin could never threaten her again, she couldn't stay here any longer than necessary. Clint wouldn't want it; he was a hermit.

"This chicken is great," he said. "I have to remember your recipe."

"Thanks. It's easy."

He smiled. "Easy is great. And it doesn't make the recipe less worthwhile in the least."

She bit her lower lip, realizing she was doing it again: devaluing herself and her abilities. An overwhelming sense of despair washed over her. Was there any way in which she wasn't broken? And would she ever find the energy or will to put herself back together again? Was it even worth it?

Clint paused, setting his knife and fork down. She looked at him, wondering if he'd heard something, but his ghost-filled gaze was centered on her. Had she made a sound of some kind?

"Was it awful being a foster kid?" he asked out of nowhere.

She sighed. "Sometimes. Not always."

"Meaning?"

"Well, I never felt like I belonged. Being a full-time guest is wearing."

"Did the families make you feel that way?"

"Sometimes. Sometimes they tried really hard to get past that. I was probably a big part of the problem."

"How so?"

"I couldn't feel permanence. Maybe that was because after my grandmother died I was…difficult. Angry, bitter, striking out. So I went through a couple of families fast."

"They didn't expect that kind of stuff? I mean, what were they thinking? You can't take in a kid who's been through the things you have and not expect some adjustment problems."

She shrugged, then winced a little as muscles twinged. "I think some families get into it because if you take in enough kids, you can get a decent chunk of change from the state. Especially if you're careful about how much of that money you actually spend on the kids."

"Ugly," he said flatly.

"People are people. Some better than others." Which was a far more philosophical attitude than she usually had. "So anyway, I was difficult. I admit it. I wasn't suitably grateful, or quiet or willing to accept the way those families thought things should be. I went through three homes in rapid succession because my foster parents couldn't handle me. Or didn't want to. I honestly don't know. I was too young to have any perspective on it."

"Of course you were, which placed a bigger burden on them, and they should have known it."

"I don't know, Clint. For all I know, I was more difficult than most. Anyway, by the time I got to my fourth foster home, I knew I was a trespasser, and that it was just a way station."

"That's sad."

She shrugged again. "It just *was*. I got to the point of existing only to reach adulthood so I could get away and have my own place. It was like suspended animation. I didn't even make friends, because I knew I could be changing schools in just a couple of months."

"That stinks." He said it so harshly that she blinked and stiffened. No, he wasn't mad at her, she realized. She was learning that, finally. About Clint Ardmore, anyway, even if not about the rest of the world.

Something made her continue. "I *thought* that once I was on my own I could put down some kind of roots. I thought I could be normal." She shook her head and looked away. "It didn't happen."

"Tell me." His voice was almost gentle.

"Call it 'child interrupted.' I don't know. I kept trying, but I couldn't believe it. I rented a place, but I barely unpacked. I couldn't even bring myself to hang a picture. I made friends at work, I always had friends. I'd hang out with them, but even so, I look back now and realize there was a part of me I never shared. I never let them really know me, even though when I had to give them up, it hurt. But it didn't hurt as much as it might have if I had let them really close. I was still in suspended animation."

He nodded, his mouth set. "Then Kevin."

"Yeah, then Kevin. The answer to all my prayers." She shook her head and swore softly. "God, I was an idiot."

"Will you please stop saying that?"

"It's true!"

"It's not. It actually makes a ton of sense. So…Kevin. Let me guess. He was warm and friendly and caring, and he made you feel safe. At first."

She closed her eyes. "Yes," she whispered.

"He made you feel as if you'd found an anchor you could really cling to."

"Yes." She dared to open her eyes and look at him.

"And he flattered you, because he was intensely interested in you. In everything about you. He chipped at your walls, and you let him in, because like everyone else on this planet, you were desperate to be cared for."

She nodded, feeling unshed tears burn her eyes.

"You didn't do a damn thing wrong. You were conned."

"Clint…"

"No, you were conned," he repeated. "He could have done the same thing to just about anyone, but you were easier prey than most because of your background. Don't you dare take responsibility for anything Kevin did, because Kevin and his kind are born predators. He used you. That's all on him, and it wouldn't have made any difference who you'd been."

"But…"

He shook his head. "No buts." His eyes grew narrow. "There are people in this world who are born with a gift. They inspire trust, they always seem to know the right thing to say. Some of them use it for good. Others use it to take advantage. And the bad ones…well, their victims are blameless. Don't you see? There's no crime in trusting people to be who and what they say they are. There's no stupidity in that. Most of us start from a position of trust until we find out there's a reason not to trust. This world couldn't function otherwise."

He gave a short, bitter laugh. "I'm probably one of the least trusting people you'll ever meet, but I still trust you. I trust you're telling me the truth. If I didn't, you would have been out of here already."

Her mouth sagged open a bit. "Really?"

"Really. So does that make me an idiot?"

She shook her head slowly.

"See?" He picked up his fork again. "So along comes Kevin, and with a predator's instinct he senses easy prey. Being easy for him doesn't make you stupid, it just makes him meaner."

"Why?"

"Because he could have picked on somebody his size. But he's a freaking coward. Take it from me, lowlifes like him are all cowards. He plays a con game against easy targets, not difficult ones. And he gets his kicks out of it."

She didn't know how to respond to that. It was certainly something she was going to think about.

"So he knew you were already wounded, and he was mean enough to take advantage. Creep."

Almost in spite of herself, she felt a smile tug at the corners of her mouth. "He *is* a creep," she admitted.

"And that's the most printable word I can find for him." He paused, then said, "I rarely make promises, but I'm going to make one now."

"What's that?"

"That I won't rest until Kevin is out of your life for good. Whatever it takes. Prison, a new identity. Hell, I'd probably grin as I was breaking his neck."

Once again she faced the deep well of violence in this man, a well that seemed so contradictory when she thought of how he'd cared for her. She should have been frightened, but apparently some part of her hadn't been totally broken, because she discovered, strangely enough, that she could still trust. One man at least.

"Clint?"

"Yes?"

"I don't want you to do anything that will make you feel worse about yourself."

"Like I'd even notice."

It hurt to hear him say that. "You're a good man."

"You don't know me."

"I know who you are now. Who you've been for the past couple of days. You're a good man. I know you feel bad about things you've done, but they don't define who you are now."

He snorted. "You're one to talk."

"Exactly."

He went perfectly still for a half-minute, then surprised her with a faint smile. "Hoist on my own petard, huh?"

"Maybe. But all the things you've told me to make me feel better about myself? Maybe you should listen to them, too."

He insisted on cleaning up after dinner, telling her to rest.

She sat on the couch, watching him ferry dishes back and forth, then listening to the sound of running water and the clatter as he washed up.

He *was* a good man, she thought. Most emphatically. Bad men didn't feel troubled by conscience. Kevin certainly didn't. She wished there was some way she could make Clint believe that. Psychological mess that she was, though, there was no reason he should listen to her.

She sighed. Then she noticed something else. As the evening deepened, Clint seemed to be coiling tighter in some way. Even when he finished the dishes and returned to his armchair to read, she sensed he was strung as tight as a bow.

"What are you waiting for?" she finally asked him.

"Kevin."

Her heart sputtered, then resumed beating, only faster. "Tonight?" she asked hoarsely.

"Probably not. A predator with an ounce of decent hunting instinct will want to case the place for a couple of days."

"You talk about him as if he's an animal."

"He's worse than an animal. Animals, by and large, hunt because they need to eat, not because they get a charge out of it."

She really couldn't argue with that. "I guess you'd know better about these things than I would."

His gaze darkened. Even in the lamplight she could see the ghosts in his eyes again. She wished she knew a way to exorcise them.

But she couldn't even exorcise her own.

He set his book aside. "Listen, I want to warn you about something."

She tensed. "Yes?"

"I'm going to be wound up tighter than a spring, especially at night. There's no way I can hide it from you. I'm going to be pacing this cabin like a lion in a cage. I'm going to go outside frequently to check things. I just want you to know, because the simple fact that I'm on edge doesn't necessarily mean that I know something is happening right then, okay?"

She nodded slowly, feeling a hollowness inside her.

"I'm going to be hyperalert, hypervigilant. That means... Well, try to avoid startling me, okay?"

"I'll try."

"I'm going to be operating on instincts honed by years of experience in dangerous situations. Unfortunately, that makes *me* dangerous, too."

"I think I understand."

"Maybe you do, to some extent. Maybe not." He shook his head. "I hope you do, because when I react it'll be fast. Thought won't even enter into it."

"Okay." She tried not to let him see that he was making her uneasy. She could get hurt if she startled him? How could she be sure not to do that?

But he seemed to want to move on. "I suggest you take a shower now. Get into some clean clothes. I have more sweats you can wear. Get comfortable. Because later on I'm going to be on guard duty. Speak before you act. That's all I ask."

"I can do that."

The ghosts in his eyes eased a bit. "I know you can."

"But you don't think it'll be tonight?"

He shook his head. "Not tonight. Too soon. He can't be sure how many people are in this cabin. So he'll have to watch. And I'm going to do my damnedest not to scare him off."

Kay took the shower he suggested. It was a relief to be able to get in and out on her own, unlike a bath. The heat of the beating spray helped, too, like a mini massage. Feeling looser all over than she had since Kevin had first beaten her, she dried and dressed in the clean sweat suit Clint had given her. She even managed to comb out her own hair.

The improvement in her ability to take care of herself pleased her, and she was actually smiling when she came out of the bathroom.

Until she realized Clint was gone. Fear gripped her hard, and she backed up against the hallway wall, as if she could press herself right into it. "Clint?"

No answer. What now?

She needed the tire iron. Protection. Slowly she eased down the hallway until she could see the living room. Nobody there, unless someone was hiding on the far side of the couch.

She darted across the room as fast as she could and grabbed her weapon from the couch where it still lay. Then she backed up against the wall again, to ensure nobody could get at her from behind.

Her heart was hammering so hard she was sure it must be audible throughout the entire cabin. She was panting audibly.

She'd always wondered how someone who was terrified could possibly hide. Now she knew—it was impossible.

She gripped the tire iron harder, glad of its weight in her hand. God, where was Clint?

Then she heard the front doorknob rattle and start to turn. At once she shifted her grip, holding the iron bar at the ready in both hands. If Kevin came through that door...

But it wasn't Kevin. It was Clint. He stepped in, locked the door and kicked off his boots. As he was tugging off his jacket, he turned and saw her.

For an instant they both stood locked in a frozen tableau; he astonished, she ready to kill.

Then relief swept through her like a tsunami. The makeshift weapon clattered to the floor, and without a thought for her battered body, her natural inhibitions or anything else except that he was here, she flew across the room and launched herself into his arms.

To her amazement, she didn't bounce off him as if he were a brick wall. Instead he caught her and clutched her close in arms that felt like steel, the best kind of steel in the world.

"It's okay," he whispered. "It's okay. I guess you didn't hear me when I said I was going out."

"I thought...I thought..." She couldn't get the words out. She dug her fingers into his shoulders, then slid her arms around his neck, pressed her face to his shoulder and hid in his strength. *Don't let me go,* she thought desperately. *Please, don't let me go.*

As if he understood, he slipped his arms down until they cradled her bottom. He lifted her high against him, and she wrapped her legs around his waist. If she could have, she would have melted right into him.

"Shh," he said, and only then did she realize she was crying softly, little hiccupping sobs.

"Shh," he said again.

They moved, and the next thing she realized they were sitting on the couch, and she was still wrapped around him like a vine, straddling him and clinging.

His hold shifted as he placed one arm securely around her back and with his other hand held her head close to his own. Cheek to cheek.

"I'm sorry," he said. "I called to you when you were showering."

"I didn't hear." She squeezed the words out.

"God, I'm sorry."

She heard real caring in his tone. Not that he hadn't been caring before, but now there was a note of some kind of recognition. Maybe the recognition of one wounded soul for another. Maybe he'd found a way to liken the demons that drove him to the ones that drove her.

She hardly cared what it was. It was enough that she felt the shared connection between them and knew that he felt it, as well. It had been forever since she'd felt a true connection with anyone. What she'd felt for Kevin had never approached a meeting of hearts. Never.

She leaned against Clint, gradually relaxing into his embrace. For the first time she noticed how good he smelled: of man, soap and fresh air. Intoxicating scents to a woman who hadn't let anyone this close in a long time without the blinding pall of fear in the middle.

Bit by bit the tension seeped from her, and in its place came awareness of other things: his hard, muscled chest; the gentle strength of his hold; his steady breathing near her ear. The aroma of his shampoo. His warmth. How big he was, how powerful. But even that couldn't scare her now, because all that power had devoted itself to protecting her. A godsend.

An amazing godsend, just as she had been about to give up hope.

Then she noticed the heat.

A warmth where their bodies met at the loins as she straddled him. It was as if her attention took a sudden nose dive to her very center, pushing away everything else.

Oh, man, she'd never thought she would feel this way again. Kevin had long since crushed desire out of her, or so she had thought, but here it was, as alive as ever it had been. Acute. Weakening. Demanding an answer.

Two layers of fabric, at least, lay between them, but that only aroused her more. Made her feel safe enough to acknowledge her excitement.

Moist heat. She was spread wide, with her legs on either side of him, and she realized even the slightest movement would brush cloth, and him, against her most sensitive flesh. She held her breath, waiting, waiting, hoping against hope to feel just the slightest brush of fabric as one of them moved. Everything inside her focused on that point of almost-contact.

Oh, please…

Her heart skittered, as if afraid of what she was thinking. She couldn't. She was broken. She would only get so far before she would inevitably frustrate them both. She couldn't do that to him. Not again.

But, oh, how she needed to know that Kevin hadn't utterly destroyed this part of her. Needed to feel hope. Needed Clint. Needed him the way she had needed nothing since her grandmother's death.

She needed him so much it was frightening.

She gasped, drawing a breath finally. And then, hardly moving, afraid to let him know where her mind and body had wandered, because he would have every right to push her away after what she'd done before, she lowered herself the tiniest bit.

Ahh!

Just that little whisper of contact, that little brush of fabric…heaven! Enough to awaken a long-forgotten ache.

"Kay…" he whispered.

No! Please. No. Don't bring back reality. Not now. Not when she was trembling on the lip of a discovery she needed as much as she'd ever needed anything.

His hand slid down her back. Slowly. Carefully. She bit her lip and buried her face in his neck. Hoping. Waiting. *Please take me there!*

His hand reached her bottom, rested there for a few seconds, then gently, oh so gently and carefully, pressed her a tiny bit closer.

A soft groan escaped her as she felt him hard against her, as she realized he wanted her, too. Her fear of being soiled and ugly forever went up in smoke. *He* didn't feel that way about her, and he was letting her know that, letting her know she wasn't alone in this moment of madness.

She pressed her face even harder against his neck, signaling her yearning. Everything deep inside her throbbed now in a way she'd almost forgotten.

She didn't know how to do this, she realized hazily. She didn't know how to reach out for this. She'd never been allowed to. It had always been Kevin who decided, whether she wanted it or not. She had not one bit of knowledge about how to seduce a man.

Nor could she be completely certain she wanted to.

But Clint seemed to understand. Somehow, as if he plucked the thoughts from her very mind, he knew.

The hand on her bottom pushed her a little closer, and another soft groan escaped her. Had anything ever felt this good? Then, driven by an instinct she didn't even know she had, she rocked her hips against him, just once. Just once because she needed something deeper.

"Easy," he whispered.

She almost jerked back as fear spiked in her, but his hand held her close.

"Easy," he whispered. "Slowly. Take your time."

Time was the last thing she wanted to take right now. She was afraid, so afraid, that this moment would suddenly shatter in a burst of fear and self-hatred.

For an instant she thought he was about to push her away, and horror gripped her. But before it could gain control, she realized all he had done was move her a bit. Just a little bit, so there was some space between them. Oh, Lord, he *was* telling her no.

But then he surprised her. His hand slipped between them, between her legs. And with the gentlest of touches, he stroked her through the fabric. Through that layer that not only protected her but seemed to heighten the sensation to a dizzying level.

Oh, heavens, no one had ever touched her that way before. Kevin had always been in a rush, tearing away her clothes to get at what he wanted. This was…this was…

No words would come to her. She lost herself in feeling as Clint's hand continued to stroke her as if she were the most delicate rose petal. Softly. Safely. The guardianship of clothing protecting her from the memories.

Infinitely patient, ever so careful, giving but never taking. Over and over his fingers touched her lightly, until she thought she might go mad from wanting more.

Quiet sounds began to escape her, but she felt safe enough to let them free. The hand on her bottom, the hand between her legs, offered her that freedom in a cushioned, secure place.

Nothing he did caused memories to surface. This was entirely new, entirely different. Helplessly, she gave herself over to his touch. Letting the feelings race through her, carrying her to places she'd never been before. Even when her hips began to helplessly rock, his touch never changed, remaining gentle and sure, giving her freedom to find *herself* again.

Higher she soared, discovering an unexpected joy in opening herself, in surrendering to him and the feelings he evoked.

The ache reached a crescendo close to insanity, but his touch never deepened. Teasing, promising, caring, he took her over the top into an explosion that rocked her to her very core.

She lay boneless and weak against him. His arms cradled her, and the kisses he brushed against her cheek told her she did not need to hide from him. Or from herself.

Finally she found breath to whisper, "I never knew."

"No," he said quietly, "I would imagine you didn't."

He knew her better than she knew herself. Or maybe he just knew Kevin, as he'd said.

But she didn't want to think about Kevin right now, didn't want him intruding on what suddenly seemed to her to be holy ground. She crushed him into the mists of memory, and focused on the here and now.

On the powerful arms that held her so gently. On the big man who had just showed her that she wasn't entirely broken, and had asked not one thing for himself. Not in her wildest imaginings could she have believed a man like Clint existed. Generous. Kind. Undemanding.

But finally one thought wouldn't leave her alone. One thought had to be spoken. "That was selfish of me." She barely got the words past her lips, as shame once again tried to rear its head.

"No," he murmured. "Not at all. You can't imagine the pleasure it gave me."

She lifted her head just enough to see his face. Something there said he wasn't kidding. "But you…"

"Shh," he murmured. "Not every man gets a chance to take a woman to the stars. Especially one who thought she'd never visit them again."

A sigh escaped her, and she let her head fall back to his shoulder. "You took me to the stars," she admitted. "And beyond."

"It's a nice place, isn't it?"

"Wonderful." Then a surprising little imp, long buried, surged in her. "What if I want to go again?"

"I'll gladly be your rocket ship."

Her strength was returning, and she pushed herself up with her hands against his shoulders. At once their loins met again, this time firmly. Oh, she liked that.

"What if…?"

He waited. Then prompted her. "What if?"

She bit her lip and met his gaze from beneath lowered lashes. This was hard to say, but she refused to let herself out of it. She'd been running from too much for too long.

"What if," she said hesitantly, "I want even more?"

A smile began to curve his lips. "Then I'd say I'd love to give it to you."

She almost smiled, but embarrassment overcame her, and she sought refuge again in his neck. "Really?" she asked huskily.

"As much as you want. However you want. But I have a ground rule."

"What's that?"

"We go only where you're comfortable, and we move slowly."

"You'd need the patience of a saint."

"I have plenty of patience. What I absolutely want to avoid is causing you to take any backward steps. You've already had to take enough of those in your life."

She thought about that, then announced, "You're amazing."

"Not really."

"Stop it, Clint. You forget where I've been. I know a good man from a bad one now."

A long breath escaped him, and she almost thought it broke a bit. Concerned, she raised herself upright and looked straight at him. His eyes were closed, hiding his ghosts. Ghosts she wished she could rip out of him with her bare hands.

"Clint?"

"I'll be okay." After a moment he swallowed and opened his eyes. The ghosts were still there, but now something else had joined them. Something warm. Something that made her toes curl.

A few more seconds passed, and then he spoke again. "But there's something I need to do first."

"What's that?"

"I'd be an idiot unworthy of your trust if I didn't take a look outside. It's been an hour."

That long? Fear slammed her again. "But you said it should be several days."

"It should be, and it probably will be. But that doesn't mean I can act on that judgment. There's always the astounding chance I could be wrong."

Despite the return of her fear, she had to smile. He was poking fun at himself, and she liked that. "What if I don't want to let you go?"

"Sorry, lady." Then, with that amazing ease, he lifted her off his lap onto the couch. "First things first. If you haven't changed your mind by the time I get back, we can explore the rocket ship further."

Before he left, he gave her the tire iron again. "Lock the door after me."

Outside, Clint took a few deep breaths of cleansing air. Not because he needed to wash the scent of Kay out of his nostrils, but because he needed to focus single-mindedly on his own prey—Kevin.

The trust Kay had just given him had wrenched those internal cracks even wider; they were beyond hope of cement now. Forever after, even if she left in a few days, those cracks would be filled by Kay.

And he couldn't exactly regret it. The return of feelings other than self-damnation was painful, but it was also good. Maybe he could change.

But first things first, as he'd said. In the garage he had a pair of infrared binoculars. Not the souped-up fancy kind, because he had never needed them, but a basic pair. Just enough to tell him if there was any heat around the tree line.

But first he walked around the house, pretending to check things while keeping an eye out for any movement. He tested the breeze with his nose, like an animal. Years back he'd learned the importance of smells. Your enemy might be on a different diet, which would make him smell different. And in an area like this, which should be empty of anything but animals, even the merest wisp of a human scent of any kind would be important.

Nothing.

He'd cleared the trees back nearly a hundred yards from the house. Not that he disliked trees, but inbred caution from many years on the dangerous side had made it impossible for him to leave cover so close to his home.

As he returned to the garage and picked up the infrared binoculars, he was glad he had been so compulsive. If anything had approached the house tonight, he would be able to tell.

He caught some faint heat signatures from the woods but was pretty sure they were animals. With his regular binoculars he scanned the snow all around and saw no sign of footprints. If Kevin had been watching the place earlier, he hadn't approached the house.

But the absence of sign didn't mean Kevin hadn't been there during the daylight hours to watch. In fact, given what he suspected, he would be willing to bet the man would do his scouting when it was warm—or at least warmer—and clear, even though he would probably save his attack for the middle of the night.

So far everything was okay. But he would have to check again later. Much later, when Kevin would presume the cabin's occupants were soundly asleep.

He returned both pairs of binoculars to the pegs in the garage and made his way back to the front of the house. As he did so, he looked up. The new moon had almost arrived. That would make it a lot harder to see Kevin's approach with regular vision. But it would also daunt Kevin, just a bit, even though the starshine would provide enough light as it magnified itself by bouncing off the snow.

Yeah, Kevin might wait for the cover of the new moon. It would fit, and it would occur about the time Kevin would be getting most anxious to take care of his little mess.

And Clint, despite several years of trying to rein in his impulses toward violence, actually felt a bitter pleasure that the confrontation could not be far off.

Chapter 10

Kay waited for Clint, a morass of emotions. Everything from embarrassment to hope to a new kind of budding fear filled her. She felt so vulnerable right now, and the feeling made her uneasy. Kevin had taught her what it meant to be physically and emotionally vulnerable. Since she had sent him to jail, she'd been busy building protective walls of every kind so that she couldn't be hurt again.

But Clint had slipped past those walls with a delicate touch. She had opened herself to him in a way she had sworn never to do again. If anything, she had opened herself more than ever before, simply because Kevin's approach to sex had always been rough and impatient enough to keep some of her innate barriers in place.

But Clint had slipped past even those. She couldn't help feeling both frightened and exhilarated. Experience and instinct warred inside her, the first warning her not to trust, the second telling her she *needed* to trust. Needed to trust Clint. Needed it for her own survival as a person.

She jumped up when she heard Clint knock on the door. "Clint?" she called when she reached it.

"Just me," he answered.

She opened the door, letting him in with the cold, and watched as he locked it behind him.

"Everything's okay out there," he said immediately. "No sign of him."

Only then did she realize she hadn't been getting wound up only about what had happened between her and Clint. Always, at the back of her mind, no matter how far away he might be, Kevin hovered like a shadow, ever ready to pounce.

"You look cold," she said finally. "Should I make some coffee?"

He paused in the process of kicking off his boots to search her face. For once she could see past the stony facade to the thoughts behind it as clearly as she could look into her own mind. He wondered if she was regretting what they had done.

Was she? Certainty settled in her heart. No. Unable to find another way to respond, she stepped close and hugged him. There was no hesitation in his answering hug. None at all. She was a little amazed, all of a sudden, not just at the barriers she had leaped, but at the barriers he had apparently leaped, as well. When she had met this man, he'd clearly been determined not to let anyone into his life. Yet here she was, if only for a brief time.

He brushed a kiss on the top of her head. "I'll take you up on that coffee," he said huskily.

Slow. He'd said they had to take it slow. Appreciation for him wrapped around her heart. "Okay."

He followed her into the kitchen and helped to make the coffee. While they waited for it to finish, he drew her against his side and held her as he leaned against the counter. Forgetting everything else, even if only for now, she wrapped her arms around his narrow waist and leaned into him. A traitorous thought slipped through her mind; if only she could stay like this forever.

But life didn't offer any forevers, and she knew it. That didn't, however, mean she couldn't pretend for just a few hours or days, whatever time life gave her with him.

They carried their mugs into the living room. This time he didn't take his easy chair but instead sat right beside her on the couch, his arm draped loosely around her shoulders.

Letting her know he was open to her, to being touched, to being hugged. That she didn't have to hide herself or her needs. All at once she felt a glorious sense of freedom unlike anything she had ever felt before. She felt free to be herself without expectation of disapproval.

Tears sprang to her eyes, tears of happiness.

But Clint saw only the tears, not the feeling behind them. "What's wrong?" he asked immediately. "Did I do something?"

"No, no." How could she possibly explain this? "You make me feel…as if it's okay to be me."

A quiet oath escaped him. "Of course it's okay to be you."

"But don't you see?" She looked up at him, tears still hanging on her lashes. "I can't remember ever feeling that way before."

"My God." He whispered the words. "Never?"

"Never. But what about you?" she demanded. "Do you feel it's okay to be you? Have you ever?"

"I used to," he answered after a moment of hesitation. "Maybe I'm working my way back to it. I don't know."

She reached up and palmed his cheek. "It's okay to be you," she said fiercely. "You're a lot more okay than most people."

"You don't know."

"You keep saying that, like I can't see what's right in front of my eyes. You're a born protector. You're kind, generous, thoughtful. Whatever you were before, what you are *now* is the man who's been taking care of a stranger since he found her by the roadside. A man who probably would have been a lot happier not to have his bastion invaded. But you never hesitated. That's the man you are now, Clint, and he's a good man."

His mouth framed a crooked smile. "Maybe."

"No maybe about it." Then she took her newfound courage into her hands and tugged his head a little, just enough to bring him close for a kiss.

She felt him tense, and for an instant she felt a flutter of fear that he would reject her for her forwardness. But when his mouth settled gently onto hers, she realized his tension was because he was controlling himself, trying not to frighten her or bring back bad memories.

"Oh, Clint," she whispered against his mouth. "Oh, Clint." In that instant she would have given anything to heal him the way he was helping her to heal. He didn't deserve the ghosts that haunted him, the demons that he believed lurked within him.

No more, she realized, than she did.

"Easy," he murmured, when she tried to deepen the kiss.

Easy? She was ready to attack him and leap every last wall in one bound. But even as she realized that, she knew he was right. Neither of them knew what might trigger one of the land mines Kevin had planted in her, and she would hate herself if she pulled away again. Because if she did that, he might justifiably never let her this close again.

Patience, she told herself. Patience.

"Are you ready?" he asked huskily.

"Ready?" She pulled back a little, looking at him from heavy-lidded eyes that didn't want to stay open.

"Are you ready to be with me?"

Her heart skipped several beats. For a moment the ugly memories tried to rise, but she beat them down and answered honestly, because he deserved it. "I want to *try.*"

"Then let's explore the rocket ship a little more."

She nodded, waiting, wondering where he would begin.

He began by rising, then lifting her into his arms. "I've never," he said, "been one for making love on a sofa."

Somehow that comment made her want to giggle. "Why not?"

He carried her toward the back of the house. "Something about getting so preoccupied that I'd probably knock us both to the floor."

The giggle escaped her then, and she was glad to see him smile. His gaze met and held hers.

"Do you have any idea," he asked, "just how beautiful and sexy you are?"

She felt her cheeks grow hot and pressed her face to his shoulder. "No," she mumbled.

"Then let me put it this way. I'm having to fight an almost overwhelming urge to behave like an animal in rut. It's been a helluva long time since anyone made me feel this way. You make me hotter than a blacksmith's forge."

"Oh." She liked that. She liked that a lot.

She opened her eyes when he started to lower her feet to the floor.

They were in his bedroom now, dark with night, curtains drawn against the world. The only light came from the hallway behind them.

He had a king-size bed. Well, of course. He was a big man. She only vaguely noticed a dresser, a chair and a doorless closet. The bed gripped her attention, and once again she felt the merest shudder of anticipatory fear.

"We can stop right here," he said, as if he read the fear on her face.

She looked at him. "Right now all I'm afraid of is disappointing you."

"That's impossible," he said flatly.

"How can you know that?"

"Because the only thing that would disappoint me right now is myself, if I do something stupid and scare you."

"I'm not worried about that." Well, only a little. Realizing he wouldn't carry her any farther because he needed to know this was her own choice, she walked over to the bed on rubbery knees and lay down.

A moment later he joined her, reaching out for her hand and clasping it. Minutes ticked by as they remained like that, looking up at the ceiling.

"When is launch time?" she asked finally.

A chuckle escaped him. "That's up to you."

"Hmm. What if I said I don't know how to...launch?" It embarrassed her to admit it, but she sensed that truthfulness was the only thing that would serve both of them right now.

"Do you want me to lead?" he asked.

She rolled onto her side and looked at him. "I never had a choice," she said. "I might as well have been a plastic doll with Kevin, and there's never been anyone else."

"Son of a bitch," he said, though his tone was mild enough.

"Yeah, he was."

"Not supposed to be that way." Now he rolled onto his own side to face her, leaving only a few inches between them. He propped his head on his hand so he looked down at her. "Wanna play a game?"

"What kind of game?"

"Let's pretend you've never done this before. Any of it. This is your very first time."

She swallowed and nodded. That might be hard. But the idea held a certain appeal. "Okay."

"And let's pretend I'm the big bad seducer of young maidens who have no experience."

"I don't know about the bad part."

He shrugged a little. "Most people might think a seducer is bad."

"But what if I need one?"

"Then maybe it's not bad at all." He reached out to brush her cheek gently, to push her hair back. Then he traced the outline of her ear with his finger, and a shiver of longing ran through her.

"Just make me one promise," he said.

"If I can."

"Tell me if I do anything you don't like for any reason at all. You don't have to explain a thing. Just say no, okay?"

She nodded and swallowed again. Her heart had begun to beat heavily and her breathing accelerated. "I promise."

"Good." He smiled a little and ran his finger around the shell of her ear once more, before letting it trail down to the pulse in her neck. A soft gasp of pleasure escaped her, as sparks seemed to run from his fingertip to her center.

"See?" he murmured. "This can be a fun game."

"Have you played it before?"

"I never needed to before. But I think I'm going to like it a whole lot."

She thought she would, too.

"Close your eyes, darlin'," he said quietly. "Just feel."

And oh, he made it so easy to do exactly that. She lay there, her breathing growing quicker as he continued to stroke her face and throat. Deep inside a different kind of pounding began, a pounding that wanted answers.

Answers he didn't give. He continued to stroke her ear and throat until she found her whole body willing him to touch her elsewhere, anywhere, because instinct and need demanded more.

But he was patient, maybe too patient. Even so, she was afraid to rush him as he slowly and surely carried her into a whole new world of hunger and beauty.

"Easy now," he murmured, almost a warning, and then his hand left her throat. Slowly it swept downward, along her side to her hip, then back up again. He repeated the movement until a long shaky sigh escaped her and her body, of its own accord, tried to move closer.

"Easy," he said again. "Just enjoy the feelings. We have plenty of time."

But it was so hard. He'd barely touched her, really, yet he'd awakened so many feelings that she had thought were lost to her forever. Never had she imagined that passivity could be so difficult. With Kevin she had frozen inside, allowing herself to feel nothing at all as she did exactly as he asked.

This man was asking nothing, and he was unfreezing her. Fast.

"Clint," she whispered.

"A little more?" He obliged before she could answer. His hand stopped wandering her side and brushed over one breast. The electric shock was so sudden and unexpected that she arched and gasped.

"Oh, that's nice, isn't it?" he said, his voice throaty. "Very nice. You have beautiful breasts, you know."

Did she? Hazily she remembered Kevin thinking they were too small and complaining about it. But Kevin wasn't here. Not in this place. And Clint seemed to think something else entirely.

"See," he murmured, closing his hand around her. "You fit perfectly in my hand." Then his thumb rubbed over her nipple through the fabric, and a moan escaped her. "Perfect," he murmured. "So perfect I want to kiss it."

"Yes," she whispered. "Yes." Oh, please, yes.

His hand dipped down, sliding across her belly, striking more fire, and as it moved upward again it slipped under the sweatshirt. She gasped, loving the feel of his callused palm against the soft skin of her midriff. Loving how it scratched ever so slightly as it moved tantalizingly upward. Slowly upward. Giving her ample time to object.

But objection was the last thing on her mind.

Now his hand cupped her breast without the fabric barrier, and without a thought she pressed herself harder into his palm. This was what she wanted. This was what she had never known.

His thumb brushed back and forth, teasing, taunting, satisfying and dissatisfying all at once. And then she felt the merest breath of cool air before his tongue replaced his thumb. He flicked her nipple, cool and swollen, with wet heat until a small groan escaped her and she tried to reach for him.

"Shh," he said. "I'm nowhere near done seducing you."

At that moment she would have said she didn't need any more seduction. Already she was getting close to the stars he'd shown her for the first time just a short while ago.

Then she jerked in astonishment and relief as his mouth closed over her nipple. He sucked gently on her at first, then more strongly, until it seemed there was a direct line between his mouth and the point of sensation between her legs. Her whole body throbbed in time with his mouth, and her legs loosened, then tightened, as she tried to find relief.

"You are so sweet," he whispered. Then his mouth moved to her other breast, giving her attention she had barely realized she needed.

"Clint," she moaned, getting more impatient by the second. Yet he would not hurry, not even when she grabbed his shoulders and tried to pull him closer.

"Not yet," he said softly. "I want you over the moon with me."

He was going over the moon? Something in her healed over in an instant. Another wordless moan escaped her as her body took over, rocking her hips, seeking more and still more.

A little laugh escaped him, as if he were pleased. Then, as he continued to tongue her nipple and suck her breast, his hand slipped down along her hip and back to the place it had touched before. Still outside the fabric, shielding her from intimacies that might come too soon. And again he stroked her as if she were the most delicate flower.

She was caught, strung on a wire of fire running from her breast to her core. Her body shivered and struggled toward the stars, but he wouldn't quite let her go there.

Almost, but not quite. Who would have thought torture could be so wonderful?

"Clint…"

"Are you really ready, darlin'?"

Her eyes flew open and looked straight into his. "I've never been this ready in my life."

He chuckled softly. "Be sure. Very sure."

She had no doubts, not even when she felt him begin to tug the sweatpants down. She even lifted her hips to help, glad to be rid of them.

Then his fingers found her petals, and the pleasure-pain sensation was so exquisite that a cry escaped her.

He stopped at once. "Are you all right?"

"Oh, please, don't stop!" Past all thought and reason, she knew what she wanted. She reached for his shirt with one hand, his belt with the other. "Clint…"

"Easy." He rolled away briefly, and when he came back to her, he was nude. In the dark she could see very little, but at last she could touch him, learn him, try to make him half as crazy as he had made her.

He pulled the sweatshirt over her head, the sweatpants from around her ankles, then tugged her close so they met, skin on skin from breast to thigh. She felt his hardness against her and threw her leg over his hip, wanting that hardness inside her as she'd never wanted anything in her life.

She felt him press against her, an answer but not enough. Instead his hands and mouth continued to roam her body, as if he wanted to memorize every silky inch.

"Anything you want," he murmured just before he kissed her mouth. "Anything. Just let me know."

She wrapped her arms as tightly around his neck as she could and thrust her hips against his. "I want *you.*"

No doubt, no question. He'd carried her to the point of no return.

"Then hang on just a second." He rolled away, and she heard what sounded like a drawer, then something tore. A familiar scent assailed her nostrils, and for an instant, just an instant, she remembered another time. Another first time when simple precautions had struck her as caring. She froze.

But then he came back to her, and before she could become totally locked in memory, he began again to caress her in those amazing ways, ways that took her so far out of herself that she was in a universe where Kevin had never existed.

"Clint, please," she begged, her voice thick with need. "Please. Now." She didn't think she could bear another minute of this exquisite torture.

He surprised her. He didn't push her onto her back. No, he lifted her so that she straddled him and had to brace her hands on his shoulders. He held her waist, stilling her.

"As much as you want, no more," he said, his own voice husky with passion. "You're in charge. You lead the way."

She knew exactly where she was going now. She positioned him with her hand, feeling the latex, accepting that he cared enough to protect her, wishing he didn't have to, and then she lowered herself.

Slowly. He was big. So very big, and her muscles stretched as if this was the very first time for her. That, too, made it special, seeming almost to cleanse the stains on her spirit.

Certainly it was her first time with Clint. And she reveled in it.

She took him slowly, but once he was fully within her, a sigh of sheer pleasure escaped her. Then, with his hands on her hips, it was she who took them both to the stars.

"I need to take care of something," he murmured in her ear.

She lay hot, sweaty and utterly sated atop him. "No." The last thing on earth she wanted was to be separated from him by even so much as an inch.

"Yes," he said, and there seemed to be humor in his voice. "I don't want to give you an unexpected present."

She sighed, letting him reach between them to remove himself cautiously from her hot, wet depths, then allowed herself to be rolled gently to the side.

"I'll be right back," he said, and showered a few kisses on her face and breasts.

She didn't want to move. Not one single muscle. She didn't want to lose one bit of what she was feeling right now.

Eyes closed, she listened to Clint go into the bathroom, listened to the water run, and sensed the exact instant he returned to the room. How had she lived so long and never realized it could be like this?

He lifted her, surprising her eyes open, then put her back down, this time on a sheet. He pulled the covers over her, then slipped under them with her and drew her close. She snuggled into him, into the safe haven he had made for her.

And finally she said, "That was some rocket ride."

A quiet laugh escaped him. "I've never had a better one. Ever."

Moments she never wanted to end stretched before her in a golden glow. The transformation inside her seemed almost impossible to believe, yet there it was. She had changed. Forever.

The phone rang. This time it was Clint who groaned. "Hell," he said.

She felt the same, but only for an instant. *Kevin.* It had to be about Kevin. With one ring of the phone he came slamming back into her world. Her heart skittered, and every muscle in her body coiled.

And this time Clint didn't tell her to relax. Even in the dim light from the hallway, she saw the return of the stone mask.

He hurried out to get the phone, which was in the living room. She could only hear the sound of his voice, not the words. She lay stiff and waiting, afraid of what he might be learning. She squeezed her eyes shut and hoped it was just an old friend, nothing about Kevin.

But even so, Kevin had returned to her mind, with all the terror he had taught her. She couldn't banish him. She might never be able to banish him.

"Kay."

She opened her eyes and saw Clint in the doorway. He was still naked.

"Get dressed," he said. "I'm not going to turn on the light in here. Can you see well enough?"

"What's going on?"

"Just get dressed. I got the mud off your shoes earlier while you dozed, so your feet will be protected."

Terror rose in her as Clint grabbed his clothes from the floor and disappeared while she scrambled into the sweat suit. The socks he had loaned her lay on the floor, forgotten. They wouldn't fit inside her jogging shoes anyway.

Her legs felt like lead as she went to the living room. There she saw something that made her freeze and gasp.

Clint was standing there, snapping his jeans, his back to her as he jammed his feet into his boots. But what she saw on his back gave a whole new meaning to "wounded." Burn scars, deep dips in the flesh that suggested he had been shot and might even be missing parts of himself.

He heard her gasp, and he turned. More scars on his belly. Old ones. How had she not felt those scars with her hands?

He saw where she was looking. "Sorry," he said roughly. "I know it's not pretty."

Her mouth felt dry, but she found her voice. "It's the pain, not how it looks. God, you must have suffered."

"Morphine is a wonderful thing." But he was hurriedly reaching for his shirt, trying to hide the scars from view.

She wouldn't let him. To hell with Kevin. She crossed the room fast, before he could button his shirt, and reached out with both hands, pressing them to his belly, then sliding them around to trace the scars on his back.

"Don't hide from me," she whispered, tightening her hold and pressing her face to his chest. "Please don't."

He stilled and let her hands trace the old scars. Then a sigh escaped him. "Kay, I need to recon. Now."

She lifted her face and looked up at him. "You're beautiful, you know. You really are."

Something in his expression shifted, but only briefly. The stone returned hard and fast. "I've got things to do," he said.

She didn't know if he was trying to escape her, silence her, or simply reacting to the pressure, but regardless, she stepped back and let him finish dressing.

"Your shoes are in the den," he said. "They should be dry by now."

"Okay."

"Keep the door locked. And grab that tire iron."

"What happened?"

He paused halfway to the door and looked back. "Kevin was seen in town today. The sheriff has been showing his mug shot around, and apparently a merchant ID'd him."

"Oh God! He'll hear they're looking for him."

He shook his head. "Not in this county. People might talk among themselves, but they never gossip with strangers—*any* strangers—and especially not about something like this."

He started toward the door again. "Lock up after me," he reminded her. "And finish dressing."

She did as she was told, trying to keep a handle on her fear. She wasn't alone this time. She had Clint. And Clint would, by any measure, be more than Kevin could handle.

But that didn't keep her from picking up the tire iron after she tied her shoes.

The wait seemed endless, but at last there was a knock at the door.

"It's me," said Clint.

She opened the door and let him in. She wanted to throw herself into his arms, let him hold her and drive away the terror once again, but something about him made her pause. She watched as he locked the door, then shed his coat and boots.

"Did you see anything?"

"Not yet."

He walked past her, and she noted the shift in him. He was no longer the lover who had been so gentle. Now he moved like a large cat coiled to spring at any moment. It was almost a relief when he knelt before the fire and put another couple of logs on. That at least seemed normal and ordinary.

But the ghosts were back. She saw them the instant he straightened and faced her.

"You can relax for now," he said. But the gentleness was gone from his voice, and his eyes had a distant look to them. As if he were focused somewhere else.

"Maybe," she said hesitantly, "you should call the cops to come get me. Or take me to them yourself."

Now his gaze snapped into focus, and she knew for certain he saw her. "Why do you say that? You were dead set against it."

"Because I'll never forgive myself if something happens to you. Or if you have to do something you'll regret later. I've been selfish. So selfish."

"No."

No? She stared back in astonishment. "No?"

He shook his head. "This ends soon, and it ends here. If I take you to the cops, there's no telling when that bastard will find you again. No. This time it's *my* way."

Before she could begin to muster an argument, he started to move. Window by window he removed the obstacles he'd laid out.

"Why are you doing that?"

"I only put them there so you could sleep easily. So you wouldn't be lying awake in terror that he might get in while you slept. They're not necessary."

"No? Then how the hell will you know if he breaks in?"

The smile he gave her was chilling. "I'll know. I'll know as soon as he makes the attempt. And the last thing I want to do is scare him off."

She didn't know if she liked this, but he seemed so certain.

"You only need a perimeter warning system when you don't have enough sentries to cover the entire perimeter," he said, as if trying to get her to understand. "You have a sentry. Me. Just trust me on this, Kay. The bastard is counting his freedom in days now, if not hours."

She certainly hoped he was right about that. But Kevin had taken on such monstrous proportions in her mind that he seemed superhuman.

But then, Clint was taking on those proportions now, too, and for a much better reason. Finally she sagged onto the couch, still holding the tire iron, and let him do whatever he thought necessary.

Because Clint was right about one thing, if nothing else, this had to end. Over the last few days, Clint had taught her so much about the kind of life she wanted to have, a kind of life that was actually possible if she could get out from under Kevin's shadow for good.

And she couldn't think of a better reason than that to make the stand here and now.

Clint finished up at the back of the house. When he returned, though, he took his easy chair instead of sitting beside her, and she ached, feeling dismissed.

Yet some part of her realized that wasn't fair. He had gone into some kind of mode that precluded distractions. He had the look of a hunter, she thought, and it wouldn't be wise to break that concentration.

She ought to know. Intense focus had saved her more than once.

"Kay?" His quiet voice pierced a silence that had been punctuated only by the crackle of the fire for what seemed a long time now.

"Yes?"

"I want you to know…" He hesitated.

She waited, sensing he was struggling with something. No point in pushing him.

He tried again. "The part of me you'll see until we get Kevin...*you* don't need to fear it."

"I know that." Her own certainty came as a surprise.

"Do you?" He searched her face. "But some of it may...horrify you."

"After what I've been through? For the love of God, Clint, I've been beaten, burned, kicked, raped, strangled, kidnapped, starved and pursued across half the country. Maybe there haven't been any guns or bullets yet, but I have a nodding acquaintance with what men are capable of."

"I guess you do." His face darkened.

"So let's be clear on something I've finally figured out."

"What's that?"

"That sometimes, just sometimes, it matters *why* people do bad things. And self-defense, or the defense of another, seems like the best reason anyone could have."

One corner of his mouth lifted. "Well, that's Just War Theory in a nutshell."

The remark came at her sideways, but then she caught his reference. "Really? I came up with something that smart on my own?"

He shook his head and sighed. "When are you ever going to believe you're not stupid? You don't need a wall full of degrees to be smart, Kay. Believe me. You're smart."

"I'd still like the degree."

"When this is over, we'll make that dream come true. God knows, you have everything it takes to get the piece of paper."

That lit a little warm glow in her heart. But there was a bridge to be crossed first. A scary bridge.

"So," she said hesitantly, "what's the plan? What do we do?"

"We wait." His gaze grew distant again. "I don't think he'll come tonight. It's too soon after the blizzard. He couldn't have scouted enough to be sure how many people are in the house."

"Tomorrow night?"

"Possibly. If I were him, I'd wait for the dark of the moon, but he doesn't have my training. My guess, and it's only a guess, is that he'll want another day to make sure there are only two of us here."

"And then?"

"And then he'll come when he's sure we'll be asleep. I'm betting somewhere between two and four in the morning."

"But we won't be asleep."

"No way."

She nodded, compressing her lips. "That sounds right," she said after a few moments of thought. "He used to come after me at night, when he hunted me down. Twice he caught me in bed asleep. The last time…well, I was out jogging. Some of those country roads can be pretty empty. I thought I'd be safe because I'd hear any cars coming."

"But you weren't?"

She shook her head. "Obviously. He was waiting for me, not following me. He jumped out from behind some bushes and hit me on the head before I realized what was happening."

"Hell." He met her eyes. "Let's get something clear right now."

"What's that?"

"You saw that my only closet doesn't have doors. So when I tell you to hide, you get under the bed. No ifs, ands or buts."

"Why?"

"Because there are two of us in this house, and he's going to know it. Because he wants to end this. My guess is he's going to come armed with something more than a tire iron or a knife."

"Oh my God." She breathed the words. "Clint, you've got to take me to the police. I don't want you to risk your life!"

"No," he said, stone-faced and impassive.

"Dammit, don't give me that Sphinx crap! If he shoots you…" Oh, God, she couldn't bear to even think about it.

"First of all," he said levelly, "Kevin isn't going to know I'm waiting for him. Secondly, I have body armor, a relic from the past. I just wish I had some for you. So you're going to get under the bed, right?"

She nodded. "If there's time."

"There's going to be time. That's where you're going to be *before* he gets into this house."

"How can you know that?"

"Because I'm going to be awake and waiting."

It sounded like a Möbius strip of thoughts to her, but he seemed so self-assured that she couldn t doubt him.

Helplessly, she looked at the pendulum clock ticking on the mantelpiece. It was the first time she had honestly cared what time it was, but now that clock had become all-important.

Because she knew he was right. Kevin would come in the dead of night. The only question was which night.

At midnight Clint went outside again. Ten minutes later he was back with an odd-looking pair of binoculars. "Night vision," he said shortly when she looked curious.

Then he walked through the house, turning out the lights one after another, until the glow of the flickering fire was the only illumination. The shadows grew deep, moving as if with a life of their own.

He had begun to pace in deadly earnest now, moving from room to room with surprising silence.

She watched him, growing increasingly on edge, wishing for distraction but knowing it would be dangerous now.

"Damn fire," he muttered at one point.

"What's wrong with it?"

"I can't look out the front windows. If I pull the curtains back even a bit, he could see, because there would be light behind me."

"Can we put it out?"

He shook his head. "No central heat. Besides, I might as well send up a flare, letting him know we're on the lookout."

He paused, obviously thinking. "Okay, I'm fairly certain he won't come from the front. He might be seen.

Sarah said they're increasing road patrols in this area. Not heavily, but enough. He won't be familiar with the usual patrol patterns, so it shouldn't alert him."

She nodded, trying to follow.

"No, he'll want maximum cover. That means the back."

"And you nailed the windows shut," she reminded him.

He shrugged. "That was mostly for you. Breaking a window would announce his arrival, and sliding one open makes noise, especially with wood frames. And then it takes time to climb through, time when he'd be exposed. No, he's going to try to jimmy a door lock. Maybe pick it." He looked at her. "You think he knows how to pick a lock?"

"Probably. He got into my apartment twice without alerting the neighbors. Afterward, there was no sign of damage to the locks."

"Good." His smile was unpleasant. "He'll be counting on that, then."

He paced through the house once more, then glanced at the clock. It was almost one. "In a little while I'm going to ask you to move to the bedroom. If anything happens, anything at all, promise you'll get under that bed."

When she looked as if she might object, he went on.

"Look," he said sternly, "I don't want to have to worry about you. I want you safely out of the way so I can do my job."

"Okay." But she rebelled at him taking risks for her, though the more reasonable part of her knew she wasn't capable of handling this on her own. Experience had taught her that. No matter how she had fought, Kevin had always gotten the upper hand, until finally she had learned not to fight at all. But one thing she was sure of, although she didn't tell him, and that was that she would not simply hide. Not anymore. If she didn't fight for herself, she would lose something essential and never be able to get it back.

She sighed. Then something else rose to the forefront of her mind. "How were you wounded?"

For several seconds he didn't answer. "Which time?"

Her mind balked. "More than once?"

"More than once," he agreed. "Let's see. Shrapnel and burns from a roadside bomb. A bullet from a sniper. A knife in the back during a covert op."

"But didn't you have armor?"

"When you're undercover, armor could give you away."

"Oh." Her heart squeezed. "So how many parts did you lose?"

"None that matter. Spleen, a chunk of lung, part of a rib, some bits of muscle. Nothing I can whine about."

She hated to imagine what *would* make him whine. "Does it still hurt?"

"Sometimes. Old injuries do that, even when you get them from basketball or soccer."

Feeling her own dulling aches and pains, she could only marvel at his acceptance. "How do you make yourself go back after something like that?"

"Go back to the job, you mean?"

She nodded.

"The same way you're making yourself face this mess right now. Because you have to."

She could see a commonality in that, although there was a huge different in degree.

"And we need to be quiet now," he said. "Our voices could be heard."

Fear slammed her again, but this time she forced it down. When he offered his hand, she took it, and allowed him to lead her back to the darkened bedroom.

"You can sit on the chair or lie on the bed," he murmured. "Just stay awake so you hear me if I tell you to hide."

"I don't think anything could make me sleep right now." And she didn't. Adrenaline and fear were coursing through her so powerfully that she was sure even lying down would be impossible. She found her way to the chair and sat, wondering if even that would drive her crazy.

Clint pulled off his socks and resumed his prowling on silent bare feet. At first she wondered at that, then realized he didn't want to slip on his socks. At one point, as he passed the bedroom door, she saw that his dark silhouette had changed, had grown bulkier. No doubt the body armor he'd mentioned earlier.

Rarely had a few hours seemed to drag by so slowly, and every time they had, it had always been bad. Why couldn't time slow down when things were wonderful, like when they'd made love earlier? Why did those moments seem to slip by so quickly?

Her thoughts wanted to return to that interlude, to relive it again and again, holding it up as assurance that life could be beautiful, that she could be whole again. Finally she just gave in and let it, while her eyes watched the red numbers on the digital alarm by the bed change minute by minute.

Clint was an amazing lover, and she didn't need a whole lot of experience to tell her that. Her body recognized it as surely as if her experience had come with a million testimonials. Maybe better.

He'd awakened feelings so long dormant she'd begun to believe they had died. And now she knew one thing for certain—she wanted to live long enough to make love with Clint again.

If that meant sitting here in the dark, terrorized by a memory and a threat, then she would do it. She shifted her hold on the tire iron, cherishing the bit of protection it offered, but cherishing more the man who prowled the house like a giant cat, on guard and ready.

After years of running and hiding, she'd found someone who was willing to stand up for her, willing to stand *with* her, even at huge risk to himself. Someone who hadn't even wanted her here in the first place, but had a huge enough sense of duty and honor to care for her anyway.

How many places could you find a man like that? Very few, as well she knew. She'd faced impatient prosecutors, impatient cops, people who thought they had much more important things to deal with. People who cared, but not enough, who were perhaps too busy to care. When they told her they didn't have enough evidence, she'd wondered if she was somehow supposed to provide more than her own battered, abused body as proof. But Kevin, all but that one time, had had an alibi. And he'd left nothing behind to betray him.

She'd especially hated it when they had been hinted that maybe *she* was somehow letting Kevin know how to find her. That maybe *she* got some sick pleasure out of the horror of her own life.

Her hands tightened so hard on her weapon that she had to force them to relax before they started to weaken.

Then came the dawn, and with it the sickening realization that she still had to look forward to the threat and another night of endless tension.

God, she wanted to be sick.

"Get some sleep," Clint said from the doorway. "I'm good for a few more hours, but then I'm going to need you to spell me."

She would have liked to ask him to sleep with her, to feel the security of him wrapped around her, but she understood his concern. Everything had to give way to vigilance now.

Unless the cops found him. But Kevin was smarter than that. He'd already proved that several times over.

Clint was right; Kevin would come at night, and he would come from the rear. He would come from where he was sure nobody could see him.

Because while he might be crazy, he wasn't stupid.

She put down the tire iron and crawled into the bed. She could still smell the musky scent of their lovemaking, and it soothed her somehow. At last she found forgetfulness in sleep.

Chapter 11

He woke her around noon with coffee. Sitting on the edge of the bed, he called her name quietly until her eyes fluttered open.

Even though he tried to mask it with a smile, she could see weariness in his face.

"You shouldn't have let me sleep so long!" At once she sat up and tried to swing her legs to the floor, but he was in the way.

He was still smiling when he reached out to touch her legs. A gentle, tentative touch. She felt warmth run through her like syrup.

"My turn to sleep," he told her. "Do you want your coffee here, or would you be more comfortable elsewhere?"

What she wanted was to grab him and drag him down onto the bed with her. Without the guardian of full wakefulness, desire rose up like a tidal wave. She could feel her cheeks heat.

"What I want," she managed to say, "isn't on the menu this morning."

At that a quiet chuckle escaped him. "At least not right now." His eyes held a warmth she'd almost never seen there.

"So everything's okay?"

"So far."

She decided she had to get out of the bed or everything was *not* going to be okay. With the way he had distracted her yesterday, she was quite certain that if they went there again, Kevin would be able to bash his way into the house and she would never even hear him.

With a reluctant sigh, she climbed out of the warm bed and padded into the front room.

"Breakfast, too?" she asked as she emerged from the hallway and saw the table.

"Hot and ready," he said.

She almost giggled at his choice of words, even though he probably hadn't meant them as a double entendre. But when she stole a glance at him, she amended her judgment. Maybe he *had* meant them that way.

A touch of shyness overcame her then, enough to get her to the table and seated before a plate of steak and eggs. "This looks wonderful!"

"I was surprised you didn't wake up while I was cooking."

"Now that I see what you've been up to, I'm surprised, too."

Her own hunger also surprised her, and while he'd served her far more than she would have chosen on her own, she devoured a surprising amount of it. They didn't talk much as they ate, but what were they going to talk about?

Not their lovemaking, not now. Not Kevin, because he couldn't be allowed to ruin this meal. Not the future, because right now neither of them was sure if they had one, or what it might be. But somehow the silence that had initially been a regular part of this household now seemed uncomfortable.

Too much on their minds, she decided. Too many subjects to avoid. And she found herself actually hoping that Kevin would come that night. She wanted this over with.

At last he finished. "Wake me at four," he said.

She looked at him. "Will that be enough sleep for you?"

"Absolutely. And I want to be wide-awake before it gets too dark." He paused. "Look out the windows from time to time. Just don't get too close to them."

She nodded, suppressing a shiver as the darkness moved into her mind again. She watched him disappear down the hall, then, moving slowly because the bruises still ached and some new aches had been added by their unexpected lovemaking, she cleared up and washed the dishes. It kept her busy.

She looked out all the windows, copying what she had seen him do, barely twitching curtains aside so she could see the empty areas around the house. No sign of danger that she could see.

When she went back to the couch at last, she found a surprise waiting for her, a thick hardcover book. There was no jacket, but the cover was dull green, and stamped into it in black were the title and author: *Just War Theory: a Survey and Reflections*. Below the title, in smaller print: Clint Ardmore, PhD. USMC (Ret.).

His book!

She sat and eagerly opened it. When she got to the flyleaf, her breath caught and her throat tightened.

Kay, he'd written in a bold hand, *you understand far better than you know. Clint.*

She stared at the words, feeling a throb in her chest. Nobody had ever given her a gift like this, a gift that said she was bright enough to understand.

She clutched the book to her breasts and closed her eyes for a minute, hugging the feelings, hugging the intent, wishing she could hug Clint right this minute.

Then, cautiously, sure she wouldn't begin to understand this kind of book or even this kind of writing, she opened to the preface and began to read.

Much to her surprise, she was drawn right in.

Hours later she looked up to realize that the day was darkening. A glance at the clock caused her heart to skip.

He'd said four. It was already four-thirty. Where had the time gone?

She put the book aside and jumped to her feet. She hurried back to the bedroom, aware that night was already beginning to encroach. She hoped he wouldn't be angry with her.

"Clint?"

He sprang out of bed as if launched and settled into a crouch.

"Clint, it's me."

Slowly he relaxed and straightened. The first words he spoke were, "It's getting dark."

"I know. I'm sorry. I was reading your book and lost track of time. Don't be mad at me." She was already tensing, moving backward, shaking.

"Why the hell would I be mad at you?" It was almost a bark, making her jump back farther. "Kay…" He adjusted his tone. "I'm sorry," he said quietly. "I'm not mad at you. I can't imagine ever being mad at you. I was just startled."

She began to breathe again, although she still felt shaky. "Because I was late getting you?"

He shook his head. "If things like that made me mad, I'd be nuts."

"Or Kevin," she admitted.

He swore quietly. "I'm sorry. What you just saw was my own demon at work. I still wake up as if I'm under attack."

"I know what you mean."

He nodded. "I think you do."

She hesitated. "Thank you so much for the book. I'm enjoying it."

"You're just saying that to be nice. It's as dry as bones."

She shook her head. "No. I really am enjoying it. It's slow reading, but I'm learning a whole lot. That's why I woke you late. I got absorbed."

"Well." He sounded almost pleased. "That's really nice to hear. People say it about my novels, but I think you're the first person, other than a professor or two, to actually say that about the textbook."

"Well, I'm certainly not a professor."

"Wouldn't surprise me if you took that route someday." Evidently deciding they'd both relaxed enough by now, he approached her and slowly slipped his arms around her. "I need my head examined," he said almost to himself, then bent to kiss her.

She sailed away again to a far planet, a place where nothing existed except Clint. And she would very much have liked to stay there, except just as she started to wind her arms around him, he broke the kiss.

"Damn," he said almost ruefully. "I gotta get rid of that guy. He's interfering with my desire to sweep you off your feet and right into my bed."

She felt a current of joy mixed with desire zap through her. "Really?"

"Really," he admitted. "But first things first. I want the bastard off my plate. And off yours. Then we'll have time to decide if we both just went temporarily insane."

Well, Kay thought as they headed to the front of the house, that was always possible. If so, she wanted to go permanently insane.

But the shadows were deepening, and with them her fear. She wondered if she would ever feel truly comfortable in the dark again.

But Clint surprised her. He headed straight for the kitchen, turned on a few lights, and asked her if peanut butter sandwiches were okay with her.

"Sure." She hesitated. "Um… Why did you turn on the light?"

"Because we've got to make it look normal in here. It's supper time. Lights in the kitchen. Go turn on a light or two in the living room."

"We want him to think we don't expect anything?"

"You got it." He flashed her a smile, though only a small one.

"Are you going outside to look again?"

"Not tonight."

"Why not?"

"Because if he's been watching, he knows I've been on alert. I want him to think I'm asleep at the wheel now, feeling safe."

She had never imagined how much psychology went into this sort of thing. "Have you been planning this all along?"

"Lady, that's what they used to *pay* me to do."

She was still standing on the kitchen threshold. Questions kept bubbling up. "But…"

He raised a hand. "Give me five to make sandwiches. Then we'll talk about what I've been doing, and why I'm changing the pattern now."

"Okay." She could agree to that. She went and turned on a few lights, signaling even through the curtains that the people inside the cabin were up and about and busy.

She would have felt safer with less light, despite her fear of the shadows, but she trusted Clint to know what to do.

And that brought her up short. She trusted Clint a whole lot, she realized. She trusted him completely. Was that wise? Her heart said it was.

They ate their sandwiches at the table, accompanied by tall glasses of milk.

"Okay," he said. "I've been listening to you and building a picture of Kevin in my head. A profile. I think I know what he's thinking and what will draw him in."

She nodded. "Okay."

"I realize you know him better, but I know predators, obsessives and bastards. I'll allow I could be wrong, but I don't think so."

She nodded. "Go on."

"I've been keeping an eye out in part to catch some sign of him. The need for that evaporated yesterday when Sarah called to say he'd been spotted in town. Whether or not I catch sight of him in the woods now is irrelevant. He hasn't run away to try again another day. He's here, and there's only one reason for that—he knows you're still around."

She nodded, and peanut butter suddenly stuck in throat. She reached for her milk and took a few swallows, wishing she could be anywhere near as clinical about this as he was.

"Am I disturbing you? Upsetting you too much?"

"No," she said. "Well, yes, but I want to know. I've got to know."

He nodded, measuring her. "Okay. We know he's out there. So he's going to come. If he's watched this place at all since the blizzard stopped, he'll know I've been out there checking around. Of course I did it partly to see if I could get a sense of where he'd come from, or where he might be watching from. But I also did it to send the signal I was alert. To hold him off. But now I'm going to send a different signal. The new one is that I think we're safe now."

"So he'll feel safe making his approach?"

"Exactly. Like I said last night, I don't want to scare him off. Not now." His hands flexed a bit, as if he could feel them around Kevin's throat. "Tonight or tomorrow night, he's going to make his move. I'd bet money on it."

Kay drew an unsteady breath and looked down at her plate. She didn't think she could eat another mouthful. The moment she'd been both dreading and hoping for might only be hours away.

Clint surprised her by reaching out to grasp her hand. "Trust me, Kay, he isn't as smart as he thinks he is. And he's not nearly as smart or capable as *you* think he is."

"Probably not."

"Trust me," he said again, and squeezed her hand. "If you can't eat that, I can get you something else."

She shook her head. "It's hard to swallow anything right now."

"Don't let fear overwhelm you. Use it, don't let it use you."

She wondered how many times he'd had to say that to someone and decided there were some things she didn't want to know. At least not tonight. "I'll try."

"Anger is a good substitute. If the fear gets to be too much, work up a good mad."

She smiled weakly. "That should be easy to do."

"Unless the fear takes charge."

She realized he was right about that. If ever she'd needed to be angry, now was it. But somehow fury kept slipping away before the force of memories. Memories of all the times Kevin had gotten to her despite her fleeing, despite locks, despite her going into hiding. And now he once again knew where she was.

So she looked at Clint, reminding herself of his strength, his confidence, his experience. He was a pillar, and she had to cling to that or slip away into the dark, icy waters of fear.

"You can do it, Kay," he said with the same calm confidence. "You figured out how to get away from him, and you ran with as much determination as I've ever seen. Despite a battered body, despite a concussion. You've got the right stuff."

That, she supposed, was a compliment. It *did* settle her a bit, and she was grateful. One thing she knew with absolute certainty. "He's not going to take me alive. Not again."

Clint's head jerked a little. "Have a little faith in me, woman."

"I do." In spite of herself, a small laugh escaped her. "I'm just saying."

"Well, that's okay, but it won't come to that."

Not as long as Clint was in one piece, maybe. But if Kevin came armed with a gun… A shudder shook her. "It's going to be bad," she whispered. "He *must* have a gun by now."

"Probably." It didn't seem to concern him at all. "And that's why you're going to be under the bed. If I get… momentarily disabled, you be sure to go for his ankles as soon as he gets close enough. Break them. He won't be expecting that."

This time it was *her* hands that clenched, feeling the weight of the tire iron that she would be holding. "I can do that," she said with conviction.

"Of course you can. And he's going to find me harder to put out of action than his worst nightmare."

His tone conveyed such certainty that she absolutely, completely believed him. He would know. He'd been there.

Something like calm passed through her and remained. With its arrival, fear seeped away. "Okay," she agreed, sounding firm for the first time. "But, Clint?"

"Yeah?"

"Don't let anything happen to yourself. We've got a few more rocket trips to take."

He laughed then, a genuine laugh. "Bet on it, lady. Bet on it."

Chapter 12

Night seeped into the house. Even with the lights on, Kay felt it. Night had always been a fearful time for her since Kevin, and she seemed as attuned to it as a mythical vampire. The thought almost amused her. If only she hadn't felt the fear seeping in with it.

At ten, after hours of pretending to read, she heard Clint stir.

"Time," he said. "I want you under the bed. Sorry the floor's so hard."

"I can take it."

And under the bed, perhaps she would feel safe in the darkness. She headed at once for the bedroom, carrying the tire iron with her. It hadn't been out of her reach all day.

Once there, she waited while Clint turned out lights one after another. Then he reached the bedroom and took her into his arms for one tight hug and a deep kiss. The kiss even managed to bypass her fear long enough to make her toes curl.

"Okay," he said huskily. "Get under the bed. Do you want a pillow or something?"

"It might get in the way." Still holding her weapon, she got down onto the floor and slipped beneath the bed. "Hey, Clint?"

"Yeah?"

"You're compulsive."

"Why do you say that?"

"Every self-respecting bed needs some dust bunnies. You don't have any."

The sound of his laugh cheered her. They were going to do this. Yes. Most definitely.

She had to believe that.

Then the bedroom light went out, too. She could tell he was still standing there for a moment; then he left the room on bare feet. Prowling. Much as she strained her ears, all she could hear was the crackle of the fire in the living room, and he'd even let that burn low.

She wiped her palms on the sweat suit and gripped the tire iron anew. Loosely, so her hands wouldn't cramp. Then quietly, slowly, she eased out from under the bed. She still lay on the floor beside it, so he couldn't see her as he walked by. But she knew one thing for certain—if Kevin got in here, Clint was not going to face him alone. She would never forgive herself.

Slowly her eyes adapted to the darkness. The little bit of orange glow that reached the room from the living room was enough. Just enough. If she had to go for Kevin's ankles, she would be able to see them. And she wouldn't miss.

She thought she heard Clint's voice murmuring quietly. Phone?

The floor was hard, especially where she was bruised, but she ignored it. Something filled her, something like a fierce pleasure. This time Kevin wouldn't catch her unawares. This time she was going to be ready. And if she had to use that tire iron, it was going to be a long time before he walked again.

And he deserved it. He was going to deserve everything he got when he came into this cabin. Because he had hurt her. Because he wanted to kill her. Because a man like that didn't deserve to walk around free.

Oh, yes, the anger was building. Slowly and surely, she was getting mad enough to seriously hurt someone.

She saw Clint's bare feet as he came into the room. "Clint?" she whispered.

"Yeah." He kept his voice low.

"Do you have your armor on?"

"Yes. Just put it on."

Something in his voice alerted her. "What happened?"

"I called Sarah."

"And?"

"The cops are close. Very close. They're tightening the noose right now."

"Oh, God…"

"Shh."

"Clint…"

"No more talking." His whisper was firm. "Not a sound, hear me?"

So she didn't make another sound. When she had to move, she did so as stealthily as she could, rising slowly to her feet, grasping the iron rod as she moved silently across the floor to stand just inside the bedroom door. If Kevin came this way, he was going to lose his face.

God, the waiting was endless. If the minutes crept by any slower, she would die of old age before dawn.

What was that?

She thought she'd heard a scratching from somewhere outside the room, but she was unable to tell any more than that. It could have come from anywhere. She held her breath and strained to hear, but the night was silent save for the distant crackling of the fire.

And then she thought she heard it again. Oh God. Her heart climbed into her throat. Dimly she saw Clint pad silently past the door, on his way toward his den—and the back door.

He'd heard something, too. Her heart nearly stopped. Once again she wiped her palms dry and gripped the tire iron. And once again she wished Clint had trusted her with a gun. What if he got hurt? What if she couldn't hit Kevin hard enough?

Clint's promises that nothing would stop him sounded weak now, even exaggerated.

But he would know, she reminded herself. He'd been wounded multiple times. If anyone could know what he was capable of, it was Clint.

She forced herself to quiet her breathing. To stand perfectly still. To wait, when waiting seemed impossible and every nerve in her felt stretched to the point of snapping.

Another sound, more like a snick. A lock? Her mind threw up images of Kevin slipping through the back door, invisible in the dark, bigger than Kevin had ever really been, some mythical, indestructible creature....

Stop! she screamed at herself silently and fought down the fear. *Don't let the fear use you. Use it.*

Good advice. The best advice. Adrenaline began to thrum through her, winding her tight. She could do this. She *would* do this. Because never, ever again was Kevin going to come after her.

"Over my dead body," she promised herself under her breath.

There it was, the faintest squeak of a hinge. The back door must be opening.

Why didn't Clint act? She squeezed her eyes shut for an instant, remembering the layout of the house. Of course, Clint wanted Kevin all the way inside, at least as far as the den door, where she suspected he was waiting.

Then he could take Kevin from the side.

It seemed like a brilliant plan. As long as Kevin didn't get off a shot. Because the idea that Clint might get hurt scared her more now than fear for herself.

The anger was strong in her now, making her ready, clearing her head until every sound, every sight, every thought, was as clear as if it were etched in glass.

Another squeak. The hinge? The sole of a shoe on the wood floor? She couldn't tell. All she knew was that the threat had entered the sanctuary of this house.

She bit her lip, barely daring to breathe.

Then it happened, so fast that her impressions were impossible to sort through. A thud. A grunt.

She stepped out into the hallway, weapon at the ready, and could make out two struggling figures, the bigger one undoubtedly Clint. She stepped closer, determined to hit Kevin with all her might the instant she could do it without hitting Clint. That man was going to pay.

Then the most fearsome sound of all—a gunshot.

She pressed closer, looking for an opportunity, but they were struggling together, both so close....

More grunts. Another shot.

God in heaven! She gripped the tire iron as tightly as she could, then watched in horror as the larger figure began to sink toward the floor.

He'd hurt Clint. The thought filled her with fury. Just a little closer, she thought. *A little closer, you bastard. A little closer.*

"There you are," said the all too familiar voice.

Panting hard now, she watched as he stepped over Clint. Oh God, Clint was dead.

Something in her snapped in that moment. She raced toward Kevin, screaming. Apparently her reaction startled him. He must have been expecting her to turn into the usual bundle of terrified passivity. But she didn't care anymore, didn't care about a damn thing except that was Kevin and he'd hurt Clint.

She swung the tire iron with all her might, wielding it with the power of all the terrified nights, all the anguish, all the pain, all the hatred she felt for him and what he had turned her into.

The iron bar connected with his forearm just as he was raising it, recovering enough to aim at her. She heard the satisfying crunch of bone, the yowl of pain, but, still maddened, she went after him again, this time catching him on his shoulder. She heard something heavy and metallic hit the floor, and then Kevin sagged, falling.

But just as she would have struck him again, Clint rose up behind Kevin and hurled himself at Kevin's back, knocking him over completely, driving the breath out of him.

Kevin shrieked as Clint rose up again, straddling him, lifting his head and banging in on the floor.

Clint and Kevin. Struggling on the floor.

"Light," Clint gasped. "Now!"

She ran a couple of steps down the hall and flipped the switch. And by the illumination of the overhead light, she could see that Clint was blood-soaked. His arm, the side of his face.

The fury that erupted in her went beyond anything she'd ever felt before. In an instant she became something more, or less, than human herself. She hardly felt the snarl that twisted her mouth. She had one aim and one aim only as she closed in on the men, waiting for her moment.

"Clint," she said in warning.

He pulled back just a bit, getting out of the way as the tire iron came down on Kevin's shoulder again. Hard. Kevin screamed. She raised the weapon again, ready to strike, but Clint's warning stopped her.

"No," he barked. "No. Stop."

She stood there, ready to kill, but Clint grabbed Kevin again, this time wrestling him onto his face. Kevin shrieked as if his shoulder were broken, but Clint ignored the sound. He shoved a hand into his pocket and pulled out a plastic tie. Ruthlessly he wrapped it around Kevin's wrists and locked it tight enough to evoke another howl.

Then, rearing back, he pulled out another tie and wrapped it around Kevin's ankles. Kevin howled again.

"Kay?" Clint's voice sounded a bit thin.

"What?"

"Call the cops now. The emergency number."

"But you're bleeding!" The true horror of that was beginning to penetrate, and rage began to give way to fear. A new kind of fear.

"Just call them!"

She dropped the tire iron and ran for the phone in the living room. 911 answered immediately, and she told them Clint was shot. A reassuring voice said, "They're on their way."

Message delivered, she went to unlock the front door. Then, numbly, she hurried back to the hallway. And Clint.

She didn't care about anything else right then.

He was sitting on the floor, leaning against the wall, knees up, staring at Kevin, who cried out every time he tried to struggle against his bonds.

Kevin saw Kay. "You bitch!" he spat. "You're going to pay for this!"

"Say that one more time," Clint growled, "and I will kill you with my bare hands right now."

The tone was so steely, so hard, that it left no room for doubt. Apparently even Kevin heard the death sentence there, and with an inarticulate sound of rage, he fell still.

Clint looked at Kay. "My belt. Now."

She knelt beside him swiftly, fought her way under the body armor and unbuckled his belt. Pulled it off.

"Wrap it around my arm above the wound and pull it as tight as you can. Now."

Her hands had begun to shake, making the task more difficult, but she managed it, even managed to ignore his groan when she yanked the belt tight and held it. "They're coming," she said breathlessly. "Clint, hang on. They're coming."

"My God!"

Kay turned and saw a woman with beautiful black hair, like a raven's wing, and wearing a deputy's uniform, standing in the bedroom doorway. Behind her was Micah, and beside him a man with a scarred face who looked as if he'd visited hell but had returned.

The woman immediately came over to Kay. "Are you all right?"

"Clint," Kay said. "Clint."

Then the man with the scarred face and Micah were pulling her to her feet and easing her away, then kneeling beside Clint. And Clint was looking pale, sweat beading his brow.

"Damn fool," Micah muttered as he yanked the belt even tighter.

"I'm okay," Clint said.

"Brachial artery," Micah said. "You could bleed out."

"I'll be fine, dammit!"

"Yeah, sure," said the man with the scarred face. "Just as soon as the bleeding stops and we get you a transfusion, then get the bullet out."

Kay sagged, and only the female deputy's grip saved her from collapse. "Clint," she said.

And somehow she managed to break loose and take two steps toward him. When she fell to the floor, she didn't care. She crawled the last few feet and pressed her head against his leg. "Clint."

A hand touched her hair. "I'll be fine, darlin'. I'll be fine."

"You better be, or I'll kill you."

Somebody laughed. She didn't know who, nor did she care. Because for some reason she seemed to be sinking into darkness.

She wasn't out for long. She woke to find EMTs checking her out. "I'm fine. The injuries are old. Clint?"

"He's being transported by air to the hospital," the man said. "He was still kicking and complaining when we took him out."

"Thank God." Her voice shook, and tears began to run down her face. "I need to get to him."

"I'll take you," the female deputy said. She squatted down beside Kay and smiled. "Hi, I'm Sarah Ironheart. You already met by brother-in-law, Micah."

"Yes. He's nice."

Sarah smiled. "I'll second that. And that scary guy over there?"

Kay turned her head and saw the man with the scarred face standing over the bed where EMTs were checking out Kevin.

"That's our sheriff, Gage Dalton. He takes it personally when someone like Kevin hurts someone in this county. I think he's already called the Feds in, too."

"I wanted to kill him," Kay admitted, looking at Kevin and realizing he no longer seemed mythically powerful. In fact, he looked downright puny.

"I'm not surprised," Sarah said. "There are a few of us who would gladly have done it for you after we heard what he'd done."

"Clint wouldn't let me."

Micah turned and looked at her with ebony eyes. "Clint's a wise man. You don't want to live with that."

He would know. She remembered him saying he'd killed his wife's ex-husband to protect her.

Assured that Kevin was well-guarded now, Kay let her eyes close, let go of one terrible tension and gave in to a new one. "Clint," she said again.

"Come on," Sarah said. "Let's see if you can stand. Then we'll follow them to the hospital."

The drive to the hospital seemed endless, though of course it wasn't. Sarah understood her need for quiet, though, and didn't try to converse.

Kay herself was wrapped in the memory of those nightmare minutes from when Kevin had entered the house to when she had crawled to Clint's side. He had to be all right. He *had* to. Her fists clenched on her lap, and she willed the car to fly.

But even at the hospital, she couldn't see him. He'd already been taken to surgery. Sarah waited with her, bringing her coffee.

"Clint's tough," the other woman said at one point. "He'll make it, Kay."

"He's human," she answered. Her eyes felt swollen with unshed tears, hot and burning. "He's only human."

Sarah squeezed her shoulder and let it lie. "We'll need to talk to you in depth. Later. When you're ready."

Kay managed a jerky nod. At the moment she doubted she could manage a simple coherent sentence. All she wanted to know was that Clint was all right.

Dawn was just breaking through the windows in the waiting room when a young doctor finally approached. He looked tired, but not upset, and Kay felt the first ray of hope in hours.

"Clint's fine," he said before she could ask. Then he sat beside her and looked at her. "I'm going to treat you as next of kin, because that's what he was demanding when they brought him in. He's in recovery. The bullet nicked the brachial artery in his arm. The blood loss was bad enough, but probably not as bad as it looked, okay?"

She nodded, unable to speak.

"He's going to be a hundred percent fine in no time. In fact, we should be able to release him tomorrow, if we know he has care at home."

"I'll take care of him."

The doctor nodded. "He needs some time to wake up, then I'll have someone come get you and take you to him."

"Thank you." Relief washed over her so strongly that she had to lean forward and put her head between her knees. God, what was wrong with her?

The doctor touched her shoulder. "You've been beaten, haven't you?"

"A few days ago."

"Then I want someone to take a look at you. I don't like that bruise on your head."

"I'm fine!"

"You sound just like Clint."

"I can't afford it, anyway. I don't have insurance."

"That doesn't matter here. Let someone take a look at you. It'll help pass the time until you can see Clint."

So she let Sarah lead her away to an examining room, where another young doctor, who introduced himself as David Marcus, checked her from head to toe. And Sara took photos.

She didn't care anymore how many photos were taken of her purpling, green and black bruises.

All she wanted was Clint.

"Well," said Dr. Marcus finally, "I wouldn't have believed it, but you seem to be fine."

"That's what I said."

He gave her a smile that penetrated the blanket of fog that seemed to layer her mind, a fog that allowed only concern for Clint to penetrate. "I doubt you were as fine a couple of days ago. But it's good to know we don't seem to have anything to worry about."

She let that little bit of offered warmth wrap around her heart.

At long last they took her to Clint. He was lying on a bed, his arm bandaged from shoulder to elbow, and held to his side by gauze wrapping. He had more color now, she noted, as she sank into the chair beside the bed.

Then, carefully, she reached out and took his hand. His eyes fluttered open. "Kay?"

"I'm fine," she said. "Sleep."

His eyes closed again, and she laid her head on the pillow beside his, still clinging to his hand. She let fatigue claim her then. Her guardian angel was safe, and nothing else mattered.

Sometime during the afternoon, she woke. Lifting her head slowly, blinking, she found herself looking into Clint's gray eyes.

"How are you?" he asked.

"I'm fine. You were the one who got shot."

"It's nothing. I'm ready to get out of here."

"Not until tomorrow," she said firmly. "At the earliest."

One corner of his mouth lifted. "Afraid you can't handle me?"

Her jaw dropped a little, and then she started to smile. "I think I can handle you. But I want what's best for you."

"And that means getting out of here. I'm all stitched up. I want…" He hesitated. "Well, maybe I want too much."

What could he possibly mean? She drew her brows together. "What?"

"I want," he said, his voice low, "to be somewhere we can talk."

"Oh." Probably because telling her she would have to move on soon wouldn't be easy to do when a nurse could come walking in at any moment. Well, she thought, as her heart squeezed with pain, did she want to delay that another twenty-four hours, or did she want to face it now?

Either way, it was going to practically kill her.

"They won't let you go," she said finally.

"Actually, they can't stop me."

"Umm…there's this whole transportation thing, Clint. No car."

"Hell." He sighed.

At that moment the sheriff—Gage Dalton, she seemed to remember—limped in. He was smiling crookedly, one side of his face seeming to have lost some mobility to the burn scar that marred it. "Well, well, the hero's awake."

"I'm no hero," Clint grumped. "Cut that out."

"I thought it was a damn good operation," Gage remarked. "We were only a couple of minutes away at the critical point. And we got the guy."

"I hope he's hurting."

Gage's smile widened as he limped to the other chair and dragged it closer. "He's definitely hurting. We've got him cuffed to a bed down the hall. Broken shoulder, broken collarbone, broken ankle. Plenty of bruises and cuts. Somebody did a number on him."

"Thank the Valkyrie here," Clint said, nodding toward Kay. "I think she'd had enough."

"Evidently so." Gage's gaze turned to Kay. "We've been working while you were hiding. Do you want to know?"

"Please."

"Well, we got his priors. We got the other complaints you filed against him. I still don't understand why he kept getting away with it."

"Some cops," Clint remarked, "have too much on their plates to worry about one little lady."

"Evidently so. Lack of evidence." Gage snorted. "They could have had it with some effort. We got it." He looked at Kay. "You can't exactly travel cross country and leave no trail at all. Anyway, I thought you'd like to know he's being charged with stalking, multiple batteries, attempted murder, kidnapping—which will probably be handled by the Feds, since he took you across state lines—and I don't think he's going to breathe free air for the rest of his days."

Relief caused her to sag as every bone in her body seemed to turn to rubber. "Thank God," she whispered. "Thank God."

"Then, of course, there's the attempted murder of Clint, a second attempted murder charge for you, breaking and entering of a domicile... The prosecutor is having a field day with this one. If it's in the books, he's going to get charged with it."

"Good!"

Gage smiled, clearly satisfied. "Clint? Still sure you don't want to be deputized?"

"No thanks, I like my life."

In that, Kay heard the death knell of her hopes. Feeling crushed, she hoped only she didn't show it.

"Well, I've got some more good news," Gage continued. "The doc says you can go home now, if you promise to be good—and if you have a nurse." He arched a brow at Kay. "Will you mind being a nurse?"

She started to smile. "It's the least I can do."

"That's settled, then. We can take your statements in a couple of days." Gage pushed himself out of the chair, a faint grimace of pain crossing his face. "I'll get someone in here to help you get dressed, Clint. Then I'll take you both home."

Chapter 13

Home. Gage had used the word so easily the day when he had taken them to Clint's place from the hospital. But it would never be her home, Kay thought sadly. Even as she took joy in every little thing Clint let her do for him as his arm healed, she knew this would be the last time she could do anything for him.

He liked his life the way it was. He'd said so.

Since he couldn't yet move easily enough to get in and out of bed, he'd settled grumbling into life on the couch. Clearly a man who didn't like being unable to do exactly what he wanted when he wanted, he put up with being an invalid as if it were the worst thing in the world.

Finally she snapped at him, "It *could* be worse, you know. You might be dead."

At that he laughed, surprising her, and tried to give in with good grace when he needed help, much as it went against his nature.

But the third afternoon, when he seemed to have recovered from his surgery and the loss of blood, when he started to look bright-eyed again, he asked her to come sit beside him on the couch.

This was it, she thought. He was going to tell her he could manage without her. And he probably could, even if being temporarily short an arm hindered him.

So she sat beside him, on his uninjured side, and waited for him to lower the boom. Her chest ached with the awareness that grief was approaching.

"I'm awful," he said.

Startled, she looked at him. "What in the world are you talking about?"

"I'm awful."

She frowned at him. "Would you like to clarify that?"

"I'm talking about the kind of person I am."

"Well, I beg to differ."

"You've only seen part of me."

"I've seen more than you think. Do you honestly think I don't see the ghosts in your eyes? The predator you can become?"

It was his turn to look shocked. Then he said, "I've seen and done some pretty horrible things. Things I couldn't tell you in a million years."

"We're entitled to some secrets." One corner of her mouth quivered. Rejection came in all forms, and apparently Clint was trying a different version. She just hoped she had a chance of fighting it.

"Some secrets are corrosive. They eat at the soul."

She didn't try to argue. Her throat was so tight it hurt, and she didn't know how to argue with this, anyway. So she waited, fingers twined together so tightly they ached.

He sighed and closed his eyes momentarily. "Okay," he said. "I've been a bad guy more often than not."

"In your own estimation."

"That's the only one that matters."

Again she couldn't argue, nor could she tell him how much it hurt to hear him talk about himself this way.

"I came to hide in this place so I could try to work things through. So I could avoid being a bad guy again."

When he didn't continue, she said softly, "Tell me."

He paused, as if trying to find a way to make sure she understood. "When you've been a trained killer, when you've been at war too much and too often, things inside you get a little broken. I don't trust myself."

"Why?"

"Because I've seen some of the best men I know find it impossible to come back to civilian life. Because when it hits them, they take their pain, their rage, out on their families. We're not fit for the regular world anymore."

"You *believe* that, but—"

"I've seen it. Believing has nothing to do with it."

She nodded, beginning to truly grasp his problem. "But, Clint, have you ever gone off like that on a friend? Or a lover?"

He jaw tightened. "Not yet. But it helps that I stay solitary."

"Maybe."

"There's no maybe about it. I don't put myself in situations where the beast could get loose."

"Except to protect a woman who landed on your doorstep."

He passed his hand over his face. "You saw what I became."

"I saw what *I* became. You're the only thing that kept me from killing Kevin."

"I didn't want you to have that on your conscience."

"And you didn't kill him, either."

"I wanted to," he murmured. "Oh, God, how I wanted to."

"But you didn't. And I wanted to, but you stopped me. That ought to tell you something."

"Kay, don't you understand? I'm trying to tell you that you can't trust me!"

"And I'm trying to tell you that I already do! Completely. Implicitly. Like it or not, Clint Ardmore, I trust you. And I have every confidence in your self-control."

He looked at her again, doubtfully, then almost fearfully. "I'm afraid of taking advantage of you."

"In what way?"

"You're free of Kevin now. You could go out there and have a whole glorious life. Instead you're sitting here beside me, a crusty old hermit. You should go and try your new wings. And not let me take advantage of you."

She twisted a little so she was looking directly at him. "How are you taking advantage of me?"

"You were dependent on me for a while. It creates feelings in you that might not be real."

Her heart sped up. She didn't know whether she was angry or feeling the first stirrings of hope. All she knew was that this was one fight she intended to win. "Do you really think I'm that stupid?"

"You're not stupid at all!"

"So you keep saying. I'm also not a princess who's spent her life in a tower. I've had enough experience to know a few things. And one of the things I know is that you're a good, a *very* good man."

"No."

"Yes." She rose up on her knees and put her face close to his. "I know I've been looking for you, just you, my entire life."

"You can't know that."

"I already do. You have absolutely no idea what you've done for me, and I'm not talking about Kevin. You've made me feel worthwhile again. You've made me feel smart, not dumb. You've given me back a kind of confidence I haven't had since I was a kid, and all because *you* thought I mattered enough to shake up your routine and take a huge risk with your own life. To talk to me like an intelligent adult. To care for me when I was almost helpless." She grabbed his shirtfront, taking care not to jar his wounded arm. "Don't you see? Not since I was a kid has anyone cared that way for me. Not since I was a kid has anyone thought I was worth even a smidgeon of that kind of effort."

"But…"

She shook her head, silencing him. "Throw me out and go back to your solitude if you want. But no matter what you do, you can't prevent me from being in love with you."

"In love?" he repeated in an almost-whisper, and closed his eyes. "How can you know that? How can you be sure?"

"Try this," she said fiercely. "I ran more than once. I could have run from you the instant the blizzard was over. I could have called the cops and told them to come get me. I was *never* as helpless as you seem to think."

"You couldn't run. No money. No place to go."

"Dammit, I've always found a way to run. I've spent my whole life running. I would have figured something out within a day if I had wanted to. I wasn't your prisoner!"

He opened his eyes, his gaze boring into hers. Finally a long, unsteady sigh escaped him. "You mean that?"

"Of course I mean it. I ran from a killer. Do you think I couldn't have run from you? Listen, Clint, please. I mean it. I love you. I trust you. If you don't trust me, that's fine. If you want to give this a trial run for six months, a year, ten years, fine. Whatever it takes to make you comfortable. Because the one thing on this earth that I absolutely do not want to do is walk out your door for good."

A few seconds passed in silence, and then she saw something new blazing in his eyes. Something bright and beautiful.

"Ghosts are hard to live with," he said.

"I'll live with them. You may have noticed, I have some of my own."

"And you'll leave if ever you want to?"

"I always have."

He started to smile, the stony facade giving way piece by piece. "I love you," he said. "I love you, Kay Young."

"I love *you,* Clint Ardmore. Now, are you done trying to get rid of me?"

His smile broadened. "I give up."

"Good." She settled back on the couch and leaned against his shoulder. Her heart began to do a happy tap-dance of joy. He wasn't going to get rid of her.

"In fact," he said slowly, "I want to marry you."

She caught her breath as joy surged in her. "When?"

"I don't want to rush you." But his voice held a tentative note of happiness.

"Next week would be fine," she said.

Suddenly it was as if he'd never been wounded at all. With one arm he lifted her onto his lap and kissed her hungrily, deeply.

A forever kind of kiss. Because they'd both found their forever kind of home.

* * * * *